The House of Lost Souls

F. G. Cottam

The House of Lost Souls

First published in Great Britain in 2007 by Hodder & Stoughton
An Hachette Livre UK company

1

A CIP catalogue record for this title is available from the British Library

ISBN 978 0 340 95386 0

Typeset in Sabon by Palimpsest Book Production Limited,
Grangemouth, Stirlingshire

Printed and bound by Mackays of Chatham Ltd,
Chatham, Kent

Hodder & Stoughton policy is to use papers that are natural, renewable and
recyclable products and made from wood grown in sustainable forests. The
logging and manufacturing processes are expected to conform to the
environmental regulations of the country of origin.

Hodder & Stoughton Ltd
A division of Hodder Headline
338 Euston Road London NW1 3BH

www.hodder.co.uk

For my girls and for my boy, with love and pride.

One

Hull, October 1995

Nick Mason thought it ironic that he had always been so skilled at the covert aspect of the craft. Not so much skilled, really, as talented. He had a natural aptitude, an instinct for concealment. He watched his sister, pale at the graveside, from his hide a hundred feet away and it never even occurred to him that he might be discovered and compromised there. He knew how good he was at doing this. The proof lay in the fact that he'd done it so often and was still alive.

It was ironic because he had never thought to employ these skills in carrying out surveillance on his own flesh and blood. But there it was. There he was. Here he was, spying on his little sister. His instinct told him there was every reason for doing so. He was doing it for her own good. And ironic or not, it was bloody convenient to possess the sly and patient cunning necessary to do it so successfully.

He'd gained the expertise in the 1980s in Northern Ireland. They loved a burial, the Paddies did. They loved a martyr properly honoured and, to Mason's mind, were melancholy by nature, always hankering after a proper excuse to mourn. All the major players attended the big ones. And you learned a lot from the body language, watching them pay their respects to one another. You watched them greet one another and offer their condolences and you learned about their hierarchy. And so he'd seen a lot of IRA heroes go to their final resting places, hidden in hides just like this one, sometimes feet away from the boyos posted as sentries, sometimes close enough to smell the breath on them from the steadiers they'd sunk in the pub on the way to the church.

He had to admit that this particular funeral was different from any of those, though. There was his sister, for a start, a pale, broken little presence in her black coat, with her clasped hands and the grief running in raw streams of redness down her face. She'd wanted to come on her own. He'd had to respect her wish to do so. It was why he was smeared in cam cream and wearing enough webbing to conceal a sniper in a combat zone. It was why he was dressed in jungle fatigues and had remained entirely still for two hours now in a narrow depression behind a thick cluster of twigs and thorn bushes adorned by an orange and russet litter of October leaves.

It wasn't just his sister that made it different, though. Watching the funeral procession walking to the graveside had been for Mason like watching a film with several of the frames missing. The light was odd and there was a jumpy quality to the way the mourners moved that made it hard to keep track of what was going on. Funerals usually had their own morbid choreography. Even when they buried one of the boyos in Belfast, the event had always possessed the same slow, deliberate decorum.

Here, one of the pallbearers had staggered from under the burden of the coffin and vomited with his head twisted away from the procession and his hands on his knees as soon as they exited the church. The other bearers had looked as sallow and nauseous as their colleague had, lurching and struggling on. The parents had not appeared to notice. Mason, mindful of the manner in which the girl had taken her life, tried not to look at the parents. But the priest followed the coffin like a man striding towards his own death, stiff-legged and sweating, gasping out the liturgy in little gulps of breath.

There was something not right about the sound of the ceremony. The church bell was a muffled, sporadic clang, dim-seeming as though travelling an impossible distance before being heard. If he really concentrated, he could just make out organ music, emphysemic from under the church rafters. But odd melodies kept drifting over it, reminding him of the piano rags and vapid crooning his old grandfather had liked to listen to.

The light was odd. Twice, the jump-cut procession of clergy and mourners and undertakers seemed to fade to black and white in their progress and when this effect occurred, it seemed to Mason that he was watching men in top hats and starched collars carry a black casket on a sombre march to oblivion through a throng of mourners massed in broadcloth and gabardine.

He rubbed his eyes. There was nothing wrong, Mason knew, with his eyesight. When he looked again, the procession was normal. And the dead girl on her final journey had reached the edge of her grave. The weather was strange. There was a fitful wind that swirled fallen leaves in cones and eddies like kaleidoscopic little whirlpools on the grass between headstones. This wind was unseasonably warm, as well as capricious. It carried a light scent, too, Mason thought, subtle but rank. Oddest of all, though, were the girls. There were three girls mourning their dead friend. Strictly speaking, there were two girls and a woman, because the American student was a few years older than Mason's sister and the student from Merseyside. But there should have been three figures recognisable as students in their youth and togetherness and grief, shouldn't there? Except that Mason kept counting four.

He knew about pattern recognition. It was one of the most useful of the disciplines the army psychologists had drilled into the men operating in the field. Nature was random.

Organised human behaviour wasn't. The IRA liked people to think that their cold assassinations were spontaneous acts of valour, but everyone knew they were rehearsed until perfected. Pattern recognition could enable you to spot the nondescript car you saw too often in your rear-view mirror, or the bland face that passed yours too frequently on the street. It could help you to come out the winner against a fruit machine, or complete a crossword puzzle miserly with its clues. It could also, on occasion, save your life.

Mason's training insisted that the pattern at the graveside was wrong, that it was somehow out of kilter. But if he tried to concentrate on the mourners he seemed to lose some of the detail in heat ripple, which was ridiculous, because it was a damp day in late October. There was no heat ripple. There were bereaved family members as stiff-limbed as the walking dead, and there was a fearful-looking priest and burial professionals sallow with some kind of collective sickness. And there was a mourner too many among the girls. He risked moving a hand to wipe his eyes, which were gritty now with sweat and leaf fragments blown into his face by the wind. And he began to feel the ground beat underneath him like impatient hands, cold and flapping.

He had never worried overmuch about death. He had killed three men in Ireland and two in Central America and never given any of them another living thought. Colombia had been a contact, a legitimate firefight, ambushed by foot soldiers from the Medellin cartel when the regiment had been helping out the Yanks with their marching-powder problem. The training had kicked in and he'd scored two hits. It had been kill or be killed. Northern Ireland had been what it was, the Province and its long and dirty, often clandestine war. He'd had nothing to be remorseful about. They'd even given him a medal. None of it had ever troubled his conscience. And he could honestly say that he'd never been frightened.

But Mason was frightened now. And he was spooked. He looked up and through dim ripples of light, thought he saw a team of snorting, black-plumed horses crossing the cemetery pulling a glass coffin mounted on a carriage hearse. He blinked and the apparition was gone, but the ground still seemed to throb with horrible life underneath him and he knew that it was his own pulse, thumping, his whole body cold and urgent now with foreboding.

Then he heard his sister scream from the graveside. Sarah screamed. And the sound pierced Mason's heart in his hide among the tombs with its terror and its bewilderment, carried to him on the stink of the sorry autumn wind.

Paul Seaton knew it was back when a gust of rain lashed with vindictive fury at the windows of the bus he was on. They were halfway over Westminster Bridge in a stalled procession of bleary rush-hour traffic. The squall shuddered at the bus windows and left them dripping without. It rocked the old Routemaster on its springs. And Seaton knew. There was nothing unusual about rain in London on a raw evening early in November. It didn't signify anything other than itself and the bleakness of the season. But Seaton knew then that the thing he'd almost come to believe he had escaped was back, had returned to seek him out. He stood and threaded through the obstruction of standing passengers there on the lower deck and stepped from the tailboard on to wet London pavement. The wind whistled through the gaps between the bridge balustrades, the rain it drove soaking his trousers from the knee so that the fabric gathered and clung with the rhythm of walking against his shins and calves. The cloth of his trousers felt cold and greasy and he was aware of rain scouring off the river into his hair and the collar of his coat.

Since he was headed south, the famous view, the sweeping fairytale of House of Commons and clock tower was behind him to his right, obscured anyway by the throbbing convoy of buses. The river was to his left. But he resisted any temptation to look at that. He didn't look at the river until he reached the foot of the bridge and descended the steps to the Embankment under the pale stone gaze of the Southbank Lion. He risked a glimpse at the statue on its plinth, at the lion's fierce and familiar head. Rain ran through its stone mane and dribbled from the corner of an eye.

The river dimpled under the rain. Seaton shivered, already soaked. He looked up to the lamps strung along the Embankment, for comfort. But there was nothing cheerful this evening about their light. The tide was uneasily high and the water close and pale in the cast of the lamps. There were old mooring rings in lions' mouths in lions' heads all along this stretch of the Thames. They were green and imperious with algae and invisible, now, in a strung pride of bronze along the bank beneath him. When the river was high, it rose to reach the rings in the lions' mouths. It was how you measured the height of the tide. Now, he thought, tonight, the lions guarding the bank beneath him were surely engulfed. The river was drowning them. He fancied he could hear the dim clank of their rings against the current.

He looked at the water. The dark width of it was stippled in ribbons of urgent force. In other places it was black and still. Odd bits of debris carried past him borne on the current, half-sunk, ambiguous in the rain and the cast of light from the lamps on the bridge. As he stood and watched, his eyes were taken by a patch of something on the river surface, its shape shifting, more a contrast in texture than a solid object, whatever it was absorbing rather than reflecting any light. From out towards the far bank, it drifted closer. It began to look like the dark material of a garment, a floating slick of tweed or gabardine, a coat lost on a bad night to lose one. Only would cloth stay on the surface like that, Seaton wondered, as the shape in the water wallowed and shifted, resolved into a meagre body, the scant ballast of the corpse keeping the fabric that wrapped it only just afloat. Then, still thirty feet from him, the shape seemed to sigh in the water and it sank from sight and further speculation. There was an odour on the rain, a long-forgotten river smell of coal tar from chugging funnels and hemp and oil spillage in the lapping scum. Then, like the ghost it was, that odour, too, was gone.

He shuddered in the rain seeping through his clothes and flesh and dampened bones. And he turned away and raised the collar of his own coat hopelessly, about to head for home on foot, with no great distance to travel and everything in the world to try to come to terms with. Except that the music stopped him before he was able to take a step. Seaton stood, quite unable to move, his skin crawling with gooseflesh, listening at the river's edge to the mournful drift of the song. The melody was old, even elderly. And it was familiar. In a high tenor, with the crisp enunciation of an evening around the wireless, a voice from sixty years ago was singing 'I Wonder Who's Kissing Her Now'.

If I turn around, I'll see a Thames party boat, Seaton thought, antic figures partying through the glass and condensation in the lights of its long cabin. It was November, after all, and the run-up to Christmas had begun and the works celebrations were already beginning to occur.

Except that he knew in his heart he wouldn't turn around and see anything of the sort. There wasn't any party boat. He could hear the shellac of the old recording crackling with static under the needle of an antique gramophone as the song grew louder from behind him through the rain. The song was playing for an audience of one. The last thing he wanted to see was whatever sight might accompany it. And instead of turning around, he found he was able to move his feet away from the river and the sound, and so he answered in his mind the question posed by the title and lyric, instead. I don't know who's kissing her now, he admitted to himself. All I know is that it isn't me and won't be, ever again.

The feeling of foreboding aboard the bus had been very strong. And when he got home, the message light was flashing on his phone. He got messages very seldom. And so he dismissed all thought of rationalising that gabardine-clad corpse he thought he might have sighted in the river.

Home to Seaton was a one-bedroom flat on the top floor of a seven-storey block in Waterloo. The building was dilapidated, served by a single, piss-haunted lift that seldom functioned for more than a few consecutive days without breaking down. Tonight, though, it was working. He unlocked his door, trying not to be depressed by the smell of stale occupancy familiar to cheap spaces indifferently let. He could see the phone message light blinking out of the corner of one eye as he closed the door behind him. It cast a green, intermittent glow from the sitting room. The wind was stronger up here and he could hear rain spatter hard against the sitting-room window. The view through that window was the principal reason he had taken the flat. The location had appealed for sentimental reasons. The rent had been an important factor. But what he could see from a window the width of the sitting room had been the clincher. He had ignored shabbiness verging on squalor for the sake of his view.

He walked on into the room, past the beckoning phone, looking out and down at the night. The block was at the southern end of Morley Street. Seventy feet beneath where he stood, a neat boundary garden with a low perimeter wall gave on to St George's Road. Directly opposite, there was a terrace of four-storey Georgian houses. Immediately to the left, the bulk of the Catholic cathedral massed and brooded. A block beyond the terrace, over to the right, he could see the dome of the Imperial War Museum, cleverly lit by its floodlights through the stir of trees surrounding the old building. To the rear of the cathedral, the lights of a bar were a small patch of yellow brightness across from the museum grounds. It was a failed pub, gaudily repainted and rechristened Zanzibar. Seaton went there some evenings. He had preferred it when it had been a pub. But the beer was cold and the staff were friendly enough. This area was strong with associations still familiar from his happy past. Usually, he took great comfort in them.

Behind him, the green glow of his message signal nagged at the gloom. As it would continue to do, until the content of the message was revealed.

Or erased.

I could always erase it, he thought. A swathe of rain bleared the glass in front of his face and made him blink and recoil slightly. And what, precisely, would erasing the message achieve? It might buy him an hour of queasy ignorance. These things were best confronted, weren't they? You could not hide from them. The decision made, he was trying to will himself away from the window when the phone behind him began to ring.

He ignored it. He just waited until it stopped. And then he turned and went across and played the message.

'Hello, Paul.'

The voice of Malcolm Covey.

'What I have to say concerns the Fischer house.'

A few items of dull furniture occupied the room. Two of these were armchairs. Seaton dumped himself heavily in one of them. Covey had paused, perhaps for effect. But more likely it was to allow Seaton to accommodate himself to the shock. It was coming on for twelve years since he'd seen or heard from Malcolm Covey and in nine words, the man had got right to the point.

'I'm sorry to intrude on you. But there really isn't a choice. Like you, probably, I was under the assumption that the place had been long demolished. But apparently it hasn't been. A party of students went there a couple of weeks ago.'

Were lured there, Seaton thought. There was music in

Covey's background. He had Handel on, distinct and plangent in his silences. But then, Covey's background was plush. In Seaton's background, there was traffic noise and the distant roar of a 747 slowing in its descent.

'One of them is already dead. The others are in a desperate situation. Four of them visited the house.'

Five, Seaton thought.

'Five,' Covey said. 'If you count the tutor who was supposed to be monitoring their course. He was the idiot who took them there.'

Seaton had his head in his hands.

'Paul? I need you. They need you. There is no time for prevarication on this.'

Another silence.

'There's a bar, improbably named, not far from where I believe you live these days.'

Zanzibar, Seaton said to himself.

'Zanzibar,' Covey said, and he chuckled. 'Who'd have thought it, Paul, in Southwark?'

But Seaton's mind was on the Fischer house.

'I'll meet you there at eight this evening. Please be there. Be there, Paul, for God's sake.'

Seaton rose from his chair thinking that God had very little to do with anything that had ever occurred within the grounds or walls of Klaus Fischer's gloomy domain. He walked back to his window. He turned his wrist so that his watch face showed in the flare of the sodium lights from the busy intersection below. He studied the hurl of indifferent traffic for a moment. It was just after a quarter to eight.

If he thought about it objectively, his life did not amount to very much. He occupied a rented flat in a block that smelled of frying onions and old semen stains and rodent droppings and damp. He commuted by Underground to the British Museum where he scraped a few hundred pounds a month checking facts for writers too idle to carry out their own research. He didn't own a desktop computer or a credit card or a decent suit of clothes. He didn't possess a television set. His only diversion in the flat was a second-hand cassette player he'd picked up on a market stall in Lower Marsh, and he didn't tend to play that often because the tapes he owned brought reminiscences unbearable to him. He'd plugged the machine into a wall socket and put on Everything But The Girl, heard the opening song of the album *Eden* and cried salt, self-pitying tears on his knees with his face between his hands. He hid in a part of the city fondly remembered, known from his own young adulthood. He hid there because he'd been confident there once, and happy. He hid there because its familiar streets and tender memories were the only consolation left to him now. It was no sort of a life at all, when you thought about it. But it was the only one he had. He believed that Malcolm Covey's intervention, now, could take it away from him.

You exited the lift and took your life in your hands crossing St George's Road against the traffic hurtling from the right. Then there was a gated passage flanking the cathedral that led to the made-over pub. This short walk was always an ordeal, the cathedral's length a sinister mass in the darkness. He shared the passage with no one. Odd doors and gated entrances punctuated the length of the building to his right. Leaves and city debris stirred and floundered on sets of descending steps and in dark recesses. There was a Gothic, deliberate atmosphere about the place, a sepulchral character to the mass of its stone buttresses and retreats. Shapes snatched inexplicably at his eyes as vagrant shadows shuffled and sulked in the night there. And he heard laughter, high-pitched with contempt or teasing mockery, that made him hurry on, even as he rationalised the sound into the squeal of brakes on the road beyond, or cold wind gusting through elaborate masonry.

Malcolm Covey sat smoking a cigar. Even in the crush, he'd found a table, kept a vacant chair. In the intervening decade, Covey seemed not so much to have aged as to have grown even more comfortably into himself. The hair and the beard were silvery grey rather than salt and pepper. He had looked distinguished before. Now he looked almost eminent. His huge body was buttoned into a dark-grey, three-piece suit. Rings adorned two of his thick fingers. One was plain gold. The other housed a fat ruby. The whole impression was of ease and stature and affluence, until he spoke. The voice was betrayed slightly now by the weight he carried and, Seaton assumed, by the number of Havanas he had burned his way through over the years. There was a shrill, short-of-breath quality to it that Seaton didn't remember from before and that hadn't been noticeable earlier over the telephone.

Seaton knew he was someone prey more than most to easy sentimentality and, particularly, to the cheap warmth of nostalgia. But he felt neither sentimental nor nostalgic facing the figure in front of him. He did not even feel the faint pleasure of familiarity assumed lost. This was partly because of the urgency that had brought Covey so abruptly back into his life. But it was mostly because he had always felt ambivalent about the man. It was hard to warm to any person instinct warned you not to trust.

'You look good, Malcolm. Wish I could say it was good to see you.'

Covey puffed and nodded. He had risen to greet Seaton with a handshake. Now he sat back down. 'You look pretty good yourself. All things considered. You've every right to look like hell.'

'Thanks.'

'Which is where they're going, Paul. Those girls who went to the Fischer house. Unless you can help them?'

Seaton shivered. 'I was a victim, Malcolm, not an adversary. I did not win. I merely survived. You surely know that better than anybody does.'

'Survival was a sort of victory.'

'If you'd been there, you wouldn't think so. And if you were me, you would certainly know differently.'

'Perhaps going back can help you get closure.'

'I'm not after closure.'

Covey frowned.

'I'll help them if I can. I just don't know how I'm equipped to.'

The three surviving students had attended their dead friend's funeral. And they had all seen her there.

'An open coffin?' Seaton asked, misunderstanding.

'No. They saw her attending,' Covey said.

They each thought they saw her among the mourners. Each of the three put it down in the moment to private anxiety, or grief. They were shocked and very upset, after all. The girl who subsequently tried to take her own life got the worst glimpse. She saw her dead friend loitering at the graveside in a hat and veil, her mouth a dim contortion shaping incoherent curses, soil slithering into the grave under the toes of her pointed leather shoes. Afterwards, the three discussed what they'd seen. 'And,' Covey said, 'the real terror began.'

Seaton thought about what he'd been told. 'When did they go to the Fischer house?'

'Almost three weeks ago. The dead girl killed herself a week later and was buried a week after that.'

'And the attempted suicide?'

'Two nights after the funeral,' Covey said. 'She's out of hospital now, recovering with her brother at his house in Whitstable.'

'Recovery being a relative term,' Seaton said.

Covey shrugged.

'What were they doing there?'

'They're not students of the paranormal,' Covey said. 'They attend a legitimate university. In Surrey. It has a charter. It receives government funding. It awards recognised degrees.'

'And employs morons,' Seaton said.

'The moron to whom you're referring teaches ethics,' Covey said. 'The girls were – they are – philosophy students. They were examining the possibility of evil, apparently. They got on to the notion of evil as something communicable. Something that can, as it were, contaminate. They began to discuss the possibility, then, of residual evil. And they sought and were granted access to the Fischer house as part of their study.'

Seaton put his head in his hands. 'Oh, Christ.'

'Most of the time, as you must long have concluded by now yourself, the place is benign,' Covey said. 'On this occasion, it wasn't. Unfortunately, they found exactly what they were looking for. It's out, Paul. It's abroad.'

'They're out, you mean.'

'Don't confuse evil and its manifestations.'

'I'll do what I fucking well please.'

'You haven't done that for some years, Paul. You haven't been allowed to.'

Seaton was silent for a moment. The bar they were in was smoky and loud. Garlic had burned in the kitchen to the rear of the bar and its smell was pungent in the other smells of wet clothing from the rain, scent on warm skin and beer and damp hair, all compressed and heating between nicotine walls. There was a steady thrum of conversation, the chink of glasses, laughter. He had to speak loudly himself to be heard. 'What exactly would you like me to do, Malcolm?'

Covey sighed. 'I think you should see the Whitstable girl.' He reached for his briefcase under the table between them and pulled a thick Manila envelope from it and placed the envelope on the tabletop. 'The address is in there. Along with twelve hundred pounds in cash and the keys to a car parked in a lock-up under the railway arches around the corner from here in Hercules Road. You are a psychologist and an expert in trauma. The envelope contains identification in your own name. There's a letter of accreditation from the BMA and some other departmental stuff from the Guys St Thomas Hospital Trust.'

'And her family are amenable?'

'Her brother is the only family she has. And he's more than amenable. He's desperate, Paul. He doesn't want his sister to die.'

Seaton put his hand on top of the envelope. 'I'd like to see the tutor first.'

Covey nodded. 'And so you shall. Your appointment with him is at two tomorrow afternoon. It was arranged using the same set of credentials. I'd suggest you drive straight on to Whitstable after that.'

'It will mean getting to Whitstable after nightfall, Malcolm.'

'You'll find the brother interesting, I think. From what I've heard of him, I don't necessarily think you'll bond, as the current terminology has it. But he's a formidable chap. After his fashion.'

'I'll be arriving there after dark.'

'There's no time to do otherwise.'

Seaton thought about this. 'Whitstable is on the coast, right?'

'Right.'

That was something. He pulled the envelope towards him. He could feel its contents shifting. Its keys, its forged documentation and, of course, its cash. Twelve hundred: four hundred for each tender life. The ethicist was outside this equation, his life beyond consideration, forfeited by his having taken them there. As though money could save them. As though their lives could simply be bought.

'Why the Whitstable girl?'

Covey looked at him. He looked almost amused. 'Your bedside manner wouldn't offer a shred of comfort or salvation. We both know that. To visit them all would be an enervating waste of time. But the brother of Sarah Mason might prove an ally. As I say, he's formidable. And, of course, you'll find him at his ailing sister's side.'

'Why me, Malcolm?'

'A naïve question, Paul.'

'Seriously. Why me?'

'Because you beat it, once. Because you have the power in you to beat it once again.'

'I won't do it,' Seaton said. 'I'm not qualified.' He dropped the envelope back on to their table. 'I won't do it.'

'You've no choice,' Covey said, reclining magisterially in his seat amid the loudness and the crush of Zanzibar. His voice was flat, devoid of inflection. He extended his arm and flicked ash from his cigar on to the floor. With his free hand, he pushed the envelope of cash and bogus credentials back towards Seaton. 'Now listen very carefully to what I have to say,' he said. He held Seaton with his eyes. 'Listen to my every word.'

Three

They parted thirty minutes later on the street, Covey folding his bulk into the cosy refuge of a black cab. Seaton leaned into the open doorway to say goodbye in the rain and Covey blinked in the glow of the cab's interior light and gestured at the cathedral building looming over where they stood, a few feet of pavement away from the yellow pub. He nodded. 'Insurance?'

Seaton shook his head. Rain, hard in a dancing thrum on the roof of the cab, made him blink. 'It would only make things worse. They'd see it as provocation,' he said.

'You really think they're that . . . informed?'

'Yes. I'm afraid I do.'

Now, Covey blinked. He looked more sad than shocked.

'I'll think about what you've said, Malcolm.'

'No time,' Covey said. 'No time for thought.' He tugged hard at the door handle, Seaton let go of its frame and the door slammed shut and the cab was away in a spray of water from its rear tyres. Seaton straightened up. For the second time over the course of a single evening, he was soaked to the skin.

He'd been in bed half an hour when he heard the music playing softly from his sitting room next door. He'd bought a duvet cover and sheets, offering the enveloping childhood comfort of cotton fleece, on taking the tenancy of the flat. He'd bought them expensively from the Army & Navy department store in Victoria along with soft pillows and a plump goosedown duvet. The plan had been to bury his solitary nights in cosy oblivion. And it had worked. Until now. Now, the music from his sitting room made stiff shrouds of his sheets against his rigid body. He listened to the same, faintly relentless song. He counted seven minutes off the luminous dial of his wristwatch. He started to sweat and to grow cold in his bed. He recognised the song. Or he thought he did. And it continued. It wavered through the wall and door-frame in strained, distended chords and choruses, swelling and fading, ragged and persistent. The door was to his right. On the wall to his left, behind the heavy drape of his curtains, he could get out of bed and look out at the night view spread below. At the busy thoroughfare and, beyond it, the War Museum dome, floodlit beyond the drip in its tended grounds of sodden, autumnal trees. The older locals still called the place Bedlam. The building that housed the museum had once been a lunatic asylum.

But the madness now was coming from the right. So Seaton pulled back the duvet and got out of bed and walked through the door into his sitting room.

Where the music was louder.

He had no curtains there. The room was lit in whitish monochrome from the sodium lights on the intersection down below. Shadows jumped and scattered on his walls and ceiling as traffic slid by. And the music persisted, repetitious, frightening him.

It was the Fairport Convention song 'Tam Lin'. Poor, dead Sandy Denny was singing it. It was her slightly disembodied voice, or a voice at least sharing the perfect pitch and cut-crystal enunciation of the late Sandy Denny. Seaton could hear the whoops and whistles of the band, the Fairports – or their facsimile – in full cry, with their virtuoso fiddle-playing and frenetic picking of guitars and mandolins and drum rhythms. And something under that, unruly and discordant. An occasional noise like the close snagging of cloth and what sounded like the odd snicker of vindictive laughter.

Seaton sank into his armchair. He stared at his cassette machine, on the floor, over by the wall. The plug was still pulled from the socket and lay where he had left it after his tearful failure weeks earlier to listen to *Eden*. There'd been no batteries in the machine when he had bought it from the market stall so he knew bloody well there were none in it now. It didn't even play with the pretence of a lit red power light to signal genuine electronic life. Denny's roused ghost sang and her band went through their antic thrumming of the tune, and Seaton thought about the old couple who manned the weekend junk and bric-a-brac stall in Lower Marsh and had sold him the player. They were ordinary people, he had no doubt. Ordinary people plying an innocent trade for pin money.

He got up and pressed the 'reverse' button that would play the other side of the tape he knew the machine didn't really house. And after a pause, he heard laughter and the sibilant hiss of his own name, repeated, recited, delivered like the punchline of some dark and secret joke. Then that stopped and there was only the spooling of phantom tape. And then there was a snatch of conversation he recognised from what dialogue he had shared in Zanzibar with Malcolm Covey. More laughter followed, viperish, and that noise again, familiar like the tearing of cloth. The bump of furniture. The drag of thin chair legs across a polished hardwood floor. He pressed the 'stop' button, and there was abrupt silence. He pressed 'open' and the cassette tray opened, empty. He stood and turned to get a glass of water from the kitchen tap and behind him heard the cassette tray snap shut again. The ghost of Sandy Denny wavered back into voice and sang 'Tam Lin'. She was unaccompanied now. And she sounded bedraggled and somehow abject.

'It's a good trick,' Seaton said, out loud. 'If a touch domestic.'

The singing stopped. There was a moment's silence. Then Seaton felt the shudder through the darkness of the cathedral bell as it pealed, once, booming between buildings in the rain and then reverberating into rest. He looked at his watch. It was fourteen minutes past one in the morning. It was no time at all for thc cathedral bell to toll.

He nodded in acknowledgement and appreciation. The bell had been somewhat more than domestic. And instinct told him it was circumspect, just now, to pander to their vanity. He didn't think he could be hurt from this distance. Not physically hurt. But he was very shaken. If the intention had been to disconcert him, then that had been achieved with great effect.

Seaton drank a glass of water drawn from the tap in his kitchen sink and went and lay back in his bed. For a time he feared that the song would groan back into its gruesome pastiche of life on his little cassette player. He thought that the bell in the cathedral might suddenly start to toll its iron angelus, defying calendar and hour through the depths of the night. But he was a long way away from the Fischer house. And there were three students of philosophy and their foolish tutor far more deserving of attention now than he. So he lay in bed and waited for sleep to come. But he lay for a long time and it came only reluctantly. Through his bedroom window, he was aware in their reflection on his roof of lights going on in the secular part of the cathedral building over on the other side of St George's Road. The dean or the deacon, possibly, roused from their quarters. Possibly the warden. They'd discover no bell-ringer. Unless they were really very unlucky indeed.

He'd been no more than twelve or thirteen years old at home in the family's two-storey tenement on the northside of Dublin. It had been at the most desolate period of his mother's divorce from the father he was never to see again. She was getting through it only on heavy dosages of Valium. She drowsed a lot at times she shouldn't have. She left food simmering on the stove. She left the fire untended in their open grate or a bath still running for one of her boys upstairs. On this particular night, she'd fallen into a deep sleep on the sofa.

Paul didn't mind. The big TV mast on Winter Hill at the northern edge of the Pennines meant that they got the English channels. With his mother asleep, he could tune into filth like *Take Three Girls*, or *Country Matters*. The latter, in particular, was a series so packed with female nudity it was spoken of in the playground at school with nothing short of awe. He sneaked a look at his mum. He went across and turned the television's tuning dial. Granada and BBC2 were always the best bets for nakedness. He heard his younger brother, Patrick, creep down the stairs. Granada were showing some sort of documentary about the Troubles in the North. On BBC2, the weatherman was finishing up.

'Just what I need to know,' Patrick whispered from behind him. 'I'm bound to rest easier, confident that East Anglia is looking at a fine late afternoon.'

'Shush,' Paul said.

They squeezed into the chair facing the TV, pushed together by the sagging springs, Paul putting an arm around his brother's flannelette shoulder as he always did, waiting with some excitement.

It was *The Old Grey Whistle Test*. And what the two boys saw on it that night seemed to them more sinister than entertainment had any right to be. The band were costumed like medieval minstrels, in high pointed hats with bells and harlequin tunics and woven leggings. When they moved, they adopted the antic postures Paul recognised from the paintings of Hieronymus Bosch in his school history books. The song they did was 'Tam Lin', though he didn't know that then. The evil-looking band performed as if under some kind of spell, their playing growing ever more possessed in its fire and frenzy as their singer chanted the verses. Her voice did not describe the Flemish world of Bosch, though. To the young Paul, it was a voice that belonged instead to the dark England of ancient and malevolent spells. It was an incantatory chant that evoked the Green Man and spiteful elves and John Barleycorn and cursed souls, shrieking, lost in the mists of moors and impenetrable English woods.

The sight and the sound of this performance truly dismayed him. He sat snuggled against his brother, disturbed and petrified, the television screen a grey window on a world of warped magic.

It was only eight or nine years later, at Trinity, that he heard the song again and was able to make sense of what he'd seen. They were called Fairport Convention, he learned. The boys were mostly from North Oxford and their singer had been a girl from Wimbledon called Sandy Denny. Among their players had been the guitarist Richard Thompson and the fiddle player Dave Swarbrick. And their appearance on the *Old Grey Whistle Test* had unlocked in an impressionable boy a series of dreams so vivid and disturbing he had never really been able to forget them.

What Patrick had made of it, two years the younger, he had never thought to ask. It had not been something he had wanted, afterwards, discussion reminding him of. He did remember that after turning the television off and putting a cushion under their mum's head and a coat over her, they had stolen upstairs and crammed into a single bunk in their bedroom together.

That had been the start of it, he thought now, lying in his nest in his rented flat in the night in Waterloo. Rain whickered and spat on his bedroom window. That had been the start of it. Not the Fischer house nor any of the other subsequent things, but that. It had been 'Tam Lin', all those years ago, that had sparked the fear in him that eventually found its proper cause and terrible justification.

'How flattering that you remembered,' Seaton lay on his back in bed and said aloud, descending into sleep, perhaps emboldened by the beer consumed listening to the loquacious Malcolm Covey. But despite the bravado, he wasn't really thinking this. He was really thinking how awful, how defeating, that they should have known in the first place. As they knew everything, every detail, each debilitating flaw. Above him, in the puddles of the flat rainy roof of his block, he heard a skittering sound. It could have been the claws of some capering demon. But, more likely, it was a crow or a feral cat night-scavenging. It was much more likely that, Seaton thought.

And sleep claimed him.

He sat sipping coffee outside a café on Kennington Road at nine thirty the following morning, glad it was a Saturday. He didn't pursue his research work at weekends. He had tried to simplify his life, to reduce it to a series of habits and routines undeserving of challenge or even rigorous thought. But life was going to be vastly more complicated now, after Covey's intervention. It was going to be more dangerous, too. To his surprise, Seaton found he almost welcomed that. The prospect of action was almost a relief to him, after the months and years of concealment and dread. Wakeful in the small hours, fearful after the tape-machine cabaret, he'd decided he was unlikely to survive what he intended to try to do. But his bitter conclusion had been that his life was not worth living anyway. Not as it was. And, unchallenged, he knew its condition would never greatly improve.

The café was an Italian place called Perdoni's. It was double-fronted and had an optimistic array of metal chairs and zinc tables placed on the pavement outside. And it was at one of these tables that Seaton sat, the pavement flags under his feet still wet with rain from the previous night. Inside, the trade was mostly black-cab drivers, sharing the red leather bench seats with a smattering of tourists just off the Eurostar. On the other side of the road sat the brutalist brick and glass edifice of Kennington police station. To the left of the station, from where Seaton sat, was Lambeth North Underground station. To his right, he could see the black railings and leaf-thinned trees of the War Museum grounds. The War Museum was the attraction for the Germans and Dutch and Belgians in Perdoni's, chain-smoking over their empty espresso cups, to the general irritation of the cabbies in the café. Most of the cabbies smoked, of course. When all was said and done, they were cabbies. But they were more furtive about their habit than the tourists were when they dragged on their crimped and hidden gaspers.

Overhead, the morning sky was a vivid blue, intersected by fading vapour trails. It was a bright enough blue, the sky. But it had a depth and stillness suggestive of the steady retreat of sunlight and warmth through autumn. Halloween was not long past. In the newsagent's window a few doors down from the café, they were still trying to sell leftover werewolf gloves and pointy hats in a cut-price window display. The British had really taken to Halloween over recent years, the kids trick-or-treating in their witch and skeleton costumes and ghoul masks in faithful imitation of their American counterparts. It threatened to become a bigger celebration than Guy Fawkes Night. Maybe it already was. Seaton could see the irony in All Hallows Eve becoming no more in the public mind than an excuse for children to beg sweets at the doors of strangers. But he couldn't enjoy it. He had seen real ghouls. Magic was something that could be harnessed and exploited and there were people in the world with hunger for power and influence enough to risk dabbling in its dark, cruel possibilities.

It was easier not to think about it. It was much more enjoyable to think, instead, of the psychological warfare being waged inside Perdoni's between the cabbies and the foreigners. He sneaked a look through the glass. The cabbies huddled, bellicose behind their swinging brass badges, in front of stroke-inducing fry-ups and mugs of sweet tea. The foreigners were pale and impassive in spectacles with narrow black frames and dark clothes he knew would have costly labels. They tinkered with expensive camcorders in preparation for their museum visit. These were taken from and put back into little leather knapsacks embossed with discreet logos. Occasionally, their owners checked the time on their expensive wristwatches. And all the while they smoked.

There was one particularly good-looking couple at the periphery of this chic cluster. Both the man and the woman were tall and very slender. You would have said that each was even beautiful in a pale, bloodless sort of way. She wore black lipstick and it capped half the cream-coloured stubs in the teeming ashtray on the table in front of them. Something about this pair intrigued Seaton. He would have felt self-conscious, rude even, scrutinising them. But they seemed to be staring through the window back at him, brazenly enough. Then the weight of a passing lorry shivered the glass of the café window, making the tableau behind it blurry and indistinct for a moment, and Seaton turned his attention elsewhere.

After Perdoni's, he packed a few things into an overnight bag and then walked the short distance to the lock-up under the arches in Hercules Road. There was a key to the padlock on the door in Covey's padded envelope. The car key the envelope contained had already told him that he would be driving a Saab. The car was fairly new, black, its exterior spotless and its carpets and upholstery freshly vacuumed. The tank was full and Seaton had studied the route using a road atlas in the morning at his table outside the café.

He had not driven for a while but had barely drunk anything the evening before with Covey and driving was a skill he considered rudimentary enough. Nevertheless, he had one bad moment on the journey. It occurred on the A3, the bulk of Guildford cathedral looming monolithic to his left, when the Saab's radio switched itself on. He looked down at the green lights of the display, so shocked that the wheel seemed to convulse in his hand, veering the car violently to the left. A furious horn blatted from behind and he saw the lorry he'd almost hit shuddering under the force of its air brakes in his rear-view mirror. He corrected his steering with sweaty hands and could feel his heart, light in his chest, as he waited for Sandy Denny's cold and ragged delivery of the posthumous 'Tam Lin' through the speakers behind the door panels. But when he made sense of the sound, it was a white soul song he didn't know, the station innocent, the presenter talking inanely about the weather or his wife or something over the melody as it faded in and out of coherence with the strength of the signal. Some piece of software built into the Saab's dashboard had elected to turn the radio on, that was all. The last person to use the car must have preprogrammed it. He pushed the radio's 'mute' button and the music and talking stopped as his pulse began to slow reluctantly to its normal rate.

The university was new, half-timbered buildings with thick panes of tinted glass, set amid gravel paths and thickets and avenues of mature trees on one side of a slope that grew less gentle the higher and more exposed to the weather it became. A chapel and an administration building topped the rise. The chapel surprised Seaton. He thought that perhaps it meant American or Catholic funding. The blue sky of the London morning had become a mournful November grey en route to Surrey in the afternoon. Now, when Seaton looked up, the cloud was blank and low and bruised heavily with its burden of impending rain. Gravel, in larger fragments than he thought usual for paths, crunched or was squirted stubbornly out from under his feet. He could feel the sharpness of individual stones through the soles of his shoes. Halogen lamps had been wired high at intervals in some of the trees and he was glad of the light. He had been obliged to park at the very bottom of the hill. The humanities building was closer to the top. His breathing became more laboured as the incline steepened. The path seemed to narrow and the trees grew denser, limiting the daylight through their crisp brown and orange autumn foliage. So he was glad of the halogen lamps. And particularly grateful for their flat, white glare when he thought he heard the approach of something large and stealthy through the ferns and branches, over the dead leaves and damp grass behind the wall of trees rising along his left, parallel to the narrowing path along which he walked. He stopped and the sound ceased. He could hear his own breathing and the whisper of water dropping on to leaves as the rain began to fall. Up ahead, above him, lights flickered on and off in the humanities building that was his destination.

He looked around, half-waiting for the sound to stir again. The rain strengthened. He heard drops begin to drip from stiffening leaves and dribble down runnels of bark. It occurred to him that he was soaked, again, for the third time in less than twenty-four hours. And it occurred to him that the wood on the hill was a great deal older than the university buildings so sympathetically designed to blend in with their austere and gloomy surroundings. He waited in the rain to hear again the predatory prowl of whatever was concealed in the trees to his left. He waited for five minutes, glancing a couple of times at his wristwatch. It was growing darker. But no sound came. After five minutes, he moved on up the hill to his meeting with Andrew Clarke, the ethics professor. He did not want to be late. Though he was confident Professor Clarke would have no further, pressing engagements after this. It was a Saturday, after all. And Saturday was a quiet day in academia.

There was moss spreading on the wood of the building. It furred the sills of the windows and encroached across the stone surround of the main entrance, soft and deeply green. And there was mildew inside. Seaton smelled its scent of subtle decay as soon as the glass door closed behind him and he paused in the blink and stutter of failing fluorescents overhead, wondering which way he ought to go to find the ethics man. There was no one in the long corridor in front of him. There were doors to right and left, numbered he saw, as he progressed along the passage. But none of them bore a name. The mildew smell grew stronger. He saw two doors marked WC with male and female symbols under the initials and went into the Gents because he needed to pee.

Mildew blotched and spotted the porcelain of the urinals. In the sinks, the mouths of the dripping copper taps were stained and swollen with mould. The mirrors above the sinks reflected black. Seaton saw all of this in the feeble glow of an emergency light screwed into the plaster above the door. The fluorescents were out in here. He peed calmly and then deliberately washed his hands. The paper from the dispenser, when he dried them, felt dusty between his fingers. He liked the mirrors above the row of sinks least. There was a temptation, very compelling, to look into them. He'd glanced at one of them on walking in and thought he'd glimpsed in its dark reflection a grinning flapper under a glitter-ball. It would be a terrible mistake to look into the mirrors in here. He compressed his paper towel in his palm and aimed it at a bin screwed to the wall. It missed. He was reaching for the door handle when he heard a snicker of laughter from one of the stalls, which he now saw was locked. He was suddenly aware of the smell of strong tobacco smoke. It was very rich, Turkish, perhaps Egyptian. He crouched and looked under the stall. A pair of feet faced him. They were shod in shiny leather shoes. Above the shoes, skirting each, rose the grey anachronism of canvas spats. In the dim light, Seaton could just make out the ridges of buttons rising taut at their ankles.

He saw the sole of one shoe lift and slap the floor and heard more laughter from the stall's occupant.

'I say,' said an empty voice.

He straightened and walked out of the lavatory as calmly as he could.

The ethics professor was in a room at the very end of the corridor. It was his office, and he sat behind his desk flanked by shelves of books with his name on their spines and photographs of occasions he'd dignified with his attendance in an academic gown. There was a lit Coleman lantern on his desk and it deepened the shadows in the room with its steady flare of flat brightness. Light gleamed off the glasses the professor wore, making it impossible to see his eyes or read his mood. He was probably in his mid-fifties, with grey hair and grey cheeks. There was a careworn, threadbare look about him entirely absent in the pictures of him on his walls. Seaton felt very sorry for him, sitting there. He had a view through his window of dark, encroaching trees. He cleared his throat, stood and turned and looked through the window now.

'Are you aware, Mr Seaton, that there are more trees in Surrey than in any other county in England?'

'No. That I didn't know, professor.'

'An Irish accent. Dublin?'

'Dublin. Though I was born in Bray, which is to the south of Dublin in the north of County Wicklow.'

'On the coast.'

'On the coast.'

The professor nodded. He was still looking out of the window. 'No coast in Surrey, of course. No salt in the soil. None of those withering coastal winds. Which probably explains the concentration of trees.'

Seaton said nothing.

'The wood we're in on this hill was here long before the university and will, I fancy, be here long after it, too. Would you agree?'

'I'd say so, professor. I'd say it was a betting certainty.'

'Entropy,' the professor said.

'What?'

'Yesterday men came and used those high-pressure water hoses more usually employed to eradicate graffiti. They used them to scour the moss from the building we're in. They've been doing it a lot, lately. But this morning the moss was back.'

Seaton sat with his elbows on his knees and his fingers linked. He looked away from the professor's back, down at his own hands.

'Each day the electrician comes. Each day the lavatories are scrubbed and disinfected. But it makes no difference. Entropy, Mr Seaton. The breakdown of a pattern. The descent into disorder.'

Outside, he could hear the fizz and blink of the fluorescents in the dark corridor. 'This isn't entropy, professor.'

Professor Clarke turned from the window and faced Seaton. He took off his glasses. His eyes were very blue in the light of the Coleman lamp and for a man who studied ethics, Seaton thought, surprisingly lacking in guile. 'There's something in the trees,' he said. 'Something in this building sometimes, too. I'm being haunted, aren't I?'

'It's somewhat worse than that, I'm afraid.'

The professor groaned. 'You're afraid,' he said. He sat down.

'What possessed you to take them to the Fischer house?'

'Can you help me, Mr Seaton? Can you help any of us? You look like a priest. Like Central Casting's idea of a priest, anyway. One of those rugged, brooding, defrocked priests who rekindles his faith in a rousing final reel.'

He'd been drinking, Seaton realised. Vodka, probably. He hadn't noticed any liquor smell. He rose to go. This was useless. 'I'm no priest, Professor Clarke.'

'But you're a Catholic.'

Seaton laughed before he could stop himself. 'It's no help.'

'You're alive. And you've been there. Haven't you?'

Looking at the doomed man in front of him, Seaton said, 'What possessed you to take those girls there?'

'The invitation, of course,' the professor said. 'I took them because we were invited to go.'

Seaton took this in. 'Can I ask who it was invited you?'

'It was Peter Antrobus. A philosophy postgraduate. At least, he called himself that. But I imagine it was a false identity and his credentials every bit as bogus as those you showed me when you came in here.'

Seaton sat back down. 'Tell me everything, professor. Start at the beginning. I want to know everything you do about Peter Antrobus. And you will tell me. Even drunk, I'd say you know enough about ethics to know you owe it to those girls.' He glanced at his watch. He didn't want to be crunching across the clumsy gravel of the university's paths in the dark. He didn't want to be anywhere near this place when night fell. He did not want to risk another encounter with the visitor in the spats. Outside, it was raining persistently out of low, blue-black cloud. But it was only just after two o'clock in the afternoon. Seaton sat back in his chair and the professor began to speak.

Five

The drive to Whitstable was almost due east, so he was chasing darkness as the sun declined, anaemic through cloud when it showed itself, in the mirrors of the Saab. A few miles east of Westerham he could have joined the M25, gambling on the weekend traffic to speed his journey as far as the Boxley exit. But he stayed on minor roads. The rain continued to fall and the software behind the instrument panel of the car offered no further, unwelcome surprises.

Whitstable offered Seaton the false promise of conviviality. The girl who had tried to kill herself was a nineteen-year-old called Sarah Mason. Both of her parents were dead. Her surviving next of kin was her brother, Nicholas, who was something in the military and had taken compassionate leave to help his sister recover. She was at the family home, Nicholas's property now, one among a parade of Victorian houses built above the beach, called Wavecrest. Nick Mason was quite happy to see the trauma specialist from London. But not at home. The plan was that he would sound out Seaton while a qualified nurse monitored the condition of the girl. And the sounding out was to be done at the Pearson's Arms, a gastropub famous for its seafood in a town famous for its seafood. Mason had hired three nurses, providing twenty-four-hour professional help for his sister.

'What does he do in the military?' Seaton had asked Covey.

'I couldn't find out,' Covey said. 'Which rather answers the question, I think.'

But Seaton's mind, on the route to Whitstable, was not

on crab or lobster, or even the cloak-and-dagger world of covert military operations. It was on the story professor Clarke had recounted in his sad little refuge from mildew and failing light. As he drove, he went over and over the professor's story in his mind.

Peter Antrobus was a mature student of thirty-four who had applied to do a PhD in moral philosophy. He possessed a good first degree and the academic lubricant of independent wealth. Granting Antrobus his place required no bursaries or messy haggling over grants. By contrast, there was opti mistic talk of an endowment from rich parents with money old enough to enable them to see the pursuit of abstract thought as more than just an expensive waste of their son's time and career potential. The only problem was Peter's absolute refusal to live in student quarters on the campus. Clarke openly admitted to Seaton that the main reason for this stipulation was financial. The university charged its students considerably more to live in than it cost to keep them. The policy was rigid and extremely profitable. Once Antrobus became aware of this, he offered a gift sum equal to a year's accommodation charge to settle the matter. And settle the matter it did. He and his girlfriend moved into an old coach house at a crossroads about two miles north of the university.

Peter and his companion were both thin and pale and shared the same dark-blond hair. They both favoured a black wardrobe and, to the professor's inexpert eye, their clothes seemed stylish and expensive. He only ever saw Marthe with Peter, which was natural enough. Once, only once, he was invited to spend an evening in their company at the coach house. The couple chain-smoked and drank absinthe and ate almost nothing of the cold cuts that comprised the meal they had prepared. It was February and the coach house was uncomfortably cold. What made the evening even more of an ordeal, Clarke said, was their very public lasciviousness. They may have looked like brother and sister, but they could not keep their hands or their mouths off one another. They'd put music on, he said, and these fitful little dances would develop into the sort of necking sessions more commonly associated with adolescents in a darkened cinema.

'Their behaviour that evening was inappropriate, to say the least.'

'What kind of music?'

The professor looked thoughtful. 'Anachronistic, given their ages.'

'Be specific,' Seaton said.

'Piano music. Rags.'

'Was the coach house sited close to water?'

The professor thought about this. 'No rivers or streams, no.'

'No water, then.'

'No running water,' he said. 'There was a pond.'

Seaton nodded.

'What relevance has this?'

'Please go on, professor. I'm sorry I interrupted.'

What fascinated Clarke about Peter Antrobus was his attitude towards morality. The ethics professor said Antrobus approached the subject the way a bright toddler might approach a live hand grenade. He was full of curiosity about it, but he was entirely lacking in preconceptions or fear. It was as though he had never been exposed to the codes that govern and inhibit human behaviour. It was as though he had never been hurt and forced to learn the compassionate lesson of pain.

'As though he'd never been born,' Seaton said to himself, at the wheel of the Saab, chasing darkness on the road to Whitstable, putting his foot down now, driving faster.

Antrobus produced a speculative essay about the contagious

nature of evil. But it was not the expected stuff about demagoguery, about the charismatic leaders able to stir their followers into acts of casual atrocity in the name of religious or political commitment. There was no mention of persecution or pogroms. Instead, Antrobus argued compellingly that particular locations could infect individual people with what society termed evil. He called these people random victims of contagion. He referred to specific addresses. He mentioned a tenement in Chicago. He talked about a Venice palazzo. The atmosphere at a remote ski lodge in the Austrian Tyrol was evoked in a way that sent a shudder through Clarke when he read the description of the events Antrobus said had taken place there. Two locations in Britain were included in the essay's litany of malevolent addresses. One was a Glasgow slum dwelling. The other, of course, was the Fischer house.

'You'd have been better off in the slum,' Seaton told Clarke. But the stricken look on the professor's face rightly suggested the time for such levity was long past.

Clarke had Antrobus read the essay aloud to his ethics seminar group, where it caused great excitement. And it was there, in the discussion that followed, that he admitted that Fischer had been a second cousin to his father and that the trust responsible for the property might be persuaded to open it up.

'For a weekend,' Antrobus said. 'In the interests of enlightened philosophical debate.'

'You described Antrobus as a stranger to morality.'

'He was,' the professor told Seaton.

'Then how did he define this evil he talked about?'

'In conventional terms. Peter understood badness well enough. He understood the concept and in his essay he listed vivid examples of some of its manifestations. It's just that he never seemed remotely disapproving of it.'

'How would you say he was affected by it?'

'I don't think he was.'

'So he was never shocked or disgusted by the evil events and actions he described.'

The professor appeared to think about this. 'He was far less engaged emotionally by it all than that.'

'Intrigued?'

'Entertained,' the professor said. He put his head in his hands. 'Oh, God,' he said. 'Oh, God.' He was sober now. The memory of Peter Antrobus had sobered him.

It took months before arrangements for the Fischer house visit were complete. There was no real urgency. It was not as if the house and its history were a part of the curriculum undertaken by Clarke's ethics group. It was more of an adventure for the students. But when they researched in preparation for the visit, when they read the history of the house and accounts of the life of the man who had lived there, they became very curious to see if there was any substance to the claims being made by his young relative. The house certainly possessed sufficiently gruesome credentials to qualify as a test location for the theory put forward by Antrobus.

And it was hard not to see the visit as something of a coup. Several newspaper journalists and television programme makers had tried and failed to gain access to the house. So far as Professor Clarke could discover, it had been closed for more than fifty years. Neglected for that length of time, in such a remote location, the house would have deteriorated into ruin, Clarke was sure. But Antrobus was adamant. The Fischer house was not just securely guarded. It was scrupulously maintained.

'I take it you believe in evil, Professor Clarke.'

'I'm an ethicist. It's never been a subject that lends itself to definitive interpretation, to the black and white of easy answers, because even if you accept its existence, evil is still very difficult to define.'

Seaton nodded.

'How we think about evil depends to a very great extent on what we as individuals can assimilate emotionally. It has always been more convenient to think of Hitler, for example, as mad rather than bad because of the sheer magnitude of his crimes. It's somehow an easier option for us. It's tempting to think because it's more comfortable to contemplate than the alternative.'

Seaton nodded.

'It also depends upon the prevailing mood of the times. In the nineteen sixties, I would have bet money that the murders and mutilations committed by the Yorkshire Ripper would have been regarded as atrocities carried out by a man driven to his crimes by insanity. But he was caught and tried in the early Thatcherite years by a judiciary determined to hold him to account for what he'd done. Thatcher's government believed in the power and vote-winning popularity of public retribution. Do you remember the early nineteen eighties? Vengeance was the prevailing imperative among those who prosecuted the law. The Ripper was duly judged to be sane and convicted of multiple counts of murder. But he is still in Broadmoor rather than Belmarsh, Mr Seaton. And if you read the transcripts of the trial today, there is no doubt that Peter Sutcliffe was deeply and incurably insane.'

Seaton remembered the early 1980s, all right. They didn't remind him of the Ripper trial, or Thatcherism either. He'd been in London. He'd been a junior reporter on a local London newspaper. His brother had been a student, on the painting course at St Martin's School of Art, with a shared studio on the fifth floor of the Charing Cross Road building that led to the rooftop by a fire escape. He remembered long afternoons on that roof during the early months of a scorching summer a dozen years ago, spent drinking Italian wine bought in Soho. He recalled evenings with girls studying fashion, which travelled from the Cambridge pub to the Soho Brasserie to Le Beat Route or Club Left or the Wag Club. He remembered 'Don't It Make My Brown Eyes Blue' on the jukebox upstairs at the Cambridge. He remembered reading about the Ripper trial and the Falklands War and the simmer of industrial dissent in the pits of North Yorkshire. He recalled vividly enough the red banner outside County Hall, flagging the unemployment figure to taunt the government sitting in the House of Commons, opposite. He'd attended Pogues gigs in Kilburn on St Patrick's Day and followed Liverpool's epic form in Europe and the league. But he hadn't analysed the moral imperatives of Thatcherism. He'd been far too busy having a good time. Ethics had been a subject unknown to him. But then he'd been blissfully ignorant about black magic in those days, too.

Clarke cleared his throat and above him, the strip light in his office flickered and briefly threatened life. He pushed his glasses back against the bridge of his nose and Seaton saw that his hand was shaking. It was hard not to feel pity for him. He was seeking solace in the relative certainty of what he had studied, what he thought he knew. But soon he would have to leave the sure footing of familiar territory. He would have to wander into the darkness again, eventually.

'Society believes in the notion of places as evil, I think. And the authorities act in a way that perpetuates this superstition. So Ten Rillington Place was demolished after Christie was caught and convicted and hanged. It is almost as though we believe retribution can be exacted against bricks and mortar. Which, of course, it can't. And, by contrast, tourists pay to get into the Tower of London to gawk at instruments of torture.'

'Most of them Victorian forgeries,' Seaton said.

'Tourists travel to Auschwitz. Where nothing needs to be faked. Where you cannot exaggerate the horrors.' The professor smiled. 'And I'm told the Lubyanka has become very popular with visitors to Moscow. The black Lubyanka, where you'd think the very walls might sweat with fear and weep with remembered torment.'

'So you don't believe personally that a place can be malevolent?'

The professor's smile was brave and ghastly in the cold flare of light from the Coleman lantern. 'I didn't, Mr Seaton. I didn't. But, to be frank with you? My opinion changed during my visit to the Fischer house.'

That visit had finally taken place early in October, at the end of the long vacation, at the very beginning of Michaelmas term. Clarke's quartet of students still wore their summer tans from travel jobs and holidays abroad. A couple of the girls, God help them, wore sunglasses perched by habit in the sun-bleached highlights of their summer hair. They gathered in the college car park carrying overnight bags and borrowed camcorders and an air of anticipation close to excitement. Clarke had found the keys to the house, along with a map and other instructions, in an envelope in his pigeonhole.

Antrobus had not yet returned to the university. He was in Germany studying transcripts of the trial of Peter Kürten, the madman and cannibal more luridly known to history as the Vampire of Düsseldorf. There was a cell under a Düsseldorf police station were Kürten had been briefly incarcerated. The cell had survived Nazism, survived intact the firestorm of the Allied bombing raids towards the end of the war. And Antrobus had apparently arranged to visit it. Kürten had first murdered at the age of five, drowning two school friends in a deliberate act comprehensible at the time only as a tragic accident. Antrobus claimed to be intrigued by the man who had begun his long killing career as an infant. But he had done everything he could, despite his absence, to facilitate the visit to the Fischer house. His instructions were detailed, thoughtful.

'Solicitous,' Clarke said, as rain spattered, like fistfuls of vindictive grit, thrown against his office windows. And Seaton shivered at the tone the professor's voice had taken on.

Professor Clarke's ethics seminar group comprised three English second-year undergraduates. There was Sarah Mason from Whitstable. Rebecca Mortimer came from Southport, on the Lancashire coast. And the dead girl, the girl who had died, was Rachel Beal. Rachel had been born and buried in Hull, in the bleak and wind-blasted northeast of England, where her body lay now in one of the plots of the cemetery surrounding the church she had worshipped in as a child.

The fourth member of the student group was an American woman called Ellen Paulus. At twenty-six, Ellen, like Antrobus, was a mature student. She was also an exchange student. She had gone on the visit to the Fischer house at the very outset of her planned year of study at the university in Surrey. She was studying psychology and parapsychology on a four-year course conducted by the well-respected college she had enrolled at in Vermont. For some vague reason he couldn't readily identify, Paulus struck Seaton as a familiar name. Then he had it. Paulus was the name of the Werhmacht field marshal who surrendered at the siege of Stalingrad. Hitler had been mystified, outraged, at his failure to kill himself. 'What's a death?' the baffled Führer had asked himself out loud. What's a death indeed, Seaton thought, who considered the question far more contingent, much more complicated. Whatever, Ellen Paulus could not be held responsible for her surname. Lots of Americans had Germanic surnames. And he had a feeling the woman would need all the sympathy she could get.

'Let's cut to the chase, professor.'

Clarke opened a desk drawer and took out a bottle of Polish vodka. It was the overproof stuff and it was two-thirds empty. He unscrewed the cap and took a brazen swig. Light from the Coleman lantern flashed on the lenses of his glasses as he tilted back his head to open his throat. He coughed.

Back in the period of the Ripper trial, Seaton had smuggled a bottle of the same stuff into the Screen on the Green in Islington with a St Martin's graphics student named Claire who'd worn her hair in a peroxide beaver tail. They'd drunk most of it, watching a terrible soft-porn movie called *Tattoo*. He was quite surprised that the professor was still conscious.

There was a sound then outside the door. It sounded like something slithering against the wood. It was followed by what sounded like a giggle, suppressed, further along the corridor. There was a key in the lock on the door. Seaton got up and turned it and sat back down again.

'Bother,' drawled a voice from beyond the door. Neither man in the room reacted to it.

Seaton swallowed. 'What do you remember of the Fischer House?'

'Nothing,' Clarke said. 'Nothing at all. I've searched my memory and continue to search it. But I honestly don't remember a thing.'

Six

Seaton had left the professor, drunk, convinced that he really did remember nothing. He didn't remember it when he was awake, anyway. The booze suggested that his memory improved when he was asleep, though. He was drinking because he remembered the dreams the Polish vodka was intended to obliterate. Seaton had tried the same remedy. It didn't work, but it didn't seem worth telling the professor that. He had the moss growing on his building to contend with. He had the lurker in the woods. There was the mildew problem and the failing electrical circuitry. There was the visitor in the spats. Seaton left thinking that the professor had his work cut out with the visitor in the spats. Drunk or sober, Clarke had unwittingly given himself a great deal to contend with.

'Antrobus?' It had been Seaton's parting shot. Unnecessary, really, he thought, as the professor recoiled at the mention of the name. 'I couldn't help noticing you refer to him in the past tense.'

'He's disappeared,' the professor said. 'I sometimes wonder.'

'What?'

'Whether he was ever here, Mr Seaton. I passed the coach house the other day. Drove past it deliberately and stopped. And it's derelict, you know. It doesn't look as though anyone has lived in it for years.'

Seaton, who thought the descriptions of Antrobus and Marthe uncomfortably close to those of two people he'd seen looking back at him that morning through the glass frontage of Perdoni's, thought it best to refrain from comment.

He looked again around the professor's office. At the books he'd written and the framed citations. At a triptych of family photographs taken at a barbecue, with a playful Labrador dog in their foreground. Nothing, really, remained to be said. He stood and shook hands over the Coleman lantern and he left.

He was tired when he got to Whitstable. And it was later than it should have been. He got there shortly after seven, unable to explain to himself quite why the journey had taken so long. He came down the hill on to the high street and in the persistence of rain and a strong gust of wind off the sea the town looked shuttered and dismal. The wind rocked the car on its springs in blasts of exposure where high-street buildings were breached by the narrow lanes to his left leading to the water. If there were lights lit on Whitstable's high street, Seaton did not see them. The buildings were mostly shops, all closed, a dank, dumb procession of two-storey facades. The windsurfers and dinghy sailors who gave the place its summer life had long departed. Through the condensation and rain on his nearside window, he thought he saw the wood portal and battening sign of a pub. But he knew it wasn't the Pearson's Arms. He had precise instructions on how to get to the Pearson's Arms. Just then the radio began to play, making him jump, as John Lennon launched into the plodding piano introduction to 'Imagine'. Seaton scrabbled for the controls and found the 'mute' button, wishing he owned the Saab, because if he owned it he'd tear the fucking radio right out of the dashboard. Maybe he'd get lucky and some desperate Whitstable fucker would steal it. He hadn't seen a single pedestrian so far. Much less a skulking thief. With the 'mute' button pressed, the ghost of

Lennon singing was a just-audible nasal whisper as he pulled up and parked. Then he switched the engine off and there was silence until he opened the car door and heard the rain thrum on rooftops and the ground, and the sound of waves smacking on the granite buttress of the sea wall in the freezing darkness a few feet away. And he smelled it, too. He smelled the sea, inhaled the foam-flecked swell.

Mason was seated at a corner table in the basement area of the pub where people came to eat from the menu proper. Even in the basement's artfully limited light, Seaton knew him immediately. There were only seven or eight people in the basement. Four of those formed couples. He had studied the picture of Sarah Mason in the file given him the night before by Malcolm Covey. Nicholas Mason shared his sister's high cheekbones and brown, deep-set eyes. His clothing and hair were nondescript enough. But he couldn't do much to disguise the bone structure. He was slim, slight even, but he had taken off his coat and had his sleeves rolled to the elbow. His forearms were sinewy and strong, rising to the curve of solid biceps under his shirt. There was a packet of Rothmans on the table, Seaton saw, as he sat opposite Mason. Mason had one of them, unlit, between his fingers.

'Mind if I smoke?'

'Does it make the blindest bit of difference if I do?'

Mason smiled and lit his cigarette. 'Jesus. A Paddy. I wasn't told you'd be a Paddy.'

'You've no liking for the Irish, then.'

'Not much, no.'

Seaton sighed. He made to get up.

Mason blinked. 'Sit down, mate. Please? I'm having a rough time of it right now. The manners aren't what they should be. But I'm very grateful you're here. I will be, anyway, if you can help my sister.'

Seaton sat down. He hadn't meant to go. He was here to

help if he could. Right now, he was resolved to help. He just didn't have time for the sort of macho bollocks he thought a man with Mason's background would probably consider a necessary preamble. The man had Belfast written all over him. Two, three tours of duty. But Seaton didn't have the time or the inclination to listen to or tolerate that crap just now.

'Does she remember anything about the visit?'

Mason shook his head. 'She's pretty heavily sedated.'

'Before?'

'She was extremely subdued. But I don't think so. She wouldn't be drawn, awake. And there were no nightmares I could discern when she slept. Then she went to the Beal funeral and thought she saw Rachel Beal at the graveside.'

'They all did.'

'After that, she seemed almost catatonic. And then she tried to take her own life.' Mason pulled on his cigarette. 'She walked into the sea, Mr Seaton.'

The two men were quiet for a moment. Outside, all around them, wind gathered and whooped and there was the heave of waves breaking on obdurate stone.

'A night not dissimilar to this one, a week ago. I was playing patience by the bay window overlooking the shore. I saw her because she'd wrapped—'

Mason's voice broke.

'—she'd wrapped her modesty in a bed sheet.'

Her modesty. Seaton was pretty sure as soon as he'd sat down with him that Nicholas Mason had killed men. He was equally sure now that he would help this family, if he possessed the strength to do it.

'Some of what I'm going to ask you to do, Mr Mason, you're going to have to take on trust.'

Mason looked at him.

'Faith, might be a better word.'

Mason said, 'Might as well call me Nick.'

'Paul,' Seaton said. They shook hands over the table.

'I know there's something very odd going on, Paul. Something inexplicable in any terms I'm familiar with. And it's frightening. I witnessed the Beal funeral. Against Sarah's wishes and without her knowing. But I'm glad I did. I was there when she collapsed. But before she collapsed, I saw some very strange things.'

'Anything since then? Anything here? This is important.'

Mason considered. 'There were two occurences last night, actually. In the early hours. I'd checked on Sarah just before midnight. One of the nurses I've hired was watching her, of course. I reckoned on nicking two hours' kip. But I was woken by the radio playing in the kitchen and I had to go and turn it off.'

'What was odd about that?'

'Apart from the radio switching itself on?'

Seaton shrugged.

'Before Hereford and the regiment, I was in the paras. Anyway this particular night three of us were manning a road checkpoint in a wood at Crossmaglen. We had no specific intel concerning Provo activity. It was just routine. I'd just finished my watch, was listening to my Walkman, drinking a brew, when they hit us with a mortar shell. Both my men were killed, blown right out of their kit and pasted in bits in the trees. I wasn't even scratched. I've never been able to listen to that song since. And it was the one playing when the radio decided to come alive.'

'What was it?' But Seaton knew.

'John Lennon. "Imagine".' Mason stood and pushed a hand into his pocket. 'I haven't even offered you a drink, Paul. You'll drink something?'

'You said there were two things. You said two strange things happened last night.'

'They did. I'd switched the radio off and was climbing the

stairs and I thought I heard a bell toll. It tolled only once. But it tolled louder than any bell has a right to in Whitstable.'

'I'll take a whisky off you,' Seaton said. Mason went to the bar and he put his head in his hands. It was his belief that whatever lurked in the Fischer house waxed and waned in its power. They must have gone there at a time when it was very powerful, the ethics professor and his hapless band of undergraduates.

Mason returned, carrying a double. Seaton sipped it. It was Bushmills whisky, and it tasted like the twelve-year-old.

'Who's Covey?'

'He didn't tell you?'

'Told me some bollocks about an institute for psychic research.'

'It isn't bollocks.'

'Maybe not. For all I know, he qualifies for lottery funding. But you're not who you say you are.'

'No,' Seaton said. He sipped whisky. It tasted good, seductive. It tasted of home.

'There's something else I should tell you,' Mason said. 'I said I heard "Imagine" on the radio. And I did. Or I thought I did. Because it didn't really sound like Lennon. But it didn't really sound like a cover version, either. What it actually sounded like, was a pastiche.' He shrugged. It was an easy song, after all, to mock. 'This is probably nothing.'

'Tell me anyway.'

Rain howled in the wind around the pub and the sea in its waves was a ragged chorus. The overhead lamps, deliberately dim, flickered. Seaton thought he could smell tar from the timber planking lining the walls. He thought, *Jesus. This close to the sea.* And there was a tremor in his hand he could not conceal when he raised his whisky glass to his lips.

'It didn't sound like Lennon playing the piano,' Mason said. He drew on his cigarette. 'When I was a boy, my dad had a real thing for primitive jazz. He liked the classic, early-twentieth-century stuff. King Oliver. Louis Armstrong. He was crazy about Fats Waller. He drove us mad, playing all these rags and romps from New Orleans. That's what Lennon's playing sounded like, last night. Black, barrelhouse music. Stride piano. It had the lilt and echo of the whore-house.'

Seaton downed the remainder of his drink. This time the tremor left him alone. The Bushmills had accomplished its task. He endured the heartfelt fantasy then of reaching into his pocket for Covey's money and buying the bottle from the landlord. The remainder of the bottle. Or a fresh bottle. Ah, Christ, why not the balance of the bottle opened and a fresh one, too? Why not a grand night over a full case of Bushmills? He had plenty of cash now. Twelve burnished amber bottles, filled to their necks with peaty oblivion. It was a powerfully seductive thought, as filled with foreboding and self-pity as he'd allowed himself to become, as thirsty for escape as he was, and solace. Instead, he got to his feet and said to Mason, 'I'd like to see your sister now. If I may.'

A fire of pine logs burned in the grate in the girl's room. The room was on the top of the three floors of the house. The resin from the burning logs gave the room a sweet scent. Out of the window, the havoc of the sea below was black and white, flecked under a turbulent sky. Now and then the old panes rattled in their frames, in the two windows, made fretful by the wind. The house was wooden and it groaned at the weather, and wind whistled and sighed through the attic space above them. There were fresh flowers in two vases in the room and it was cheerfully lit by bright little lamps with cloth shades in primary colours. The nurse was a plump-cheeked girl in a starched agency uniform who looked tranquil, untroubled by the one, apparently undemanding patient under her charge. Seaton felt uncomfortable in the room. He could smell cigarette smoke on his clothes from the pub and smoke and beer on Nick Mason's breath as the two men stood at the foot of Sarah Mason's bed and studied her. They were wet from the rain on the walk back along the sea wall and it was so quiet in the room that Seaton could hear rain drip from the hem of his waterproof on to the lilac painted floorboards. It was still a little girl's bedroom, this.

Its occupant was asleep. It was only looking at Sarah that Seaton realised quite what a good-looking man her brother was. Nature had blessed them both. Sarah's sleep looked deep and untroubled. But there were hollows under her eyes and her cheeks wore gaunt shadows. And the one arm visible, thrown across her body above the duvet covering her, showed the slack skin of muscle wastage where it met her shoulder. Her skin was pale. Her lips were the colour of a bruise. Her hair looked freshly washed and brushed. Her breathing was regular. But it seemed a degree or two colder in the room to Seaton than it had on the stairs, in spite of the fire. The nurse, despite being plump, wore a cardigan over her pristine tunic. You could see the temperature in the room as sinister, Seaton thought, or you could argue that you were in a room exposed to the sea on the top floor of a drafty Victorian house on the English coast at the end of October. You could cripple yourself with needless caution. Or you could die of complacency.

'We're dealing here with ghosts, aren't we?' Mason said.

They were now in his sitting room. One entire wall of the room was decorated with neat shelves lined with books. Seaton thought Mason owned a surprising number of books for a soldier. Maybe they were his father's books and he had inherited them, as he had the house. He had a shelf full of video tapes and a large-screen television, which was more predictable. And he had a very expensive stereo system, the speakers, with their black lacquered finish, angled into a listening point near the centre of the room on expensive-looking, dedicated metal stands. He liked pictures, too. And they looked like original pictures. Of all things, he had a taste for the St Ives School of English colourists. Unless, of course, it was his father's taste. They were both drinking Mason's whisky, though. And that definitely wasn't off the peg. It was Glenmorangie.

Seaton nodded at the shelves. 'Your books?'

Mason was silent, looking at him. 'I asked you a question, Paul.'

'Bear with me. Your books?'

'Mostly. A few were my dad's. I like reading.'

'Ever come across a writer called Dennis Wheatley?'

Mason chuckled. 'I've read one of his. One was enough. Supernatural thrillers, right?'

'I'm surprised you've heard of him. They're no longer in print.'

'Picked it up at a boot sale, I think. Don't think I ever finished it.'

'He was a terrible writer,' Seaton said. 'But he was very successful in his time. His peak years were between the wars. But he believed in Aryan supremacy and was quite a fan of Hitler and Mussolini and wasn't shy of saying so in his fiction, where he also argued the racial inferiority of blacks. And he was an anti-Semite. Even in the late forties, he was still trying to salvage Hermann Göring's reputation.'

'So he's not due a revival any time soon, then.'

'It's unlikely,' Seaton said. He stopped. He was struggling with a way to continue. 'From his late youth, Wheatley manifested some sort of character defect.'

'Get away,' Mason said.

'His prejudices were pretty widely shared among his class, in the period. I'm talking about something more subtle than proto-fascism. Wheatley's father was well-off, a Mayfair wine merchant. He took his son out of school and made him serve a year aboard a Napoleonic-era naval vessel to try to put some backbone into him. An ambitious father had to be pretty desperate even in those days to do that to his son and heir. Then the Great War started and the boy served as a young artillery officer at Mons and Ypres.'

'That should have done the trick,' Mason said. 'Backbone-wise.'

'It should have. But apparently it didn't. Not long after the armistice, his father died and Dennis inherited the wine business. This in the early nineteen twenties. He ran with a very louche crowd. At a very louche time. Do you know much about the twenties and thirties in England?'

'Educate me,' Mason said.

'There was a great deal of social unrest.'

'I know about the Jarrow March. The General Strike.'

'Wheatley drove a London bus during that. And wore a pistol on his belt to combat the Bolshevik menace.'

'He sounds like a wanker.'

'He was a toff,' Seaton said. 'If you've read your Orwell, and I'm guessing you have, you'll know that the judiciary and the police had their hands full in those days suppressing a very large and sometimes very militant working class. The government was unnerved by what was going on in Russia in the years after the Bolsheviks murdered the Tsar and his family. They were frightened by the pithead shop stewards in Wales and the north, tough men pissed off after four years of combat in the trenches, only to come home and discover none of the promises concerning social injustice were going to be kept. These were the years when a peacetime army confronted striking dockers in Liverpool and Tilbury and Chatham with their bayonets fixed. If you were a toff, in the years between the wars, the law didn't really touch you.

The law had its hands full. You were outside it, irrelevant to it, really. And this state of affairs led to some very decadent behaviour.'

'Cocaine and caviar?'

'A bit more extreme than that,' Seaton said. 'Satanism.'

Mason raised an eyebrow. 'And this Wheatley character was involved?'

'He almost bankrupted the wine business supporting his recreational habits, including a mistress he set up in a London flat, with the obligatory accounts at Harrods and Fortnum & Mason. Then, after his wife divorced him, he remarried. His second wife supported him financially until the novels started to pay. That happened when he began to write about black magic and its English practitioners, a group he called followers of the Left Hand Path. He wrote his first bestseller in 1934. And he never looked back.'

'And he was a satanist?'

Seaton hesitated. He cleared his throat with a cough. 'Wheatley knew a great deal about black magic ritual. He certainly knew black magicians. He was an intimate of Aleister Crowley. But he always denied being personally involved in the rituals, in the ceremonies. I think he was lying.'

'Your point being?'

'He was a friend of Klaus Fischer. He advised Fischer on the purchase of his property on the Isle of Wight. He may even have acted as his intermediary in the sale. He seems to have had a way about him when it came to striking a deal. He was a frequent guest of Fischer's, so it's a safe assumption he was invited to the parties thrown there. Dennis Wheatley was Fischer's calling card on London society. And he was the reason, ten years ago, that I visited the Fischer house myself.'

The two men were silent for a while. Seaton felt tense,

despite the alcohol. He kept expecting to hear a scream from the top of the stairs. He kept expecting 'Tam Lin' or 'Imagine' to start seeping out of Mason's lacquered stereo speakers. 'Imagine' would have a sardonic, ragtime lilt. He glanced down at his wristwatch. It was a little after midnight.

'To get back to my original question,' Mason said. 'Are we dealing here with ghosts?'

Seaton stifled a yawn. He was tired, as well as tense, as well as scared and intimidated by the prospect of what he thought he was going to have to do. Quietly, he said, 'Why? Do you believe in ghosts, Captain Mason?'

'I've sat here in my own home tonight,' Mason said, 'listening to a lecture in English social history delivered by a Paddy drinking my Scotch. At this moment, given the circumstances, I think I'm ready to believe anything.'

Seaton smiled to himself.

'I've got a story to tell you,' Mason said. 'I'm going to tell it to you, because it might be important in how things develop between you and me. And then you're going to tell me about your visit to the Fischer house. Aren't you, Mr Seaton?'

'We'll be up all night,' Seaton said.

'There'll be plenty of time for sleep when you're dead,' Mason said.

And Seaton thought that he would have liked very much to be able to say amen to that. 'Talk, captain,' he said. 'I'm all ears.'

It was a covert job, helping the French sort out some tribal trouble on the Ivory Coast. A team of three had been seconded from the regiment and attached to a company of Gurkhas. The terrain was dense jungle, the Gurkhas chosen because they were tough and silent and uncomplaining about the country they would have to live and fight in. The two blokes with Mason were NCOs, good soldiers, veterans of special ops in the Falklands and Northern Ireland and the Gulf War, men coming to the end of their lives on active service still fitter than most fit teenagers. There was no hierarchy among the trio, despite Mason's rank. It just wasn't the regiment's way. They were equals in the field, all reliant on each other, the same hardware and the same intel – French on this particular occasion, piss poor as always and suffering in translation, as if things weren't already bad enough.

The way it went in these conflicts was always pretty much the same. The tribes squared off over disputed land, or cattle or a waterhole or whatever. The skirmishes and ambushes escalated into attritional war. Wells were poisoned. Villages were burned. Cows and goats were stolen until things peaked with the rape of women and the hacking off of limbs. There came a point where cost started to outweigh potential advantage and the elders of the opposing tribes got together and reached a settlement involving as little loss of face on both sides as possible. Then they went home to mourn their dead and bandage their wounds until the next time.

'Why couldn't the French sort it out themselves?' Seaton said.

Mason smiled. 'The French are very attached to their bits of Africa.'

'You don't mean they're still empire-building?'

'You have to remember how long they've been there. Anyway, they've no plans to leave that I've ever been aware of. But they have learned some things. One of the things they've learned is not to be seen as one-sided in tribal debates. It's much easier to let foreign troops take the blame for partiality. It's why Paris will pay for Gurkhas. To the tribespeople, Gurkhas don't look French. French intervention in the Ivory Coast means French troops leaving their garrisons in convoys of troop lorries. We arrive at night aboard Chinooks. We could be anyone.'

'It can't be a cheap way of doing things.'

'I don't suppose it is. But sometimes it's the only way.'

'Because this tribal conflict wasn't petering out,' Seaton said.

'No,' said Mason. 'It wasn't. This one was rather different.'

They were in the north of the country, in the hilly region west of Touba, maybe a hundred kilometres from the border with Guinea to the east. The border was far too remote there to be anything more significant than a dark squiggle on a map. Certainly it meant nothing to the warring tribespeople. At first, all Mason and his company of Gurkhas could find was the aftermath of fighting. They found scorched villages and corpses, and dead beasts bloating and alive with maggots and blow flies. So far, so predictable. But the really odd thing, the bizarre thing, was that all the fatal casualties they came across were from the same side. The two tribes were ethnically distinct. The corpses were all from the taller, paler-skinned Kesabi tribe. The Tengwai, their opponents, were either uncharacteristically fastidious about collecting their fallen comrades, or they were close to invincible. The shadow-chasing went on for six days and seven nights. Never once did Mason or any of the force he commanded see a single protagonist in the fighting alive. They would always arrive in the silence and death of the aftermath. And it began to unnerve the two regimental NCOs because they were experienced jungle fighters and had never in their professional lives encountered anything like it. The silence under the tree canopy was almost palpable. The smell of death seemed to permeate their clothing and kit and their sleeping bags. They began to feel more like prey than predators – or that laughable compromise, mediators. There was nothing to mediate. There was no conflict to resolve. They felt like witnesses to an ethnic-cleansing campaign carried out by murderous phantoms.

'What do you know about Gurkhas, Paul?'

'Valiant little fighters from Nepal. Bloodthirsty mercenaries in the cynical pay of the Brits.'

'Neither of those stereotypes really fits them,' Mason said. 'Oh, they're brave enough. And they're as tough as fuck. And they're very disciplined. But they're a long way from being just hired guns. They're extremely loyal. But they do like to know what's going on. In fact, they insist upon it. Back in the Korean War, a company of Gurkhas refused to fight in a particularly difficult engagement because they felt they'd been sold an optimistic lie about the strength and disposition of the forces opposing them. So their commander, who was a Sandhurst man, decided on what's still today a pretty novel approach in the British army. He opted to tell them the truth. He told them that they could expect casualties of around sixty per cent. But that he would personally lead them.'

'I'm sure that reassured them.'

'It did. That's their mentality. They fought and they did

take around sixty per cent casualties, and they won one of the bloodiest battles of the entire war.'

'The Sandhurst officer?'

'Killed,' Mason said. 'Early on in the engagement. But that's not the point.'

On the morning of their seventh day in the jungle the Gurkha soldier nominated to speak for his comrades voiced their general disquiet. They were not comfortable. They did not feel they knew everything they needed to know to make their mission one they could successfully execute. Mason agreed. He asked SAS sergeant Tom Dillon, who was carrying their coms equipment, to break radio silence and appeal to the French for any information that might possibly assist them. Two hours after the request, the French came back on and gave Dillon coordinates for a missionary outpost about twenty kilometres from their position.

'Crafty, the French,' Mason told Seaton. 'The only thing you can say with any certainty about them in the field is that they always know more than they let on.'

It was the early hours of the following morning before they reached the outpost, a shack on stilts on the banks of a tributary of the Sassandra River.

Seaton frowned. 'Actually over the water?'

'Why? Jungle architecture an interest of yours?'

Seaton just looked at him.

'Yes,' Mason said. 'The priest's house was over the water. You reached it via a pontoon of logs and old oil drums roped together.'

'And the priest was there?'

'It was night when we arrived. He was on his knees, praying by candlelight, fingering a worn set of rosary beads in a tiny tin-roofed chapel built above his living quarters. You climbed a ladder to enter it. It was consecrated, a holy place, but desperately poor. A zinc pail for a christening font. His Mass paraphernalia, the goblet and hosts, in a wooden footlocker embellished with gilt paint on top of an old linen chest for an altar.'

'But a holy place?'

'Yes. In a careworn sort of a way. It was a holy place, all right. But it felt weary. Weary, like its occupant.'

The priest showed no surprise on seeing armed men enter his tiny place of worship in the early hours. The Gurkhas had removed their bush hats, perhaps as a sign of respect. The priest nodded slightly and rose slowly to his feet and measured his place on the beads of the rosary with his fingertips and kissed its crucifix tenderly before placing the rosary around his neck and kissing the crucifix again. He looked educated, sallow-skinned, high-born, blue eyes fierce in the candlelight in his ancient bony face; his priestly humility both the gift of, and the penance paid for, his enduring ancient faith.

'A Jesuit,' Seaton said.

Mason nodded, remembering. 'Not just a Jesuit. A French Jesuit,' he said.

He twisted his rifle on its strap so that the butt faced forward and he took both hands away from the weapon and held them out in front of him with the fingers splayed. He recited his name and his rank. 'We mean you no harm, Father,' he said.

The priest merely nodded. He showed no sign of being remotely afraid of uninvited visitors, armed to the teeth and smeared in camouflage cream. His composure was completely unruffled. Indeed, the look on his face when his eyes met Mason's seemed almost to suggest a sort of amusement. 'You will take tea?' he said in English. 'They slaughtered my goats a fortnight ago. So I can offer you no milk with it. But you are welcome to the fortification of tea. And you will need, gentlemen, to be fortified.'

Seaton said, 'Was there anything unusual about the church?' and he could see that his question broke Mason's reverie, his reminiscences, annoying him.

'Doesn't it sound unusual enough for you already?'

'Anything else,' Seaton persisted.

Mason looked reluctant to consider the question. It was his story, after all. It was his telling of it. 'It was cold. It wasn't cool, it was cold in there. It was dense with night heat and humidity outside and the place had a tin roof and wooden walls with chicken wire nailed over gaps in the planking for windows. It should have been stifling, but it was as cold as the grave.'

'Anything else?'

'Yeah. No insects. They are always around you in the jungle, the flies and moths and mozzies, buzzing, crawling, biting, especially at night. But there were none in there. It was still and cold and the air was subdued in that chapel, in the proximity of the priest.

'The sound of running water carries at night. But when I think of it, you couldn't even hear the trickle of the water in the tributary underneath us,' Mason said.

Both men were silent for a moment.

Mason said, 'His name was Father Lascalles. He had spent a great amount of time in Africa. He had been in the Congo in the nineteen fifties, he told me. And that was when he asked me whether the trader Philip Mason had been a relative of mine.'

'Your father?'

Mason nodded. 'The question at least explained the look on his face when I barged in on his meditations with a rifle in my hands. Lascalles had spotted the resemblance immediately.'

'Was your father famous in the Congo?'

'Notorious, would be a better word,' Mason said. 'But we

were a long way from the Congo here and decades on from my father's mischief there. He's got nothing to do with this story, Paul.'

Seaton nodded. 'Go on,' he said. 'I'm sorry I interrupted you. I won't interrupt again.'

The priest told them that the chief of the Tengwai had entered into a pact with a demon. He had sacrificed five young, first-born sons of the tribe in return for invincibility in battle against their traditional enemy. The Tengwai warriors would be invulnerable in battle against the Kesabi, on the condition that they remembered each day properly to honour the Kheddi the demon had instructed the Tengwai chief to house in the best-appointed hut in their principal village.

But the Tengwai had become afraid of their own prowess on the battlefield. They mourned bitterly the loss of their five beloved tribal sons. They saw no honour in defeating an enemy with the diabolical intervention that made their own proud fighting skills obsolete. They admired the obdurate courage of the Kesabi, struggling to continue to wage a war that had become, for them, suicidal. And in their hearts they felt that the demon had tricked them, had reneged on the bargain. This because they were so deeply afraid of the Kheddi, enthroned in pomp in their midst, honoured, fêted daily. The Kheddi made slaves of them in its baleful presence and their dread obligation to it. They hated their chief and despised him for the foolishness of his dabbling with diabolical forces. They muttered about killing him, about deserting their own homes and lands and suing for peace with their enemies. They were grief-stricken, remorseful, ashamed and sleepless at night with their own convulsive, deepening terror. It goes against nature for a warrior to know his enemies cannot harm him, the Jesuit said. Men become unbalanced, forced to consider the prospect of their own immortality.

'I'd have laughed at this stuff,' Mason said to Seaton, 'before I got there and saw the evidence with my own eyes of how that tribal war was being fought. But it didn't seem funny, drinking tea and listening by candlelight that night, the way the old priest told it. And neither of the lads were laughing when I sneaked a look at them. And more to the point, since they outnumbered us, none of the Gurkhas were laughing, either.'

'This idol. This . . . Kheddi?'

Mason shook his head, slowly. 'More than an idol. A kind of golem, the priest said. The bogeyman made flesh. He wasn't very specific about it. He hadn't seen it himself. For some reason I imagined the tales from my own childhood of the tar baby, extricated from his tarry lair, grown-up and grown nastier. Certainly the Kheddi sounded like more than a totem, though. Animate, somehow. Malevolent. A Jesuit priest was never going to see the devil's dealings in a charitable light. But even given his theological bias, he made it seem like the Tengwai chieftain had struck a very sticky bargain.'

Sticky. Tarry.

'Animate?'

Mason nodded. He reached again for his cigarettes. He had chain-smoked throughout his story. There was a pall of cigarette smoke, thin and bitter, in the room where they sat in the house on the seafront in Whitstable. Rain scrabbled on the windowpanes like thrown grit in fierce, fitful gusts of wind. Seaton remembered the girl, then, sleeping her troubled narcotic sleep in her room at the top of the stairs.

'The priest said it killed his goats,' Mason said. 'Gutted them, drank their blood, ate their livers and hearts.'

Wind howled outside, rattling the windowpanes in their painted wooden frames with a fury that made Seaton jump. He thought suddenly about the man he had left late that afternoon, about the ethics professor and his terminal case of entropy in his building gathering moss behind its enclosure of dripping trees.

'By dawn, fortified by Jesuit tea, we had a plan,' Mason said. 'Our strategy was based on the old "cut off the head and the body dies" principle. Our Jesuit ally was able to provide a very detailed hand-drawn map of the village where he insisted we would find the Tengwai chieftain's quarters. He sketched a route that would take us there in less than a day's march undetected, an old hunting trail neglected and unused for decades, but there, if you knew where to pick it up. We would surround the village, do the necessary surveillance, establish a field of fire in case everything went pear-shaped. Then, after dusk, one man would go in and slot the chief. All the Gurkhas wanted to do it. There were nine Nepalese in our patrol and every single one of them volunteered. Either of my noncoms from the regiment would have gone in just as willingly. But there were two compelling practical reasons for having a Gurkha do it. They don't eat the meat-based diet Westerners do and so their scent is harder to pick up than a European's typically would be. That's a big consideration in the heat and humidity of the jungle; just ask any of the old American or Aussie combat vets who ever fought in Vietnam.'

Seaton said, 'The second consideration?'

Mason looked at him. 'The kukri knife,' he said, eventually. 'Everything you might have heard about Gurkhas and knives, from the trenches in Flanders to Port Stanley in the Falklands, is likely to be true.'

His name was Hindip Roon and he had followed his father and grandfather into the Gurkha Rifles. He was no more than five feet tall and, wet through, wouldn't have weighed above fifty kilos. Mason watched the trooper walk away, becoming as light and insubstantial as a ghost, until he disappeared completely into the foliage skirting the perimeter of the village. There was a sort of fog, a vapour that glazed the soldiers' skin and smelled sulphurous and made the branches of the trees and hanging vines gluey against clothing and kit. On the grass, its residue dragged at boots as sticky as the slime that trails a snail. But it was useful, this mist that made phantoms of men and coated the jungle in its suffocating hush. It made concealment easier. According to the priest, the chief of the Tengwai wore an emerald-studded collar as his badge of office. It was not something he would be likely to relinquish willingly. Mason had ordered trooper Roon to bring back the collar when he returned as physical proof of the deed done. Roon might feel compelled, he knew, to take other trophies. It was a grisly and long-cherished custom among the Gurkhas. But he'd volunteered for the task and what he did with the bastard's extremities was, to Mason's mind, entirely his own prerogative.

Except that, by midnight, Roon had not returned. Through the weeping mist, through his night-vision binoculars, Mason could discern no movement in the village. But then, since his unit's arrival and careful disposition around it there had been no sound or visible sign of life in the village at all. The jungle was quiet, too. But that had been a feature of their mission, when he thought about it. They had heard no birds singing or earthbound beasts crashing, startled, through foliage. There were no monkeys capering and calling up above in the trees. They hadn't seen so much as a squirrel or a bat up there in the canopy. There'd just been biting insects and the odd distant bark of a scavenging jackal and, a couple of hours earlier, the coils of a fat snake wound indolent around a heavy branch a few metres to the left of the path the priest had put them on.

He sent a two-man scout party to assess the level of defensive fortification and sentry disposition at the two entrances to the village compound marked on the Jesuit's map. And they returned after an hour to report that there were no sentries. There were no defences. The village gave the appearance of being entirely uninhabited.

As commander of the mission, Mason knew he had to go in after their man. Their belief in their own invulnerability could just about explain the defensive laxness of the Tengwai fighters. But Mason's men were not Kesabi, hampered by bad magic, crippled by juju terror. They'd go in hard and fast and it wouldn't be subtle or diplomatic and the Tengwai wouldn't know what had fucking hit them. They'd only hope to Christ trooper Hindip Roon was still in one piece and, if he was, they'd get him out and fuck the French and their fucking colonial games, Mason thought, as he gave the signal to attack.

They found only two men in the village. Both of them were dead. The Tengwai chief lay, headless, in his hut. Hindip Roon sat cross-legged outside the hut with the severed head facing away from him on the ground between his knees. In the grip of Roon's right fist, the chief's collar of office glinted green and gold in the darkness in thin beams from the torches screwed to the assault party's rifles. Roon had a slacker grip in death on the handle of his kukri knife, which he had used left-handed to slice open his carotid artery before bleeding to death in apparent repose.

The chief had not died in repose. Mason settled on his haunches and examined the face of the dead man by torchlight. The sides of the head were dark and bloody and the hair there matted with gore where Roon had sliced off his ears. But you only noticed that after taking in the raw, red nakedness of his skull. Because Roon had scalped him, too. His lips were drawn back in a snarl of agony from his teeth. Worse, though, were his eyes. They were black, dismayed, lost as the life dimmed in them to the dawning consequence,

Mason thought, of what his bartering with evil was going to mean for him in death. Mason rose and spat on the ground and went into the dead chief's hut.

It was more than a hut, of course. It was vaulted, timbered in hardwood, the high dome spreading above a spacious circular room, flagged in smooth stone under strewn rugs, opulently furnished in teak and ivory and marble and blood. The headless torso of the chief lay in a thickening pool of gore, small and still at the carved feet of the ebony throne on which the Kheddi sat, shambolic and grotesque, much worse a sight in the anaemic light of Mason's torch beam than the priest had led him to believe it could ever be. Its skin was some greyish animal hide, scraped and seasoned, maybe the softened hides of boar or buffalo, crudely stitched over its stuffing in the rough shape and posture of a man. Standing, it would have been about eight feet tall. But it would never have stood, Mason thought, thinking of the priest's butchered goats. It was a lifeless thing, an abomination slouched on its throne, with its cloven buffalo hooves for feet, with its hands taken from some slaughtered ape and clenched now, the fingernails black with rictus and crafty decay. It was an abomination, right enough, but crudely inanimate.

Mason raised his torch beam and studied the head. It was large and pale and bald, sunken in places in shallow depressions where the stuffing didn't seem to be sufficient and gave it a deformed and almost sullen aspect. The eyes were blank discs of ivory perforated at their edges and stitched on to the face. And the mouth under them was a black, leering gash. Mason shook his head. He turned his back on the thing. And he felt the hairs rise on his neck in dread as he heard the Kheddi shift behind him in its seat.

'I was wired anyway, so pumped with adrenaline I thought my heart was going to explode out of my chest. I spun, already squeezing the trigger, and gave it the full mag,' he told Seaton. 'High-velocity rounds. Point-blank range. I hit it with a burst that cut the fucking monstrosity in half. Next thing I knew there were half a dozen very jumpy blokes in the hut with me, safeties off, trigger-happy as fuck, shouting their heads off in the dark. It was fucking bedlam.'

'What did you do?'

'We buried our dead comrade. We torched the camp. We marched on no sleep for two solid days and were air lifted out at our agreed rendezvous aboard a Chinook.'

'Did you tell anyone what happened in the hut?'

Mason laughed. A bitter sound. 'Back in Blighty at the debrief? No.'

'On the march out of the camp?'

'I didn't need to. Like I said, I fired a burst that cut the thing, the Kheddi, in half. And we all saw the contents of its stomach. Straw stuffing, like you'd expect. Other random things, bits of gold, plaits of old rope, rags, coins, what looked like a couple of dozen semi-precious stones. And five small human skulls. And the skulls were partially digested.'

Seaton sat and considered what he was hearing. 'You mean in a state of decomposition?'

'No, Mr Seaton. I mean what I say. We all saw it.' He reached for another cigarette. 'I can close my eyes and see it now. It's what makes me broad-minded, you see, about whatever's going on now with these poor girls.'

Both men were silent for a while. Seaton had questions about the story to which he wanted answers, but he thought Mason looked exhausted in the chair opposite his. So he didn't ask them. But the silence began to unnerve him with the fitful wind outside and the imagined noises from the room occupied by the sleeping girl upstairs. And so he was compelled to speak.

'Did the priest give the demon a name?'

'My name is Legion,' Mason said. His voice was flat, devoid of emotion, spent after the telling of his tale. 'He seemed to think it's always the same demon, irrespective of what it calls itself. But you'd know that, wouldn't you? So I don't really know why you bother to ask.'

'What do you think he saw, the Gurkha?'

'Roon,' Mason said. 'Hindip Roon. Tough bloke. Third generation. His grandfather won the Military Cross fighting the Japanese in the 14th Army counteroffensive at Meiktila. He was very proud of what his granddad did in Burma, was Roon.'

'What do you think Hindip Roon saw?'

'I think it's what he heard, Mr Seaton. We found the ears he took as trophy tucked into one of the ammo pouches strapped to his webbing. He did that, and the rest of his blood work, in the hut. That was obvious from the mess around the chief's corpse, even to me, wired as I was. But he worked with an audience he didn't know he had. What I think, is this. I think the Kheddi spoke to him. I think the Kheddi spoke to Hindip Roon. And I think, perhaps, he might have heard its laughter.'

'You've lost me,' Seaton said.

'Its glee,' Mason said. 'Its happy appreciation of Roon's craft.'

Eight

A cry from above took them back up the stairs and on to the threshold of the girl's room. She was propped against her pillows, awake, alert. Her cheeks were flushed above a bright smile which contrasted dismally with the look of sly and ancient mischief dulling her eyes. The nurse, to one side, her back to her patient, busied herself with a glass-topped trolley crowded with the apparatus of the sick room. There were pills in white plastic cylinders and medicine bottles and a thermometer propped in sterile fluid and a thing with rubber coils and a glass gauge for calculating blood pressure. When you looked at the girl's face, Seaton thought, you couldn't blame the nurse for turning her back.

The girl clutched a radio in her lap, a portable with the aerial extended. She'd taken it from her bedside table, where Seaton remembered seeing it earlier, behind a box of tissues. The tissue box was now on the floor. He thought the scream they had heard the nurse's, alarmed perhaps at the suddenness with which her patient had roused to consciousness and moved. The girl blinked and her head snapped back against her raised pillows. She stabbed at one of the preset buttons on the radio and sound assaulted the room at a volume that caused the nurse to jerk and send her trolley crashing sideways to the floor.

'I'm so sorry.'

Her voice was audible only because it carried as a whisper under the anthemic assault of Joy Division, the baritone of Ian Curtis incanting 'Love Will Tear Us Apart'.

Mason had crossed the threshold of the room and guided the nurse, with a gentle grip insistent on one elbow, as his sister punched another preset on the radio and Nick Drake intoned something whispery and acoustic that filled the room and with its gentle rhythm and rhymes rocked the girl back and forth against her pillows. The girl was panting, her face awful to look at now, and against the walls and windows of the house the wind had roused itself once more with shuddering, uncertain violence. Things moved in Seaton's mind, shadowy in the wainscoting. The shadows themselves spread and encroached. Gravel was sprayed against the windowpanes as if in antic glee. Mason had not returned from taking out the nurse. There was a smell of rottenness. Like something stagnant, this dead odour carried on the breath of the panting girl. Seaton had still not dared take the step that would deliver him into her room. But he needed to get the radio away from her. As if reading his mind, the girl punched a preset. He heard Sandy Denny singing 'Who Knows Where The Time Goes?'.

From the bed, the girl leered at Seaton. 'They know where the time goes,' she said. 'They're so very keen to tell.' She belched, with a look of surprise, and her breath was the rank air of the crypt. 'Dying to tell,' she said.

And Paul Seaton fled.

Mason found him hunched over the wheel of the Saab in the pub car park, his seatbelt buckled but the engine cold when Mason opened the passenger door and sat heavily beside him. Both men were soaked from the hard, heavy rain on their separate journeys there. The car radio was playing. The music was jazz, a weary four-in-the-morning ballad infused with a faint bebop energy. Someone very good was making a trombone sound as subtle and sinuous as a tenor saxophone. 'My Funny Valentine', Mason thought. He looked at Seaton. He didn't think he had ever seen anyone look so frightened in his life.

'Cigarette?'

'I don't smoke.'

'Me neither,' Mason said, lighting one. 'Gave up five years ago. Read the Allen Carr book, but it didn't work. Not for me. Hypnotherapy did the trick, though. Clinic in London, not far from Regent's Park.'

'You must have really wanted to stop.'

'Oh, I did,' Mason said, inhaling deeply. 'Cost me an arm and a leg. But it was worth it.'

'Congratulations.'

'Cheers.' He exhaled. 'Thanks for waiting.'

'Just deciding where to go.'

Mason nodded, trying to keep his voice calm, the welling desperation out of it. If necessary he would drag Seaton out of the car, subdue him with the sap he'd put in his jacket pocket on leaving and carry him back to the house on Wavecrest over his shoulder. The fucker was going nowhere, not with Sarah in this condition, not if he had anything at all to offer them. 'Right,' Mason said. He kept on nodding. He pushed a hand deep into a pocket and fingered the raised stitching on the leather grip of the sap. 'Right.'

'Your sister?'

'Sedated. Our nurse is a stoic.'

'I just lost it, briefly,' Seaton said. 'I'll be okay in a minute.'

Mason studied the glowing tip of his cigarette. Wind rocked the car on its springs.

'The music—'

'All suicides,' Mason said. 'Ian Curtis hanged himself. With Nick Drake it was painkillers. And that singer with Fairport Convention threw herself down a flight of concrete steps.'

'You know your music.'

Mason nodded towards the car radio. 'I don't recognise this.'

'Frank Rosolino. Trombonist. Big on the West Coast, once. Well, big by bebop standards. Which means he was a virtuoso who just about scraped a living. Pretty much any jazz player's lot, in the era of James Taylor and the Eagles and the Doobie Brothers.'

Fear took some people like this, Mason knew. Made them loquacious, verbose. Sometimes it was all you could do to shut them up. 'You a jazz fan, Paul?'

Seaton nodded. 'Radio turned itself on a second after I got into the car.'

'Frank Rosolino kill himself?'

'Late one evening. Shortly after he put a bullet into the head of each of his sleeping infant sons.'

Seaton reached for the switch to turn on the windscreen wipers but his hand gave up before touching it, as though he lacked the will. The trombone died in the speakers and Mason, a pause after, straightaway recognised the mournful Roy Buchanan blues that followed it. He thought that the volume might jump, suddenly. He thought that he might scream if it did.

'Walking after you in the rain, I wondered about the odds against that kind of thematic coincidence with the songs on the bedroom radio.'

Seaton turned to face him. 'Outlandish,' he said. 'The odds, I mean. I'm not an actuary. And I'm not a betting man. But I would think those odds incalculable.'

Mason nodded.

Roy Buchanan sounded other-worldly, the chords enfeebled now, the strings of his old Telecaster guitar distorted and loose.

Mason had cajoled and caressed and bribed the nurse back into his sister's charge. She had slumped into unconsciousness again by the time they got back to her room, thin against her pillows, her breath shallow and her face wearing the dead sheen of pewter. The nurse had taken the radio from her sleeping grip and then wrenched the plug that powered the thing from its socket on the wall. She dumped it in Mason's hands with an expression on her face that was a complex stew of fear and understanding and resolution. She was a Celt, he remembered, the nurse. She was a girl from County Meath and acquainted, perhaps, with talk of magic and certainly with folklore. And the nursing was a vocation in her and so her conscience would resolve her now to stay. With no point in speculative talk he merely nodded his thanks and relief to her and went to find Paul Seaton.

He knew Seaton wouldn't have got very far. He had cut the Saab's fuel line while the Irishman was in the Pearson's Arms lavatory to make absolutely sure of that. Whitstable had become very fashionable over recent years. But it was far too small a place and the trade it attracted was far too smart for it to support a local mini-cab firm. The nearest would have to come from Herne Bay or Canterbury. It was late, and going though the pockets of Seaton's coat after hanging it on a hook in the house earlier, he'd taken Seaton's wallet. So getting a lift out would be a problem for him, with the railway station long closed. It was almost 2 a.m. It was dead time in Whitstable.

Mason was almost surprised to find himself descending the cellar steps of the Wavecrest house before going after Seaton. He hated the damp, salt odour of his father's old refuge from his children, from domesticity. It was the part of the house that most unnerved him. But his thoughts were vague on this, as he reached for the weight and threat of his father's sap, and felt the scrutiny of the hardwood idols brought back by his father from Africa, as they watched him through their carved, incurious eyes from where they were huddled on their shelves against the far wall.

He heard the rumble of the sea, underneath it now, underneath the heavy reproach of its waves broaching on the shingle above. He slapped the lead shot and leather sap into his palm and cursed himself for the futile bravado of the gesture. Nobody was watching, after all. Nobody was here to be impressed, or daunted.

The truth was, his father's house had always unnerved him. He had slept under this roof with a night light on until the age of fifteen, despite the old man's taunting. And it wasn't just the house. He had always felt the small town of his birth a malign and frightening place. He hated its narrow alleys and the gibbet swing of its pub signs in the dark. He grew up loathing the slither of the wind through its winter nights. He thought there was something odd, unfettered, out of kilter about the place. It was cold, underpopulated, meagre. There was a starkness about the shadows and the light. There was the feeling he always had of being followed. There had been two, really terrifying, childhood incidents he fought not to recollect with any clarity. One had taken place at the tea garden in Tankerton. The other had occurred in the old ice-cream parlour on the front when he'd been ten or eleven years old. It had been a relief when his father had sent him away to the boarding school in Cumbria. He hadn't minded the dark, there. There was night comfort in the sound of the other boys, breathing, asleep in the dorm they shared. And there was something cleansing about the bleak regime of fell-running and forced treks and orienteering on frozen mornings by torchlight. He wondered sometimes if his whole professional life had not been some sort of reaction to, or compensation for, the fears he felt so plagued by as a child growing up here. Maybe. And maybe not. There were plenty of other men in the regiment, rightfully prone to night terrors of their own. Now, in his father's cellar, amid his father's stores and stashes of secret collusive things, he slapped the sap against flesh again and self-consciously chuckled at the bite of pain with the impact into his palm. And something shifted softly over by the shelves against the far wall. And Mason swallowed and sauntered with exaggerated slowness towards the dim flight of cellar steps.

'The sea,' Seaton said, in the Saab. 'They find it more difficult to summon their mischief, near the sea. They're fierce fond of music, so they are. And, of course, they love to have their little joke. But at the edge of the sea . . . well, it's always been safe. Safer, at least. Not entirely safe, nowhere is. But certainly safer. Until now.'

'You're going to tell me what's going on,' Mason said. 'You are. Aren't you?'

'You look about ready to beat it out of me, captain.'

The Irishman had that right. 'If I had to, I would,' Mason said. 'But I don't need to. Because you came here to tell me. Didn't you?'

'We can't do much about things, about the prevailing circumstances, until I do.'

Mason waited. Eventually Seaton said, 'Any of that Joseph Conrad meets Rider Haggard Congo bullshit true?'

'Not Congo,' Mason said. 'It wasn't the Congo. It was the Ivory Coast.'

'Just a yarn spun to buddy the two of us up? A grand tale, captain. But that Kheddi stuff was nonsense, wasn't it?'

Mason seemed to tighten under his sodden clothes. He dripped rain and indignation. 'Blarney isn't my style, Seaton,' he said. 'I'm sorry to say that every word of it was true.'

Wind rocked the car in a savage upward gust despite the buttressing shelter of the sea wall and, a moment after, a wave pounded like a canon battery against the wall itself and hit the fabric roof of the Saab in a heaving spatter of brine. They saw it gush down the windscreen, a living element, foam-flecked, shaped in sinewy cascades of black water. The radio was quiet now. Roy Buchanan, who had hanged himself in a police cell in America in 1988, had apparently returned to his troubled rest.

'It began twelve years ago,' Seaton said. He had extended his hands and his fists were tight on the wheel and his knuckles white in light that glowed like phosphorescence through the dripping car windows. 'That's when it began for me. It's all my fault, really. Everything that's happened can be brought back to me. And yet, you know, it began with the noblest of intentions.'

Mason crushed the orange ember of his cigarette between finger and thumb. 'Tell me,' he said. 'Come back to the house on Wavecrest and tell me all of it.'

Nine

He met Lucinda Grey in the upstairs bar of the Cambridge pub one sunlit evening in the warm spring of 1983. When he walked into the bar, Crystal Gayle was singing 'Don't It Make My Brown Eyes Blue' on the jukebox. He remembered that. It could have been Van Morrison singing 'Brown Eyed Girl' or Julie London singing 'Cry Me A River' or Nina Simone singing 'My Baby Just Cares for Me'. The upstairs bar at the Cambridge had just about the best jukebox of any pub in London. But it was Crystal Gayle. And Lucinda's eyes were neither brown nor blue. They were green and remarkable, appraising him from the other side of the bar when he walked in. Closer, he could see that the pupils of her eyes were encircled at the inner limit of the green by iridescent flecks of gold. Her dress was gold, too – raw silk, slubbed and pleated. And her hair was the colour of dark honey, cut into a heavy bob.

It was a flamboyant year in a flamboyant decade and most of the crowd in the bar were students from the St Martin's School of Art building a hundred yards along Charing Cross Road. It was bright in the bar in the early evening through the big windows overlooking Cambridge Circus. Dressed for the night, in the late daylight, the fashion course students were self-consciously poised and picturesque in their buttoned shoes and bias-cut skirts and tailored jackets and hats.

They formed separate groups, or orbits, the students in the Cambridge in those days, in that year. So those on the graphics course were deliberately monochromatic in black

Levis and white Hanes T-shirts under their MA-1 flight jackets, the girls among them distinguished only by their peroxide rockabilly quiffs. The girls on the painting courses wore rah-rah skirts or jeans purposefully distressed with artfully torn sweats over tight white singlets, while the boys all dressed in the Jackson Pollock ensemble of jeans and plaid shirts and denim jackets. Footwear was crucial. To a man and woman, the graphics lot wore Doc Martens. The painter girls wore clumpy black engineer boots. The would be Pollocks wore Jackson's Bass Weejun loafers carefully saved-for and purchased on their pilgrimage to an American-owned clothes shop called Simmons, in Covent Garden. Flip on Long Acre had made authentic Americana generally cheap. But the Flip merchandise came over tightly packed aboard container vessels to be pressed back into life when it arrived. So, of course, they didn't sell the shoes.

Seaton was there to see his brother, Patrick, dressed tonight in a zoot suit and painted silk tie because they planned to go to a club and didn't intend either to queue or to pay the entrance fee. If you were picturesque enough, it was a time and London, and particularly Soho, was a place where that could be done. The suit looked good on Patrick, who was broad-shouldered enough to carry the cut. Seaton was less convinced by the straw trilby tilted back on his brother's head. As Patrick walked towards where he stood, Seaton saw that his brother had adopted a swaying sailor's gait. You made yourself up, in those days, at the age they were. Some people were someone different every single night of the week.

'Who is the tall blonde in the pleated dress?'

'I'm fine, thanks. Well, fine other than the terminal illness they broke the news to me about this afternoon.'

'The tall girl with the green eyes.'

Patrick sipped beer.

'The straw trilby is a mistake.'

'Makes me look like Felix Leiter. The CIA man in the Bond novels.'

But Seaton's eyes and attention were again on Lucinda Grey.

'Sinatra wore a hat like this on the cover of "Come Fly With Me".'

'Makes you look like a Yank tourist,' Seaton said.

His brother thought about this and shrugged.

'In a Norman Wisdom film.'

'She's a bit of an enigma,' Patrick said. 'A blonde of the glacial persuasion.'

'So you can't even introduce me.'

'If I could, then obviously, I wouldn't.'

Seaton pondered this, wondering was it a double bluff. He decided it wasn't.

'I can only tell you she's on the fashion course,' Patrick said. 'And she keeps herself very much to herself.'

'Evidently.'

Seaton didn't get to speak to Lucinda Grey that night. He went with his brother to the Mud Club and the Wag, where they played Kid Creole and Animal Nightlife and where the air smelled intensely of the smoke of Marlboro Reds and hair gel and brilliantine and dance sweat and where everyone, as Seaton got drunker, looked like they were extras in a film set in Cuba before Batista was overthrown and Che Guevara and Castro set the long-prevailing fashion in the hot unruly places of the world for jungle fatigues. And sometime after midnight he picked up a black dental receptionist from Woodford Green whose style was somewhere between Carmen Miranda and the model in the Bounty Bar television commercial current just then. And he took her home and forgot almost entirely about the fashion student with iridescent green eyes from earlier in the evening in the upstairs bar at the Cambridge. He almost forgot her. But he didn't quite.

And then he saw her again the following week at a club called the Wharf, which occupied a derelict warehouse building on an empty stretch of the Thames near the Shadwell Basin. It was the era of warehouse parties, word-of-mouth and flier events like the Dirtbox, floating notoriously between vacant tenements in King's Cross, with its sound systems and zinc bathtubs full of ice cubes and tins of Saporo beer. But the Wharf had a gentler and more contrived atmosphere of tidal drift, almost of permanence. And its clientele reflected its status in contrivances of their own.

There was a boy in a matelot shirt and a canvas yacht cap like a Jean Genet caricature on the door. A scar blunted the bridge of his nose and his tattooed arms were sinewy and tanned. The spring was hot that year, warm already with the intense promise of the burning summer to come. The club was lit by yellow oil lamps, and starlight cast on to its ceiling in pale ripples reflected through the windows from the river below. Patrick was there with friends from St Martin's. Stuart Lockyear was there. And Greg Foyle, whose pictures would one day sell for hundreds of thousands of dollars and hang in the Metropolitan Museum of Modern Art in New York. They were seated at a table on the other side of the dance floor and Patrick said something to Greg and Greg looked at Patrick and Paul knew from the look that his brother was very drunk.

He saw the mysterious girl from the fashion course, Lucinda Grey, sipping a viscous green drink from a shot glass in a flamboyant huddle of people by the bar. He became aware of the music, as the final notes of the Jacques Brel song, 'Amsterdam' faded. It was the version of the song sung in English by David Bowie. And in its histrionic aftermath he recognised the first bars of 'Bad Day', a new song sung by the English torch singer Carmel McCourt. She came from Manchester and she lived in Paris. Her songs were becoming very popular in the clubs that year. He breathed in the smell of the place; the mingled aromas of tar and timber and tobacco and dank night river. And he walked over to Patrick's table and Greg poured him a drink from one of the bottles of Lambrusco they were sharing.

'You'd be on the scent,' his brother said to him. Patrick blinked, but the blear remained across his eyes.

Paul sipped wine.

'In the hunt,' Patrick said. 'The chase. The game's afoot, is it not?'

'Don't sound so disapproving. It's hypocritical. You'd shag anything with a pulse.'

Patrick appeared to ponder this. 'Wouldn't necessarily insist on a pulse,' he said. 'Don't want to over-egg the pudding.'

Paul laughed. And from the other side of the room, he saw Lucinda Grey smile at him above the shot glass held poised beneath her lips. She raised an arched eyebrow and, with the fingers of the hand not occupied with the glass, she beckoned him across.

'Your fat rockabilly friend looks drunk.' She sipped her drink and looked at him over its turning rim. The drink was iridescent, like her eyes.

Seaton looked back to his group. And back again at Lucinda Grey. She had her arms folded across her chest and the posture pulled the leather sleeves of her jacket, taut and soft. It had a mandarin collar, the jacket, and her neck was long under her jawline, the hair cut close, razored to a velvet nap above the hollow at the back, rising above her collar.

'He isn't fat. And he isn't a rockabilly.'

Patrick, who was powerfully built but cherubic of cheek, had made the fatal mistake of wearing a letter jacket with some collegiate logo displayed across its back in his first week at art school. It had cost him thirty-five quid at Camden Market. And it had cost him any shred of credibility. He'd been the first to admit, afterwards, that this particular item of Americana had been a misjudgment. But despite the peach zoot suit he'd teamed with a hand-painted tie tonight, despite the careful strokes of eyelash dye he'd brushed into his pencil moustache, he'd been the Fat Rockabilly, at least in the third person, ever since.

'You're right,' Seaton said. He sighed. 'The Fat Rockabilly's definitely had a few too many tonight.'

She lived in a hard-to-let council flat. She'd queued all night outside County Hall to get the tenancy, she told Seaton. It was in a walk-up block on Old Paradise Street, just on the south side of Lambeth Bridge. She told him this as he walked her home along the river an hour after meeting her, an hour after speaking to her for the first time. They passed an anchored barge in the darkness and the smell of gunpowder drifted up off the breeze on the river. It was one of the fire-works barges used in the GLC's sporadic extravagant displays. A party boat wallowed by, over near the far bank, its lights pearly now through thickening mist and the voice of Boy George, thin and tremulous, singing 'Do You Really Want To Hurt Me?' over its sound system.

He looked at her. He couldn't stop looking at her. She was tall and slender in her black leather jacket and a cream silk blouse and a black calf-length skirt that hugged her hips, and there was something in her hair, brushed back from her face, that gave it an oily, intricate gleam when they passed under the bright globes, every few yards, of the Embankment lamps. Her skin was very pale and her mouth full under deep red lipstick. The Culture Club song carried over dark water and light jigged through mist on the distant boat. And Seaton smelled the scorch of dead rockets and burned-out

Catherine wheels and his skin pricked and his heart hammered in his chest with the hurtling joy of life and youth and possibility. He'd never felt so alive. His life was a brimming adventure. A sensation accelerated through him and he took it for sexual anticipation, for lustful excitement. But it was more than that, he realised. It was a pure untrammeled anticipation of all the life he had to come. Later, he would remember this moment often. Later, much later, this moment and the remembered joy of it would come to visit him, unbidden, all the time.

There was a Stockman in the sitting room of her small second-floor flat. It was partially clothed in ruched pinned silk that looked blood red in the moonlight through the window but faded to something between terracotta and taupe when Lucinda switched on a standard lamp. The floor of the room was littered with pieces of dress patterns and swatches of cloth and sketches of clothes. She could really draw, he noticed. There was an electric sewing machine on a table with a pedal underneath. Her other furniture comprised an expensive-looking hi-fi and a small vinyl-covered sofa he thought he remembered having seen in the window of Practical Styling.

'Sit down,' she said. 'I'm sorry about the mess.' She took off her jacket and hung it across the Stockman's headless shoulders. 'Would you like a drink?'

He could hear music coming from one of the flats of the floor above. The somnolent UB40 cover of 'Red, Red Wine'. He looked at his watch. It was just after one in the morning. She took a record from its sleeve and put it on her turntable. Julie London began to sing 'Cry Me A River'.

'Do you have any beer?'

'No boy drinks, I'm afraid,' she said. She stood with her jacket off and her hands on her hips and her weight on one leg. Her breasts were small and high against the fabric of her blouse. Julie London was quietly histrionic through the loudspeakers. 'There's Chartreuse or Armagnac,' she said.

Chartreuse. The green drink she'd been drinking in the Wharf.

'Armagnac would be grand,' he said.

'Grand,' she said.

'It's what they say at home.' He felt foolish.

'In Dublin's fair city,' she said. 'Where the girls are so pretty.'

But he had never in truth seen a girl in Dublin with the looks on Lucinda Grey.

After a week, he moved in with her. Her flat was small, it was true, but they didn't want the space to be apart. When they weren't attending clubs and parties, they would sit through the lightening evenings on one of the wooden benches outside the Windmill pub nearby and sip beer opposite a peach tree that blossomed pink all through a perfect May. They rented videos, still a novelty, from the newsagent's shop on Lambeth Walk. They rented *Hammett* and *One From The Heart* and laughed their way through *Dead Men Don't Wear Plaid* and *Trading Places*. They played tennis together in Archbishop's Park on one of the two public courts surrounded by high elms and beech trees. At the end of the month, they hosted a ridiculously intimate cocktail party. Girls from Lucinda's course wore paste jewellery and cocktail frocks and their hair piled and sculpted in gelled and sugared confections. Kid Creole cavorted on the stereo.

'It won't last,' Patrick murmured, drinking a vile concoction called a Dark and Stormy, which Greg Foyle was dispensing from a steel shaker misty with cold in the heat of the tiny kitchen. 'I doubt if your doomed romance will see out the summer.' But he smiled as he said it. And Paul knew the remark must have seemed absurd, even to him.

Ten

During the day, Lucinda attended college and Paul worked at the second job he'd ever had, as a crime and local government reporter on a local London paper called the *Hackney Gazette*. He was a stringer for the *Evening Standard* and for the TV news magazine programme *London Tonight*. And he had proposed a feature to the features editor of *The Face*. And *The Face* had accepted his proposal. The world seemed so alive with novelty and hope that some mornings the light and hurtle of London seemed to gasp with it, having to catch up with itself, with its own gathering thrill and momentum. Life was a movie, of course. He was at that forgivable age of self-obsession. And he felt like his role was shifting in it from an extra to one of the principals. He didn't want a starring part, his ego wasn't that big. But, he thought soberly, Lucinda might be destined to occupy one. And he thought his own might be a telling cameo.

Seaton kept only two things from his past. The one was his brother, of course. The other was his boxing. He'd boxed as a youngster, scrupulously and well, learning at and then competing for the St Theresa's club on Dublin's northside. He enjoyed the rigour, maybe even the pain. The discipline of it seemed to seep into his soul. So he kept up his roadwork when he moved to London and, in Lambeth, he ran laps of Archbishop's Park and trained at the Fitzroy Lodge club housed in a railway arch on the corner of Hercules Road. Two nights a week and on a Saturday morning he would skip and hit the bags and work the speedball and do floorwork on one of the canvas mats. The club was run by a thin chain-smoking trainer called Mick. Mick's office was a plywood and Formica den poised on a shaky balcony above the floor and twin training rings. Now and then he would emerge from its bitter Benson & Hedges fog to ask Seaton to spar with one of his prospects. So it was that Paul Seaton kept his body hard, attending his church of choice, honouring vanity and faith, always doing his regular penance.

On a Friday, his habit was to leave the *Gazette* office on Kingsland Road never later than four. He would head up West, meet his brother, have a Friday-night drink with the boys. But he'd taken to doing this early, curtailing it, besotted as he was with Lucinda Grey. So he'd meet the boys and then seek out Lucinda later, in the Dive Bar or the Cambridge or the Spice. She wasn't hard to find. And it didn't matter how packed with other people a place was. She was impossible to miss.

So it was at five o'clock on a Friday early in June, he sat drinking Lambrusco from a big two-litre bottle bought from an Italian deli on Old Compton Street. They were on the flat roof of the St Martin's building on Charing Cross Road and London undulated around them through heat ripple and the smells of softening tar and street cooking and pollen from the flowers and leaves of summer trees in the squares. Hank Williams sang, keening and plaintive on a tape playing on Foyle's paint-spattered beatbox. Seaton sat on the low wall surrounding the roof, at a spot above the open windows of their studio. Now and then, the smells of oil and turpentine rose to clash and coalesce on the hot breeze. It was very hot. The sun was very bright above them. They all wore Ray-Bans, except for Foyle, whose habit it was to narrow his eyes and squint into the light.

'I saw a rehearsal for Lucinda's degree show this morning,' Lockyear said. Lockyear was dressed entirely out of Lawrence

Corner, in a khaki shirt with pleated pockets and voluminous Desert Rat shorts. With his blond slicked-back hair, Seaton thought he looked like Franchot Tone in *Five Graves To Cairo*. 'Her show was really good. The knob of the donkey, as they say in fashion circles. I wouldn't be at all surprised if she gets a first.'

'I'll be surprised if she gets a pass,' Foyle said, who looked like Kerouac, like Kerouac would like to have looked, in his 501s and his print shirt and the haircut he still had then.

'Some disparity there, boys, between a fail and a first,' Seaton said.

'I'd forgotten about the dissertation,' Lockyear said. 'Greg's right. It's a shame, because her degree collection is really strong.'

'The knob of the donkey,' Patrick said, nodding, sipping Lambrusco from a plastic cup. He was looking towards where the Post Office Tower undulated through heat ripple, from this distance like some frail and improbable movie prop.

'Every silver lining has a cloud,' Lockyear said.

Foyle was nodding, agreeing with him. 'It's a shame,' he said. 'A damn shame.'

'What are you all talking about?'

His friends looked at Seaton and at one another. It was his brother who said, 'Her dissertation. She hasn't done it. She's asked for and been given an extension on it and she still won't get it in by the deadline. If she doesn't, it's an automatic fail. I can't honestly believe she hasn't told you.'

'Well, she hasn't.'

They looked at him, trying not to.

'What's it on?'

'Pandora Gibson-Hoare,' Foyle said.

The name meant something to Seaton. There was some old, almost involuntary memory there which stirred at the name, but remained opaque as his mind struggled through heat and wine drunk too early in the evening. Something he'd read or seen, some forgotten association stirred in the dimness of recollection but would not reveal itself. He gave up. 'Who is she?'

'Fucked if I know,' Patrick said.

'She was a photographer,' Foyle said. 'Portrait and fashion photography. She was one of the pioneers in fashion. But she did all her meaningful work very young. And she died young.'

'Inconsiderate of her,' Patrick said. 'Dissertation-wise.'

'She's pretty obscure,' Foyle said. 'Hard to research. I've heard Lucinda hit a wall with her. It wasn't laziness. Lucinda just got stuck.'

Seaton climbed down to the roof. He looked up at the sky, at vapour trails expanding and distorting miles up in the blue void. And he looked back to the group, noticing how clean-cut and absolute was the blackness of the shadows they cast on the flat surface of the roof. Hank Williams sang a song of dusty heartbroken longing on Greg Foyle's beatbox. Beyond them, London toiled in the early-evening heat. You could look out from here across its shimmering topology and feel its energy and promise running through you like a charge. Pandora Gibson-Hoare. For some reason the name itself evoked in Seaton images of cars with running-boards and roofs of taut canvas and waxed bodywork sleek under black rain. He saw a convoy of them, the headlights yellow through an avenue of whispery trees. He could smell tobacco and cologne in the dark spaces behind the windscreen, see the motion of curved mudguard as the wheels they housed bounced and shivered over uncertain roads.

'It'll be a shame if Lucinda fails her degree,' Lockyear said.

'A travesty,' Foyle said, swallowing wine.

'Lucinda won't fail her degree,' Seaton said, dragging

himself back into the here and now. And he knew that she wouldn't. Because he wouldn't allow it to happen.

The extension gave her a deadline that was still a fortnight away. He reckoned if he took one of the two weeks' holiday he was owed, it would be more than enough time. But he reckoned without Lucinda's principles, her integrity and her embarrassment at his finding out in the way he had about what she saw as a shameful academic and intellectual failing. Pride had made it a secret between them. He wondered that she could have hidden something so worrying, so well. But he only wondered briefly. Mostly he was just determined to help her. And not, honestly, just for her. Research and writing was what he did, after all. He wanted to help her, but he wanted to impress her, too.

He didn't say anything until the following day, the Saturday, until after they had played tennis. They didn't go for a drink after tennis on the Saturday. They had booked the court for the late afternoon. And the Windmill didn't open on a Saturday evening. So they walked home and drank tea in their small sitting room with the window wide. Lucinda wore the white pleated tennis dress she had played in, her hair held back from her face by a white band. On anyone else, a dress for tennis in the park would have seemed to Seaton like an affectation. On Lucinda, it seemed the only possible attire. Her hair was still damp at the hairline with heat and effort as they sat and drank their tea.

'Why didn't you tell me about the dissertation?'

The colour drained from Lucinda's face. So pale did she become that he noticed with surprise that pale-green eye shadow sculpted the shape of her eye sockets between the lashes and the brows. He hadn't been aware that she wore make-up in the daytime. She laughed, 'I didn't tell you because there is no dissertation to tell you about.'

'Why isn't there?'

Lucinda looked down at her hands. They were resting in her lap. She raised one and peeled the band from her head and freed her hair and shook it so the damp ends clustered in dark-blonde points around her face. 'I chose the wrong subject,' she said. And Seaton could hear how upset she was in the way her accent had reasserted itself in her speech. Her words sounded flat and northern. 'I thought I was going to write something brilliant about a forgotten artist. I've ended up chasing a ghost.'

'I can help you.'

Faintly, there was the familiar sound of music, 'Red, Red Wine.' from the flat upstairs.

'Help me do what? Cheat?'

'Help you get the degree your talent merits.'

She looked distressed. He had never seen her look so distressed. She looked trapped, in the heat, in the room, in his scrutiny.

'Show me her pictures,' he said, saying it to deflect attention from Lucinda, to get her out of the glare of her own exposure. She went over to a shelf above the television they had bought and took down a slim book with stiff card covers and handed it to him. Then she left the room. He could hear her fumbling in the bathroom cabinet for her asthma inhaler as he held the book between his fingers.

It was a monograph. The author was a man named Edwin Poole, his name etched in a typeface reminiscent, Seaton thought, of the Bloomsbury Group. Past the contents page, Poole had written around twelve hundred precise words about the photography of Pandora Gibson-Hoare. There followed twenty plates of formal portraiture taken in a rigid monochromatic universe that smelled of dust and remoteness rising in the heat of the bright June day from dead and brittle pages. There was a picture of a doleful escapologist burdened by chains on a bridge on the Seine, the river and city made recognisable by the skeletal tower in the distance behind the manacled figure. There was a picture of a circus clown, seated on a drum in a sawdust arena, the pompom buttons on his tunic absurdly large, somehow pathetic under such detailed scrutiny, what looked like blood sprinkled and dotted in the area around his giant feet. There was a picture of a ballerina poised in the wings of a lit stage. Her limbs were sinewy against the white flounce of her tutu and her face cadaverous under her black drawn-back hair as she sucked on a cigarette screwed into a tortoiseshell holder. A New York cop held the butt of a heavy revolver between finger and thumb with the disgust a man might display holding the tail of a suspended rat. A corpse was bundled in an overcoat at his feet. You could only guess at the sex of the apparent crime victim from the smallness and paleness of the one hand visible under the bulk of the coat. Seaton recognised the great French boxer Georges Carpentier, pictured eating a cream bun at a café table with brilliantine in his hair and a long gash over one eye coarsely stitched. There were some studies of a female cabaret artist with a fat python and one of a conjurer displaying a decaying smile and a glass orb that seemed to hang by magic in the air above a card table. A man posed half in shadow on the deck of a liner. There was no convenient lifebelt displayed to give the name of the ship. But Seaton recognised the subject as the English occultist Aleister Crowley. He was smiling at something. Or for the camera. Elsewhere, at an atelier, an audience of frosted women studied a thin mannequin pinned by fussing seamstresses into a gown.

There was power in Gibson-Hoare's pictures, Seaton thought, but mostly it was the fascination the viewer felt at the sight of death, rather than any intrinsic quality in the work. There was something compelling about extinction, and these pictures, of course, documented a vanished world. It was what all the subjects had in common. They were gone. It was not a world, though, anyone was likely to feel much nostalgia or sense of loss for. It was too sad and grotesque for that. Maybe that was her art, her gift, to get not just under the gilt and glamour but beyond the nostalgic cosiness that characterised so many old photographs. Pandora Gibson-Hoare's vision was not cosy or quaint. It was stark and unsettling. This was no sepia-tinted series of artful reminiscences. Her world was not one Paul Seaton would have liked to have lived in. It was not one he would have even liked to visit, he thought, as he closed the thin book, wondering what on earth it was could have intrigued Lucinda about the woman's work.

He read the monograph again. Edwin Poole had surprisingly little to say. His point seemed to be that Gibson-Hoare was technically accomplished in a way that few women photographers of the period were. And that she eschewed emotion in a way that few women photographers were capable of doing. Seaton was left with the view that the argument was more a way of dispelling the author's prejudices than shedding any light on the artist under discussion. If Gibson-Hoare qualified as an artist. On this evidence, Seaton wasn't sure that she did. Julia Margaret Cameron's photography predated this stuff by more than fifty years and was just as technically accomplished. And if you wanted the triumph of narrative over emotion, you could do a lot worse than look at Lee Miller's war photographs. And Lee Miller had been all woman. He looked at the contents page again as Lucinda came back into the room, changed out of her tennis clothes and carrying two mugs of tea for them. Poole's monogram had been published in 1937.

'Her cousin,' Lucinda said, sitting down. 'There was just a decade between them. He had no artistic pretensions of his own. He was twenty-seven and something important at

Lloyds of London when her messy suicide looked like it might hurt his career.' She sipped tea. 'So he produced this, at his own expense, and had a few hundred copies printed.'

'It's pretty worthless.'

'On the contrary, it's quite valuable. It was printed by some Bloomsbury offshoot on a press set up by Lytton Strachey.'

'I meant it's worthless as a source.'

Lucinda nodded. They both sipped tea. It was strong and malty. Like her vowels, her tea had a northern character. 'Most of her best work is in the British Museum.'

'So she did do good work?'

'Oh, yes. She did great work. For a period.'

'What were you hoping to find?' He was aware that in saying this he was putting Lucinda's efforts into the past tense. And she must have noticed because, for a moment, she didn't reply.

'More than exists in the public domain. Pandora painstakingly learned photography, the craft and science of it, to meet some artistic need or yearning in her that wasn't being satisfied. She certainly didn't need whatever income or profit her work could provide. And women photographers were regarded as dilettantes, so she wasn't after status. She was an artist. And then she stopped.'

'And you were seeking to explain why she stopped? To solve the mystery? That was the thrust of your dissertation?'

'No, Paul. I think there's a cache of work, somewhere. I think there's important work of hers still to be discovered. And, stupidly, I was hoping to be the one to find it.'

Seaton put Poole's book on the floor and held out his free hand and took hers and was gratified to feel his grip returned. 'Does this conversation mean you're going to let me help you?'

'Help me cheat, you mean?'

'If you like.'

'Yes,' Lucinda said. 'I suppose it does.'

Later, Seaton walked to the newsagent's shop on Lambeth Walk and rented *An American Werewolf In London*. And they wound back the tape and watched the scene when the two hapless Americans seek refuge in the Slaughtered Lamb three times, laughing more with every viewing.

'I'll bet you had a crush on Jenny Agutter,' Lucinda said.

'Ah, come on,' Seaton said. 'There's barely a man alive didn't have a crush on Jenny Agutter.'

Later, they walked into Kennington and met Stuart Lockyear and Patrick at the Black Prince pub where a singalong was staged on weekend nights. And Patrick sang 'Blueberry Hill', improvising the words because he didn't know them, scat-singing in the end, Seaton watching his brother perform, weeping tears of laughter, with a Guinness in one hand and the other over his eyes, only daring to look through the gaps between his fingers. And Patrick finished to a standing ovation and, at closing time, Seaton and Lucinda walked home under a high moon, the pavements still warm from the heat of the day, the sky paler over where they knew the river reflected the moon, the two of them happy, he thought, to have survived their first row without really having had to row at all.

On the Sunday, he asked Lucinda to give him all her notes, the whole file, everything she had on Gibson-Hoare. It was a scant archive. There was a photocopy of a *Times* obituary and Xeroxes of some of the fashion plates kept at the British Museum. There was an ancient copy of *Vogue* containing a spread of fashion pictures she had taken on what appeared to be a touring-car and picnic theme. Brogued shoes and flat caps accessorized tweed and gabardine in pictures that cried out to be in colour. But colour in those days would have meant hand-tinting. Another feature, this one in *Harper's Bazaar*, was a swimsuit story shot on what looked, from the intensity of light, like the Riviera. Beautiful people lounged on chairs and a diving board against the bleached cement of a deco pool. You could see her skill in this shoot, in the tactile way she handled skin and light, like a sculptress with her camera.

Finally there was a photograph of Gibson-Hoare herself. She wore her dark hair woven in plaits around her head, under a glistening tiara. There were pearls around her neck in a thick rope. And her shoulderless dress, sewn with beads, winked and glistened in the light from a chandelier. The picture was a group shot and had been taken at a table at the Café Royal. Café Royal insignia embroidered a curtain behind the smiling group. All the figures in the shot with her were male. There were five of them, they were in evening wear, and Seaton recognised two. One of the two was Crowley again, smiling again, his deep eyes holding an expression entirely at odds with the bland ordinariness of his other facial features. Also recognisable was Oswald Mosley, younger and thinner in the face than he became when he was notorious, but still unmistakable.

Seaton turned the photograph over. The names of the individuals in the group were pencilled on to the back of the print. Lucinda was leaning over her sewing machine, biting through a length of cotton thread. She tilted her head in a way he found funny when she did it, like a cat, worrying at something.

'Who is Wheatley?'

'A thriller writer. His books are all out of print.'

He nodded.

'Fischer?'

'Some sort of industrialist. An arms dealer, I think. Made a fortune in the aftermath of the Great War out of weapons patents. I've no idea about the fifth guy. But she ran with a pretty louche crowd, did Pandora.'

Seaton nodded. He had shifted from the sofa to a chair under the window to see the picture in better light. The eyes of the men in it all seemed to share the same lazy malevolence the eyes of big cats have when they doze, half-awake, between kills. It was a look that gave the lie to ever relaxing in the truest sense. There was a lethal indolence there, a sort of predatory alertness only lightly disguised. Except for Crowley. To Seaton, Crowley in the Café Royal picture simply looked deranged.

There was no sincerity in any of the smiles. Pandora Gibson-Hoare had that in common, at least, with the people with whom she shared her table. But when Seaton looked closely, he didn't think she looked truly one of them, not really. Under the jewellery and elaboration, he thought she manifested two characteristics unique to her in the group. She looked very beautiful. And she looked afraid.

He started first thing on Monday morning, just as soon as he had opened what post he had at his desk and phoned the press bureau at Scotland Yard to learn of any crimes committed over the weekend on Hackney's ground. There were several, of course, but none that merited following up. They got an edition out twice-weekly and Monday was a press day. But the paper was pretty full, looking only for a front-page lead. There was a gruesome court report about a revenge killing already on the stocks, and one of the boys was working on a human interest based around a toddler rescue from a canal. At ten thirty, the owner of a pet shop at Hackney Downs called in with a story about how a monkey had escaped its cage and run amok, trashing the pet-shop interior and liberating most of the stock, the previous day.

'We'll lead on the furry felon,' the editor said at ten forty-five, putting his head around the newsroom door in one of his whimsical moods. He wouldn't have done it for the Friday edition. But he must have thought he could get away with it midweek. It certainly made a change from blues-party stabbings and arson attacks and tower-block suicides. And Seaton wasn't on it, so he climbed the stairs to photographic to pick brains on how he might discover more about Pandora Gibson-Hoare.

There were two staffers up there on the fourth floor. Mike Whitehall was the junior of the two and had been dispatched to record the furry felon's carnage in glorious black and white. It had occurred to Seaton that monkeys were actually covered in hair, but their readers were unlikely to argue the distinction and their editor was notoriously partial to alliteration in headlines. Anyway, he was glad Mike had gone. Mike possessed a born reporter's curiosity and would want chapter and verse about why he was asking his questions. Eddie Harrington, an indifferent veteran close to retirement, would not. And he was the more likely of the two to know the answers.

The darkroom light was off when Seaton got to the open door of their set of offices at the top of the stairs. That was good. It meant Eddie wasn't developing. He walked along a narrow corridor and found their chief photographer polishing lenses on a stool in a walk-in cupboard full of camera equipment and stoppered glass bottles of chemicals. Eddie nodded at him over his spectacles but didn't stop polishing. Dust rose in tiny particles and danced around the yellow dusting cloth in his fingers in what light crept there from the corridor.

Seaton knew Eddie liked him. He wore a suit for work. He was polite, respectful still to his elders, because it was how he had been brought up to be. There was still a punk hangover among the young reporters in the newsroom that manifested itself in mohair jumpers and a sort of sneering generic insolence. They thought of themselves as pioneers of new-wave journalism as they tapped out wedding and funeral captions on the newsroom's ancient typewriters. And they kept threatening lightning strikes, mumbling darkly about pay parity and demarcation. None of them was well-paid. Not compared to the printers in the building's basement, anyway. But that wasn't the fault of old staffers like Eddie. So Seaton made sure he was smart and respectful. And he knew that Eddie liked him for it.

'You say she died in obscurity?'

'In poverty. Which, I suppose, pretty much amounts to the same thing. It was odd, because she had plenty of wealthy relatives who would have helped her. But she was penniless when she took her life. And she didn't do that wherever she was living. So I don't have an address.'

Eddie pondered this. 'Why is that address so important?'

'It's a long shot, to be honest with you. I need to find any papers she might have left. Her final address might give me a clue as to their location, if they still exist.'

The expression on Eddie's face suggested he thought this shot particularly long. It occurred to Seaton that Eddie was probably by now fondling the best-polished lens in the history of his department.

'I'll give you a list,' Eddie said. 'Professional guilds, associations, organisations to which photographers generally belong.' He finally put down his polishing cloth and began to pat his waistcoat pockets for a pen.

'Did she use a printer?'

'I don't know.'

'Portrait photographers often do. Printing is an art in itself, beyond a particular point in the photographic craft. And printers mean invoices and invoices mean addresses. She very likely would have had an account with a printer. If she did, that printer would have to have had her address.'

'I'll phone my girlfriend and ask if she knows.'

Eddie nodded. 'I'll have your contacts list by the time you get back.'

Lucinda was at home, sewing frantically for her degree show. Outside their flat, the relentless sun of that relentless summer had turned the grass a brittle yellow. But she was inside, toiling over her patterns, her fabrics, her little electric machine. He pictured her in the light through the muslin drapes she had run up for their windows. And Seaton felt a surge of love for her as she answered the phone with her slight, northern formality. She was living for this bloody show of hers. He loved her. He did. And he would help her all he could. He spoke in a hushed voice in the presence of the other newsroom reporters as they clattered fingers on their typewriter keys and smoked and pretended not to listen to anything worth listening to.

'No printer,' Lucinda said.

'Fuck.'

'She printed all her pictures herself. Many of them were private commissions and the fact that she printed them, that they were never in the hands of a third party, was apparently a prerequisite of the commission itself.'

'How do you know that, Lucinda?'

In Lambeth, there was a silence. In Hackney, the newsroom clattered and scraped with busy chairs.

'What?'

'How do you know that?'

'It's anecdotal. Some of her work was very risqué by the standards of the time, apparently. And some of the subjects rather well-known. Why?'

'How can you know so much about this woman? And so little?' Lambeth was silent again. So was the newsroom. 'I'm sorry,' Seaton said. He replaced the receiver on its cradle and looked at the pinboard on the wall next to his desk for inspiration. It was covered in clippings and flyers. There was a signed print of Henry Cooper pushing over a pile of pennies on behalf of some charity next to a grinning pearly queen in a Shoreditch pub. There was a leaflet for the Save Wapping campaign. There was Princess Di in puffball sleeves at a bedside in Homerton Hospital. Children face-painting; fund-raising fire fighters, a headline claiming pharaoh ants were terrorising a Clapton estate. No inspiration there.

He went and got Eddie's completed list and did a ring around. And he discovered that Pandora Gibson-Hoare had been a member of several photographic bodies and associations. But all of them, when the people he spoke to obligingly went to look, had her last address as the house in Cheyne Walk where she had lived in the period when the Café Royal picture had been taken. Seaton located and rang the number for the Chelsea Arts Club.

'Oh dear,' said the elderly female voice on the end of the

line. 'We don't keep records that far back. But I do remember her, vaguely. And I remember that she lived in Chelsea. She had a rather grand address, in Cheyne Walk.'

He looked at his watch. It was twelve o'clock. He'd been on this only two hours, which was no time at all. But he had a bad feeling about it, a feeling of discouragement. When her body had been found, according to the one obituary, she had been officially described as being of no fixed abode. It meant she had been destitute. London in the 1930s was a grim place to be homeless, a cruel place to try to find refuge in without the money to pay a regular rent. So many of the population were poor. Not genteel poverty but the relentless, widespread, worsening desperation of the Great Depression. Compassion was scarce and charity almost totally arbitrary. It had required the welfare state to provide a proper safety net. But, more importantly, it had required the welfare state to provide individuals with a paper trail it was possible to access and research and follow. And that had not been established until 1948, eleven years after the death of the woman whose trail was looking colder to Seaton by the minute.

He got up and offered to make a round of teas. He ran into Mike from photography in the staff kitchen.

'How was the furry felon?'

'Hirsute. Felonious.'

Seaton nodded, washing cups. Mike had a superior vocabulary to anyone on the writing side of the staff. But tabloid writing was all about the words you rejected. And he was a snapper, so the talent was doubly redundant.

'Arthur's café for lunch in an hour?'

'Why not?' Seaton said. Arthur's was just before the pie-and-mash shop on Kingsland Road as you headed towards Dalston Junction. After the Favourite, next to Camden Town Underground station, Seaton thought it the best café outside of Dublin. One of Arthur's mixed grills might just provide the necessary inspiration.

She was found in the river, low tide leaving her corpse stranded on the pebbles near Shadwell Stair, not far from the Prospect of Whitby pub. And that was probably as close to a common public house as someone from her background had ever come. How could she have descended so far as to die destitute? Did none of her eminent friends try to help her? Had she gone mad? The stigma of insanity was the only explanation Seaton could think of for the blanket neglect of her former circle. He looked at the obituary again, which stated with genteel disdain that she had died from a self-inflicted wound. That was an odd way even for the *Times* in 1937 to describe a drowning.

He called Bob Halliwell, the desk sergeant at Bethnal Green nick and one of his better-cultivated contacts. Though cultivated was not a word you would associate with Halliwell generally. Halliwell had told him once he spent his spare time fly-fishing. Seaton thought Halliwell probably the sort of angler who dynamited for trout.

Bob Halliwell listened patiently. Then he said, 'Forty-six years. Mick, even by your standards, this is a pretty stale lead.'

Halliwell called him Mick because he came from Dublin. Worse, the policeman thought this was genuinely funny. 'It would have been Whitechapel's ground back then, that stretch of the river.'

'But you'd have the paperwork since the consolidation. And the file would have been transferred and archived and put on to your computer records.'

Halliwell sniffed. 'In theory,' he said.

'Go on, Bob,' Seaton said. 'It's worth a drink.'

'It's worth more than one,' Halliwell said. And then, reluctantly, 'Give me the name again. I'll call you back if I can find anything.'

He was looking out of the window, to where Mike Whitehall waited for him for the walk down to Arthur's when Bob Halliwell returned his call fifty minutes later.

'She didn't drown, Mick. She cut her throat before jumping and bled to death in the water.'

Through the window, in the car park, Mike was adjusting the knot of his tie and patting down his hair in the wing mirror of the editor's Granada. Mike, tall and slim and dapper in his black suit from Robot in Covent Garden and his crêpe-soled Robot shoes.

'So it was suicide?'

'It certainly looks that way.'

'Anything else unusual?'

'Malnutrition. She had starved herself.'

Through the window, Mike had taken the pager from his belt and was playing with it.

'She was destitute,' Seaton said.

'No, she wasn't. We still have her effects here. I've got them in front of me. She was wearing diamond earrings, was madam. She was wearing a ring set with emeralds and rubies and a Cartier watch strapped to her wrist. Stuff like that was easy to pawn back then. Still would be. She wasn't a candidate for the soup kitchen, if you want my professional view. She was starving herself out of choice.'

'How come you've still got her effects?'

'According to the accompanying note, her cousin was supposed to collect them.'

'But he never did?'

Halliwell laughed. 'Hasn't so far. They're still waiting.'

'And she cut her own throat?'

'That's what the surgeon said.'

'I owe you one, Bob,' Seaton said.

'Chivas Regal,' Halliwell said. 'No half-bottles, mind.' He hung up.

Twelve

In Arthur's café Seaton sat opposite Mike, while the proprietor strolled between the crowded tables telling his customers what it was they were going to eat. There were menus in Arthur's, printed in brown italics on heavy yellow paper in transparent plastic sleeves. But once you'd been there often enough, Arthur, dapper in his white waiting-on coat and short-back-and-sides, would dictate your order to you. In the beige décor and stifling heat of the café, Mike worked through the mixed grill Arthur had ordered on his behalf while Seaton neglected a plate piled high with meat lasagne. He sipped from his glass of Coke. The café, from the door in, occupied a long narrow rectangular space. Bench seats were arranged to either side of a central aisle that ran the length of it, so you were either facing the door to the kitchen or you were facing the entrance and, beyond it, Kingsland Road. Seaton looked at the traffic through the windows rising from waist height to either side of the door. It wasn't moving. Palls of diesel hung about above the pavement in the heat and brightness from buses and lorries gridlocked out there. He could feel his thighs sticking through the light wool of his suit trousers to the plastic-covered padding of his seat. He drained his glass.

Arthur passed their table, tapping its Formica surface twice with a forefinger, taking Seaton's empty Coke glass and wiping away the circle of condensation from underneath it with a cloth before winking and moving on. He always referred to them to their faces as his Gentlemen of the Press.

He liked them enough to extend them credit at the end of the calendar month when funds were apt to run a little low. He'd offered to do so out of the blue, months earlier, without their asking. Seaton was from Dublin and Mike came from a town in Merseyside called Formby. They'd been surprised by the offer. But London was a collection of villages, when you got to know your way around them a bit. And in this part of London, they were mostly made to feel at home.

Arthur would have made a good subject for Pandora Gibson-Hoare's camera, Seaton thought. He had a face carved from mahogany, an urban metropolitan face that was somehow ageless. You could see him astride a bicycle, sweep's brushes balanced over one shoulder, dark-skinned with soot on a cobbled street a century distant. You could see him wearing a billboard in a lost newsreel, advertising to a stunned world that the *Titanic* had foundered, many lives believed lost. But there was more to his features than their timelessness. His face had the deadpan inscrutability required for convincing magic. So you could see him as a hypnotist, say, levitating some pretty, rigid volunteer in petticoats and buttoned boots. That was more Pandora's line, wasn't it? Something unsettling and improbable; an image begging more questions than it was capable of answering. In the prints in the monograph he'd seen, she seemed to specialise in precisely the opposite of what the revelatory art of photography was supposed to do.

'Aren't you going to touch that lasagne?'

Seaton picked up his fork and put sauce-covered pasta into his mouth and began to chew. He just couldn't stop thinking about Pandora. He had this image in his mind of her pale body, naked and bejewelled, her fine skin wrinkled and stained from its time in a river still poisonous in those days with its cocktail of industrial filth. Jesus, you'd have to hate yourself, then, to jump into the Thames. The Cartier watch would have stopped at the precise moment her body entered the water, an entirely redundant clue since the killer had been herself. The time of death was immaterial. He was half-tempted to take Bob Halliwell over that bottle of Scotch, see if he could have the detective take from their strongroom the drawer of artifacts claimed from Pandora's corpse. Touch them and, in doing so, touch her. But what would be the point of that, beyond a sort of ghoulish perversion?

'You know, it's one of those clichés vindicated every time I sit down with you,' Mike said, from miles away, on the other side of their table.

'What is?' He saw that Mike had cleared his plate of everything but a small puddle of egg yolk. He heard the sound of the transistor radio from the café kitchen, loudly tuned as always to Capital, a song by ABC playing, Martin Fry singing their histrionic hit 'The Look Of Love'.

'The stereotypical Irishman,' Mike said. 'The silver-tongued Celtic charmer. I mean, you lay it on a bit heavy sometimes, the way you weave in all those spellbinding aphorisms. But, personally, I have to say I'm a willing audience. I suppose I'm just a sucker for a monologue from the bog.'

Seaton smiled. 'I'm sorry.'

'Stand me another Coke. Tell me what's on your mind,' Mike said. He looked at his watch.

The thing was, for a moment, he'd been there. He'd been on the strew of pebbles by Shadwell Stair, the body under a tarpaulin at the edge of a grey tide of lapping scum, barges passing in low procession pulled by squat long-funnelled tugs billowing smoke into a low November sky. He'd smelled the river, the damp gabardine of policemen's raincoats, the sour pickled odour of waterlogged flesh, breathed the air, heavy with its burden of sulphur and soot. It had been raining. It had been raining in London on the morning the fact of Pandora's death revealed itself.

With effort, he dragged himself back. Back to Arthur's. Back to the heat, to the here and now. 'Got much on this afternoon?'

Mike grimaced. 'I'm actually thinking of calling it a day, after the furry felon. Bringing the curtain down on a brilliant career. I might as well go out on a high. A man at the top of his game should know when he's peaked. I mean, the mad monkey. Come on, professionally speaking, it just doesn't get much better than that.'

'It could be worse. It could be a pile of charity pennies toppled in a pub.'

'Depends who's doing the toppling,' Mike said. 'Last Tuesday night in the Anchor and Hope it was a woman who used to be in Pan's People.'

They were both silent for a moment. Seaton picked up his fork and then put it down on his plate and pushed away his plate of uneaten food.

'So what are you doing this afternoon?'

'The most boring sodding job on the planet,' Mike said. 'I'm taking the camera bodies in for a service. It means I've got to drive to sodding London Bridge.' He looked over his shoulder. 'In this bastard traffic. In this bastard heat.'

'Isn't there somewhere more local?'

'Undoubtedly. But Eddie insists on using the same place the company has used since about the turn of the century.'

'Tradition,' Seaton said. He was half-rising, fishing in his pockets for coins to pay for the lunch.

'More than that,' Mike said. 'It's always been renowned as the best place, with the best technicians, used by the best photographers. Which is great if you're handling Hasselblads and Leicas and your work is featuring in *National Geographic*, but a bit wasted when you're generally pointing the lens of a 35-mil Pentax at a grinning Syd James opening a garden fête. Or taking a mug shot of a delinquent primate.'

Seaton sat down. He took his notebook out of his jacket pocket and put it on the table and offered Mike his pen. 'Write down the name of this place, would you?' he said.

Mike took the pen. 'You'll have trouble finding it. The entrance is an unprepossessing little green door with no number in a ramshackle brick building dwarfed by the brutalist monstrosities erected in the sixties to either side. It's staffed entirely by gnomic Swiss lens-grinders and ancient tinkering Scots. The average age there must be about ninety. They make Eddie look boyish and carefree, the staff at Vogel and Breene.' He laughed. 'What do you run to anyway, Paul? A Kodak Instamatic?'

'It's not for me. It's for my girlfriend. It's for Lucinda.' Lucinda owned a good camera. Mike knew she did.

'She should have kept the guarantee,' he said, writing down an address. 'These people might be old-fashioned, but they're far from cheap. They'll charge her a term's grant just to take the lens cap off.'

Seaton nodded. He took back his notebook and pen. Pandora Gibson-Hoare had used Leica cameras. She hadn't been destitute and so may have owned them still at the end of her life. She had stopped working professionally. She had stopped having her pictures published. But what if she had continued to use her cameras? Or merely to have owned them? Wouldn't she have had them serviced, if only out of force of habit? And wouldn't the company that serviced them have had an up-to-date address for her?

'Thanks,' he said to Mike, in Arthur's café, the June heat sending a trickle of sweat between his shoulder blades. He looked at their plates. 'I'll get this one. This one's on me.'

He phoned as soon as he got back to his desk, asking, as Mike had advised him to ask, for Young Mr Breene.

'Young Mr Breene is about a hundred and seventy years old, but he's reasonably cordial. He doesn't have a first name, obviously. No one there does. But if you're deferential enough and try not to sound too young, he might condescend to book Lucinda's camera in before this time next year.'

He had the newsroom to himself. The other reporters generally went to the pub around the corner for lunch and had a pint and played pool and listened to The Clash on the jukebox while the bread hardened around the ham and cheese in their sandwiches and rolls.

At London Bridge, Young Mr Breene was summoned to the telephone. There was a cough and then an elderly voice with a hint of Aberdeenshire.

'How can I be of assistance?'

'I am putting together a story about the pioneer photographer Pandora Gibson-Hoare.'

There was a pause. 'Are you indeed.'

'It's for a magazine called *The Face*.'

But Young Mr Breene was unfamiliar with *The Face*.

'I wonder, did Miss Gibson-Hoare ever have her equipment serviced by Vogel and Breene?'

There was another, long pause. 'Why would you wonder that?'

'There's a peculiar quality to her work.'

Young Mr Breene chuckled. 'That was her eye, Mr Seaton. Her talent. It had nothing whatever to do with her choice of camera or of film.'

Seaton swallowed.

'You sound very certain of that.'

'The prototype of the 35-millimetre Leica was created in 1913. The Great War prevented it from going into production. It was 1924 before the camera was ready for mass production and the following year before it became widely available throughout the world. Miss Gibson-Hoare bought two of them. And you are right to suppose that we serviced them for her. In fact, I believe we still have one of them here.'

Seaton's heart was audible to him against his chest wall. 'Am I right to think she lived in Cheyne Walk?'

'In Chelsea, yes,' Breene said, and Seaton's heart descended to his stomach. 'But not in Cheyne Walk. That wasn't the address we had for her towards the end of her life.'

'Could you tell me where she did live?' He could hear the boys from the pub clattering up the stairwell, could smell the beer-and-tobacco-smoke pub smell that would cling to their clothes and hair and breath for the rest of the afternoon.

Young Mr Breene had paused again. 'You want to know where it was that Pandora Gibson-Hoare resided. Now why on earth would you want to know that?'

'I just want to paint the fullest possible picture, Mr Breene. To do that, I need to be in possession of all the detail I can accrue.'

'I see. Well, I don't profess to see the use of the information, but I don't see it can do any harm to tell it to you. That said, I won't give you the detail you seek over the telephone. Come here personally. Ask for me. Present your press credentials. Do that, and I will furnish the address.'

Thirteen

The following morning, Seaton did something he had never done before and rang into the office sick. He'd spent the small hours lying awake next to a sleeping Lucinda as light gathered in the sky and filled the room with a milky luminescence that gradually grew into dawn. At five thirty, he'd had to steal carefully out of bed and make himself a cup of tea. He drank it, looking out of their sitting-room window down at Lambeth High Street and the chink of Embankment, visible to the right where the edifice of the old government office building opposite ended and Lambeth High Street intersected with Lambeth Bridge Road. He'd never known himself feel remotely so excited by any professional pursuit.

What did he honestly hope to find?

If the flat had been provided by a friend or lover, there might be some legacy of Pandora's left behind. There might be a cache of letters shedding first-hand light on her work and the reason it so abruptly ceased. There might be half a dozen little cylinders of yet-to-be-developed film containing pictures no one had ever seen. He thought this unlikely, 35-millimetre stock probably having perished to nothing after better than four decades of neglect. But there might be prints. And that was his greatest hope. She might have shot whole stories that she edited out of what the world thought of as the Gibson-Hoare cannon. And commenting on the rediscovered work would give Lucinda's dissertation real distinction.

Two small worries nagged at Seaton as he sipped tea and looked out over the deserted dawn intersection of streets.

The first was that, in all likelihood, he would find nothing at the new address. The building could have been bombed in the Blitz or bulldozed during the wholesale redevelopment of London in the 1960s. How likely was it that, even if they survived, a set of furnished rooms would still harbour such fragile and reclusive keepsakes? It would be unlikely he'd find anything at all other than a suspicious and hostile landlord or a clueless tenant occupying impersonal space on a short let. Or a company let; because Chelsea wasn't any longer the bohemian haven it had been before the war. It was a succession of coveted postcodes and record-breaking property prices. If he found nothing, he would have to rely on the sparse facts and thin conclusions of Edwin Poole as the basis for work that would inevitably be undermined by the insubstantiality of its spun-out speculations.

And this brought him to the second, honestly more troubling, of his two concerns. Because he knew that this pursuit was about more now than helping Lucinda, however important that had been to him when he'd originally had the idea. As soon as he'd looked at the Gibson-Hoare pictures in the Poole monograph, he'd been hooked, hadn't he? Or perhaps it was the plea for help in her frightened eyes in the picture taken of her at the Café Royal. He wanted to know what troubled vision of the world informed her disquieting work. He wanted to know what it was had made her stop working with such abruptness, when her reputation was at its apparent height. He wanted to know the reason she had hidden subsequently from her former life. And she had been hiding, hadn't she, if poverty could not be blamed for forcing her into obscurity? And finally, Seaton wanted to know the reason for that ghastly suicide. He knew now that he would ask Bob Halliwell if he could see the artifacts taken from her corpse at the Whitechapel mortuary. It couldn't remotely help with the framing of Lucinda's fraudulent dissertation.

He could think of no reason for doing it beyond his own prurient curiosity. But if it took a big bribe, a litre of Chivas, he'd do it now, he knew.

From their bedroom next door, he heard Lucinda sigh in her sleep. And then he thought he caught sight of a shape, dark in space and light, through that chink in the buildings that gave a glimpse to the far right through their window of the Embankment. From where he looked, to his right, at the intersection with Lambeth High Street there was Lambeth Bridge Road, which at this hour was still empty of traffic. On the other side of it was the ornamental garden fronting the church of St Mary's at Lambeth. And beyond that was the Embankment itself.

Embankment was where now he saw a tall figure in what he could have sworn was a black top hat, staring directly back at him. He saw with surprise that the still figure was dressed formally in a black morning suit. And then, with a movement so spasmodic and sudden it made Seaton clatter the lip of his tea mug hard against his teeth, the man raised his top hat and Seaton saw that its brim trailed crêpe tails of mourning ribbon, before it was put back on his head and he turned and started to walk eastward, out of sight. But he was followed. Horses, a team of four black-plumed horses followed him into view, pulling a glass carriage hearse at the solemn funereal pace the figure had set. It progressed silently, the clop of hooves and trundle over the road of iron-bound wheels sounds that would not carry over the three or four hundred yards of distance that separated Seaton from what he saw. The whole weird procession passed out of his limited view of it through the window in no more than a fraction of time, a couple of seconds. It was twenty-eight minutes past six. It was no time for a funeral procession of such stately flamboyance. It was no time for any kind of funeral procession at all.

He'd dismiss it, he decided, as one of London's passing enigmas. There was much about the complexity and ritual of the city he did not understand. But for a junior reporter on a local London newspaper, he felt he was doing okay with his latest story. True, it was about as far off-diary as a story could get. And, as Bob Halliwell had said, he was pursuing it forty-six years after the fact. But he was making significant progress. Lucinda sighed again, dreaming he supposed, stirred from deep sleep into listlessness by the encroaching light, her warming skin and dormant senses roused by the rising heat of another day. He felt a stir of excitement grip his belly as he made the decision, then, to call in sick and call in at the premises of Vogel and Breene at London Bridge. He stroked his chin. He would shave and iron his crispest shirt. He wanted to make the best impression he could on Young Mr Breene and suspected that manners and appearance would be important in accomplishing that. Lucinda moaned and uttered a word he couldn't make out in her sleep. She didn't waken, but the one lonely word sounded anxious, he thought, afraid. He went and opened the bedroom door a chink and looked at her lying there in the diffuse light of a summer morning gathering strength and intensity through her home-made muslin drapes.

He loved her. He wanted her. What was new in him, he knew, was that he felt for her. He thought it was a shame the way that taking a degree tested people at such a tender age. He was only three years past the ordeal himself. But he didn't think Trinity College had provided quite the pressure with modern literature that St Martin's did with its fashion course. He could understand the stress she must be suffering and he sympathised with a depth of emotion and a tenderness so real and novel to him that he knew it must be love.

This glorious summer was going by as Lucinda, lovely, toiled and fretted over her little electric sewing machine in the flat. But it would be over soon. And Stuart Lockyear had called her degree collection brilliant. And Stuart wasn't one for pointless flattery. She'd done it all in shades of yellow and cream and taupe; pleated flowing dresses and bias-cut, calf-length skirts worn under waisted jackets. Already, Whistles had ordered three keynote garments from the collection for their flagship store in Marylebone. And the buyer from Harvey Nichols was said to be interested, too. The auguries were good. Seaton closed the bedroom door softly on Lucinda and stroked his chin again and went into their small bathroom to shave so that he would look the part when he rang in sick and went to London Bridge for his audience with Young Mr Breene.

At some stage of his life, Breene had been badly burned. The skin of his neck above his tie knot was pink and smooth in rivulets like spoiled wax. His eyelids were lashless and had an almost oriental cast to them. Seaton guessed that his own eyelids had been burned off, lost to the fire that had consumed most of his facial features and replaced by skin prised and shaped from painful grafts. His nose was short, almost comically arbitrary, the nostrils crude, and he had no lips at all. He didn't blink. Under his shock of still thick and unruly hair, his face looked at first glance like that of a badly put-together child. A wood counter separated them. He lifted a section of it and beckoned Seaton through. Seaton held out his hand and Breene shook it and the gash under his nose stretched across his teeth in what Seaton supposed was a smile. His grip was strong. If his hands had been burned, they had recovered their strength and aptitude. They must have done, for the man to be able to handle the intricate task of camera repairs.

'Tea or coffee,' he asked when they got to his office. His office made it plain to Seaton that Young Mr Breene did not concern himself with the day-to-day mechanics of calibrating shutter speeds and repairing light apertures. It was too big, too well-appointed. There were some good Scottish landscapes on the walls. There were pictures of Breene with various civic dignitaries at events Seaton supposed had been organised by the London Chamber of Commerce or the Lord Mayor's office. There were signed prints of photographs taken by Beaton and Bill Brandt and even Cartier-Bresson. There were half a dozen golfing trophies in a glass display cabinet. And there was a view from two high broad windows cut into the side of the building out over the river, London Bridge a resplendent curve of stone and painted iron to the left in the light of the ascending sun.

'Coffee would be very welcome.'

'But first, your credentials,' Breene said. He sat down behind the mahogany splendour of his desk in a swivel chair. Seaton, still standing, took out his NUJ and IOJ cards and the laminated pass with his picture on it the Met Police Press Bureau insisted you carry. Breene leaned over and looked. 'A very nice likeness. But you're not English, are you?'

'Dublin.'

'A wonderful city, Mr Seaton. Sit, please.'

Seaton sat in one of the two straight-backed chairs facing Breene's desk. He put his press credentials back into his wallet. Breene pressed an intercom switch and leaned into the machine. 'A pot of coffee, Mary, when you have a moment. Two cups. Thank you.'

He smiled his ragged smile again. 'You don't mind staring, Seaton, which is to your credit. How do you think I got to look such a sight for sore eyes as I do?'

'I'd say you were in the cockpit or fuselage of an aeroplane when it came under enemy attack and caught fire. You baled out, which is why you can still smile and appreciate coffee. You baled out, or your pilot got you down. But you were badly burned.'

'Very good. You've an instinct for what you do.'

'Not really. I live near the Imperial War Museum. I've spent a couple of idle Saturdays in there.' Seaton regretted the use of the word 'Idle' the moment it came out of his mouth. But Breene didn't look offended. 'May I ask about the specifics?'

Breene bowed his head, as if studying the grain on the polished surface of his immaculate desk. Which Seaton knew he wasn't. 'South Downs. Nineteen forty-three. I was the pilot. Five kills in nine missions had made me about as complacent and cocky a twenty-six-year-old as ever flew a fighter aircraft. How old are you, Mr Seaton?'

'Twenty-Five.'

Breene nodded. 'Well, then, you know how comfortably in youth the mantle of arrogance fits. Don't you?'

Seaton swallowed and nodded. This man was not the fool Mike Whitehall had led him to believe he would be meeting. But then the building wasn't exactly some squat Dickensian relic, either. Mike found a bit of embellishment amusing. A bit of understatement, evidently, too.

'I didn't see the chap who shot me down. I was on a homeward course, thinking already about a bath and a beer. When you were cruising, a Hurricane practically flew itself. I'd lost concentration for a moment and I didn't see him. But he saw me. By God, he did.'

They all had faces like this. Some pioneer plastic surgeon had worked on them. They had survived, most of them, because they were young and resistant to secondary infection and because most of them were too callow at the age to appreciate the implications of being maimed through the long life to follow. Some had even returned to active service. Seaton found himself liking Young Mr Breene. He took a deep breath and regretted having lied to him over the telephone. Breene deserved better than the crude pretence.

The coffee arrived. A woman in a liveried blouse and pinafore carried it in on a silver tray. She poured them a cup each and added the cream Seaton requested. The woman withdrew and they both sipped in silence for a while. Then Breene opened a drawer and put on a pair of white cotton gloves and, after doing so, took from the same drawer a small worn leather case fastened by a single press stud. He opened the case and a Leica camera slid into his palm, a stiff card tied by string to one of the rings from where a strap would attach. There was writing on the card, neat script written by the nib of a fountain pen, the ink aged to violet from the original blue or black by oxidisation and the passage of time. Seaton tilted his head and so could read what had been written: 'Miss Gibson-Hoare. Service and routine overhaul. 28/05/34.' The spring of 1934. Almost fifty years ago. The date was six or seven years after the composition of her last published photograph. And it was almost three years before the discovery of her body on the bank of the Thames.

Seaton looked at the camera. The iconic Leica logo was etched on to the body, of course, but the whole small assemblage looked more intricate and old-fashioned than he had seen from Leica adds in the colour supplements and the windows of the better class of camera shop. The lens housing was made of brass and there was a brass viewfinder which raised on a hinge and looked a little like the rear sight of a rifle. The black-painted body was chipped here and there to reveal the metal alloy beneath. The instrument looked more a slightly crude prototype to Seaton than the finished article. But he was guilty of investing it with the expectation of technical embellishments he knew must have come much later.

'We're in the business of repair and maintenance rather than restoration here,' Breene said. His Scottish accent sounded much stronger when he spoke now. 'You're looking at a Leica One from 1925, Mr Seaton. It may appear a little weathered. But it's perfectly serviceable.'

It was what it was, unmistakably, but it looked old, from a remote time, and sat with the mute power of a relic on Young Mr Breene's wooden desk.

Breene peeled off the gloves and left them on his desk blotter and went and stood over by one of the windows overlooking the river. His doing so didn't noticeably diminish the quantity of light in the room. The morning was very bright and Breene made a small dapper figure, his hands clasped behind his back now, against the great Victorian pane.

Seaton made no attempt to touch the camera. A part of him wanted to pick it up and heft and study it, feel the cold weight and mass of the metal and glass in his palm; sniff it, smell the scent of the thing, scent the ghost of its dead owner. But he knew that to do so would be some kind of gross violation in Breene's fastidious mind. He thought that the strengthening accent was a sort of clue, that there was a reason the man in the room with him had been taken back in time. In his mind, he did the maths. Breene had been twenty-six in 1943, so twenty at the time of the Gibson-Hoare suicide. And, Seaton would have bet money, studying then at university in Edinburgh. The accent wouldn't have survived so intact the great English seats of learning. He would have been seventeen years old and undoubtedly at school when the camera had been brought in to Vogel and Breene. But it was worth a try. Something had pulled his mind and emotions back across the decades. It was why he stood now with his back to Seaton. He was hiding the changed expression his feelings had inflicted on the pink ruin of his face.

'You knew her, didn't you, Mr Breene?'

Breene's shoulders stiffened under his suit coat. He cleared his throat, but replied still facing the window.

'You were too modest earlier, Mr Seaton. You do have an instinct for what you do. It's quite profound. And what you're doing has nothing to do with a fashion feature in a magazine I've never heard of. Does it?'

Touché, Seaton thought. 'No,' he said. 'No, it does not.'

There was a long silence before Breene said anything more. In the silence a horn wailed from a boat on the river and became faint as it passed underneath them and faded away. 'My grandfather was one of the founding partners of this business and was followed into it by his son, my own father. And my father would bring me here as a child in the school holidays sometimes to learn something of it. Typically, I would spend the morning at some attraction like the Tower or Tussaud's. And then I would come here and tinker and absorb information during the afternoon in that easy way children have. Anyway, it was the Christmas holidays. December. I remember it was cold for London, had been snowing, though it didn't really stick. I was about ten—'

Which meant 1926 or '27. The glory years for Pandora Gibson-Hoare. Her golden period.

'She arrived, late one afternoon, in full evening wear. She had on a cloche hat and a fur stole and there hung a rope of pearls around her neck heavy enough to tow a barge. She left a Bugatti, a convertible, with its engine running on the pavement outside. A Bugatti! I believe it was a Number 38. This was at dusk. The lights of the car were left on. No traffic wardens in those times, Mr Seaton. Not for the likes of Miss Gibson-Hoare. She walked in trailing perfume and pink gin and tobacco. I was in the reception area, which was bigger then. Better appointed. It was considered important in those days to maintain a grand entrance and we did, with ornamental pots and much panelled wood. All gone now, of course, in these days of utilising space efficiently. All ripped out after a visit from the time-and-motion people back in the nineteen sixties during the folly of the efficiency drive instigated by myself.'

Seaton looked at the camera on the desk. He imagined the throaty purr of an Italian roadster on the pavement outside, its headlights yellow orbs fierce with glamour as night descended on the staid city.

'Our vestibule was quite something in those days. And she was quite something in it, shaking the snowflakes from her gray mink stole, glittering, it seemed to me, under our crystal chandeliers. She was quite tall and very slender, the very epitome of the fashion at the time, far more beautiful, my father commented more than once, than any of the celebrated models she photographed. I remember she caught my eye and smiled at me. I was at the desk, practising fair-copy, trying to perfect my copperplate just by duplicating by hand the entries into the service log we kept in those days on the front desk. She was wearing lipstick. It wasn't red, it was wine-coloured, the stain on her mouth. And she smiled at me, revealing perfect teeth.'

'Why was she here?'

'She had apparently dropped a camera into the sea. She had been getting out of a speedboat or launch at a jetty and dropped her camera. The water wasn't deep and the camera was retrieved. But it had been fully immersed in salt water and needed stripping and the parts cleaning properly to allow everything to dry out.'

'Did she arrive driving the car herself?'

And Breene's shoulders stiffened again. 'What you mean is, was she alone, Mr Seaton. And the answer is that she wasn't. There wasn't a chauffeur. But she didn't arrive alone. There was a chap with her, some flashy fellow in evening wear and a silk scarf and a pair of buttoned spats. Like her, he was tall. I remember he had on an astrakhan coat and carried a cane. He didn't really look at anything, had this restlessness about him. I think they must have been on their way to a party or reception somewhere, the way they were attired.'

'There's something else, isn't there?'

And now, finally, Young Mr Breene turned around. And Seaton really could see him as the alert and curious child he'd been.

'She really was very beautiful. She had pale skin and dark eyes and auburn hair with the gloss of silk about it when it shook and caught the light. She was a remarkable creature, even to a child such as I was. But you're right, it's something else I remember most vividly. As they left, the fellow winked at me. It was a wink full of lasciviousness, a look almost entirely lost on a little boy. And he stuck out his tongue. And his tongue convulsed and cavorted between his teeth like some chopped pink eel, unaware of its death. And then he walked out with her across the parquet. Except that he more glided than walked. It was a curious affect, or trick, he possessed. As though his feet didn't actually touch the floor. To this day, I don't honestly think they did.' He laughed. 'And to this day, Mr Seaton, spats give me the shivers.'

'We're largely spared spats, these days.'

'Thank the Lord.'

'Who was he?'

Breene indulged in one of his silences, before answering. 'I asked my father. And my father told me he was thought by some to be the wickedest man in the world. And I didn't ask anymore. I left it at that.'

Seaton said nothing.

'We don't all share your curiosity, you see.'

'Why weren't you more curious? Why aren't you?'

Breene looked across to the camera reposing on his desk. 'Because curiosity killed the cat. And the cat had nine lives. And that's eight more than I've ever been able to boast.'

Seaton nodded. He remembered then what Young Mr Breene had said about the mantle of arrogance. About how comfortably, on the young, the mantle of arrogance could fit.

'Come. Since it was what you came here for, I'll give you that address.'

Fourteen

He went there straightaway. He looked it up in his heavily thumbed and dog-eared *A to Z* in the bright sunlight on the street outside Vogel and Breene and then jogged towards London Bridge tube with only a glance at his watch. It was eleven fifteen. He'd been with the old man over an hour. It had seemed less at the time, but he was in a hurry now to recover the vestiges of an enigmatic and elusive life. And he could not wait to do so.

It was just after midday when he crossed Fulham Broadway at the junction to the right of the station exit and walked up Harwood Road, the Town Hall building on his left a high jumble of stained ornamentation in the unforgiving light and still-rising heat of the day. Left again into Moore Park Road and the traffic sounds from the junction he'd crossed seconds earlier retreated into something like a rumour. He didn't know this part of London at all. He was relieved to see that Moore Park Road comprised two facing terraces of three-storey Victorian houses. The angle of the sun cast the road between the terraces into shadow. It was suddenly cool, as well as quiet. There were odd parked cars. But there was no road traffic moving. At the end of the block, at the first intersecting road, he saw there was some kind of shop. There was a pub next to it, the sign obscured by hanging baskets of flowers and plants that, even from here, he could see the dry summer had defeated. But the road itself had been spared bomb damage, redevelopment and other urban catastrophes. It was intact. He started to study the numbers over the knockers on the doors.

Ten minutes later, his knuckles tender from rapping on solid oak, he walked into the shop a block down the road. The knocker on the door he wanted had been too stiff with clumsily applied paint to make much noise on impact. It suggested whoever lived there didn't get many visitors. But his hammering fist hadn't aroused anyone either. And there was no bell to ring. The curtains had been drawn and when he'd stooped and tried to look through the narrow letterbox, the interior had been dark, with a dank odour somehow discouraging to the notion of life, let alone domesticity. The smell had reminded him of the smell of the high-rise slums he sometimes had to go to with Mike Whitehall, doing conditions stories on damp or cockroach infestation on Hackney's neglected estates. It was the smell of squalor. It seemed odd to encounter it now, here. This wasn't the opulent riverside Chelsea of Cheyne Walk; that was obvious. The parked cars had some mileage on them and there were patches of graffiti celebrating the Second Division heroes of Stamford Bridge here and there on walls. But most of the addresses looked well-maintained, smart in the discreet way prosperity usually manifests itself among people used to being prosperous.

'How's it going,' he said absently, walking into the newsagent's shop, fishing for change, his mind on his summer thirst and the Diet Coke that would quench it.

'You'd be a Dublin man, I'm thinking.'

Seaton looked at the figure behind the counter. He'd expected an Asian proprietor, because in London that was what you almost always got. The man behind the counter was flanked by Chelsea FC pennants on one side and a giant colour poster of the centre forward Kerry Dixon rising for a header on the other. His shop was like a small shrine to the Blues. Except for one sly little shield tacked to the rear wall, visible above his left shoulder and bearing the three-castle crest of the Dublin gaelic football team. You'd have to know what it signified even for it to register, so discreetly placed was it. But Seaton knew it all right. The proprietor himself was blue-eyed, long from the girlish lower lip to the tip of the chin, dark curly hair tumbling down his forehead as far as his eyebrows. And his waistline was winning the battle to force his tucked-in shirt out over his trousers. He looked like all of Paul Seaton's uncles rolled into one and the thought made Seaton smile.

'You'd be a Dublin man?' he repeated.

There was a way to play this. 'I wouldn't be after coming from anywhere else, now. Yourself?'

'Ah,' the newsagent said. 'There's not a town to touch it. Not at all. Nowhere.'

'Not even London?'

'Oh, London's a grand place, right enough. Sure it's grand. There's only the one thing London's lacking.'

'It'll never be home,' Seaton said.

'As long as I live and breathe,' the newsagent said, 'it'll never be home.' He sighed. There was a silence.

'And the Guinness,' Seaton said.

'Right enough,' the newsagent said, nodding his head. 'And the Guinness, too.'

He spread his hands across the newspapers and magazines on his countertop. The ritual greeting was complete. Dublin had been duly honoured. 'Now,' he said. 'What is it you'll be wanting?'

He sounds to me, Seaton thought, like I must sound to Lucinda.

'You don't happen to know the people live at number eighteen?'

The Dubliner stared at him. 'Ah, man. You wouldn't be a copper, now. Would you?'

Seaton pulled out his NUJ card. 'It's a routine thing.' He nodded to a wall rack hung with papers folded to show their mastheads and the first line of their front-page banner headlines. 'We've got to fill 'em. For you to sell 'em.'

'You're looking for a scruffy old guy. Lives there alone. Tall, wears a beard. We deliver him the *Telegraph* daily. He also takes the *Racing Post* and *Punch*.'

'Deliver? The man doesn't live more than a minute away.'

'He's a recluse, so he is.'

'What time does he get home?'

'Sure, he's home now.'

Seaton looked at his tender knuckles. He didn't think anyone was that reclusive.

'You'd be better knowing what time he comes round,' the newsagent said, grinning. 'It's fair to say the feller takes a drink. I'd say he drinks well into the small hours. I've never seen him surface before five in the afternoon, when he'll sometimes brave the light for a pint of milk. But you're better catching him around six. The later you leave it, the better the humour he's apt to be in.'

Seaton looked at his watch. It was only twelve thirty. 'Thanks,' he said. 'That's grand.'

'Semi-skimmed,' the Dubliner said.

'What?'

'The milk.'

'That's grand,' Seaton said. He was at the door, had the door held open, when the obvious occurred to him. 'Would you happen to know the feller's name?'

'Gibson-Hoare,' the Dubliner said.

But he pronounced the latter part of it, whore.

There was nothing else for it but to go back home to Lambeth. He couldn't entertain himself window-shopping in the King's Road for five and a half hours. He had to stay out of North London altogether unless he was spotted, fit and mobile, when he was supposed to be bedridden with a stomach bug. He'd get a district line train to Embankment and walk over Hungerford Bridge. Then he'd walk along the South Bank, under Waterloo Bridge, under Westminster Bridge, up the steps at Lambeth Bridge, across the road and home. He'd take a glorious stroll along the summer river, trying to calm himself, trying to contain his swelling sense of excitement and anticipation before returning to Moore Park Road by later simply reversing the route.

Early on a Tuesday afternoon, Lucinda wouldn't be home. She would be at college, still frantically putting together the finishing touches to her degree show. It seemed to Seaton a superhuman amount of work for one student to accomplish on the timetable and the grant. But it was the same for everyone on the degree course. The standards set were the reason St Martin's had such an exalted reputation. And he was taking care of her dissertation. At least she didn't have to worry about that any longer.

He shivered, realising he'd reached the point, about forty feet from the steps leading up to the bridge, where he'd seen the odd incongruous funeral cortège not long after first light that morning. There were low-walled rectangles of grass here, where the Embankment widened, decorative features for the tourists to sit on at the weekend and enjoy the view and their cornets when the ice-cream van parked here. He walked between two of them, out to the side of the road, where the iron-rimmed wheels of the carriage hearse had trundled a few hours ago. The heat was intense. Molten bubbles of tar glistened in the sun in odd places where the road surface had been hastily patched in repair. But the weird apparition from this morning had left no physical evidence of its passing. He looked across towards Lambeth High Street, to their block of flats, finding with his eyes the window he had watched it all through, the window looking blackly back.

He picked up his kit from home and walked along Lambeth Bridge Road to Fitzroy Lodge. And alone in the gym, he skipped eight five-minute rounds as the game's deities looked down on him from the fight posters decorating the walls. He needed to dissipate some energy. There were Hagler and Hearns and Leonard and Duran tacked up there on the walls. As trains trundled above through the weary heat on the lines in and out of Waterloo, he watched the timer on the wall tick by the rounds and skipped.

It was still only three thirty when he finished at the gym. He dumped his gear in the flat and walked along Lambeth High Street to the Windmill pub. He thought Lambeth High Street as ill-named a thoroughfare as he'd ever come across. It carried no traffic. It was bordered along one side for most of its length by a large green of parched yellow grass and indolent trees with a jumble of old tombs and headstones half-buried by bushes and thorns at its eastern boundary. You had to go down Old Paradise Street or Whitgift Street, through the railway arches to Lambeth Walk, to encounter shops. He didn't know how Lambeth High Street had ever earned the sobriquet. They had early photographs taken there hung on the walls of the pub. Victorian children with the bruised pallor of poverty stared at the camera from bedraggled awnings. It had looked no busier then. The biggest difference in that black and white world had been the mud in the gutters and between the cobbles on the road.

In the couple of months he'd lived there, the Windmill had become not just Seaton's local, but his pub of choice. Most of the regulars during the day were firefighters from the station that neighboured the pub, coming in for a homeward-bound pint at the end of their shift. There were office workers at lunchtimes and in the early evenings from the government building opposite the block in which he and Lucinda lived. And in the evenings proper, there were eight or ten locals who propped up the bar with expressions made stoical by the sheer entrenchment of their nightly beer ritual.

Seaton ordered a cheese and ham roll and a pint of Director's bitter and went to sit and eat and drink on the bench on the pavement outside the pub. Opposite, at the western limit of the green, was a small walled public garden containing a single cherry tree. The bloom had gone from the cherry tree now. He bit into his roll. The butter was fresh and the ham moist and tender in his mouth.

It was a lovely spot, this. It had almost the seclusion of a secret place. He loved its quiet, so close to everything. He had spent hours in the evenings here with Lucinda, as the light had lengthened over the late spring, after tennis usually, before the approach of her degree show had robbed him of her time.

Faintly, through the window behind him, he could hear the familiar tape the landlord seemed to favour most often, playing through bookshelf speakers perched behind the bar. The tape was a soul compilation. It had always seemed to Seaton a particularly melancholy collection of songs. Now, he heard the Isley Brothers' 'Harvest For The World' segue into Billy Paul singing 'Me And Mrs Jones'. He sipped bitter and chewed on the fresh bread of his roll and looked at the thinning blossom grown pink and dusty on the tree in the garden opposite while Billy Paul sang his hymn and, Seaton thought, probably his requiem to his clandestine lover and their affair. And then it was Marvin Gaye and 'Abraham, Martin And John'. The song had been a big hit for Smokey Robinson in America. But nobody could sing as plaintively as Marvin Gaye about promise wilfully lost.

Seaton didn't know whether the landlord had compiled the tape or bought it. He'd been tempted to ask, half-resolving to seek it out and buy it for himself. But he'd decided it was better heard at, and associated with, the pub. It wouldn't have sounded the same at home. Through the window, now, it had a melancholy charm you couldn't duplicate, heard above the conversation of the lunchtime stragglers, against the occasional ring of the till, faint through a summer window, all the more poignant for the fragile way in which it carried to his ears.

Seaton sipped beer and listened to the loop-tape, faint through the pub window, and looked at the cherry tree in the little public garden opposite through drowsy heat. He considered the time on the face of his wristwatch. It was a quarter to five. It was about time to go. He drained the last of his beer and brushed his lap for crumbs. And he wiped his mouth with a paper napkin from his sandwich plate.

In the future, he would often look back to this exact moment, sometimes with the nostalgia and grief and self-pity mingling so intensely in him he wept at the recollection, considering it to be for him the last departing day of what he would have called a normal life. He knew, in his heart, the sentiment was self-deceiving, the creeping damage already by then at least partially inflicted. He didn't really enjoy his moment that day outside the pub as he had so often in his recent past. He lacked the capacity for relaxation. The excitement in him over the address in Moore Park Road was too urgent and compelling to allow it. He swallowed his food and drank his beer without savouring either. But, like everyone else, Paul Seaton sometimes took refuge and comfort in a lie. When all was said and done, he was only human.

Fifteen

In Chelsea, this time, the door was opened, answering the stiff knocker almost straightaway.

Sebastian Gibson-Hoare was tall and thin and middle-aged, and flamboyantly undressed for the late afternoon in a Chinese silk print dressing gown. He opened his door in a cloud of competing odours. Under cologne, his breath was a mingling of brandy and the liquorice smell of French cigarettes. The cologne was Vetiver and he had on far too much of it. His breath was all the richer because he was panting. Looking past him into the hallway, Seaton supposed it was descending the stairs that had winded him so. They were steep. On the other hand, he'd been coming down them. With the long tobacco-stained teeth his smile revealed and his thinning combed-over hair, the effect of him altogether in the daylight should have been shambolic and terrible. But it wasn't, somehow. Maybe it was his smile, which was easy and disarming. Perhaps it was his height and build, which gave his greeting gestures a sort of easy elegance.

'A cold caller,' he said. 'How novel. Now, your patter may be persuasive and I might even be in dire need of double glazing or complete sets of encyclopedias. But I ought to warn you, I'm an undischarged bankrupt.'

Seaton said nothing. He thought there was likely more to come.

'And I'm an unrepentant bankrupt, too,' Gibson-Hoare said.

Seaton said nothing. He'd had a speech prepared, of course. But it didn't now seem to suit either the man or the circumstances. He lifted his hand to reach into his pocket for his wallet and his press card but then let it drop again. Officiousness did not seem the right route, to his instinct, to this man's real whereabouts, or confidentiality.

Gibson-Hoare sniffed. And he introduced himself. And the two of them, on the threshold of his house, shook hands. 'You'd better come in,' he said. 'You'd better come in and tell me why I've so mysterious a visitor.'

His sitting room was at the top of the stairs. Before they ascended, Seaton took in what detail he could of the gloomy entrance hall as his eyes tried to adjust after the brightness of the day outside. At the far end was a kitchen, one side of a beaded curtain in the doorway pulled back to reveal the chipped enamel of an old stove. To the right was a doorway, curtained off by a heavy brown drape. That led to the cellar, Seaton supposed, going on the faint smell of damp clinging to the velvet curtain fabric. He could smell mouse droppings, too, the overall atmosphere of decay, of squalor, he'd sensed peering through the letterbox depressing now he was inside the place.

But there was nothing squalid about Gibson-Hoare's sitting room. It was large and light through two handsome windows and richly coloured with original art and the scattered plush of rugs and cushions. His furniture was clearly antique and very substantial. The room was spacious enough not to be cramped by the presence of a Steinway piano. The lid was lifted over the keys and from the patina of wear on their ivory, it was obvious that the piano was frequently played. Gibson-Hoare seemed to like antique weaponry. A pair of duelling pistols had been mounted in a glass-fronted case on one wall above a row of swords. He owned a claymore and a cutlass, but the rapier appeared to be his weapon of choice where cold steel was concerned. His booze occupied cut-glass decanters in the bottom half of a large globe of the world, the upper hemisphere pulled back on a hinge in readiness. Each decanter wore a silver necklace with an engraved plate telling you what it contained. Seaton knew next to nothing about antiques, but it was obvious there was a lot of valuable stuff here. Either its owner was lying about being a bankrupt, or the bailiffs assigned to his case were criminally negligent.

'Tea? Or something stronger?'

'Tea would be grand.'

Seaton thought he was probably about sixty years old. If he was, then almost everything he owned here pre-dated him. When he served the tea, the sleeve of his dressing gown rode up to reveal the rectangular case of a Rolex wristwatch with an age-mottled face, hanging from a gold bracelet with too many links for the thinness of his wrist. What else had he inherited, Seaton wondered. A cache of pictures? Personal memories shedding light on the life of the enigmatic relative he may well have known as a child and adolescent?

He sipped tea. Sunlight warmed the room through the windows. Dust motes rose in Vetiver-scented air. He wondered how to begin. 'You're very trusting, Mr Gibson-Hoare. This being London and all.'

'No I'm not, my young friend. I'm not trusting at all. You're very presentable. You've a charming brogue and honest Irish eyes, but you wouldn't have got through the door without what Young Mr Breene told me about you when he was considerate enough to call.'

'He called you after my visit this morning?'

'He called me after you telephoned him yesterday. Without my permission, he wouldn't have given you this address. A firm doesn't thrive like Vogel and Breene has over the years without manifesting some measure of professional integrity.'

Or discretion, Seaton thought, wondering what the man in front of him would have made of Breene's description of his one childhood sighting of Pandora. And more to the point, of her date, on that winter evening long ago.

'There's no cache of pictures for you to discover, Mr Seaton. Antiques is the business I've dabbled in during those infrequent periods of my life when I've summoned the necessary energy for trade. I know a little about commerce, something about collecting, a fair amount about art. Copyright would be mine by ownership and default. With Horst prints selling as posters in every branch of Athena, I know what such pictures could be worth, potentially. I know what the originals might fetch at auction. But they don't exist.' He sipped tea. 'If they ever did, they're long perished.'

'Did you know her?'

Gibson-Hoare laughed. He threw back his head and his teeth were stained brown against thinning enamel. 'Goodness me. Why don't we get right to the heart of the matter?'

He was lonely. He might or might not be queer as well, Seaton thought, but the key to it was the loneliness. He didn't see many people. And he enjoyed company, after his peculiar fashion. Seaton felt suddenly depressed, deflated. Because he knew now that Gibson-Hoare had not known Pandora. If he had, he would have answered rather than avoided the question. It would have given him more to say. It would have provided him with the company for longer in which to inflate and indulge his reminiscences.

'She was a distant cousin,' he said. He took his teacup over to the globe and took the stopper from a whisky-coloured decanter and poured an inch or so into his tea. He stirred it and sipped. 'I never met her. I never even knew about this house until I inherited it in 1963. But in the twenty years I've been here, if there had been hidden treasure, I'd have found it by now. All I have discovered is damp. And rodents, latterly. I'm keeping the death-watch beetles and woodworm at bay, but it's altogether a terrible fag, domesticity.'

Seaton said nothing. He didn't think inheriting a London house a plight he could sympathise with wholeheartedly.

'She had no talent for it.'

'For what?'

Gibson-Hoare chuckled his throaty smoker's chuckle. He rummaged for cigarettes in a pocket of his dressing gown and found the packet. 'Thought that would get your attention. For domesticity.'

'How do you know?'

He proffered the pack with a cigarette clenched between his teeth. Seaton smiled and shook his head. Gibson-Hoare lit up with a large silver lighter shaped like a swan he took from the table with the tea things on it. He exhaled smoke, blue in the dusty sunlight in the room.

'I didn't meet her. But my late neighbour did. And he had some rum things to say about the hours she kept. And the noise she managed to generate. Always at night, apparently. She was a disruptive little soul, was our Pandora.'

'Did she occupy the house alone?'

Gibson-Hoare smoked and picked something imaginary from between his teeth with a thumbnail. 'I can't imagine what possible business that can be of yours.'

'None of it is my business, sir. And viewed one way, this visit, uninvited, is an intrusive and wholly unnecessary interruption.'

Gibson-Hoare frowned and smoked. Pacing back and forth across his rugs, he looked to Seaton like a character from one of those plays John Osborne's work a mile down the King's Road had made obsolete decades ago.

'Viewed another way, my being here could be the first small step in the rediscovery of someone whose work should never have been forgotten. Pandora was a pioneer. She possessed technical brilliance and the courage to be original. Even Mr Breene commented on what a singular and gifted eye she had. And I'd say he's an experienced judge, fairly grudging in his praise.'

Gibson-Hoare sat down. The frown had lightened to a more thoughtful expression. But he still didn't speak.

'These things have their own momentum, so they do. Who knows? If you can summon the necessary energy, in a year's time you might find yourself curating a retrospective exhibition of your late cousin's work.'

Gibson-Hoare looked skyward and Seaton read the look as one of patronised exasperation and feared he'd probably gone too far. But then he said, 'There are some of her things here, still. One characteristic of families like mine is that we never throw anything away. I can assure you there are no photographs. Those she destroyed herself, I was told. And with some enthusiasm, apparently. That according to my late neighbour, who watched her light the brazier in the garden one December afternoon and was forced the following morning to complain about the acrid smell of the smoke as it still smouldered through a shower of rain. There are no photographs. But there are some clothes and other artifacts. You're welcome to look at them if you think it will help you paint a more vivid picture than the one you have.'

Seaton thought of the smell that had permeated the thick velvet drapes concealing the cellar steps, contaminating the hallway even in the current heatwave with the clammy languor of damp. He wondered how much of a stomach he would have for rummaging through mildewed coats and mould-spotched dresses; the rotting gladrags of a suicide. Her camera had been a relic, sterile, pristine between Mr Breene's white cotton hands. And he had coveted its touch. Her decaying ephemera, folded into closets at the bottom of the basement steps, seemed altogether less beguiling.

In his mind, Seaton visited again the stretch of river where the tide had abandoned Pandora. He could smell the sodden wooden supports of the landing stages behind where the group of them stood in the still, chilly absence of breeze. Small stones slithered in the mud and puddles of oil slick dumped by river vessels, under their leather-shod feet. In the mist on the water a foghorn sounded blindly and the police doctor opened his bag between his feet with a click of its lock and a waft of surgical spirit from the small bottles and wound rolls of lint and shiny instruments within. The doctor plucked his fob watch by its chain from his waistcoat pocket and made a verbal note to a plainclothes man of the time. The man nodded under his trilby and looked briefly at the body, uncovered now. He took off his hat in a gesture of respect for the dead. And he looked at the wound, bloodless and wide after its time in the water, dividing the flesh of her throat.

Out towards the centre of the river, there was a sudden commotion like the rumble of a storm and the surge of a cascading unseen torrent. It was a fire boat, the water pulled up through its pumps and pushed through the brass tips of its hoses, the noise the scream and impact of the deluge steepling down and crashing against the surface of the Thames. They were practising out there, rehearsing. They were preparing for the conflagration that would come with the looming war. Pandora Gibson-Hoare had elected to miss the performance. She was missing even this sombre rehearsal for it.

'Cold feet, Mr Seaton?'

'What?' He blinked. He sipped at his tea, which had grown cold. His host had lit a fresh cigarette and was at the centre again of his blue aura of French tobacco smoke in the light bathing his sitting room. 'Not at all,' Seaton heard himself say.

'It's all in the attic. One floor up. There's a ladder. I won't go up there myself, it's a few years since I've had the required agility. So you'll be climbing solo, as it were. But you're welcome to take a look if you so wish.'

Her stuff was in a trunk. It wasn't damp up here. Light entered through a single pane of glass. The skylight looked welded to its frame and was spotched on its exterior with rain stains and years of pigeon shit. But the illumination it allowed was a help as well as a relief. The attic wasn't as crowded as Seaton had expected. The house had a flat roof and it was a relatively large and regular space. He'd expected a jumble of Gibson-Hoare's antiques, a rejected arsenal of rusting weaponry and old keyboard instruments, perhaps. But there wasn't much and it all looked personal. A few pictures were propped against one wall. There was an oriental frieze on articulated lacquered panels showing a stork in a rocky stream. There were some elderly 78s in faded paper sleeves in a gilt rack that had tarnished badly. Her trunk stood in the furthest corner from the light, hide-bound and studded with ornamental bronze rivets, her initials picked out in mother of pearl above the lock mechanism. She'd been fond of pearls, he remembered, looking at the lock, fingering the key to it Gibson-Hoare had given him. She'd worn a rope of them thick enough to pull an ocean liner out of dock.

The lock surrendered easily and he opened the trunk inhaling Pandora's scent, what was left of it, the smell of her ghost, perhaps, but hers, he knew, as old perfume and tobacco and perhaps the dust from her skin rose and filled his nostrils and lungs with an odour from a dead time. He was reminded of leather and cinnamon. There was candle wax and expensive soap and something underlying it all, harsh and indescribable. He thought about the Café Royal picture, then. And the thought came into his mind that the sourness he smelled might be the sweat of fear, secreted fifty years ago.

The thought startled him.

Something scurried in the corner, in the shadows and concealed space behind the stacked paintings, and Seaton was reminded of the mouse droppings he'd smelled in the gloomy vestibule of the house. He listened for it to repeat, poised leaning over the trunk, for the skitter of rodent claws. But all was quiet again. He was so tense, he realised, he was forgetting now to breathe. He pulled in a deep breath and knelt down and put his hands into the trunk and pulled from it three slithery silken piles of old frocks and scarves and underskirts and stockings and camisoles and put each pile on the floorboards next to him.

It felt wrong, doing this. Not sacrilegious exactly, but a spiritual violation nonetheless. Seaton thought it might be the vestiges of child Catholicism that made him feel it. But this was Pandora's intimacy, in this box, protected by her suicide, now trespassed on, by him. One of the piles of her things subsided and spread over the floorboards in a slither of elderly satin and stitched ornamental beads. The rodent in the corner chewed at paint and canvas, quietly, so as not to be heard.

A scatter of heavier, more solid items lay on the bottom of the trunk. There was a tarnished silver cigarette case and a pair of opera glasses in a case of Morocco leather. There was a flattened cloche hat and two pairs of shoes with faded French embossing still visible on their footbeds. He didn't recognise the label. Many of the old, pre-war labels would have perished with the fall of France. But the shoes were immaculately crafted. There was a pewter brandy flask, this tarnished, too, with a dog's head engraved on one side. Seaton thought it might be a spaniel. Encased in a velvet box, he found a Cross fountain pen with her initials engraved in the gold of its clip. There was a cigarette holder, made of tortoise-shell and densely stained with tar. And there was a litter of coins: French francs and centimes and an English shilling and a twelve-sided threepenny bit.

Restoring this pile of junk into contents now neatly packed, Seaton was forced to ask himself precisely what it was he thought he was doing. Suicides did not deliberate, did they, about their legacies? People driven by the compulsion to destroy their own lives did not, by definition, consider their existences worthwhile. So why would a suicide contrive to leave anything worthwhile behind? The cold fact was that they wouldn't. And the answer to the question of what he was doing was, surely, that he was wasting his time, intruding on a lost and private life by sifting through its sad detritus. He should stop.

He shook his head. He breathed in another deep lungful of dusty air. He reached for the trunk lid to close it. And it almost was closed, when he paused and opened it fully again. He leaned carefully over the contents and stretched out his palms and felt around the smooth insides of the trunk itself. And doing so, he felt the subtle protrusion of the thing concealed under its fabric lining, under the lock mechanism, thinking, *now this is more like it.*

His fingers had found a flat, solid shape. It measured about seven inches by five and protruded about an inch proud of the trunk lining. He sat back on his heels to gather himself. He took everything out of the trunk again, careful not to let any of the solid objects thump against the floor. He lifted the trunk slightly and angled it to the light. The lining was faded and worn and running threadbare in a line around the lip of the trunk. But it was intact. Whatever was concealed beneath it had been hidden there for a very long time.

He squeezed sweat out of his eyebrows with his thumb. A moment ago, he had been on the brink of giving up, the trunk lid a fraction of an inch away from being closed and locked forever on Pandora and her mysteries. Except that he hadn't been about to give up. Not really, he hadn't. The closing of the trunk lid had been a gesture made to common sense and common decency. But it had only been a gesture. He couldn't have given up, not until all hope was exhausted.

His instinct simply wouldn't have allowed it. A sensation ran through him like a strong and vibrant current. Asked, he would have called it the thrill of vindication. But what it actually felt like, up there in the heat and the dusty light, was triumph.

He heard music, then, the notes drifting upward from two floors below as Sebastian Gibson-Hoare played the piano. The effect of it was instant on the rodent sharing the attic with Seaton. There was an explosion of sound over in the corner and the canvas of the paintings stacked there seemed almost to ripple with shock in its aftermath. Then nothing, the creature having apparently fled. Seaton recognised the tune, which was 'I Wonder Who's Kissing Her Now?'. And even as his fingers scrabbled for purchase against the fabric lining the trunk, he thought what a very cultured method Sebastian Gibson-Hoare had of pest control.

It was a nonsensical thought and its intrusion into his mind almost caused him to laugh out loud. He was giddy with excitement. He was damaging property that wasn't his. He was humming the tune to himself at a speed that kept forcing him to loop back to the melancholy tempo set by Gibson-Hoare at the piano downstairs. The old cloth gave with a rent like a gasp of asthmatic breath and he held up into the daylight a flat package tightly wrapped in oilskin bound with twine. As he lifted his jacket, as he pulled his shirt free of his belt, he could feel the sweat glossy on his back in the heat, and the enormity of his crime. He tucked his shirt back in over the package, his find held snug against his spine by the tension of his belt. He closed and locked the trunk and then turned it around so that the lock faced the wall and the hinges faced the room. As though such a childish ploy could conceal the theft. But then, how could you be accused of stealing something no one living had even known was there? He pulled the trunk back around to its original position, wiped his hands on his trousers and took a deliberate breath. He buttoned his jacket. It was an absurd thing to do in the heat, so he unbuttoned it again. The song on the piano had wandered into 'I Get A Kick Out Of You'. The light in the attic had subtly diminished. Gibson-Hoare could really play the piano. It must be talent, pure and simple, he thought. The man would never have possessed the application for painstaking practice. Seaton looked at his watch. He'd been up there only fifteen minutes. He climbed down the ladder carefully, closing the hatch softly above himself as he descended.

It was a quarter to seven when he was shown cordially out of the house, Gibson-Hoare almost apologetic that the visit hadn't been a success, but managing to suggest subtly also that Seaton's expectations had been naïvely optimistic. 'History isn't as convenient a calling as journalism, my boy. Your sources tend to lie beyond the reaches of a contacts book. And my distant cousin was precisely that, wasn't she? Pandora was elusive both by nature and design.' He shrugged. They shook hands. And doing so they brought to its conclusion what Seaton supposed for Sebastian Gibson-Hoare had been an amusing, if forgettable, interlude.

Sixteen

He had to find a phone box. On an average Tuesday, he'd have been home half an hour ago. By the time he got home, he'd be well over an hour late. Lucinda wouldn't exactly be tearing her hair out, might well be working late herself at college, but he had to oblige her with the courtesy of a call. He saw a phone box at the crossroads, diagonally opposite the small newsagent's and shrine to Chelsea FC he had visited that morning.

Fishing for change, with the number dialed and the receiver against his car, his eyes wandered over to the shop's busy facade. In his pocket, he fingered a ten-pence piece. And he saw the shape of the big Irish proprietor, standing perfectly still behind the glass of his window.

'Hello?'

'It's me.'

'Hello, you.'

Except that he wasn't standing perfectly still. He was standing on the one spot right enough, with his arms hanging at his sides. But he seemed to be swaying, ever so slightly, gently rocking from side to side.

'You've got a murder mystery to crack and you won't be home till midnight.'

'Jesus. You're psychic.'

Lucinda laughed. The sound was music, after the hacking laughter of Gibson-Hoare. 'Is she tall and blonde? Your murder mystery?'

And Seaton had to laugh himself. 'Listen, she doesn't have

me forking out for Chartreuse or Armagnac every time I go to the bar.'

A hundred yards away the Irishman was a dark shape, swaying ever so slightly behind the glass of his shop. Seaton was aware of the bump of what he'd stolen, pressing and unfamiliar against the small of his back. Across the road the Irishman's face was in shadow, you couldn't really make it out. But his mouth seemed to be hanging open as he swayed and watched. It was hot and close in the phone box, but Seaton shivered. The pips went and he shoved another coin in the slot.

'I suppose she drinks cider,' Lucinda said, 'out of the can.'

'In the street,' Seaton said.

'In the gutter. What time will you be home?'

'Nine at the latest.'

'Your dinner will be in the dog.'

'We don't have a dog.'

'I'll go out and pick up a stray.'

The Irishman had lifted one arm and seemed to be pointing his finger in the direction of the phone box. Seaton blinked sweat out of his eyes. You couldn't really tell. He wasn't much more than a hulking swaying silhouette behind the busy display and reflection of the glass.

'Where are you really, Paul?'

'Just doing a shit boring job with Mike. All around the houses for no more than an extended photo caption, probably.'

'Poor you,' Lucinda said.

He didn't have a clue as to why he had just lied. He had surprised himself with the lie, with its casual conviction. Ordinarily he was a hopeless liar. At least, he was when he cared about the person he was lying to.

'See you about nine, then.'

'See you then.'

He pushed open the stiff phone-box door and turned his back on the strange apparition haunting the shop over the road. He'd decided he would get the Underground to Embankment station and then walk to the Victoria Embankment Gardens and examine the package, sitting on one of the benches there. He wanted to see what he had in daylight and in the open air. He needed to be away from Gibson-Hoare's house, away from him and any other potential witnesses to his theft, before he did it. In the gardens he would be almost home, practically within sight of home, but on the other side of the river from where he lived. Lucinda sometimes walked along the river, but she never crossed it on her walks. He could go and examine what he had, undiscovered, there.

It was a favourite spot with him. He sat on one of the row of benches facing the Embankment wall and the river beyond. He sat in the shade of one of the great trees that bordered the green and the path. Some of the trees trailed leaves from branches so burdened by their own weight that they bowed and dipped beneath the surface of the river at high tide. The tide was high as Seaton sat. And he could hear the soft lap of water and leaves on the other side of the wall. The package lay now on the weathered black wood of the bench, next to him. The twine knotted around it looked still taut but, he knew, would have been weakened by time. He picked the package up and hefted it, smelled the yellow oilskin and the faint must of what it protected and concealed. He tested and snapped the twine between finger and thumb and let it unravel, and unwrapped the oilskin and let the contents into the light for the first time in what he knew must be close to fifty years.

A couple walked by, tourists speaking softly in Italian. Big Ben, off through the tangle of trees to his left, boomed the quarter-hour. Office staff at the end of their working day were playing a scratch game of football in the gloaming somewhere on the green behind him, using traffic cones for goals. Dimly, he was aware of their shouts and cajoling. There was passing traffic, faint on Millbank. He heard the river-water lap, the lazy wake of a passing boat.

He held a notebook in his hands. Its cover was blue, marbled board and it measured about eight inches by five. Its pages were lined, flimsy, each page covered by neat handwriting in black pencil. There was some mildew spotting on the rear cover of the book but when Seaton flicked through it he saw that the pages were intact, whole, complete. On the inside front cover, there was a hand-drawn map of a section of the southwest coastline of the Isle of Wight. Seaton recognised the Needles, stretched out to the west beyond Freshwater Bay. The coastline from Freshwater to Ventnor had been described in this small sketch with superb detail and draftsmanship. The map ventured inland, to scale, only as far as Brightstone Forest and Calbourne and Chillerton, where it stopped. At the northern border of Brightstone Forest, a circular mark had been made. Underneath this mark, the cartographer had identified the spot with two words. Fischer's House.

Seaton had known the package did not contain photographs. The dimensions had been wrong for prints of the period, along with the solidity and density and weight, something he sensed even before removing the oilskin wrapping. But he felt elated, much more than disappointed, at what he had discovered. He flicked through the notebook. She had numbered each of the pages, two hundred of them, neatly in their top right-hand corners.

Behind him, the footballers were putting on their track tops now and picking up their bags in the aftermath of their game. The good-looking Italian couple had drifted off. A breeze soughed in the high branches of the trees at the edge of the river. In the last of the light, in the creeping twilight, Seaton turned to the opening page of Pandora's journal and began to read.

6 October, 1927

The crossing was ghastly. There was a lurching sickening swell on the Solent and the boat we crossed aboard was small and thrown about by the pitch and toss of the waves. There are steam ferries for the summer excursionists, apparently. But they stop their runs early in September. There's a mailboat after that and the mailboat books passengers. But Fischer, with his talent for the clandestine, wanted everything necessarily hush-hush. Dennis, of course, revelled in it. He was in the artillery in the war. But he was a sailor before that for a year, a time he describes, I think with irony, as his time before the mast. He was very nostalgic about Portsmouth. Pompey, he called the town. He insisted on taking us to a harbour bar there after dinner on the evening before we crossed.

We walked from the restaurant. The streets were full of sailors. They looked very picturesque in their blues but were uncouth with drink and there was violence in the air. A drunk ranting in the bar Dennis took us to made a loud remark about Jews with his furious drunken eyes on Fischer. He stood over our table and glowered. He was a powerful fellow, massive through the chest and shoulders, his sleeves rolled to reveal the sort of forearms I've seen before only on circus strongmen. Except that the flesh of the sailor's arms was heavily etched with tattoos. The name of each ship in which, I presume, he had served was inked along smooth hambones of muscle. Dennis actually stood, I think intent on facing off the fellow. But Fischer merely chuckled and murmured something to Dennis. Dennis sat back down. Deprived of confrontation, the sailor spat on the floor between his spread feet and walked away. Fischer took a carton of toothpicks from a waistcoat pocket. My God, I thought, he isn't so ill-bred, surely, as to start picking his teeth in our company. He tapped a toothpick from the carton and fingered it. They were of the wooden disposable kind. He grinned. But instead of lifting the toothpick towards his mouth, he looked over to where the sailor railed, now, among his shipmates. And Fischer held the little wooden spear between his fingers and, with his grin turning savage, snapped it. And forty feet away, the sailor convulsed, stricken, his agonised howl keening through the drunken hubbub so loudly that it wholly silenced the place.

Dennis ushered us out. He conjured a taxi from somewhere and it took us back to our hotel. They tried to persuade me to have a nightcap with them when we got there but there was nowhere in the hotel a woman could enjoy a drink in male company respectably. Instead, I left them to it over billiards in a games room and retired, sleepless, uncomfortable with Fischer's mirth in our cab over the bar-room insult, and his retribution.

Far from being a Jew he is a Jew-hater, one of the new breed of Germans apt to blame obscure conspiracies for their defeat in the war. And I was surprised at how tolerant Dennis seemed of his views, having seen the slaughter on the Western Front first hand. But there is a charm about Fischer, a magnetic quality in the face of which one is apt to forgive his brutality. He tears the tips from his cigars with his teeth. I saw him hawk and spit in the street while we waited for our cab. He curses, albeit in German, at great length and irrespective of the company he finds himself in. He is physically obese and the smell of fat, alive and labouring, is always there under his expensive soaps and colognes. But he has energy and the charismatic quality of someone who absorbs attention and at the same time seems to radiate his own kind of dark light. It's almost as though with him, you share his orbit. It isn't a quality one could photograph, I don't think. It's something invisible, almost hypnotic. It's like a parlour trick, but played with enormous power. He has power.

Though I don't believe he is wise to use it in the vindictive playful way he did with that hapless sailor. The charisma might be entirely lost on Dennis, who was drunk again after the restaurant. But Fischer's wealth and influence have made a deep impression. Klaus Fischer is an important, influential man. And then there is his mystery, a quality which is not lost on Dennis, one feels, at all.

I don't believe Dennis really shares Fischer's conspiratorial beliefs about the origins and outcome of the war. It's just that there's a general cynicism about him that makes him a sympathetic audience for this kind of talk. He won't challenge it because he lacks any strong principles or even beliefs of his own. He has no religion. Certainly politics provides him with no hope. Perhaps that's the attraction for him of Fischer. Perhaps Klaus Fischer can provide Dennis Wheatley with a kind of faith. And perhaps he craves that. Along with power, which he certainly covets enormously.

On the morning of the crossing I joined them both for breakfast, early, the gaslights in the hotel restaurant lit to defeat the darkness and the unaired smell of the previous evening's cigars still present in the chair fabric and curtains there, and in the air above us beneath the dark crystal of the chandeliers. And when Fischer went to settle the bill, Dennis boasted about the way Fischer had felled the insolent sailor of the night before with no more than a vindictive gesture. He had inflicted a crippling blow on the man, Dennis said, with some relish, cutting bacon and slicing sausages on his plate. He had done it with nothing more concrete than a thought. That was power, he said. But sitting there, listening to the squeak of cutlery in that dismal hotel restaurant, it seemed to me not so much power as a petulant abuse of it.

Our boat cast off from a slipway to the east of Portsmouth Harbour, its engine labouring against the run of the tide in the cold and damp of the morning. Warships loomed at anchor to our right as we chugged along and, at the wheel, Dennis offered them a stagy salute. They looked like ragged grey castles in their stillness in the soft light. The water around us was glossy with floating slicks of oil and yellow in patches with scum from the bilge tanks of the anchored fleet. Hooray for the Empire, I thought, loyally. Seagulls flapped above the water in ragged squadrons, diving now and then. We passed a lifebelt, thrown overboard probably for a jape, Dennis said. He'd put on a white canvas cap with a peak. Watching the circle of painted cork bobbing on the surface, it didn't look much to cling to. Monosyllabic since his arrival at breakfast, Fischer seemed to contemplate the lifebelt, gripping the rail atop the gunwale with both hands. He grunted and spat into the sea.

We were well into the Solent, about two miles out, when the squall hit. It hit suddenly. The wheelhouse was very cramped with the three of us sheltering in it. Dennis tapped a glass tube that displayed the barometric pressure next to the ship's compass and asked quietly had I ever been to sea before. Only aboard a liner, I told him. Liners don't count, he said, with a dry sort of laugh. Looking out over the rising sea, I began to think him a frightful bore for this old-salt stuff he kept indulging. But I was grateful too, suddenly, for his expertise. On our projected course, he intended to round the Needles, expose us in this weather to the open seas of the Atlantic. This was no Cowes Week jaunt aboard a well-appointed yacht.

He sent us both down, to the boat's single cramped cabin, neither of us inclined to protest against our sudden demotion to below decks. As the boat lurched and the wind capered and roared about her timbers, Fischer's complexion took on a greenish tinge. He didn't look frightened. He didn't look particularly nauseous. He looked sinister and sulky, still in his overcoat, hidden inside his gloves and Homburg hat and woollen muffler. The small portholes misted with our breath in the cold and we sat on the hard wooden berths silent and uncomfortable for a while. Then, with nothing to look at or do, he instigated our first real conversation. He asked me about Crowley and about what I'd seen Crowley do, and I confessed it was why I was there, aboard that wretched craft at the mercy of the squall. Because of what I had seen Crowley accomplish that evening in Brescia and because of what Dennis had subsequently told me about his friend Klaus Fischer, a far more powerful adept than Crowley ever dreamed of being. The levitation was real, I told him. The levitated man was suspended absolutely without support, six feet off the ground. I saw Houdini once in New York, was aware of the pursuasive potency of illusion. But this was no illusion. Crowley rose and lowered the man at will, at leisure, while we dined and chatted and drank champagne on a terrace at a villa in Brescia with the lake lapping on the shore beneath us.

Fischer nodded. A wave slapped at the boat and the boat juddered with the force of it and we heard seawater sluice across the deck above our heads. And Fischer said quietly that he had more respect for Houdini and his conjuring than for Crowley and his impish magic. Crowley would damn himself, was damned, he said. Houdini had tricked and entranced the world, while Crowley dabbled at the edge of an abyss, he said. Remembering, then, the sailor felled in the Pompey bar at the snap of a toothpick, I thought him hypocritical for saying it. But I didn't bring that up. I was already frightened of him by then, I suppose. Not frightened for anything particular he'd done, or said. But instinctively afraid. Fearful in the way a rabbit outside its burrow might fear the approaching howl of a hungry wolf.

Fischer asked me was I resolute about what we intended to do. He asked was I committed to the ceremony and I told him I was. But then I admitted, truthfully, that the sacrifice itself was a part of the ritual I dreaded. It isn't easy for any of us, he said, and his voice was a soft croon now, an intimate contrast to the elemental noise outside. He spoke about the random tragedies of fate. Take this year alone, he said. Seven hundred dead in the earthquake in Yugoslavia in February. The earth shivers and lives are randomly ended. In March, he reminded me, 1,000 people a week were dying in London at the height of the most recent influenza epidemic. Their deaths were arbitrary, unremarkable.

But not unmourned, I remarked.

And his eyes glinted with the challenge in the gloom of the cabin.

Thousands dead in the Great Mississippi Flood in the spring, he said. A quarter of a million killed by the earthquake in Quinghai Province in China. And so the litany went softly on, as Fischer crooned about human death and its meaninglessness and inevitability, until I was almost convinced. Is there much point, he pondered, in a life of want and rickets, eked out in poverty in a teeming slum, under soot-defeated skies? It would be a life inevitably prey to polio and tuberculosis, endured in the grim anonymity of shared hardship, its passing years made indistinguishable by their endless and relentless toil. And so he painted a picture of stinking privies and constant damp and squalor, the lives lived in the somnolent tenements and terraces of English cities, under the shadow of chimney stacks; the sad, incurious lives lived for the sake of existence alone, without change or improvement or hope. That was a life not worth valuing, he said. There was nothing in it to cherish, or warm to. It was a life, if you thought about it with detachment and objectivity, barely worth having at all.

And I nodded, knowing that his talk had left me no more comfortable at heart about the realities of the sacrifice. Knowing also, though, that I had been right in the hotel to think of his powers as sometimes hypnotic.

We docked at a quiet spot to the west of Compton Bay where Fischer's man met us and carried what light luggage we had brought to Fischer's car, a large Mercedes-Benz. Even on the short walk from the jetty to the car, the air felt somehow different, a different pressure and texture on the skin, fresher, the distinct and singular way it does on a small island. Blindfolded, I knew I would still have sensed the change. The squall had settled now into persistent rain driven from the east, out of a lowering sky. The interior of the car was warm and roomy, its upholstery rich with the smell of oiled leather and waxed teak after the brief misery of the boat. And Fischer's man provided rugs and hot coffee from a brace of vacuum flasks. He was deferential in his manner, but possessed the dormant power of a Carpentier, a Dempsey even, in his neck and shoulders. Looking at him, I doubted driving was the most important talent he possessed. He spoke English only with a heavy accent. He pulled on driving gauntlets and switched on the electric headlamps as soon as he started up the motor. The Mercedes was equipped with a powerful magneto. Twin beams carved a bright yellow path through the wet and the gloom. Dennis offered cigarettes, and I took one and he lit it for me. Fischer's man put the great car into gear and we roared forward. I was on my way to the Fischer House. I smoked and sipped coffee, hot and bitter, watching the sodden green fields of the island undulate to either side through rain-bleared glass, knowing now that there was to be no going back.

My thoughts during the drive were of what Klaus Fischer did and didn't know. He made a pass at me on the boat. It was subtle enough, the lightest touch with his fingers on my thigh, and could have been taken as no more than a clumsy attempt to comfort me as the boat rolled and shuddered through the angry sea. It was an easy gesture to ignore without giving the offence of outright rejection. But it was a pass. And I don't believe he would have made it, risked making the fool of himself he was, had he known as much about me as he thought he did. He only knew about me what his friend Wheatley had told him. I was sure of that. He couldn't read minds. He could no more read minds than Dennis could. He couldn't read minds the way that Brescia had convinced me Aleister Crowley was able to do.

That night in Brescia, Crowley gave me a tarot reading. He said nothing during his first turning of the cards. But when he gathered them into a pack there was something knowing, leering in his smile. And he made a remark about Sappho. He told me Sappho had been as famous in her lifetime for her lust for travel as for the distinction of her verse. He said he'd seen a vision of Sappho in a mantilla and Spanish silk. He asked me had I read an English novelist called D. H. Lawrence. He wondered if I'd ever attended a festival held under a volcano to celebrate the dead. Have you ever drunk mescal, he asked me. It comes in a bottle with a worm. He stuck out his tongue, it lolled mischievously between his morphine-stained teeth. You have to drink mescal all the way down to the worm, he said.

I know Mexico, I told him, which is the place to which he was, of course, referring. I told him I was well-travelled. I told him I was sceptical about Sappho having travelled to what was not in ancient times a part of the known world.

Crowley smiled and spread the cards a second time. We were at a card table on the terrace about twenty feet from the main group of diners. An admirer, a sometimes follower, had lent him the villa. Crowley was dressed flamboyantly, as was his fashion I'd been led to believe, whether performing some occult ritual, or promenading along the Brighton seafront. He flaunted convention out of vanity and exhibitionism, the two traits happily encouraging one another in his character. He was dressed for this evening in a coat and velvet tie reminiscent to me of the pariah playwright, Oscar Wilde. He was old enough to have know Wilde. He was around fifty years old on the evening he read my tarot. But he was addicted to heroin and had the pale and unblemished skin the habit often confers on its victims. He looked younger than he was and far healthier than he could possibly have been.

He knew the secret of my sexual predilection. He knew about Mexico and I saw with some certainty that he knew about Consuelo, too. His hair was unfashionably long and as I studied him he hid one eye behind the veil of it and then shook it back in a gesture that was Consuelo's to the life. And curiously, I didn't feel threatened by this. He was collusive in exposing me. My secrets were his, but would go no further than him, I was sure. That was our unspoken understanding. His enthusiasms ran much deeper and darker than mere gossip.

If I give the impression of liking Crowley, it's because I did. He had a charm and capriciousness the dull Germanic Fischer entirely lacks. Where Crowley had spontaneity, Fischer has only plodding and deliberate calculation. Crowley delights in magic. He cavorts dangerously amid its possibilities. Fischer seeks to use it with the calculated deliberation of an engineer.

Before I left him, I asked him if it was true he had killed those men on the Singalila Ridge during the attempt on Kanchenjunga in '05. An avalanche killed them, he told me, shuffling and re-shuffling his tarot pack. Does the rumour that you killed them make you angry, I asked him? He said that it didn't in the slightest. He said he was only annoyed because the avalanche was supposed to have wiped out the expedition at 21,000 feet. In fact, he said, we reached 25,000 feet. We were almost at the summit when fate carried out its chaotic intervention.

He was sitting with his back to the lake over the terrace balustrade and the water was entirely black behind him. A tenor sang an aria from the deck of a yacht or the garden of a villa, perhaps, remote on the opposite shore and the sound carried, perhaps for miles, the voice and accompanying music reaching us with a distorted disembodied clarity that was strangely beautiful. There were fireflies around Crowley's head now, hovering about him, like an aura. Or like the halo around the head of a saint in a Renaissance fresco.

He seemed enthused by talk of mountaineering. He asked did I think Mallory and Irvine had reached the summit of Everest, three years ago, when they were seen to disappear into cloud only a few hundred feet from the peak. They had a camera with them, he said. The camera could provide the proof of their achievement. Did I hold a professional opinion? I thought about this. Their camera was a Kodak vest camera, I said. I'm more familiar with the technicalities of the Leicas I habitually use. But it was a hardy little machine. It was purpose-built. And in the desiccated air of Everest's upper slopes, the film would not deteriorate. Up there, in the remote cold, the snow never warms enough to thaw. So there would be no water-damage to the film. If the camera was intact, if it had not been damaged by a fall and the film exposed to light, it was possible. The film could be found, developed. The mystery could be solved. I asked him did he think Mallory and Irvine had gained the summit.

I know they did, he said. George Mallory told me himself that they sat on the roof of the world, where they shook hands and shared the last of their chocolate and planted a small flag and recorded the moment with a half-roll of photographic pictures before their descent and the fall that killed them. The dead don't lie, he told me.

He stood to leave me then, my audience at an end, and when he turned I saw that a cluster of small bats had attached themselves like familiars to his velvet back.

Crowley could read my mind. Quite possibly he could read my fate, though if he was able to, he maintained a poker face concerning that. Fischer, for all his charisma, doesn't share those gifts. And Dennis is blind to anything but his own philandering ambitions. My true preferences would astonish him, I know. I saw the triumphant gleam when he took his Dunhill lighter from his pocket in the car today and lit my cigarette. In his eyes, I'm a conquest already. A conquest awaiting only the formalities of the bed. Which I fear, with him, would be very formal. But his eyes don't see much. His vision is opaque, to say the least.

I'd describe the Fischer house, here in its splendid isolation in an island forest. But I'm tired. There will be plenty more opportunity to write tomorrow, on the eve of the ceremony, when the other guests arrive. Forbidden to bring my cameras, I've been forced to write my thoughts, to chart my impressions and discoveries. It's tiring to do so. But I find there's much to be said for the unequivocation of words.

Seventeen

Seaton stopped because it was too dark in the gardens to read on any further. The sun was descending, pinking vapour trails above the river over towards Battersea. The shadows of the trees in the gardens had lengthened and grown dense and their foliage had darkened, concealing the birds that chirped now thickly as if to signal the dusk. He thought of Sebastian Gibson-Hoare, exploring his open hemisphere of alcohol in a blue pallor of French tobacco smoke. He thought of the Irishman, dark in his odd pendulous trance. He thought of the vision that had visited him of Pandora, dead on a stretch of river-bank at Shadwell. And he could not connect at all the wretchedness of that death with the vibrant life of the woman who described herself in the journal he held in his hands. He closed the notebook. He put it back as carefully as he could in its oilskin wrapper and pushed the package into a jacket pocket, where its bulk rested reasonably discreetly, just about hidden by the flap.

He needed to think. He knew he could not tell Lucinda about the theft. And sitting there, he could think of no plausible alternative explanation for the discovery of what he had stolen. He felt that the journal was likely to give him a true insight into the mind and motivations of an enigmatic talent. But he could substantiate none of it. Not without admitting the source and therefore the theft, he couldn't. It was Tuesday evening. He had till a week on Friday to come up with 8,000 detailed, fluent, plausible words on the subject of Pandora Gibson-Hoare. What he had in his pocket, in terms of what was known about her, was already sensational. Her lesbianism alone would cause the whole canon to be examined with a fresh eye for its subject matter and symbolism. That, and the hankering for magic which seemed to have seduced the woman.

He could hardly wait to read more. It was a quarter to nine. If he went home now and had dinner with Lucinda, afterwards he could read on in the Windmill for an hour before closing time at a table in the corner with plaintive soul ballads for a soundtrack. The thought filled him with an excitement and anticipation that made him realise afresh that this whole obsession was going far beyond what it had originally set out to be.

Obsession? Surely it wasn't quite that, was it? It was fully dark now in the gardens. They would have locked the gates. He saw the torch of a passing policeman strobe against the black iron railings bordering the Millbank pavement. All it really was, was his journalistic curiosity, his instinct for his craft, turned to focus on an intriguing woman who had lived through a sometimes sinister and salacious time. But it was no longer anything to do with Lucinda, was it? He had to admit that much. Standing there, under the trees in the gathering darkness, Seaton suddenly thought it very important that he didn't deceive himself about his motives, or let Lucinda down.

It went beyond Lucinda, this preoccupation with the mystery of Pandora Gibson-Hoare. But it had begun with Lucinda and with a sincere desire to help her. He would have to accomplish the essay somehow. And he would make the most plausible job of it he could. He could assimilate the Bob Halliwell information at least, suggest that the reclusiveness towards the end of Pandora's life was a deliberate choice and not a consequence of penury. He could write up the Vogel and Breene connection, which proved how punctilious she'd been in the care of her equipment. She had pioneered the use of the first mass-production Leica and he could include the forgotten poignant fact that one of her cameras still awaited its owner's lost touch in perfect working condition. He would ask Young Mr Breene about the technical limitations of those early Leicas and the film stock made for them. He was pretty confident Mr Breene would talk to him about such matters. He would write the dissertation as well as he was able to. He wouldn't let Lucinda down.

He stood in the Victoria Tower Gardens in darkness. The great bell above the Commons to his left tolled, nine times. And Paul Seaton made that solemn promise to himself. He would not let Lucinda down.

7 October, 1927

Crowley is here! He arrived this afternoon with an Egyptian woman. I was excited to see him, after the collection of dull grotesques Fischer's man has been ferrying here all day in the Mercedes. He recognised me instantly and acknowledged the fact with a raised eyebrow and a tightening of the lips that signalled: *Your secret is safe with me*. He has aged quite shockingly in the year since I saw him last at Brescia. Much of his hair has gone and his pallor is deathly. But there was mischief in his eyes. And he was flamboyant in a silk top hat and spats and morning coat, carrying a heavy silver-topped mahogany walking stick. He leaned on the stick, was obliged to do so, in shuffling up the steps to the house. And it was sad to think that he was agile enough once to climb in the Himalayas, amid those peaks on the roof of the world. All the damage done to him is self-inflicted. It was a pathetic thing to witness, nevertheless.

But I'm ahead of myself and should describe the house. Fischer lives amid ugly opulence. His walls are hung with lurid tapestries and lit by sconces fuelled with raw pitch. The floors are bare, flagged and covered in the skins of bears and big cats, trophies, I suppose. All the downstairs rooms are warmed by burning logs in huge fireplaces. They make the house smell of soot and resin. The whole effect is baronial, grand and somehow medieval, too. There is nothing deliberately or even carelessly vulgar here, nothing that signals new money. There is just a sort of picture-house phoniness, all the more phoney for being so authentically done.

What I mean is that the house looks as if it has been styled and furnished with the calculation lavished on a film set, filled with extravagant props. Fischer's house has not evolved. It has been expensively and stubbornly imposed here. But for all its air of fraudulence, everything is real. There is a pair of broadswords crossed under a shield on the wall of his library. I tested the edge of a blade and my thumb came away from it deeply sliced and painfully dripping blood. The Fischer house is the home of a man who has invented himself. That's why it seems so new and so bogus, somehow. And if it seems in places slightly unfinished, I suppose that's because the invention is not yet perfected. It is not yet complete. It won't be, until the ceremony and the sacrifice and Klaus Fischer's elevation to who and what he aspires to become.

Our Dempsey doppelgänger is an Italian American from the city of Chicago. I spoke to him briefly after he carried my bag to my room. I know Chicago slightly, and my familiarity with some of its attractions warmed him to me, I think. He used to be a boxer, had sparred, he said, with Dempsey and with Tunney too. And with Harry Greb, a fighter he said was better to his mind than were Dempsey and Tunney combined. His name was Giuseppe, he said, Joe to his friends. He had worked in Chicago for a man called Capone and asked me was the name familiar. I said it wasn't. I asked was Mr Capone a friend of Klaus Fischer and he seemed amused by that. At the conclusion of our short conversation we shook hands. Or rather, my hand disappeared into his like a finch into the jaws of an alligator. There seemed a ponderous sadness to Joe, an air of reluctant secrecy and regret. He made me feel, for the first time, the absence of my cameras. My new friend would make an intriguing subject for a portrait.

There is no distinct border between the grounds of Fischer's house and the surrounding forest. The trees simply thicken and spread, until the forest becomes remarkable. Even shorn of their leaves, the trees are so thickly placed that in parts the going becomes totally impossible. I think this is one of the few forests that has survived on English soil since Plantagenet kings and their passion for the hunt. It is not hard to imagine boar crashing through the floor of leaf mulch, driven from impenetrable thickets, shearing the bark of dripping trees with their fierce tusks. It is a place of ancient rite and seclusion, this forest. I somehow doubt Klaus Fischer has ever bothered properly to explore its shadows and glades. I think it is the sort of place that would disconcert him. He would feel lost here.

It is a profoundly English place, the wood surrounding his house. But the kingly connection is only my romantic projection. I know so little of the island's actual history. The only monarch I know to have cultivated a strong link with Wight is Queen Victoria, who spent long months at Osborne House in the years of her unstoppable grief after her husband's early death. And Victoria wasn't English at all, not in blood. She was a German, like my host. And, like him, I suspect she was chiefly attracted to the island by its surprising atmosphere of isolation. It enables easy privacy.

You can look back on Fischer's house from the wood, on its high gables and the gaunt and solitary turret rising from its roof. The turret houses a guest room, Dennis said. I told him I wouldn't like to sleep up there. I'm not easily spooked, but I wouldn't. From outside, the windows of the turret have an odd geometry. Their angles and exaggerated depth suggest menace, somehow. Darkness lurks in their panes instead of them reflecting exterior light. He smirked at my timorousness and said the room at the summit of Fischer's house was reserved for more exalted guests than me.

An exalted guest arrived today. He came in a seaplane, put its pontoons down in Freshwater Bay, flying in despite the dismal weather. It's a tribute to his skill as a pilot. He is German, like Fischer. And, like Fischer, he disguises a tendency to obesity in energetic gusto and fine tailoring. He wore splendid riding boots under a greatcoat stitched with campaign ribbons and medals won in the air over the fields of France in the war. I thought Dennis might baulk at this display, at its implications. But he plainly knew and even liked the fellow, greeting him with an embrace to follow their handshake. The German was greatly taken with the forest and I heard him ask our host over cocktails last night about game. There is no game here to distinguish those woods, Fischer told him, laughing. But he added that it always falls to the predator to find prey.

A brook bisects the wood. And the brook was as far as I was able to progress on my brief exploration after we were delivered by the Mercedes and I unpacked in my room here yesterday. It runs deep and rapidly, which is probably the effect of the rains that have persisted in their intensity since we arrived. Or it might not be a brook at all, it might instead be a smallish river with a current made swift by the narrowness of its banks. Either way, it runs dark and deep and was far too formidable an obstacle for me to think of crossing. There's no escape, it made me think. And the thought was not entirely idle. Nor was it altogether comfortable.

7 October, 1927, later

Much later! There is to be a duel in the morning. It will be a real duel involving injury and possibly even death, fought supposedly to satisfy honour. It seems so anachronistic. In a few hours the two protagonists will walk between the parked Lagondas and Bentleys and Rolls-Royces crowding Fischer's drive as the very latest and most ostentatious symbols of our technological age. They will find a secluded spot. And they will hack at one another with swords.

But even writing that, I become aware of the contradiction implicit in my own logic. We are here to practise magic, after all. We are modern people, have embraced modernity with conviction and enthusiasm and, in some instances, with substantial profit. Yet nothing could be more ancient, or more strictly bound by lore and ritual, than the black art that has brought us all together here.

Nevertheless, the duel is ridiculous, the outcome less likely the 'satisfaction' the protagonists seek than some grotesque and dangerous injury to one or both of them. One of them is actually a seasoned duellist. It is our German, of course, the fat aviator who arrived here yesterday festooned in decorations earned during his glorious martial past.

The evening began promisingly enough. Of course, it was the evening of the blood banquet, the first of the ceremonial meals we must endure before the sacrifice. There is an American here, a film producer. He had brought with him the new filmic sensation, a moving picture called *The Jazz Singer*, which comes complete with its own sound thanks to a new process called dubbing. Speech is synchronised so that the characters speak naturally on film with their own voices. In this instance, since *The Jazz Singer* is a musical drama, the actors also sing. Fischer has a projection room and the whole entertainment had been planned in advance for the afternoon prior to the banquet. Given the inclement weather, it seemed a blessing as well as a welcome novelty.

But the star of *The Jazz Singer* is Al Jolson. And Al Jolson is an Americanised Jew. Those of us unaware of this when the film began were made aware of it very quickly by Fischer's aviator guest, who loudly announced that he would not sit through a two-hour performance by a Jew from Lithuania, expected to consider the ordeal entertaining. He began to jeer and barrack and one or two of the others there, perhaps encouraged by too much wine drunk with their lunch, began to boo and handclap ponderous ironic applause. After a couple of minutes of this the American who had brought the picture here interrupted the projection and turned on the electric lights. He confronted the aviator, his face contorted with fury.

I think he was concerned more for his own dignity than for Al Jolson's reputation or the merits of the moving picture itself. He had on cotton gloves, used to handle the spools of film without damaging the film stock with secretions from the pads of his fingers. He is tough-looking, the producer from Hollywood, swarthy and sinewy with cruel eyes. He took off one of the gloves and with his bare palm slapped the German, hard, across his face. The German looked startled for only a moment, before smiling at the American and offering him a curt bow. This was the protocol, apparently, for the duel they are to fight; the challenge made and accepted in the heat of a half-drunken moment.

But Dennis tells me it is all deadly serious. The German had fought duels before, was part of a student duelling society in Heidelberg in his youth. And the American, of Italian extraction, was a college fencing champion, good enough at épée and sabre to represent his country in the Olympic Games. The men here seem very excited at the prospect of blood and steel. The women feign indifference, but are excited too, I think.

I have a small problem of my own, concerning blood and steel. The cut on the flesh of my thumb has become infected and swollen. It leaks fluid, which has a sweetish smell, like decay. I have disinfected and bandaged it, but I think I have a slight fever now and am concerned about infection. Beyond that minor worry, I have to confess to a more general and far greater uneasiness. I've prattled on about the row prompted by the 'talkie' and the prospect of the duel and my septic thumb, avoiding writing this part. But I have to write it, because it is all I can now think about. It is more urgent and important than anything else possibly could be.

I have known for months about the ceremonies and the sacrifice, have had more than sufficient time to prepare myself for what is involved in the rituals being staged here. But tonight the blood banquet was held. And it was vile. It was staged in a huge dining hall reached through the library of the house. This hall is panelled in polished wood with a heavy and elaborate burr. We served ourselves from a cold buffet displayed at one end of the room, the staff having been dismissed after the preparation of the food. There were thirteen of us, of course. We ate by candlelight at the long table running through the centre of the hall, our meal accompanied by music played loudly on Fischer's gramophone. The machine positively gleams, so new and up-to-date is it. The sound from its horn is shrill and crisp and it runs hot, smelling of metal and Bakelite. The gramophone is another of the uneasy juxtapositions in his house between contrived, Middle Ages décor and the opulent trappings of modernity. The music started staidly enough, emotional arias warbled throbbingly by Caruso and the sweet-voiced Irish tenor John McCormack. Then, with the steady intoxication of the evening, it got darker and more mischievous. It turned first to ragtime, which I've always thought sinister, somehow, in the way its simple and deliberate rhythms stalk the mind. And then, of course, it turned to jazz. I recognised a handful of tunes played by the Paul Whiteman Orchestra, Bix Beiderbecke soloing on his cornet. And then our host played a recording by the Red Onion Jazz Babies. I saw them in Chicago last year, could hear again now the brass virtuosos Sydney Bechet and Louis Armstrong competing on their crowd favourite, 'Heebie Jeebies'. I stole a glance at Göring, the German, expecting some new explosion, now about nigger musicians. But none came. Tonight, he had other things than jazz on his mind. The music got ever wilder, less controlled.

What's this? I asked Fischer, at one point, as piano keys echoed some whorehouse lament. Perhaps it was just me. I was slightly feverish, I suppose, from my infected thumb.

Fats Waller, he said, with an indulgent smile. I had never heard of Fats Waller.

As the night wore on, his guests made free with Fischer's wine and champagne, his opium and his cocaine. Much of the behaviour was drearily predictable. But some of it still held the capacity to shock. Towards the end of the evening, the Egyptian woman Crowley brought took off her clothes. A jewel sat tucked into her naval. Her nipples were pierced with thickish circles of gold shaped to look like braids of rope. She writhed half-heartedly to the music, doing a sort of belly dance. And then she lay supine on a tabletop, smoking a cigar through her vagina. Some of the men applauded this trick, which I'd heard of, but never seen before. When the cigar was half-smoked, Fischer plucked it out of her and made the ash of it glow with three or four furious puffs, before thrusting the lit end back into her. She moaned in mingled pain and pleasure and the smell of burned flesh and singed hair and sexual release rose about the room. Her orgasm earned another desultory round of cheers and table hammering before she limped off the table and slouched away to put her clothes back on. I looked at her face. But her expression was blank under the exotic application of the kohl around her eyes.

Shortly after, the sacrificial was brought in for everyone to see, not borne aloft on a bier or anything grand like that, but shaking inside the man Giuseppe's buttoned overcoat, like stolen game in the coat of a poacher. Put down, the sacrificial did not look like the key to Fischer's impending omnipotence. He was just a young child, shivering in undershorts and a once-white singlet, grey now with wear and washing. He is perhaps six or seven years old. He is undernourished. He looked confused and fearful, as though distrustful of the gaudy apparitions he was seeing. But this is one dream, if he thinks it a dream, he will not awaken from. He stood clutching at his undershorts with one hand, holding them up, the elastic having perished or perhaps snapped in his handling, protective of his infant dignity.

The assembled banqueters began to clap. And I was filled at once with compassion for the child and with heartfelt loathing for what we are here to do. Fischer's words aboard the boat came back to mock me. And then the giant Giuseppe swept the boy off the floor and made for the door and they were gone. And at once I understood the reason for the look I'd seen earlier on the face of Fischer's man. Whatever his former employer, Mr Capone of Chicago, had had him do for his pay, it wasn't this.

I looked at Dennis. His complexion was flushed and sweaty and his eyes still gleaming from witnessing the Egyptian woman's pain. He is a sadist, of course, which I had forgotten. I looked at the other faces in the room; all drunk or intoxicated in some way, except for the duellists, sullen and sober at separate ends of the table, each hoping, I suppose, that sobriety now would give them an advantage handling sharpened steel come morning. I looked at the assembled throng in their tuxedos and ball gowns and felt the pearls turn to paste around my dry imposter's throat, because I wasn't one of them.

And I'm not. And I never can be. Whatever Fischer's platitudes aboard the boat, I won't collude in the murder of a child. Absurdly, I found myself resenting Fischer for lying on the boat about the rickets. The child is sound-limbed. Thin, pale, terrified, but apparently healthy. Sound-limbed or crippled, it hardly signifies. I cannot be party to the murder of a child. I cannot.

While I was thinking this, I saw Crowley lift his head and look at me. He was sitting in a club chair over in one corner with a wine goblet rested between his fingers on one of its arms. He had on an oriental skullcap, to conceal his scalp where the hair no longer grows to cover it. He turned the goblet deliberately and one of his feet tapped in its buttoned spat, on the floor. It tapped as though with infinite patience. And then it stopped. And he smiled. And of course, he knew.

8 October, 1927

I walked down with Dennis for the duel. My fever was worse and he commented on how pale I looked. We passed Giuseppe in his shirt sleeves, raking gravel on the drive in the unrelenting rain. His bare forearms were hambones of muscle as his hands gripped the shaft of the rake. He looked at me on hearing my voice and gave me a tight smile, his eyes deferential and sad. Tarpaulins have been stretched over the parked cars on the drive and they look like the corpses of great machines, silent and still in their burial shrouds. Only one car lay uncovered, the rain spotting like dew and dribbling on the flats and curves of its black body, unable to settle on the polish.

Not everybody walked down for the duel. A few casualties from the night before were presumably still oblivious in their beds at 10 a.m., the appointed hour. Some came down wearing overcoats over their pyjamas. The pornographer from Rotterdam came and the two industrialists from Antwerp and Lille who like to play cards against one another came. The Danzig shipyard magnate came to watch as well. The casino owner from Marseilles appeared. Perhaps he had taken bets on the outcome. They made a dull troupe, pasty, bloodshot, smelling of last night's liquor and cigars as they wheezed and gossiped, trailing through the wood. None of the other women attended.

Fischer was taking few chances with the thirteen for his coven, judging by the protective clothing armouring the two swordsmen. Their torsos were plated in heavy leather and their sword arms covered in quilted padding down to the gauntlet each wore. Their legs were unencumbered, though, and they stretched and thrust with their weapons in skilled confident preparation. Their swords were rapiers; antique but deadly, undulled by age as they tore the damp air in practice strokes with a ragged swishing sound. Fischer called the duellists together and made them put on goggles and then helmets such as motorcyclists wear. They seemed very calm. They avoided looking at one another directly, but each made a joke to Fischer as he gave them their instructions and checked the edges of their blades and the buckles on their body plating and I heard him twice bark his harsh, spontaneous laugh in response to what they said to him in jest.

The duelling ground was a flat clearing covered with deep green grass in the seclusion of trees about three hundred yards from the house. I noticed Crowley wandering in the trees with apparent indifference to the spectacle. He had on an embroidered tunic such as the warlock Merlin might have worn. It trailed his feet. I realised with dull certainty that I was afraid of him now. He frightens me more than Klaus Fischer does. In Brescia I had been seduced and foolish. I looked at him gliding through the bracken and ferns and dead leaves of the forest floor and knew with a sinking heart that he had killed his comrades on that mountain all those years ago. They had been sacrificed, for something, on the Singalila Ridge. Crowley and Fischer are the same. Power is all with them. No price is too exacting.

Fischer's man appeared and unscrewed the top from a flask and I smelled hot buttered rum and the rich full smell of it almost obliged me to vomit on the ground in the nausea gripping my stomach from the fever that persisted in me. He gave the protagonists a silver cup apiece and, with their free hands, they raised the cups and drank. Their drinking hands were impressively steady, given what they were about to do. But the aviator had killed in the war, garlanded for killing. And the film producer looked, too, like the kind of man who could snuff out another's life without compunction.

I think the war has much to do with it. It is nine years since the war ended but it casts a long shadow on the world we live in. Life became so cheap as to be permanently debased. Faith was destroyed. Now, sensation and novelty are all. If the times we live in were a man, he would be a corpse, a frenzied, ersatz existence galvanised into him only by odd jolts of electricity. What were those lines of Eliot's? *I had not thought death had undone so many*.

The duel itself was over fairly quickly. It could have lasted only two or three minutes. It was fought at astonishing speed, with a ferocity to which the leisurely preamble had given no clue. The clash of steel was a bright dissonant sound in the still of the morning. Both men were clearly expert, but the American was nimbler and wounded the German to end the contest with a slash to the neck that sent arterial blood in a crimson spray across the grass. The German staggered, dropped his sword, pulled off his gauntlet and held out his hand to his opponent. His wound was bleeding copiously, but he ignored it, breathing heavily still from the exertion of the fight, honour satisfied. You could actually hear the blood droplets raining on the grass at his feet in the silence of the forest with the rhythm of his pumping heart as the German's face paled to pewter and the life pumped out of him. He staggered again. Fischer will not have his coven after all, I thought. Göring still had his hand extended. The American closed and shook it and said something I didn't catch, his tone conciliatory, the insult forgotten, all now a pantomime of manly fraternal concern. And the German smiled. And then Crowley was there, from nowhere at the German's side, as sad-faced Giuseppe gathered the discarded weapons from the ground, and Crowley was doing something I couldn't make out with his hands and a black handkerchief around the area of the wound. And the bleeding stopped, as abruptly as it had begun. It froze on the air and shrank and vanished from the grass. And spots of colour appeared like small pink commas in the German's cheeks. And his breath, which had been ragged, began to regulate and deepen.

Ja, he growled to Crowley, still weak. *Ja. Gut.*

And I heard Crowley say to him, you've lost blood, perhaps as much as a quart of it. Drink milk and porter. Eat red meat. Have the meat served to you rare. Rest and you'll be fine by this time tomorrow. And with an arm on Fischer's shoulder, the wounded German led our lurid procession back to the house for breakfast. I was at the rear, trailing Giuseppe, with his burden of discarded duelling armour and bloodied antique weaponry. My own blood pounded against my temples and there was bile, sour in my throat. I badly needed a cigarette but knew that smoking one would make me feel even worse than I did. I looked around, wondering vaguely where it was they were keeping the boy, their sacrificial. All my thoughts were becoming vague, my mind wearied by the persistent heat and sickness of infection.

And Crowley was suddenly in front of me, the vista darkened by his looming shape, his eyes on fire, the strange whorls and patterned stitching of his tunic like a maze through which my own eyes travelled and were lost. And I felt him take my injured thumb and slip from it the bandage I'd improvised, gluey now and cloying with decay. And he put my thumb into his mouth and sucked. He sucked the infection out of me. I felt the poison lifted out of me. There's no other way to describe the feeling. And I shivered and was well again.

Eighteen

In the Windmill on Lambeth High Street, the bell tolled for last orders. Through the little speakers on their shelf behind the bar, Marvin Gaye lamented his good friend Abraham. An inch of Director's bitter sat neglected in Seaton's glass. He slipped Pandora's journal into its oilcloth and put it in his jacket pocket. He drained his pint and walked the short journey home.

Lucinda was seated on the sofa, her legs drawn up under her, sketching with charcoal on a pad. The hi-fi was playing. Seaton recognised the Cowboys International album. It was an old favourite of hers, a record she played a lot. But the volume had been turned very low. She was listening to it more for the comfort of sound than for the music. She was playing it for company. There was a shot glass of Chartreuse at her elbow, casting a green shadow across the arm of the sofa in the streetlight coming through the half-pulled blind behind her.

'How was the pub?'

'Empty.'

'Just you and your cider-drinking blonde, then?'

'And the landlord.'

'Cosy.'

'It was. Very.'

'The Windmill on a Tuesday night. Nobody can say you don't know how to impress a girl.'

'No.'

She straightened her arms and held the sketch out from

her body and tilted her head to look at it. Seaton was aware of how lovely her eyes were, narrowed to focus on the quality of her work. 'Do you mind if I ask you something serious?'

'No,' he said.

'Do you really think you are going to be able to come up with the goods on my written project, Paul?'

'I'm across it, Lucinda.'

'Don't baffle me with Irish phrases.' She smiled at him over her sketchpad.

'I'm taking all of next week off,' he said. 'I'll have the thing cracked, all right.'

'Your brother rang,' she said. 'A group of them are going swimming up at Highgate Ponds on Sunday, if the weather doesn't break.'

'The weather won't break,' Seaton said. He tweaked a fret of the blind, which hung entirely still against the open window. 'This heatwave will go on forever.'

'But despite that you still put your jacket on. To go to the pub.'

'Because I need somewhere to put my wallet,' he said, taking off his jacket and going to hang it on a hook in their short hallway, only too aware of the weight and indiscreet bulk of Pandora's journal in the left-hand pocket.

'Come here, Paul.'

He sat down beside her. 'Are you going to interrogate me about the cider-drinking blonde?'

She put down her pad. She stroked his hair, his cheek. She kissed him. Her lips tasted sweet and slightly sticky with Chartreuse. 'I just want to thank you for doing what you're doing for me. Taking the week off next week and everything. It's so good of you. So kind.'

He kissed her neck. Inhaling, he could smell her perfume and skin and against his face could feel the fine subtle touch of her dark-blonde hair. He was intensely aware for a moment of the texture of her skin and hair and the delicate weight and warmth of her. He opened his eyes, which he hadn't realised he'd closed. On the other side of Lucinda, the green shadow of her glass rippled with iridescent movement on the arm of the sofa in the glow of the sodium light on the street outside. And there was the single clop of a horse's hoof, iron-shod, out there below against the night road. A mounted policeman, he thought, not really thinking about it at all. He was thinking about the grace and presence of Lucinda Grey, the thin straps of her slip, satin against tawny summer skin.

'I love you,' he said.

And he did.

Seaton sweated through the following day, always expecting an irate catastrophic phone call from an indignant resident of Moore Park Road. But it never came. His sick day had left him twice the routine work to do. So he was busy. And it was the Wednesday of Hackney borough's full council meeting in the evening, and he was on the roster to attend and cover it. They began at 7 p.m. and lasted often until the early hours. Two reporters would generally take the meeting in shifts. Seaton took the first shift because he lived furthest away. They were acrimonious and turbulent events, full of theatre and indignation. But most of it was political pyrotechnics. The Labour-led council were a long way to the left and radical enough, but most of the jaw-dropping decisions were taken at committee level. That's where the headlines were to be found, not at full council meetings, but buried amid the routine and dross of the committee-meeting agendas. Two of the staff reporters, Terry Messenger and Tim Cooper, had a real talent for rooting out and following up this stuff. They weren't just talented either, they were dogged and tenacious. Seaton knew, if he was honest, he was too lazy to apply himself properly to it. He preferred crime. Crime was easier. Even when it wasn't entirely black and white, it was easier to extract a story from a crime than from the obfuscation and shrill rhetoric of local politics. Nevertheless, he had to go. Something sensational could happen; an assault, walkout, boycott, demonstration. There was often violence in the public gallery. This stuff was meat and drink to the *Gazette* and they would never take the risk of missing it.

Before leaving the office for the Town Hall, he called Bob Halliwell.

'Micky Boy! How's the land of the leprechauns? Where's my bottle of Scotch?'

'There's a case of Chivas with your name on it, Bob, if you can answer in the affirmative to the following request.'

Halliwell was silent for a moment. When he spoke, his voice had dropped an octave. He said, 'You want to see Pandora Gibson-Hoare's effects.'

'How did you know that?'

'Because I'm a copper, Mick. And not the clueless arse-hole you sometimes seem to think you're dealing with. That's probably how I know you'd like to see the autopsy report, as well.'

'Is there any chance?'

'Because you've tickled my curiosity about this, I rooted it out and read it myself, yesterday. It's pretty routine stuff. Pretty dull.'

'Was there nothing that struck you as unusual?' Seaton held the phone against his ear, waiting for the policeman to decide what to tell him.

'The body had one unusual feature. It concerned her hands. She was missing her right thumb from the second knuckle. It had been amputated. Crudely.'

* * *

He didn't pick up the journal again until the Thursday evening. Lucinda was at a degree-show rehearsal, staged in the early evening at college. Patrick and Greg and the boys were using it as an excuse for a drink. As though they ever needed an excuse. They planned to attend the rehearsal and then go with Lucinda and a couple of her fashion course friends to a new bar opening in Soho. David Haliday had painted friezes on the walls and had been given a handful of invitations for them guaranteeing free drinks.

'I'm happy to go with Patrick,' Lucinda said to him. 'But I'd rather you came.' She liked Patrick. She never, or rarely ever, these days called him the Fat Rockabilly any more.

'I need to get on with that stuff I'm writing,' Seaton said.

'Martyr.'

'It won't write itself.'

'Give her my love.'

He got home from work on Thursday and went and trained at Fitzroy Lodge in the early evening heat for an hour. He trained under the grim ferocious gazes of Hagler and Duran, looking down from the walls. Then he took the journal to the Windmill.

<u>8 October, 1927</u>

I'm going to describe how Dennis and I met. It was at a ball not long after my father's death. Among the many things of my father's I inherited, but had no use for, was my father's wine cellar. Someone at the ball winced at tasting a bad vintage and I remarked that I had several hundred better bottles sitting neglected under Mayfair, to any of which they would be welcome. It was a stupid shallow witticism made to Edwin Poole, a young distant cousin of mine who is something in the banking or insurance world. He said he knew a man, a name at Lloyds and a wine dealer, who could help me dispose of the cellar profitably and, of course, with discretion.

Then he took me over to meet Dennis, who was holding forth about the singer Bessie Smith and the devil's music generally at a table on the other side of the room. He was slightly drunk and very cheerful, not handsome, but attractive enough in the bland open-faced sort of way common to chaps from his background. He wore campaign ribbons from the war and a monocle. He seemed too young for the monocle, screwed into his eye socket with the phoniness of a stage prop. He was after a sort of dignity, or gravitas, I thought. But in the terminology becoming fashionable then, I saw the monocle, and the ostentation of the war ribbons, as signs of insecurity. In that company, his insecurity seemed attractive rather than a weakness. He was a young man making his way in the world. And he seemed impressively knowledgeable about the devil's music called jazz.

When he met me at my father's house, I was surprised to learn that he had actually known my father. He had sold him wine. Extraordinarily, they had been on first-name terms. He kept referring to my father as 'Mr Gibson-Hoare' out of politeness and deference to me. But twice he slipped in conversation and referred to him rather fondly as 'Sebastian.'

We were in my father's cellar, when I noticed that he was wearing a bracelet. It struck me straightaway as an extraordinary piece of jewellery for a man. It was made up of tiny bronze runic figures shot through with a fine silver chain. He must have observed me looking at it. But he didn't react in the slightest to my doing so. I wondered was it some obscure insignia worn by a sommelier. Perhaps he was a master of wine, or something. Though for so Gallic a qualification, a medallion on a ribbon seemed more fitting. I wondered was he perhaps a member of the Freemasons, or some other secret society. Maybe he held some exalted rank. They all had their signet rings stamped with obscure crests, their amulets and hidden tattoos; toys and clandestine trademarks. Secret societies were very fashionable just then. Secret societies and psychiatry were the contrasting crazes of the moment.

Eventually, when I had listened to as much information about wine auctions as I was prepared to, I just came right out with it and asked him. And he smiled with a smile that stayed remote from his eyes. And he said, 'It's a contract, Miss Gibson-Hoare.'

And, puzzled, I asked would he take it off and let me look at it, properly, out of the crepuscular shadows of my father's cellar.

And he said, you don't understand. Wearing it is part of the contract I committed to. And taking it from my wrist now would be more than my life is worth.

And I believed him. Quite simply, in the stillness and the gloom down there, I knew he was telling the truth. And I wanted to know more, about the runic mystery, about whatever deal had been struck, and with whom. And over time, he began to tell me. And I met other acolytes. And I attended the ceremonies and saw the extraordinary things I've seen. And then Dennis introduced me to Klaus Fischer and I heard about the ambition Fischer had and what he apparently dared to attempt. And, of course, I met Aleister Crowley.

And I was lost, I'm tempted to write. Because sitting here in my room in Fischer's morbid temple of a house, I feel trapped and compromised and even terrified. We are a few hours away from tonight's feather banquet. It will be another tawdry and indulgent affair. I don't honestly think the reckless energy, that contagious impulse of attraction, is there for the evening to descend into outright orgy. But on the strength of last night's antics, it promises to be sordid enough. The cruel American and the wounded exhibitionist, Göring, will be in celebratory mood. I think that Crowley is bored, which is dangerous. We might see more unstable miracles than the little ones he performed for us today. It is Fischer's show, this. But Crowley is obviously jealous that the spotlight isn't his. I don't think he would try to sabotage the ceremonial, it would be far too dangerous. But his mischief sometimes seems barely his to control. I can't understand why Fischer allowed him to come. Unless his invitation was a deliberate and symbolic gesture of Fischer's assumption of superiority.

If the ceremonies go as planned, Fischer will spawn a beast that will, in gratitude, endow him with great knowledge and enormous influence. Do demons understand gratitude? Is an abomination summoned to the earth filled with a sense of obligation to any man? At the least of it, it strikes me as a volatile bargain. But it won't now be effectively struck, I don't think. And not because of Crowley's showy meddling. The spawning will not take place because the final ceremony depends upon the sacrifice. And the sacrifice will not take place.

Because I intend to save the child.

There, I've written it. And it wasn't even terribly hard to do. The truth is, I think I'd resolved to try to save the boy the moment I saw him. I've been thinking about the mechanics of it, subconsciously at least, every moment since then. At first I thought I might be able to enlist the help of the sad-eyed pugilist, Giuseppe, in my plan. But I asked the American duellist at lunch about Mr Capone of Chicago and, after hearing some of his stories concerning Capone's exploits, I doubt there's a heart in my new friend Joe to appeal to any more. So I'm alone.

Fischer has charged me with a commission. He wants me to use his camera to take a portrait photograph of each member of his coven. And himself, of course. It is to be formally staged, the subject seated on the throne Fischer is supposed to occupy tomorrow evening during the horn banquet and the sacrifice to follow. I'm to take the pictures before lunch and to present him with the undeveloped film afterwards. He has a Rollei camera, which is an excellent tool for the task of taking what will amount to thirteen snapshots. A volunteer will have to take mine. After lunch I intend to slip away and see if I can find where it is they are keeping the boy. I have to find him today. I fear tomorrow will be too late. And I feel that the longer it takes, the likelier it is that my courage might fail. If there is a God, God help me now.

8 October, 1927, later

Two things, one momentous, the other merely curious. I've found where they have the boy hidden and imprisoned. But I'll deal with events in the order they occurred. Doing so will help me stay calmer. Preserving my sanity, I realise now, has been one of the functions of writing all this madness down. Firstly, the portrait shoot, which passed off uneventfully. Crowley is vain and his pleasure in being photographed competed in his expression with a certain tautness around the mouth I took to be suspicion. I think he likes me, in so far as he likes anybody. His healing act this morning after the duel was one of compassion, as well as showing off. But he doesn't trust me.

Dennis has a pale bland face betrayed by a hint of lasciviousness. He has the look about him of tainted milk.

Fischer was serene, a squatting toad on his wooden throne, basking for his picture in the spotlight.

I think the Egyptian woman is hypnotised. There is something predetermined, trancelike about her movements. And her eyes are shallow to the point of blankness. It could be drugs, I suppose. It could be some potent narcotic someone has pumped into her veins. But shuffling on to the throne where she slouched for her picture, she reminded me of a story Dennis told about the walking dead in Haiti. When I saw her through the camera's viewfinder, the impression was strengthened to the point where I was so unnerved I could barely keep the camera still.

Fischer's German aviator wore a corset under his coat. I'm sure of it. He looked much slighter and better proportioned a figure than he appeared at any time yesterday. He was pale from blood loss, of course, but had a certain bearing about him, a certain martial dignity I thought lost on the circumstances. They are an odd lot. The remainder were equally odd, but unworthy of individual comment here.

When I took the film roll from the camera I substituted it for one from Fischer's camera box that was blank. I can't explain why I did this. I just did not want to surrender the film. There was no time to light the pictures properly, the sittings were hurried, the whole assignment executed almost in the manner of a factory production line. But I think the pictures will have something. The Rollei is an excellent camera and the film stock first-rate. I have hidden the roll and hope to recover it later. It lies between the joists, under a loose board pried from the floor of the room at the top of the stairs Fischer keeps for his most exalted guests. As I said, I can't explain why I did it. But I don't believe I will ever be held to account. By the time the deception is discovered, I will have committed a far more serious betrayal than stealing pictures.

After lunch, while almost everyone dozed, I followed Giuseppe as he carried a covered pail of our table slops outside from the scullery. We had pheasant in oyster sauce for lunch and the trailing smell of it congealing in the cold air told me what the pail contained. The falling rain was loud, percussive on the stiff leaves, dead still on the branches of the trees, and on those already fallen and not yet softened to mulch on the forest floor. And he did not hear me as I followed him. He stopped once, as though sensing he was not alone. And his huge shoulders stiffened under the rain slicker he wore and I felt the hair on the backs of my arms stiffen in response like the hackles of a frightened cat. But though he paused, Fischer's man did not turn.

He trailed through the thickening trees and I followed him. And after a while I became aware of a sound, like the rumour of running water. And it strengthened and I knew we were headed for the furious brook, or small river, that cleaves the forest. We were to the east of the trail I had followed to it before. The wood was dense, but watching the burly figure ahead of me, I was able to pick his path and avoid the snapping twigs and trailing underbrush that would have given me away.

It was on the very bank of the stream. It was built of wooden boards and felt-roofed and had no windows. It did not stand high enough for the child to have stood up straight in. Inside would be darkness, I saw, as there were no windows. The boards were bonded and weathered together by black smears of creosote, and holes had been drilled at intervals about halfway up the shelter for ventilation.

It was quite new. Even from where I stood, concealed behind the trunk of a squat sycamore tree a hundred feet away, I could see yellow deposits of sodden sawdust from the recent cutting to length of the structure's planks on the dark forest floor. The water was a chilly roar even from the distance where I hid, and I wondered what rest the child could possibly accomplish in his dark, cramped little prison. Was he clothed? Dear Christ! My fingers shook, smearing the moss grown on to the bark of my concealing tree as I fought to compose myself. I was indignant at their cruelty and disgusted at my own lazy collusion in it.

Rickets.

A slum child.

What had Fischer said on the boat? Better dead than alive. Anger and rage shook me. I trembled in the indifferent dripping forest. And I heard a voice, clear, human, pitched beyond the roar of urgent water.

'Peter,' it called. 'Peter? I have food for you, Peter,' Giuseppe said.

So the boy had a name.

And Fischer's man put the pail on the ground and sank to his haunches and I saw that a small brass padlock was all that secured a hinged trapdoor cut into the boards to confine their sacrificial.

I fled. I did not have it in me to see the boy again before my attempted rescue in the morning. And I feared discovery there, and catastrophe for us both.

Seaton looked up from the journal, aware he was dangerously close to its conclusion. There were thirty or so pages of flimsy left in Pandora's notebook. But the writing ran out in them over the course of only a couple more. He went to the bar and bought a drink and sat down and rubbed his eyes, their focus on the blue marbling of the book's cover. The story did not have a happy ending. He'd guessed that from the fact of her missing thumb. Crowley's miracle had been reversed, out of spite or revenge. She had died, self-murdered, a decade after the epiphany described in the pages he had so far read.

He thought he knew what happened next. But he sipped beer and picked up the book again with half his mind on what could be salvaged from the tragedy.

9 October, 1927, 8.15 a.m.

I misjudged poor, sad Giuseppe. I said that he would have no heart to appeal to after his work for Mr Capone, the gangster and bootlegger in Chicago, the man who likes to chastise with baseball bats and concrete boots and razors scrupulously stropped. But I was neglecting to take account of the torment done to his soul.

We found him this morning. He had seated himself on the wet ground outside the scullery and put the barrel of his pistol under his chin and pulled the trigger. There was nothing left of the top of his head, the pink slush of his brainpan exposed. The giant who held his own with Dempsey and Tunney and Harry Greb had finally been defeated by his conscience. He was a Catholic and his Catholic conscience was the one opponent he could never better with his strength, or successfully avoid.

I know the gory particulars because it was Dennis and I who found him. Last night's feather banquet was fairly subdued, everyone saving themselves for tonight's climactic activity, I suppose. The Egyptian woman, Crowley's plaything, allowed herself to be bitten on the neck by a snake charmed from a basket he produced. But Fischer mumbled some incantation to disperse the venom harmlessly. I think the event was supposed to be symbolic, a rapprochement between the two magicians. It left the girl's neck badly bitten, scarred. And the serpent was allowed the freedom of the room. It still lay in thick menacing coils around a table leg when I retired.

I ran into Dennis this morning in the grounds. Or rather, he ran into me. I was smoking a cigarette among the covered cars on the drive. He must have spotted me from his window. It was not unusual or suspicious of him to discover me there, not really. He is an habitual early riser, regardless of whatever the antics of the night before. It's an old navy habit, he says. Together, we walked around the house to see if coffee could be scrounged before breakfast at the scullery door. And together, we happened on the remains of Fischer's man. He was clothed in the pinstripe trousers and waistcoat of a blue suit and there was a shoulder holster strapped under one arm. The holster was of brown leather and rain-soaked, suggesting he had been there some time. Dennis remarked that a dumdum bullet had been used to do the damage. It was the gangster's ammunition of choice, he said. His nonchalance in the face of death did not surprise me. It is a consequence of the war, a characteristic shared by many of those with his exposure to it. They are inured to loss, hardened to violent death. This callousness has spread as a kind of fashion among them.

I would have been more upset myself, had I not followed the man the previous afternoon to the coop he built for the boy. I am in no position to judge anyone, but still think it an impossible crime to forgive. Still. At least he baulked at committing a worse one.

Dennis said he would go and break the news about the death to Fischer. They would need to find some discreet way to dispose of the corpse. And then he said something peculiar. He said it was a shame Giuseppe couldn't have elected to leave us in another twenty-four hours. I asked, why? The spawning, he said. Suicides can be very useful to the thing Fischer is to spawn.

These are the last words I shall write. I write them in my room, as the others attend the grisly cabaret of Giuseppe's death scene. His final act has drawn a full house, judging from the stillness and the quiet. But I am cautious and afraid. I dare not even go and retrieve my hidden film from its resting place in the guest quarters at the top of the stairs. There is something about that room I did not like. I would not willingly enter it again. And there isn't anyway time, now, to go up there. And I have not seen Crowley at all today, which worries me.

I must go to the boy. For the first time in my life, I must try to do something truly brave, rather than self-indulgently bold. I have stolen a brass poker from the fire-set of one of Fischer's countless baronial hearths to use to lever off the little padlock on the boy's prison. I have money. I have a rough idea of island geography. I pray the boy is as sound as he looked. My thumb has started to throb once again. It is probably only my imagination. It is like the memory of pain.

God help me.

God help both of us.

Pandora Gibson-Hoare

Nineteen

Seaton flicked through the empty pages of flimsy at the back of the notebook. But there were no more words to find. He had read the entire account. He could barely believe how brave she had been. She had been enormously courageous, given the depth of the delusion she was under. Had she been hypnotised? Autosuggestion was, he supposed, a possibility. He drained his Director's and went and fetched another pint from the bar. He sat down to 'Who's That Lady?' by the Isley Brothers. It was probably the most cheerful tune on the landlord's loop-tape, almost recklessly upbeat by the standards set by the rest of it. And the question was pertinent to him.

Who was that lady?

She had gone to see Houdini in New York. She had travelled to Italy for an audience with Aleister Crowley. She was someone who hankered after magic. It was a paradoxical feature of an age assaulted as no age had been before by the onslaught of technology. Four years of world war had accelerated scientific progress, and the stranded Edwardians of the 1920s found it difficult to cope with their new unrecognisable world. Something in them reacted against it. The craze for magic was well-documented. But it was still hard to credit the extent to which an intelligent and travelled sophisticate like Pandora had fallen for shysters like Crowley and Fischer and their assemblage of misfits and freaks. A spawning, for Christ's sake, Seaton thought. The summoning of a beast, wouldn't you know. Human sacrifice.

He was somewhat puzzled by the references to the boy. Perhaps Peter was some sort of maternal illusion fostered by Pandora's guilt over her lesbianism. But she hadn't seemed at all guilty about her sexuality in referring to it herself. She was understandably coy, but she didn't seem guilty. She was only young and her lifestyle did not exactly point to a hankering for motherhood. Neither did what work of hers he'd seen. No, he doubted the truth lay in far-fetched Freudianism. More likely it was a piece of theatre stage-managed by Fischer, the boy a child actor, the whole thing a dramatic ruse. There had been a guest from Hollywood at the Fischer house, after all. To anyone but someone as deluded as Pandora had been, that fact alone would have been a certain giveaway.

The quote from Eliot was after Dante, a reference in the first quarter of *The Waste Land* to Dante's *Inferno*. And the inference was obvious. Pandora had sought redemption in magic from a world that reminded her of hell. That was what she depicted in her photographs. Her subjects were grim isolated souls enduring damnation. What he had seen in her portraits as their subjects' stoicism and ugliness was her own expression of profound despair.

I had not thought death had undone so many.

How could he link Gibson-Hoare in his essay with Eliot's great nihilistic poem? The answer was that he couldn't. Because he could not reveal the stolen journal as his source. Seaton paced the pavement outside the empty pub. He kicked a loose stone towards a grid in the gutter. His aim was true enough, but the stone made no sound, so low had the drought caused by the heatwave reduced the water level in London's sewers. It was left entirely to his imagination to contrive a splash for the lost object.

He heard a sound in the quiet of his reverie and turned towards where it came from, to where Lambeth High Street ended in the dark T-junction of Black Prince Road. It had sounded like the snort and whinny of a horse. And he heard the metal clop of a hoof and wondered, idly now, why the mounted police were patrolling at all in so quiet a backstreet at night. They should be galloping through Trafalgar Square, providing a show to compensate the tourists forced to leave the pubs at eleven o'clock.

There had to be a convincing way for him to pretend he had stumbled innocently upon the journal. The solution to this problem was half-formed already somewhere in his mind. But befuddled by beer, it would not come into clear focus for him. He'd only had a couple. But his brace of beers had followed a workout in the unrelenting heat. And he hadn't eaten any dinner, to speak of. It had been foolish of him.

Bridle leather strained against muscle and sinew and iron-shod wheels rolled along the macadam as they approached under some thunderous burden, and Seaton's head snapped back towards Black Prince Road and he gripped the journal in its oilskin sleeve in a hand loose and sweaty now with fear thinking, *What in God's name was that?*

But all was innocent again. He heard behind him George, the Windmill landlord, whistling as he shuttered and locked and bolted for the night. River noise. It was river noise. The proximity of the river distorted and carried sound sometimes, in a way for which the senses possessed no ready explanation. Seaton sighed and relaxed.

She really had taken those pictures for Fischer. The slighted professionalism was unmistakable in her tone in the journal, even with everything else on her mind. She had even name-checked the equipment, Fischer's Rollei rather than one of her own beloved Leica cameras. Rollei, the Swiss engineer who created Rolleiflex a year or two after the autumn in which Pandora had written. Those pictures, that commission, as she called it, had been professionally executed. She'd even found space in the journal to complain about the short time she'd been given with each sitter, *like a factory production line*. The shoot had really taken place. And the film had really been switched and hidden. And, whatever her other grumbles, the pictures had been taken with film stock she described as excellent. She'd been a woman in extremis, falling back on where her instinctive craft and talent lay, when she took that set of portraits she chose to deride as snapshots. Among all the illusion during her apparent breakdown at the Fischer house, they had been real.

Seaton's eyes were drawn reluctantly back to the top of the road. And he waited for a carriage hearse to turn the corner, pulled by velvet-flanked stallions wearing black plumes on snorting heads, followed by a procession of mourners, whey-faced under their top hats because they walked in death to a long-forgotten destination.

And he shook his head and tried to slow his accelerating heart. Where had that come from? There was nothing there, at the end of the road, but night gloom. George had completed his locking-up routine behind him in the pub. The only sound was the ambient drift of night traffic along the road. He turned left and looked along Lambeth High Street to the bulk of the block where he lived, listening for their loud neighbour, for the drift of 'Red, Red Wine'. But even their neighbour was subdued tonight. Yet he did not want to tempt sight by looking again to his right. It was ridiculous. He was spooked by his own imagination, stirred by the clandestine reading matter carried in his hand. But why that? Why the funeral cortège?

He took a step towards home and cleared his thoughts.

And suddenly he had it.

The solution to his conundrum dropped neatly into his mind.

He would go to the Fischer House himself. The chances were remote that a place so large would still be in private hands. Odds were it would be a guesthouse by now, its great rooms divided; its occupants tourists, walkers, island nature lovers looking for a bit of seclusion off the beaten. It would be no bother to book a room for a couple of nights. He could leave tomorrow afternoon, come back Sunday, be back in time to make the swim on Sunday afternoon at Hampstead Ponds with the boys, and the beer after. Unless the place was full, of course. But it was still early in the season. The schools weren't off. And the Isle of Wight in June was hardly Devon or Cornwall in August. Of course they'd have a room. He'd look for the lost film and he might even find it. And if he did, what a coup for Lucinda. What he would certainly find there, though, would be the journal. He'd find that secreted under floorboards in its rightful place. Because that was where it ought to be found, wasn't it? Wasn't there a compelling logic for finding the thing in the very place where its last entry had been completed?

He lifted his head, resolute for home, no longer concerned about the beat and panoply of deadly grief rounding the corner behind him. And he stopped.

A couple of hundred feet distant, coming from Lambeth Bridge Road ahead of him, he saw the figure of a woman, turned wraithlike by the streetlamps, pale and gliding over the pavement towards him as though her feet didn't touch the ground. Her bobbed hair framed her face and her smile was a dark, night crimson shaping her mouth. Where else would you see such a sight, Seaton thought. It was Lucinda, coming home. He slipped the journal sly into his pocket, thanking fate for his having the habit of always needing somewhere to put his wallet when he went out.

* * *

He got into the office early the following morning, determined to book his accommodation at the heart of Brightstone Forest for the weekend without a curious audience. He was in at nine, confident that none of the other lads would get there until ten. Mike Whitehall tended to arrive at nine thirty or so, but his doing so was thought by the rest of the editorial staff a northern eccentricity. The lax hours the NUJ had negotiated on their behalf was the jealously held revenge, after all, for what the printers were being paid in comparison with them.

It was nine thirty before he was able to reach some clueless typist from the Isle of Wight Tourist Board who told him that there was no accommodation whatsoever in Brightstone Forest and no, she wasn't mistaken.

A brief study of the AA map of Britain told him the forest was National Trust land now. He really needed the close detail of an Ordnance Survey map, but they didn't have one in the *Gazette* office, where there wasn't much call for them and certainly not for one of Wight. When he called them, the National Trust couldn't help. As far as they knew, there was nobody domiciled in Brightstone Forest. There were visits made to it by forest wardens. And the wardens would have built a shelter. But the shelter would be rudimentary, nothing more elaborate than a hut. And Forestry only manned their phones from eleven until three, and then only on Mondays through Wednesdays.

Thoroughly frustrated, at ten to ten he went to make himself a mug of tea. Mike was in the kitchen, doing the same for himself and Eddie Harrington. 'Give me your mug,' he said. 'I'll be mother.'

Seaton handed over his mug.

'How did you find Young Mr Breene?'

'Picturesque.'

Mike laughed.

'You could have warned me.'

'I'm warning you now. You should leave it, Paul. Whatever it is. No good will come of it.'

This was unlike Mike, who was characteristically as inquisitive as they come.

'You don't want to know what it's about?'

Mike stirred sugar into his tea. He raised his cup to his lips and took an exploratory sip. 'Curiosity killed the cat,' he said. Which was a phrase Seaton had heard before. Mike didn't look himself this morning. There were these sullen unfamiliar shadows under his eyes.

'The boys are going to Hampstead on Sunday afternoon,' Seaton said. 'Swimming in the men's pond. We're all going. Patrick been in touch?'

'No,' Mike said. 'I mean, yes. What I mean is, I said no. I'm not exactly Mark Spitz in the water. I'm not even Esther Williams.'

'It'll be a laugh.'

Mike looked doubtful. 'Isn't it a bit homo, though? And a bit deep?'

'It's deeply homo. It's far more Judy Garland than Esther Williams, to be fair. But it's a lovely place for a swim in the weather. And your virtue will be safe enough among a crowd.'

'I'll bring my water wings, then,' Mike said. He sipped his tea.

Back in the newsroom, on no more than a reporter's hunch, Seaton rang a number for the County of Hampshire Civic Authority and asked for Social Services. This time, for the first time, he referred specifically to the Fischer house.

'Just a minute,' said a clerk.

Seaton didn't know if he had a minute. He looked at his watch. It was five past ten. But the stairwell outside the office door was still silent. And a spy couldn't climb through its cold acoustics without making a clatter. A ghost couldn't do it.

He heard the phone picked up and fumbled. He heard a match struck, tobacco inhaled. 'Who is this?'

'It's *London Tonight*. We're doing a piece about Home Counties provision for the elderly. And the infirm.'

'We're not the Home Counties, mate,' the voice said. 'And the Fischer house was an insane asylum.'

Seaton's heart thumped. The stairwell was still blessedly absent of feet. 'Was?'

The voice broke into laughter. 'If it was still going, I'd call it a place for the mentally challenged, wouldn't I? I'm fluent enough in the euphemistic new lingo. But it was an insane asylum when it closed. That was what they still called them back in the bad old nineteen fifties.'

'Is the building still there?'

There was a pause. 'Why? Is *London Tonight* doing a piece on Isle of Wight architecture, now? Building conservation? Who exactly are you, mate?'

'Is it still there?'

'So far as I know, it is. Derelict. Boarded-up and forgotten. It's a madhouse full of rats. Now fuck off, mate, whoever you are. You're a fucking timewaster and I've got more important things to do.'

He made a booking at a guest house in Ventnor. It wasn't ideal, but he didn't have time to shop around. Terry Messenger or Tim Cooper or someone was coming up the stairs as they told him his name and work phone number were enough to secure the booking and he dropped the receiver on to the cradle.

The afternoon was his. He was owed an afternoon or morning in lieu, for covering full council.

He'd told Lucinda he was going, the previous night, as she undressed, tipsy after the Soho bar launch. She'd nodded, immediately accepting of his story of how he'd learned that the Klaus Fischer in the Café Royal photograph had owned a house on the Isle of Wight where he was famed for his hospitality. There might be pictures of their gatherings on its walls, he'd told her, amazed at his own accelerating capacity for voicing the convincing lie. There might be something there to flesh Pandora out. Sober, she might have asked how he expected to be given access to the place. Sober, she might have asked how he could be confident that there would be anything of Pandora there, forty-odd years after her suicide, for him to find. But she wasn't sober. She just nodded and smiled with the slight diminishing of focus with which drink softened her eyes. And she didn't ask.

He knew his absence would be no loss to Lucinda. It was the last weekend she would have to prepare for her show. She would be working throughout all of it. She was probably relieved he was going to be out of her way for most of it. She didn't look relieved when he told her. But she seemed relieved when the moment came for him to go in the morning. It was concrete proof that he was working on the still-unwritten project. He was a fast writer who researched and wrote for a living. He was a professional carrying out what was, in essence, an amateur assignment. But there was only a week to go until the essay's submission.

Now, he had his overnight things in a canvas grip underneath his newsroom desk. And folded snugly among them was the journal. He didn't really need to take it. But he hadn't dared leave it behind, where Lucinda was sure to stumble on it in their tiny flat. And he couldn't leave it in the *Gazette* office, which until a few moments earlier had been his original plan. There were far too many curious eyes and probing fingers on an idle Friday afternoon in the newsroom for that to be a sensible thing to do. He occupied the couple of remaining work hours making desultory routine calls and meandering rounds of tea. At one o'clock, he made the formal note of his absence in the big diary on its tilted lectern with the Biro chained to the lectern for the purpose. And he closed the diary on his entry and nodded and waved his goodbyes to the rest of the office.

His crossing could not have contrasted more greatly with that described in her journal by Pandora. He took a train from Victoria to Portsmouth and a ferry from Portsmouth Harbour to Fishbourne. Portsmouth itself would have been unrecognisable to her, bombed into dereliction by a war she had chosen not to live to have to endure. It had been rebuilt cheaply in concrete and glass with scant regard for its history, the hulking imperial fleet she had described long towed away and broken up for scrap. Seaton's passage, enjoyed on the promenade deck in the open air, was a blue playground of smudged sails and trailing wakes out of a Dufy painting. Only the Solent forts, austere and monumental, marred the bobbing, Enid Blyton mood of the sea.

He walked the mile from the dock at Fishbourne to Wootton Creek and rented a mountain bike from an adventure shop. He used the shop's changing room to get out of his suit and into the shorts and trainers and track top he'd brought with him in his grip. He crammed his work clothes into the grip and the grip into a cheap rucksack the more easily to carry it, pedalling, on his back. And he bought the detailed island map he needed and, after riding a mile to get used to the bike, sat at the side of the road in the shade of a hedge in the heat and plotted his route. And when he'd done that, he paused. It was now just after five o'clock. There were scalloped clouds remote in the sky and the earth was warm under him. The island sky was enormous after the limited vistas of London. He could smell wildflowers entwined in the hedgerow allowing his shade. In the time he'd sat there, two cars had passed him. A 2CV had rocked by on thin tyres, its rear compartment kaleidoscopic with buckets and spades and balls and rolled beach towels, Joni Mitchell shrill on its radio through the open driver's window, singing something tremulous and folky from the album *Blue*. And a Morris Traveller, resplendent in its timber trim, had happened by towing a caravan. Island life was a lot different from Hackney, he thought, smiling as he climbed on to the saddle of the bike.

It occurred to him that it was a week to the day since he had first heard the name Pandora Gibson-Hoare. He'd been on the roof at St Martin's with the boys, Stuart Lockyear dressed like Franchot Tone in *Five Graves To Cairo*, sipping cheap Lambrusco in the indolent London heat. *Every silver lining has a cloud*, Stuart had said. The scene on the roof had been played out to a soundtrack, the broken-backed songs of Hank Williams on Foyle's paint-spattered beatbox. Over the course of just seven days he had become obsessed by Pandora, by her short life and disquieting work and tantalising mysteries. It was odd, really. He didn't feel he knew or understood her very well. Yet something in his heart and brain and even in his memory suggested that he had known something of this woman always.

Direct, he judged the distance southwest across the island to the forest to be about nine miles. But he chose to skirt around Newport, rather than navigate his way through the island's busiest town. His route was narrow and hilly and he missed a couple of crucial signposts, forcing him to double back twice. He'd been pedalling hard for over an hour when the ferns and saplings and second growth of the forest outskirts told him he had arrived there. He stopped and took a long drink from the bike's water bottle, glad the fellow in the adventure shop had thought to fill it for him.

Because he'd skirted Newport, he was approaching the forest from the north, across what the map told him was Newbarn Down. He could see the forest proper rising in front of him to a horizon where dense trees capped a high slope. He reckoned the Fischer house had to be at the bottom of the downward slope on the south side of the hill. The house was on land near a stream or river and Pandora had made no mention of a gorge, so he was assuming the house had been built on the same elevation as the stream, close to sea level. And the other side of the wooded crest in front of him would be more accessible by car from where she and Fischer had landed in the boat piloted by Wheatley. So he knew roughly where he was going. The only problem was that he couldn't get the bike over the hill. The adventure-shop man had proudly demonstrated the fact that the bike had fifteen gears. It had a tough grippy tread on its thick tyres. But so dense was the wood already that Seaton was wheeling it now rather than riding it. There were not sufficient gaps between trees to steer the thing through.

He looked at his watch. It was seven o'clock. He could double back and find a road and go around the perimeter of the forest and approach it from the seaward side. But he had doubled back enough. He could cut his losses, ride off to the guest house in Ventnor, dump his bag and find a nice seafront bar. The guest-house owner had told him a free house called the Spyglass Inn overlooked the bay and stocked an impressive range of guest ales and lagers. If he came back in the morning, he would have a whole day of sunlight in which to try to discover more than he knew. Maybe he'd find a single bullet casing on the ground by the door to the scullery. Maybe he'd find the spot where Göring and the lithe American had fought their duel as Crowley prowled like a fugitive beyond them in the trees. Perhaps he would discover a roll of undeveloped pictures taken by Pandora Gibson-Hoare of her fellow coven members gathered to practise black magic in secrecy together.

The pictures, if they were there, had waited for fifty-six years to be exposed. Surely they could wait a few hours longer? What were the odds of the Fischer house accidentally catching fire tonight, out of all the thousands of nights it had stood abandoned, and burning to the ground? What possible harm could a small, entirely practical delay do now?

It would do none at all. Waiting until tomorrow would do no harm whatsoever. Seaton knew that with as much certainty as he knew it was impossible to wait a moment longer than he was forced to. Sense didn't enter into it, the logistics of the enterprise were entirely irrelevant. He was burning with the need to see the Fischer house for himself, to explore its rooms with his own hands and feet and eyes, to solve its mysteries, to wallow in its atmosphere, to raise its reluctant ghosts, to execute his brilliant scholarly coup.

But he had to stop. He had to chain up and abandon the bike. The incline was steepening and the wood becoming thicker by the step. This was not the leaf-denuded autumnal forest of Pandora's wretched October visit. The trees were dense with leaves and the loam beneath them, veiny with surface roots, gloomy impossible terrain for two wheels.

Seaton locked the bike to a tree trunk, using the chain and padlock from the saddle bag, not at all confident he would be able to find the route back to it. The forest was so dense here that the leaf canopy allowed no shadows. It was so dark that the luminous hands glowed slightly when he looked at the face of his watch. Seven twenty. Still almost two hours of daylight. Above him, he knew the sun was setting sedately, still shining on the island. And he needed daylight. He hadn't thought to bring a torch with which to search the ruin of the Fischer house. But Pandora had not exaggerated in her description of the wildness and the density of the wood. It was remarkably silent too, he thought, for the time of year. Her account had made no mention of birdsong. But then her mind had been fraught with matters ugly and fearful to her.

He crested the rise. The climb through the wood had not tired him. He was very fit and cycling ten miles or so had only stretched his muscles and alerted his heart to the welcome challenge of extra work. But he accelerated his progress in his descent, partly as a consequence of the sly pull of gravity, partly through excitement and the pressing need to get to his destination. He heard the murmur of running water. And then at once he was upon Pandora's stream.

Twenty

A stream was all it was. The rains she talked about must have given it greater life and width and urgency in her October, but in the arid summer now it was only an eight-foot-wide surge of dimpled rushing water. There was a current to it, sure enough. And when he lay down on the bank and scooped a cupped palmful into his mouth, it was fierce cold and brackish. But it wasn't beyond a leap.

The trick was in finding the space in the press of the trees to take a run. But he walked left along the course of the water for fifty yards or so and came to a clearing of sawn and burned deadfall. It was the first evidence he had seen of any forestry. And he was grateful for it. It was run-up enough. He cleared the water by a clean foot and was on his way in the canopy twilight through the quiet darkening ferns.

As the lie of the land flattened, the forest seemed more and more to Paul Seaton a place of silence and stealth. Something about it encouraged care and watchfulness. It was a place that made a visitor alert. More, it was a place that provoked a visitor into feeling like a trespasser. It did not fill him with Pandora's fond nostalgia for the hunting blood-lust of Plantagenet kings. The forest beyond the stream made him feel like someone wilfully intruding into a dangerous domain.

He had not travelled much in the English countryside. But he had been packed off to far-flung parts of Ireland as a schoolboy. Some of them had been wild spots, remote places rich with Celtic myth. They didn't lack atmosphere. They were wildernesses, some of them studded with standing stones. They were places of obdurate inexplicable mystery. They were charged with the questions their existence posed about the lost rites for which they had been chosen and constructed. But nowhere in Ireland had made the spine tingle and the throat dry the way this dense and silent forest was doing to him now.

He'd brought the water bottle with him from the bike. He stopped for a moment and took a drink, emptying it. Oh, well. It was Fischer, he thought, looking at the still, unstirring trees. Fischer's baleful influence still spread like a faint and poisonous fog across the land he had once lorded over. This pervasive feeling of unease was his lasting legacy. There would be no picnickers or walkers here for Seaton to cross paths with, exchanging a cheery hello as he crashed by. Anyway, he wasn't crashing by. He knew he was creeping through the forest like wary prey.

And then he saw light. Ahead of him the texture of the gloom shifted and subtly thinned. And he knew where he was. He was approaching the clearing where the duel had been fought. He was on the very ground Crowley had stalked prior to performing his healing miracle on the German's neck wound. And as he approached it, the emerald grass spreading before him now in the gloaming through the boughs, he saw her. He saw Pandora in a cloche hat and a long tailored coat with a sable collar, elegant and pale, detached and watching, her eyes bright with the fever still coursing through her blood, her feet in buttoned boots on the sodden turf.

At least, he saw her in his mind. What he actually saw, as he emerged into the clearing, was the tower and gables of the Fischer house in gaunt relief against the blue of the sky three hundred feet away. And he saw that the house was massive, acres of grey slate sculpted and contorted into steep asymmetric descents above grey stone walls grown mossy with neglect. He took a breath. He had not expected it to be so huge. It was a mansion, he saw as he approached, the way it brooded and dominated there. In the way its atmosphere extended outward, like a shadow, thickly cast. Pandora would never have thought to remark on the size of the place. To her it was remarkable only in its tastelessness. She was used to grand houses. To Seaton, though, its massiveness spoke volubly about its owner and his self-importance and ambition. Klaus Fischer had been intent on making his mark. Here, in this wilderness, was his enduring monument.

The drive was no longer home to a fleet of opulent cars. And there was no moping giant to rake the gravel any longer. Grass and weeds grew thickly through the thinned remaining patches of it. Ancient oil stains darkened odd areas as though they were blotched with some black disease. Looking up, Seaton saw how, as he approached it, the house seemed to spread and settle, filling his vision. Surprisingly few of the panes in its windows were smashed. Nobody had bothered to daub graffiti on the mossy stonework of its walls. It was high, the house, five storeys from the front door, at the top of a flight of stone steps, to the attic rooms that so contorted the roof to accommodate their windows. And then there was the tower. From the drive, Seaton had to crane his neck to take in its height and narrowness and lonely crenellations. Pandora was right about the windows of the tower. They were as deep and narrow as archery slits, but curiously uneven in size and geometry. And there was glass in them still. He could see the panes glowing faintly orange up there in the setting brightness of the sun.

The door was massive. It was truly baronial, to use Pandora's ironic term. It was oak, iron-bound and bronze-studded, and Seaton could not really understand how it had survived unmolested for so long. He couldn't see why some enterprising local builder hadn't helped himself to something so formidably intact. Or why it had not been hacked at for firewood by an enterprising tramp. But then he looked around, in the stillness, in the pressing silence. The house was very remote. And it was not at all welcoming. A square of old cardboard stapled to the door spelled 'Danger' in weathered red paint. Seaton climbed the steps, praying that the secrets inside the house were as intact as its exterior had proven to be.

The flanged hinges of the door were large and elaborate, scrolled with runic symbols that, for all Seaton knew, spelled out some older, more portentous warning than the hasty legend painted on the cardboard sign. He ran a finger across engraved metal, thinking that as a ruin, the house had grown into itself. It no longer looked like the contrived assemblage Pandora had dismissed it as. Fifty-odd years on from her visit, it sat here authentically enough in its brooding dilapidation. But that was from the outside. There was surely more to discover within. He rubbed at the faint rust stains that touching the hinge had left on the pads of his fingers and leaned his full weight against the door.

It opened.

It opened on a huge vestibule paved with blood-red tiles. And then Seaton realised that the tiles were terracotta, tinted to crimson by the setting sun. What light there was in the Fischer house crept in through broken windows and the blear of filthy panes. An atmosphere of quiet gloom hung like a pallor on the place. Dead electric globes forlorn with neglect and lack of power hung down here and there, suspended on dusty chains from a high ceiling. He remembered what Pandora had said about the light, how Fischer had illuminated his mansion with wall sconces lit by smears of pitch. The globes hanging pearly from the ceiling must have been an embellishment from the madhouse years.

There was a staircase, and it was grand. Or, it had once been grand. Its spread, its dimensions, suggested something truly opulent. But whatever carved trappings had been contrived to thrill and impress Klaus Fischer's guests had long been taken away. There was a functional metal rail where once there must have been a majestic balustrade. And thirty years of neglect had taken its toll on that. It was painted an institutional green and was peeling and rusting, decaying at a rate seemingly faster than the rest of the place. Climbing the stairs, Seaton put a careful hand on the rail. The paint, no doubt cheap unstable stuff, had turned to viscous goo. And his touch left a trail on it, like slime.

Why was he climbing the stairs? He knew bloody well why he was climbing the stairs, of course. He knew where Pandora's cache of pictures was hidden. In a manner of speaking, she had told him herself. And recovering them was the reason he was here.

There were many doors on every floor, all of them shut. Darkness was stealing out of the corners of the building and encroaching at a steady creep across the interior of the house. There were many doors, and Seaton could see a flapping madman, inconsolable in the canvas and straps of his strait-jacket behind every one of them, if he allowed his imagination rein. But he didn't. Curious things instead sneaked into his disciplined mind. Stuart, a week ago on the college roof, had been more David Bowie in *Merry Christmas, Mr Lawrence*, than he'd been Franchot Tone in *Five Graves To Cairo*. They all loved Bowie, those art-school boys, sure they did. And Mike Whitehall in his water wings! It had been a joke, but there was no refuge for the weak swimmer in any of the Hampstead Ponds. They were far too deep. The men's pond was for men, whatever their sexual preference. And Mike was a weak swimmer, he knew.

On the third landing, he heard music. It was sudden and

undeniable and it withered his balls in terror with its loud proximity. It had to be coming from inside the house. He could hear the chords shake the wood on the very piano frame as its keys hammered against discordant strings. Jesus, he could identify the very room the sound was coming from. But when he walked along the landing and opened the door to it, there was only plaster and dust and shadow, and the thin decades-old reminiscence of tobacco and male sweat. And silence, of course. The silence of the Fischer house didn't hold. Like a living threat, the silence of the Fischer house impended.

I'm being teased, Seaton thought. The place is haunted. But he didn't really believe it. He didn't believe in anything unproven. And it would take a lot to challenge his wilful absence of faith. The music had come from his own provoked mind. The house was dark and atmospheric and there seemed something somehow *poised* about it. But there was no one here, living or dead. There couldn't possibly be.

The stairs were naked under his feet, scarred to either side where carpet had been roughly ripped away. He could make out wrenches in the wood from stair rods and pulled tacks. The wood itself seemed solid enough, though, under his feet. The odd stair creaked, but so far the house was blessedly free of the ravages of damp. Damp was what he had feared far more than phantom lunatics. Damp would have rotted and destroyed the film in its hiding place.

It was almost as dark as he wanted it to get by the time he reached the door he knew opened on to the guest room in the tower. It was dusk, what light prevailed scant and murky. He didn't want to be descending the staircase at night. He didn't want to be here at night at all. The door to the tower was heavy and wooden and looked original. It held an iron handle above a keyhole large enough to suggest a substantial lock. The handle shifted when he tried to turn it, but the door didn't budge even a fraction in its frame. Seaton swore to himself and looked around. He had ascended a walled-in staircase to get to the very top of the house as it narrowed towards its summit on his climb. He was on a landing now, with a single small window cut into the stone and giving out on to the dark forest stretched out below. He saw that there was a key lying on the sill. He blinked, incredulous. But when he opened his eyes, the key was still there.

The door was on balanced hinges. It opened inwards with a sigh as soon as the key released the lock. The room within was larger than he had thought it would be, the tower bigger, of course, than it looked from the ground. Opaque light, the last of the day, stole in through the glass of its three disparate windows in their deep stone recesses. The windows were also much bigger than they looked from the ground. And they were set at a curious height. They were set about eight feet from the floor, and so impossible for a man to look through.

To his astonishment, Seaton saw that an item of furniture still remained in the room. A full-length rectangular mirror stood against one wall in a wooden frame with four clawed feet. Even in the diminished light, Seaton could see that patches of the mirror's mercury backing had cracked and peeled away, so that the wall was visible behind the mirror in places through the glass.

He heard the drifting insinuation of music again. It was much more detailed this time, stride piano and a cracked black voice played under the heavy needle of an antique gramophone. His heart began to beat faster in his chest. His scalp began to itch and he could feel the hairs on his neck stiffen with fear. He was very frightened, he realised suddenly. He was truly afraid. On a shellac recording, at 78rpm, he distinctly heard from somewhere down the stairs a long-dead musician indulge in a dry chuckle.

He looked at the floor, at its seamless covering of dusty hardwood boards. You couldn't get a coin between them, so tightly were they aligned. Bluesy chords drifted up from below. There was very little light. It was almost fully dark. Seaton sank to his hands and knees and felt with his fingers for any cracks or looseness in the floor his eyes might have missed. And then something moved in the mirror. At the very edge of his vision, he just caught sight of a shape in the glass and stood and turned around to see what had been reflected. But there was nothing there. He was at the centre of the room. He turned back and lifted his eyes slowly to the mirror again.

They were behind him. There were three of them, three men in top hats and long black coats with silk mufflers draped around their necks. One of them wore a monocle. They were smiling at him and he could see that they were dead. The one at the centre had a gold incisor that looked black in the absence of light. Seaton closed his eyes because by doing so he thought he could make the apparition go away. There was a smell in the room now. The room smelled of camphor and brilliantine and cigar ash. He opened his eyes again and saw that they were a step closer to him now. The ghost with the gold tooth was almost close enough to reach out and touch him. They seemed to be finding something funny, looking at him. Each wore an empty grin, mirth cavorting in their empty eyes, their dead expressions.

Seaton fled. He fell down the narrow flight of walled-in steps he'd climbed to reach the tower. He was on the second descending flight of the stairway proper, running down it reckless with panic, when he heard a scream from above so pained and tormented that it forced him into a questioning pause.

There was a silence. It was absolute.

'Paul?'

His leg was bleeding. He had gashed his knee falling down the top steps. He could feel the blood trickling down his shin into his sock, seeping into his shoe.

'Paul?'

He swallowed. It was a woman's voice. He knew whose voice it was.

'You must be very brave now and try to help me, Paul.'

Her voice was velvety with breeding and the strong tobacco they all used to smoke back then. As if reading the thought, she cleared her throat. 'Please wait for me.'

He heard the staccato clack of high heels on wood as she started to descend the stairs from the darkness above him. Pandora's approaching footsteps sounded terribly loud in the silence of Klaus Fischer's empty mansion. As they got closer, he heard wood splinter and groan under their impact. And he began to think that whatever was coming down the stairs was certainly bearing its considerable weight on two legs. But the thing climbing down to him wasn't on heels, it dawned on him, with horror. It was coming down on hooves.

It screamed again, in anger and frustration, as he fled a second time. And now Seaton did not pause or hesitate. He ran out of the house, followed by whatever it was he had awoken and unwittingly antagonised. He could hear its bulk behind him as it marauded through undergrowth and snapped branches in pursuit. He smelled its foul breath when it bellowed, closing, in his wake. It tore the rucksack from his back, trying to take him. And then the stream was on him, he was waist-deep in it, struggling for the other bank, fatally slowed and surely done for.

But it did not follow. It screamed with bestial fury and nesting birds exploded from the forest trees in sudden flights. And on the far bank, as he lay bleeding and prone, Seaton thought he heard it finally slouching back towards the house.

'Mother of God,' he said, his head in his hands. He thought

from the pain he was in he had broken a rib against a tree branch. He knew his face and hands were pretty badly cut and his injured knee was swelling. He'd been very lucky. 'Sweet Mother of Jesus,' he said. And he started to sob into his hands. And it was a long time before he was able to stop, as the terror and self-pity competed in him for ascendancy.

When he came to, it was daylight and he saw he'd slept in a foetal crouch on the forest floor. He sat up and the grass and wildflower stems were flat on the earth where the weight of his body had lain. He was caked in dried blood from his numerous cuts. His injured knee was purple and grotesque. His cracked rib prevented him from pulling in a decent breath and his tongue felt swollen in his mouth from thirst. Pain beat through him like a pulse. He looked at his watch and the date wheel told him it was Sunday. Groggily, he made the calculation. He'd been asleep for thirty hours. He wasn't really surprised. His body had been bashed about, but his mind had needed the distance. He felt he had probably spent some of that period in shock. His body hurt but his mind felt stripped, raw.

He tried not to think about what had happened. He tried not to speculate on the state he would be in now if he had awoken in darkness and not bright morning sunshine. His world had shifted. His world was a different place suddenly, slippery and ambiguous and infinitely more dangerous than he could ever have imagined, or feared. His perceptions would never be the same and he knew that dread would always follow him now, would be with him like some grave medical condition newly and devastatingly diagnosed. He'd been very ignorant about the world. And already, he felt an intense nostalgia for the bliss of the ignorance he had so recently lost.

He could not dwell on it. He had to push it all away from

him. He looked at the soft impression his sleeping weight had left on the ground. He grasped grass in broken blades between his fingers and lifted them to his face and smelled their torn summer sweetness. He had to exist in the here and now. He had to think practically. He had to do that to preserve his sanity. And his practical problems, right now, were considerable.

Everything had been in the bag torn from his back. His NUJ and cheque cards and cash were in his wallet. So was his return ticket for the ferry. One of the two good suits he owned had been folded on top of a pair of Bass Weejun loafers in his grip. All that stuff was gone forever. And, of course, Pandora's journal was gone. He couldn't discover it now, in the Fischer house, as he'd planned. Like her final role of film, it was lost. Worse, he could not prove it had ever existed. And with its lost existence now, was lost any proof of the film.

He had nothing on him. He patted the pockets of his shorts as if to prove the point. Nothing. But in the breast pocket of his track top he found, where he had forgotten he'd put it, the key to the lock chaining the hired mountain bike to its tree on the other side of the hill. The adventure shop had kept his Access card as security for the bike. The card would get him back to London. But first, he had to find the bike.

And before that, he had to wash away the blood covering him. He limped towards the sound of the stream. He took off his clothes and walked into the cool, clear water. He crouched in the stream so that the water covered his head. He felt the current tug at his skin and hair. And when he emerged from the stream, with the blood cleansed from him, he felt the temptation extended by the warm earth and wild-flower smell of the bright day to believe that what had happened had been only some dark turmoil of the mind. It was so much easier just to consider it all no more than a lurid dream. And he might have surrendered to that temptation, if the ground all about, under the trees, had not been still thickly carpeted with the fallen feathers of startled birds.

Twenty-One

It was after eight o'clock on Sunday evening when Seaton finally reached the door of the flat on Old Paradise Street. And there was a policeman standing outside it. Lucinda must be at college, he thought, dumbly, as the police officer removed his helmet and looked into a space over Seaton's shoulder with an expression of awkwardness and pain.

'It's Mike, isn't it?' Seaton said, thinking absurdly of water wings. The police officer turned his helmet in his hands and licked his lips. 'I'm here about your brother, Patrick, sir,' he said. 'I'm afraid there's been a tragic accident.'

A researcher from *London Tonight* called him on the Monday. Someone from a number for the *Hackney Gazette* had called Social Services in Hampshire claiming to be from the programme. Hampshire Social Services had complained. Seaton didn't deny it was him. And so his retainer was cancelled, the first dent put in his reputation. The second followed a couple of hours later, when the features editor of *The Face* called.

'What's this nonsense about us doing a piece on some flapper photographer no one remembers or cares about?'

Seaton didn't know what to say. He was not equipped to defend himself, could not have done so even on a normal day. And this was far from that.

'It's the last time you'll take our name in vain, Paul.'

On the Tuesday he opened the letter from the *Gazette* terminating his contract. The reason given was failure to meet proper professional standards. He stood accused of harassing an elderly resident of Chelsea in pursuit of a freelance commission when he was supposed to be sick in bed with the flu. It was a question of integrity. It was a question of loyalties and where and with whom they lay. He was of course entirely at liberty to consult his union about the decision at his own convenience. There were channels of arbitration open to him. But Seaton knew, folding the letter, that as far as the *Gazette* was concerned, those channels would forever, now, remain closed.

On Tuesday evening, Lucinda broke down in the flat in front of him. He didn't know whether it was grief for his brother or panic over her unwritten dissertation that provoked her tears. He began to cry himself. He'd felt numb since the Sunday evening, when they had taken him to Gospel Oak to identify Patrick's body formally. He hadn't cried when he'd broken the news to their mother over the phone. In grieving for his brother, now, he felt he was grieving for his own lost life. He tried to touch Lucinda and she flinched away from him and he knew that he would never earn her forgiveness after this betrayal of her trust. She might not know it herself, yet. But he did. He knew it. It was the end of everything.

'You talk about Pandora in your sleep, Paul.'

'She's dead, Lucinda.'

'You talk to Pandora in your sleep.'

He didn't know what to say.

'You should have told me about her journal.'

'She's dead, Lucinda.'

Lucinda sobbed through bruised eyes in front of him. 'Oh, Paul. It would have been better if you'd deceived me with somebody living.' She lifted her hand to her face, as though to try to conceal this breach of her habitual composure. He saw how red and ragged her fingers and nails had become with all the sewing she'd been toiling over in the days and nights of recent weeks. He felt his heart lurch towards her. But his feet didn't shift him from where he stood.

He tried to write the dissertation for her. It wouldn't come out on to the page making anything approaching sense. After one four-hour session at the typewriter he read the sheets pulled from the roller and saw that he'd written twelve hundred plodding repetitious words about the Lindbergh kidnapping. The German carpenter who got the blame and the chair was innocent, he read. The English novelist Dennis Wheatley had snatched the Lindbergh child. Of course. Göring had given Lindbergh a medal, he remembered, vaguely. The Nazis had honoured the great aviator in Berlin before the outbreak of war.

He screwed the sheets of typing paper into balls and threw them in the direction of the waste bin. He looked at his watch. But it was useless. He was beyond concentration, beyond reason too, truth be told.

His beard started to grow, unkempt, after he saw Pandora's dead reflection staring at him over his shoulder in the shaving mirror. She'd been in the water a while by then and she didn't look so good as she had, svelte on the grass at the Fischer house duel. It grew quickly in the heat of summer, his beard. After five days he had almost the full set of a sea captain to thoughtfully stroke.

He waited for his brother's funeral. They liked to bury their dead quickly and get on with their grieving, back at home. But the British were reluctant to release the body and he was obliged to wait to escort it back to Dublin and their waiting mother. There was an autopsy report. There were statements taken from his circle by the police. Patrick had been drinking. Well, Patrick was always drinking, wasn't he? They'd all retired to a pub on Parliament Hill for a couple in the heat of the late afternoon and then gone back into the ponds for a last dip. This according to an account given the police by Mike. There were lifeguards at the ponds. And they were vigilant. But the pond they swam in was deep and surrounded by trees bowed out over the water in full summer leaf. And Patrick had suffered cramp and drowned. There were no injuries. None if you discounted death, at least. His body had been found partially snagged in weeds two feet under the surface, sunk by the negative buoyancy of his waterlogged lungs. What had he said to Mike? The ponds at Hampstead were for strong swimmers. But Patrick had been broad-shouldered, strong as a bear, the most formidable in the water of the whole lot of them.

Bob Halliwell called him. He had no idea how Bob had acquired his home number. Their number certainly wasn't in the book. He might have got it from Mike Whitehall, or Tim Cooper, or Terry Messenger. Or he might have got it from none of them.

After offering commiserations, he asked if Seaton still had any interest in seeing Pandora's stored valuables.

'I don't think so, Bob. I'm finished with all that.'

Halliwell paused on the other end of the line. 'I'll tell you this anyway, Paul.'

Bob Halliwell had never called him Paul before.

'I think she was murdered. I think she was cut and put into the river. The police surgeon who carried out the autopsy was a drinker and a locum. And there's something not right, something too pat and hasty about the coroner's report.'

'You pursuing any suspects, Bob?'

'One character witness at the coroner's inquiry who laboured the point about her being depressed.'

'Edwin Poole.'

'Right. Her cousin. A Lloyds underwriter. Murder is almost always committed by a family member. That counts for all classes of society. Though I don't think he did the deed himself. She was cut once, deeply, fatally. And, in my humble view, professionally. And then she was put into the water.'

Poole. Poole who had written Pandora's anodyne monograph. Poole, who had introduced her to Wheatley in the first place at that glittering long-ago ball.

Bob's voice came on the line again. 'Edwin Poole never committed a recorded crime in his life. I should state that he had no criminal record and was never at any time officially suspected of involvement in his cousin's death. But he was known to be a man of dubious character. That's what he was referred to as, confidentially, in the phraseology of the time. No form to speak of. But in my considered opinion, if you're looking for a prime suspect, he's in the frame.'

'Poole was a satanist, wasn't he, Bob?'

'Yes, Paul. Yes, he was.'

Seaton was crying. Not about Poole or Pandora. He tried to do it silently, but he thought perhaps Bob Halliwell could tell.

'Take care of yourself, mate. Let's not bother about that Scotch.' Halliwell cleared his throat. 'You drink it. You drink it for me.'

He knew what he had seen now in his dreams, in his imaginings in recent weeks, all that spectral stuff he thought he'd seen and heard at the edge of what was really there on the neighbouring streets outside. He'd seen scenes from Pandora's funeral, organised and paid for by Edwin Poole, her murderer; her body interred by a bogus priest after much ironic pomp in unconsecrated ground.

Patrick's body was released and he travelled to Ireland for his brother's burial. He was grateful for the rain. He did not think he could have endured seeing his brother go into a grave in sunshine. But the lowering sky wept with them and the strength of his family was a small consolation to him at the edge of an abyss of loss he could not really begin seriously to contemplate. Paul Seaton loved his younger brother very much. *I love you so much, Patrick*. He did not yet possess the necessary strength even to put his thoughts and feelings about his lost sibling into the past tense.

He got back and carried on with what was left of his diminishing life. There were telephone calls. The actor Franchot Tone called, pretending to be Stuart Lockyear. And Jack Kerouac called, persuasive in the guise of Gregory Foyle. They were good lads, the best. But they were Patrick's friends, rather than his, in truth. And because they were wary of his loss and tentative, he was able to put them off. Mike Whitehall called. And because Mike was his friend and colleague, too, and wouldn't easily be put off, he called round. He parked his company Talbot Samba in the courtyard and was persistent on the knocker while Seaton hid crouched behind the front door and held his hand over his face so he wouldn't give himself away, laughing at remembered jokes Mike had made about the comic qualities of the car. When he thought his visitor had gone, Seaton opened the door and found Mike had left a book there, on the mat. It was one he had borrowed from Seaton after picking it off the shelf on the night of the cocktail party. Returning it must have been the pretext for his visit. Mike was the sort of person who liked a pretext. The book was an illustrated history of boxing. Seaton sat down against the door jamb and flicked absently through the pages, pausing when he came to the section dealing with the life and career of Harry Greb.

A letter arrived from Lucinda. He could not make out where the stamp had been franked.

Dear Paul,

I want to say most importantly how deeply sorry I am about Patrick. He was lovely and talented and I know your heart will be broken at this terrible loss. Everything anyone says will sound like a platitude to you, but one day you might take some consolation in the happy life he led. He was full of joy and lived well on it. Most people fritter away their lives. His was always well-spent.

Please don't think badly about what happened over my degree. A third is not the end of the world. It hasn't stopped my collection from selling to some very prestigious stores. I only mention this at all because I don't think it will do you any good right now to blame yourself for my not doing better. You offered to help with the best of intentions. But the suggestion was one I should never have entertained. Cheating is cheating. I was prepared to cheat and have paid the price. It's a small price. My conscience tells me that a better degree would have been totally counterfeit in the circumstances.

I won't be coming back while you're in the flat, Paul. Please, please take your time finding somewhere else to live. God, I feel rotten saying this. But pretending things have not gone bad between us will be of no help to you. George in the Windmill will take the keys to the flat from you when you're ready to give them up. In the meantime, talk to your friends, Paul. They love you and you need them now. Take care of yourself.

Goodbye and God bless,

Lucinda

Four days after Lucinda's letter arrived, Seaton drank two pints of Director's in the evening in the Windmill and then threatened to break the landlord's jaw if George didn't surrender her new telephone number and address. Half a dozen firefighters were in the pub from the neighbouring station at the end of their shift and they overpowered him and threw him into the street. He limped over the road to the green, aware that his bad knee was getting no better. He sat down in the small paved square with the single bench and the dusty cherry tree. And it was then that the full implication of what he'd seen at the Fischer house first really hit him.

She had failed. She had not got Peter out of their clutches. The boy and the sacrifice had been real. His own experience on the Isle of Wight had been real. He had been lured and pursued and almost torn to pieces by the beast they had successfully spawned in their ceremony after the horn banquet. In their contempt, they had let her go. She had spent the ten years left to her in remorseful obscurity and then died a violent death. That was the story of Pandora Gibson-Hoare. That was the story, anyway, of its outcome.

They had done it.

The boy had died and beast been conjured. Summoned. Born.

Over the road, outside the pub, he saw an ambulance pull up. Its lights were very dull, flashing in the metallic cast of the early July evening. George had left the sanctity of his bar and was talking to the ambulance crew and gesturing over the road towards where he sat. He didn't think he had ever seen George in daylight before. The ambulance crew were nodding and looking at him, their eyes indistinct in shadow cast by their uniform caps. Perhaps they were here for the cherry tree. Its bloom had gone, after all. He wished they would turn that fucking siren off, though. He wanted 'Me And Mrs Jones'. He wanted 'Abraham, Martin And John'. He wanted 'Harvest For The World'. What he didn't want, was a fucking ambulance siren. He put his head in his hands and started to cry. He was crying a lot, lately. They had done it, he thought, entirely overwhelmed by the realisation and its implications. They had slaughtered and spawned and he had felt the hot breath of the beast and barely escaped its fury. He bowed forward from the waist and grief and dread cleaved him and he fell to the paved ground and they were on him with straps and fastenings and he saw the disapproval on the watching faces of Hagler and Hearns from their grim and sweating gym posters up above him now in some dim memory as he didn't resist and surrendered, instead, entirely to them.

twenty-two

Paul Seaton was never actually sectioned. His status remained that of a voluntary patient during the whole duration of his time at the hospital. Afterwards, he could never really understand this. It was the era of the thrilling new notion of care in the community. He thought, in retrospect, they should have had him shuffling through streets with bin bags on his feet as soon as the winter arrived. He couldn't understand why they didn't just pump him full of some sedative and parachute him into Kilburn, say. There were plenty of mad Dubliners on the streets of Kilburn. One more wouldn't have made the blindest bit of difference.

The hospital was mid-Victorian, neo-Gothic in architectural style. It was a large building and occupied spacious grounds somewhere between the wooded heights of Dulwich and Crystal Palace. From the windows of the rooms facing northwest on the top floor of the hospital there was a view on a clear day of most of London, its landmarks indistinct from this distance except when the sun reflected off the river and gave the meandering city remote perspective and shape.

There was much about the hospital Seaton didn't like. But his fall had been so sudden and appalling, he lacked the energy to hate or even very much resent the place. There were areas, though, that he could not help fearing. He feared the confinement of the narrow lifts, with their criss-cross iron gates that had to be securely drawn shut before the enclosed cubicles would drift up and down on coils of asthmatic cabling between floors. And he was frightened of the stairwells, dim stone chasms with purple marbling on the steps and bronze banister rails. He didn't like the stairwells at all. So he stayed away from the upper floors of the hospital, where the recreation rooms and library and television room were sited and all the windows were always securely locked. And consequently, the view of the city in the distance below remained pretty much lost to him.

Odd aspects of the hospital inflicted emotional wounds he did not expect and could not defend himself against. The food was not terrible. But it was institutional. And its sweetish metallic smell of steam and daily stewing would contrast mockingly with Lucinda's occasional cooking, in the cramped kitchen of their little Lambeth flat, as she conjured meals over their one bright summer together with the easy flair she brought to most things in scenes he had been complacent enough to think would go on being acted out between the two of them for years. Perhaps, even, forever.

They played music at the hospital through an old tannoy system. There seemed to be speakers everywhere and so there was really no avoiding it. And the patients were offered no choice concerning what was played. Whoever compiled the play list seemed very partial to the Marvin Gaye song 'Abraham, Martin and John'. Seaton had been fond of it himself. But that had been before recent events. Now, in the hospital, he would wait for the line about the good dying young and think of his brother under the pond at Hampstead at the age of twenty-one, and he would be broken by the simple proven truth of it.

There was a maze in the grounds. It had fallen into neglect. It was a dense and careless topiary it was not clear had been planned as a maze until you stumbled into it. Seaton could imagine some mercantile prince having commissioned the mock-Gothic splendour of the whole estate in a prolonged fit of Pre-Raphaelite whimsy. That whimsy had dictated the garden and inspired the dense and mysterious puzzle of leafy passages on its eastern border. One day, towards dusk, a fortnight after his arrival and accompanied by a pretty nurse from Dundalk, Seaton wandered into the maze and they became separated. He tried very hard to find his way out as the terror blossomed in him and the afternoon light diminished. But when he knew he was completely lost, he cracked. The orderlies located him by his screams. He had soiled himself. He had to be strapped down and sedated after, so great was the panic in him brought on by his isolation in the maze. They injected him with Thorazin and it was two days before he regained consciousness and a full week before he came properly to his senses and wept with bitter shame at the spectacle he must have made of himself and the condition he had descended to.

It was at the hospital that he saw his first ghosts. Strictly speaking, he classed the three grinning figures seen in the mirror at the Fischer house as ghosts, too. But they had been malevolent, had meant him physical harm, he was sure. The ghosts he started to see at the hospital merely watched him through eyes that were dead, stiff in their period clothes, lurking in unexpected places. But he came to anticipate them, as he grew more watchful and less easy to shock. He hated it most when he awoke in the night to sense them clustered in the far corner of his room observing him in his sleep. Moonlight would stroke their musty clothes and vacant faces. They watched him silently. But he thought their still scrutiny intrusive nevertheless. He recognized none of them as people Pandora had mentioned in her journal. Perhaps she had met them and thought them unworthy of comment. Perhaps she had never known them at all. She had been a Fischer acolyte briefly, after all, intrigued by his powers only for a short and catastrophic period in the course of her enigmatic life.

He opted not to converse with the staff psychiatrists. Instead, he gazed at the walls of the rooms where they held what they called their interviews until the time was up. He felt guilty about this, about the scarce resources in public-health provision he was wasting week after week. But the sessions were scarce enough themselves. And the waste wasn't wilful. They asked him about his dreams. In truth, he would dream about Lucinda in pleated summer silk, with the brim of a mourner's topper forced down over her tawny bob and a monocle screwed into one eye above her death's head grin. Or he would dream of a woman fleeing with a small boy through a familiar wood, the boy shivering in tattered underwear as the pearls around her throat snagged against branches thick as thorns. Or he would dream of a foul, thick-breathed beast that lurked on the edge of his vision and caused him to piss his pants, gushing, unmanned. He couldn't describe his dreams, he didn't think. If he did, he feared he would end up wearing those constraints he'd imagined being used behind the multitudes of doors spreading from the landings of Klaus Fischer's madhouse.

His mother came. She walked with a stick, he saw, since his brother's death. She patted his hand and told him he'd lost weight. He winked at her and told her he'd be okay with time. Time was all he needed, he said. Time, the healer.

'And prayer,' she said. And she rose. 'Your friend Michael keeps me informed,' she said. 'A lovely boy, is Michael. From Liverpool.'

Seaton knew that among British places, his mother approved almost exclusively of Liverpool. He nodded. 'I'll be grand in the end, Mum. Just give it a bit of patience.'

He cried after her departure, but didn't castigate himself for that. It was normal, he thought. It was nothing at all to do with the insanity.

He'd been there eight months when Doctor Malcolm Covey arrived. He'd seen the buds, tentative, breaking through the topsoil in the hospital grounds. Other than the neglected maze, the grounds were tended like punctilious tapestries, Seaton thought. A lot of people with green fingers seemed to be prey to mental instability. Maybe it was just that the mad craved neatness in their chaos.

'You're haunted, aren't you?' Doctor Covey said.

And Seaton broke his rule and looked at him. He'd seen him, of course. You couldn't miss him, with his cape and his fedora hat and the blue puff in the white room of his Havana cigar, flagrant against the hospital regulations. But Seaton looked at Malcolm Covey, made eye contact, thinking, *This one is different. This one is gifted.*

'There's a great miasma of self-pity, of victimhood, gathered around you like an aura.'

Seaton said nothing.

'Or in an image better suited to an Irishman, like the melancholy halo of a martyred saint.'

Seaton laughed. He had to. It felt good. It felt like straps unbuckling on him. 'Where have you come from?'

'I read about your case.'

'And they put a name to me? In this account you read?'

'Of course they didn't. This is an ethical profession. But the account was bylined. The author, one of the house chaps here you persistently ignore, is an acquaintance. I offered to consult. Your mother was written to and very kindly consented. Here I am.'

'Why?'

Covey shifted his considerable weight in his chair. He rolled his cigar in his fingers and then puffed at it. 'I have some experience of the paranormal. That's to say, I don't dismiss its possibilities, its eventualities and repercussions. Not out of hand, I don't, at least.'

Seaton nodded.

'What are you thinking, Paul?'

'That you're a fierce talker, so you are. For someone paid to listen.'

Covey said, 'I know something of the history of the Fischer house.'

Seaton hadn't told them he'd been there.

'You have a press contact in the Metropolitan Police?'

'Had. Bob Halliwell.'

'Exactly. And Detective Sergeant Halliwell made it his business to follow the route taken to the Isle of Wight by your credit card. He talked on the telephone to the proprietor of a shop at Wootton Creek that rents bicycles.'

Covey pronounced 'bicycles' like they were machines just invented. God knew what he made of 'credit cards' and 'telephones', Seaton thought. He looked as though he would be far more comfortable with coffee houses and light opera and horse-drawn carriages. Seaton wondered had Bob, in these inquiries of his, contacted Lucinda.

'Being the punctilious detective he is, Halliwell concluded that your interest in Pandora Gibson-Hoare put you in the Fischer house over the weekend we're assuming triggered your breakdown. When he found out where you had been, he told the people here. Why are you laughing?'

Seaton wiped his eyes. 'Because the Fischer house was once a loony bin. I'd forgotten about that. I'm just thinking it's ironic, in the circumstances.'

'You're mistaken,' Covey said. 'It was never used as an asylum. Abandoned by Fischer, it was compulsorily purchased by Hampshire County Council in the spring of 1947. And the original intention was indeed to use it as a facility for the mentally deranged. But that never actually happened. Work was begun on converting the interior of the building, but the contractors met with a series of unforeseen problems and the scheme stalled and was quietly dropped.'

'What sort of problems? Subsidence? A touch of rising damp?'

Covey studied the tip of his cigar. 'I don't know if I ought to tell you.'

Seaton laughed again. 'You mean the information might affect the balance of my mind? Bit fucking late for that, doctor.'

'The architect commissioned to carry out the conversion, a local man, was found at the foot of the cliff overlooking Freshwater Bay. It was thought to be a walking accident. But then the surveyor was discovered, dead of a fatal gunshot wound from a Luger pistol his wife said he'd brought back in his duffel bag as a souvenir from the war. It was the Great War she referred to, not the war so recently concluded. It could have been an accident. He could have been cleaning or playing with a loaded weapon.'

'Rare bit of misfortune, though,' Seaton said. 'Given that he had owned the pistol for close on thirty years.'

Covey nodded and smoked. 'Just so. Then a week after the cliff fall, two workmen disappeared from the site. They were not discovered until forty-eight hours after it was first realised they were missing. They were not searched for. It was assumed they'd walked off the job, in the manner common enough to itinerant labour at the time. Gone to a better-paid job, or to one working more companionable hours or nearer home. But they were found hanged, next to one another, from coat hooks on the wall of the billiard room in Fischer's warren of a basement.'

Seaton had started to sweat. The thought of Fischer's warren of a basement and the horrors that might lurk there had dragged him reluctantly back to Brightstone Forest. In his mind, the sun glinted, orange and baleful on the glass of the asymmetric windows of the tower through thinning trees. 'I can't go back there,' he said out loud.

If Covey thought this remark directed towards him, he showed no indication of it. He didn't react to Seaton's words at all. 'Work stopped on the lunatic scheme after that,' he said. 'The property remained an asset on the books of the county council. But I think the Fischer house is essentially an asset no one has ever known quite how to realise, or to profit from. No one since Fischer, at any rate.'

Seaton said, 'Why does my case interest you?'

'I've an interest in the paranormal,' Covey said.

'You've already told me that.'

'Klaus Fischer had a similar interest, I believe, though he pursued it for reasons very different from mine. I've learned that he held ceremonies at the property in Brightstone Forest, in the guise of parties, until 1933. In 1933, he very abruptly left. It seems that fifty years ago he quite fled from his domain. But in the seven years he owned the house, I suspect he was rather industrious, after his own peculiar fashion.'

'Psychiatrists don't believe in magic,' Seaton said.

'I'm here to be persuaded,' Covey said.

'It isn't my job to persuade you.'

'Nevertheless. I'd like to know what happened to you over that weekend.'

'I'm disinclined to tell you.'

Covey shrugged. 'You might change your mind. The man who doesn't change his mind, doesn't think. Do you know who said that?'

'No.'

'Take a guess.' *Take a card. Take any card.*

'Wittgenstein,' Seaton said.

Covey smiled. 'Freddie Laker,' he said.

And Seaton laughed again.

He saw Malcolm Covey once a week for a month. Over four hour-long sessions, he told him everything. Or he thought he did. At the end of the month, he agreed to let Covey hypnotise him. Covey told him the hypnosis was to enable him to recall details about the weekend on the Isle of Wight he might have forgotten. He might have been so shocked or scared by some of the things he had seen and heard there that he had suppressed them in the manner common to victims of trauma. The time Seaton had spent asleep on the forest floor near the stream seemed particularly to interest Covey.

Seaton agreed to the hypnosis, even though he knew that undergoing it would, in a way, break his own pledge never to revisit the Fischer domain.

He agreed because, so far, his experience of talking to Covey had helped him. He was better able to sleep, much less prey to nightmares. The panic attacks he had suffered in the shower at the hospital, and on one horrible occasion in a hospital lift, stopped occurring. Mostly, though, he was helped by Covey's demeanour, as the psychiatrist puffed on his cigar and listened to the tale unfold. Covey never once looked incredulous. He never once betrayed any doubt through tone of voice or facial expression about the credibility of the story or his patient's sanity. Maybe he believed what he was hearing, Seaton thought. If he didn't, the man was a convincing actor.

'The iconography can be explained in one of two ways,' Covey said, in their final session at the hospital, after the hypnosis.

'The iconography?'

'The stuff you thought you heard and saw. The period detail.'

'Hear and see. It's still very much with me.'

'The things you hear and see, then. The music played on shellac 78s. The camphor and lavender water and spats and morning-coat paraphernalia.'

'I wish I could dismiss it as mere paraphernalia.'

'It could simply be that you are suggestible. You are, quite, you know. It comes, of course, from Pandora's account. The trappings of her narrative inform your mind and, crucially, your imagination in ways that disturb you. Consequently, you devise your own nightmare movie and fill it with period props.'

'To what end?'

Covey hesitated. 'I don't know.'

'You don't know? You can surely do better than that, doctor. It's your job to know.'

'There's a bleaker possibility,' Covey said.

'Illuminate me,' Seaton said.

'You won't be illuminated, Paul. The alternative explanation is much darker, you see.'

Seaton exhaled. He felt frightened. Covey's voice had taken on a gentler and more sympathetic tone. He realised that he had tensed his own wasting muscles, had braced himself in his chair in the way someone might steel themselves against the delivery of awful news. He thought, though, despite his fear, that even bad news would be a welcome change from the staleness and tedium of hospital routine. Seaton knew enough, now, to know that the routine here would keep him stable. He knew, equally, that it would never be enough to make him well. This part, what the doctor was about to say, was why Covey was here. Everything else had been preamble. All of it. Sigmund Freud and Freddie Laker. Wittgenstein and Jesus Christ.

'Illuminate me,' Seaton said again.

'The second possibility, is that the thing really does exist. They brought it into being. In the terminology of their own coven, they spawned it. This would have taken powerful magic and it would have been done only at terrible risk. But Crowley and Fischer were powerful magicians. So, I believe, was Wheatley, however buffoonishly he came across to you in the Gibson-Hoare journal.

'What the demon knows of us, mankind if you will, it first learned from Fischer and his circle. We're all at our most impressionable in youth. And it was so very young and hungry and impatient for sensation in those far-off days of Fischer's house parties, was it not?'

'I don't know,' Seaton said. 'I don't know anything about demonology, Doctor Covey. I don't know why something from hell would have a taste for Fats Waller. I don't care, frankly. I'm beginning to doubt, though, that you are who you say you are.' And beginning to regret, too, allowing himself to be hypnotised.

Covey leaned back in his chair. 'Do you think your brother's death was accidental?'

'I do. It was a coincidence. Thinking otherwise is very tempting. But Patrick died because he was in a hazardous place, careless because the day had been long and hot and he was drunk.'

'Why were you not taken by the beast?'

'Because it can't cross running water. It had me. And then it didn't. It's the only explanation.'

'You've just told me you know nothing about demonology.'

'It's the reason they spawned the thing on an island,' Seaton said. 'I've had a great deal of time to ponder on this. Tides, Doctor Covey. Currents. They wanted to keep the thing corralled. After a fashion, for more than fifty years, they've succeeded.'

'Why would a demon suffer earthly constraints?'

'I think that was part of the craft of its invoking,' Seaton said. 'It was obliged to accept certain preconditions in order to come here. It would have to be. If its power had been unconfined, it would have been no use to the likes of Fischer. It's only the constraints that make the beast keep its part of the bargain. It's the Faustian Pact in reverse.'

Covey smiled. It was an impossible smile to read on a man Seaton now knew he would never really warm to. That was partly because of the horrible circumstances that had brought the doctor into his life. He would always associate the man with grief and terror. But it was also because Covey gave nothing of himself away. It was clear that, whatever else he wanted, he didn't care especially whether or not he was liked. Fuck it, Seaton thought. He was tired, exhausted, truth be told. The hypnotism had worn him out. 'What do you think?'

'About your running-water theory?'

'About any of it.'

Covey was silent. The smile held. 'I think that you're as sane as I am,' he said, eventually.

Seaton was in the hospital for just over eight months. In all that time, Lucinda Grey never came to visit him. He was greatly saddened and hurt by this. But he was also relieved. In order to leave the hospital with any hope of genuine recovery, he knew it would be necessary for him to leave his old self behind. Some decisions about the curtailed life he would lead had already been made on his behalf.

He had been summoned to the county court and had a judgment against him now over an unpaid Access bill for the sum of a hundred and twenty pounds. So he was blacklisted and, without the collateral of property, had no means of getting credit. And he had been sacked from his job, so he was unemployed, his reputation sullied in the only profession he possessed the skills to practise. He was homeless. Perhaps least importantly, but not to his vanity, he was diminished physically. The muscle had shrunk off his frame in the enforced idleness of the hospital and he felt almost insubstantial when he saw in a mirror the puny apparition he'd become. (The briefest of glimpses, this. Paul Seaton no longer possessed his past, preening attachment to mirrors.) So a lot had been done to him without his having felt he'd determined any of it.

But he was obliged to do the rest of what would need to be done. He would have to relinquish all his old pretensions, routines, associates, ambitions; his old persona in its full entirety. And he knew that it would make it much easier to deal with his new diminished existence if he made it possible to believe in his heart that he would never see Lucinda Grey again. He had to store Lucinda, as he had to store his brother, safely in the locked refuge of his memory. There, he could treasure both of them without incurring the risk of further pain. There, they could continue to live. Only there, really, could he hope to have them at all without incurring the risk of his madness coming back again to overwhelm him. And it would overwhelm him, this time. A fresh rejection from Lucinda, a single sighting of his brother's grinning spectre, and he knew he would be fit only for the deeper and more private recesses of the hospital, with their padded walls and their stiff leather constraints.

On the day of his release, he signed for his belongings at the admissions desk. A porter took him to where they had been taken from the flat, at some time after his own untidy departure from Old Paradise Street, and stored. It was a bad moment for him, this. He signed for a suitcase full of optimistic clothing and his typewriter and tennis racket and a case of albums he knew he would never be able to listen to again. In an envelope there were ticket stubs he'd saved, as souvenirs, after they'd been to see the singer Carmel, on a spellbinding Soho night in Ronnie Scott's. There was a snapshot of Lucinda, taken at a table aboard a boat that served as a floating pub on the Thames. He raised the photograph to his lips, remembering the heat of the sun on his back as he'd taken it, recalling the perfume of her skin and the lost texture of her lips on those occasions they had brushed against his. There hadn't been enough of them, of those occasions. There never would be, now. He closed his eyes and rocked on his heels under the tense scrutiny of the watching porter. Then he took from his possessions only the clothes he needed on his back and the shoes he required on his feet to walk respectably out of the place and asked the porter would he please put into the incinerator those remaining things of his he needed now so vitally to part with.

For better than a decade, Paul Seaton did no more than run away. He went first to America, to New York, where he thought the insatiable myth of the Irish diaspora made anyone with a Dublin accent fondly welcome. And the welcome there was warm enough. But it was only ardent if you had it in you to live up to the myth. You were only really warmly welcome, Seaton discovered, if you could play your predictable part in the great and panoramic drama of expatriate Irishness. But he couldn't. Not at all, he couldn't. In truth, he lacked the heart. Experience had robbed him of the easy equanimity required to enjoy the *craic*. He was a troubled soul and he could not conceal his torment. He was morose, fearful, haunted. And he was vindictive, too.

One night, an argument was picked with him by an exiled Provo in a Brooklyn bar. The man was an active-service volunteer from East Belfast with a hatred for Irish accents softened by life in London. That was his excuse, anyway, for singling out Seaton for abuse. Maybe he missed his wife or his children, back home. Perhaps, after a drink, he thought it might ease his frustration to give a Judas such as Seaton a therapeutic pasting. But when it went to the cobbles, all he got was decked twice and what looked to Seaton, running away from the scene, like a bad case of concussion after going down heavily the second time.

It wasn't a case of being the better man, he thought later, nursing a cheap suitcase and bruised knuckles in the

Greyhound station. I was just the angrier of the two of us, possibly the less drunk, certainly even more pissed off at my predicament than he had been at his.

Boston followed. He worked in a boatyard and was even cajoled into rowing in an eight-man crew in the harbour twice a week. He took shifts in an Irish bar, all the better to stop merely drinking in them. In Boston, he found himself able to be more congenial. So much so that one evening in the bar where he worked, an acquaintance got friendly enough to warn him that the East Belfast Provo he'd crossed in Brooklyn was almost entirely recovered and fully conversant with his current movements.

He travelled to Canada. An Irish passport was a wonderful thing to have, he realised, if you'd the instinct to travel at all. He discovered he didn't mind the winter in British Columbia. He'd a mind by now to believe the chill in his soul would make even Nova Scotia in the winter warm and welcoming. He sensed the scent on him from the gunman he'd hurt grown cold, in Canada. He learned to ski there. He taught English and history at an elementary school. He gave evening lectures at a college running a twice-weekly course on practical journalism. And then he had an affair with a gentle and attractive woman of Danish extraction who taught ceramics there. And the catastrophic finish of it convinced him it was time once again to run away.

They went to a cabin owned by her father in deep woods on the edge of the National Park at Banff. It was snowing hard when they got to the woods. A trail reached, narrow through the dense endless spread of conifers. The going on this trail was heavy through the falling snow. And the woods swiftly enveloped them. The hush of the wilderness was profound, as though they had strayed into some undiscovered ancient place, somewhere humans had yet to intrude upon. Trees steepled over the trail, impenetrable to either side, so they progressed along a dark abyss of them, entirely still under the burden of snow weighing on their foliage. So it remained until they happened on a gap, after an hour's hard walking, a break in the bank of trees to their left Seaton turned into, assuming it must be the path to the cabin.

'No,' the woman said. Her voice caught. She was breathless with the heaviness of the going, he thought. 'Not that way', she said. And he thought, that's fear in her voice. She's afraid.

He stopped and looked along the path forced through the wall of conifers. The snow was scattered with fallen branches and the trees themselves were pale and exposed where bark had been torn from them in great patches and strips. Closer, there were grooves and tears in the wood of the trunks. He walked over and fingered one of them in wonderment.

'No,' said the woman. He turned back and looked at her. Again, her tone had surprised him. Her breath plumed. She stood rooted to the trail. There were bright spots of colour on her face, under her hat. She had lifted her snow goggles up on to her forehead. Her eyes were pale and wide in the blank whiteness of the ground and sky. Her voice, its urgency, had made the hairs on his neck rise in the chill.

Seaton looked back along the new path rampaged through the wood. Something immense and ferocious had marauded its way through there, cleaving timber, turning nature to chaos and ruin in its strength and rage. Had the damage been done by a heard of stampeding elk, by their tossing antlers? There were no hoofprints. There were no tracks he could see of any kind, but he was no tracker and the snow was falling heavily. Now, in this aftermath, it was very still in the wood. But in the bleeding sap and dripping pine resin, Seaton could smell the violence. No. It had not been a skittish heard of elk. It had been a force far wilder and more formidable than that.

'A bear,' Seaton said.

'Not a bear,' the woman said. 'Not in the winter time.'

'Then what?'

'Come here, Paul. Stay on the trail and hurry. We are a mile away yet from shelter and light.'

Light. Seaton nodded. He could smell animal piss and sweat now strong on the snow, follow the dark stench of its fury through the tunnel in the trees of the havoc mauled by whatever creature had preceded them.

They talked and drank mulled wine and made love into the night, the cabin dark except for log embers fading in the grate and the twinkling through the window of night fishermen around their braziers, camped on a frozen lake a mile distant through trees. Maybe it was the woods and the memories they recalled in him that did it. Probably it was the path through the woods, forged by the beast. But in the small hours, in the still and the vastness as he held his Danish lover under their blankets and they drowsed, he called out a tender name that wasn't hers.

Where was home? It was a vexed and vexing question. Before his mother's death, he would have said Dublin, city of his birth and youthful bruises, education and near-indelible voice. Since then? Surely it had to be London. London was home.

And so he went from Canada to Dublin. And he knew nobody there really intimately, on the outside of a grave. He was isolated. He was, of course, lonely. But loneliness, to Paul Seaton, was by now as is an itch beyond the scratch of reaching limbs. He was resigned to his isolation. It was as normal and regular a condition to him as the regular requirement to breathe. Loneliness had been so long with him, he almost didn't notice it. And he would have stayed in Dublin. Without fanfare, the 1990s arrived. He got a research job at Trinity and a flat on the canal and life was not intolerable. Prosperity started to change the city, giving its people a pride and purpose he'd never known there as a child. He would have stayed, except that one day, he realised that he was no longer haunted. He was free of the haunting. He stood still on Grafton Street on a Saturday afternoon and sensed only shoppers and tourists and heard only the music made by chancers with acoustic instruments in their hands and caps twinkling with coins on the pavement in front of them. He turned around and looked for dim expected figures, walking dead across the flagstones. But there were none. With a wilfully steady intake of breath, as he passed Brown Thomas, he looked at the reflection cast by one of the great department store's sombre windows. He could see himself pictured in the glass. He could see, behind him, the moving panorama of the street. But nothing spectral, watching, grinned sardonically back at him. It seemed the haunting had ceased. And so he decided to go back to London, where he had been truly happiest, if only for a brief time, and where he knew he was truly most at home in his damaged Irish soul.

Twenty-Three

Seaton finished his story and then listened for a while to the silence that followed it. The night had passed peaceably enough for the patient sleeping her narcotic sleep above their heads. She had not stirred. Mason had smoked steadily as he listened, the occasional frown his only reaction to what he was being told. They were in the room with the expensive hi-fi equipment and the pretty landscapes painted by the St Ives School of colourists on its walls. The pictures had just been dark oblongs in the night. Now their detail was accruing cautiously, as November light leaked through the wooden shutters over the ground-floor windows. But the storm of the night before, which had threatened the Wavecrest panes with bursts of pounded shingle, had blown itself out. And mercifully, they'd been free of music since leaving the car. All through his story, Seaton had expected the sardonic accompaniment of uninvited song from Mason's speakers. But none had come.

'What do you think?' he said.

Mason looked at his watch. He looked up towards the ceiling, as though looking through the floors to where his sister lay. He lowered his head and levelled his eyes on Seaton.

'I've got a Land Rover garaged in Tankerton. It would take me twenty minutes to get some gear together, maybe another thirty-five to load it so it's concealed. The ferry crossing could be risky, because ammo is heavy and sometimes they'll weigh a vehicle. But it's unlikely, unless we're very unlucky. And we've both had more than our share of bad luck already. My instinct is to try to do what I did to that thing in Africa. But my intuition is that I don't know everything I need to. There's stuff I feel I've not been told. Know your enemy, they say. Fucking right, I say, if you want to survive. If you want to have a chance of coming out on top.'

'I've told you everything,' Seaton said.

'Malcolm Covey,' Mason said. 'Even his name sounds like a fucking anagram.'

'Oh, he's real enough.'

'And he sent you to me, didn't he?'

'Yes.'

'Would you mind telling me why?'

'We need to talk to the priest,' Seaton said. 'We need to go and talk to your Jesuit. Covey told me we'd be wise to do that, before attempting to do anything else.'

Mason pondered. 'Ever think that Covey wasn't coming entirely clean with you?'

'Always,' Seaton said.

'Who is he?'

'I don't know. As God is my judge, I don't know. But I spent an hour with him the other night in a bar adjacent to St George's Cathedral in Lambeth. And he was most insistent that we need to talk to the priest if we're to have any chance of saving the lives of the girls.'

'Why does he say you have to go back there, Paul? Out of the goodness of your heart?'

'He always said it. He always insisted that one day, I would have to go back.'

'Why?'

The air in the room was yellowish and bitter with smoke grown stale. The light drifting now through the shutters suggested one of those autumnal days that never brightens noticeably beyond its enfeebled dawn. Even the rhythmic slap of the water on the shingle below sounded tired. Seaton sighed with fatigue and the spent effort of all his recent reminiscing.

'Malcolm Covey said I would have to go back, because the dead don't bury themselves.'

Mason snorted. He said, 'What's that, some sort of psychiatric riddle?'

'I don't think so. I think he was just stating a sad and unfortunate fact.'

Mason was still for a moment. Seaton knew this was a man who was very seldom entirely still. Then he shifted and blinked. He looked up again; up through the layers of his inherited house, towards where he no doubt hoped his sister still slept her dreamless sleep. 'That priest must be so old and frail by now. He was very old in Africa. And Africa was almost seven years ago. And then there's the job of finding him. Christ.'

'He's at a retreat in the French Alps,' Seaton said. 'A former monastery, above the town of Chamonix. Covey told me. Covey told me that's where we'll find him.'

'Somewhere secluded he's gone, reconciled, to die,' Mason said. 'Who is Covey?'

'I told you. I don't know. I've never really known.'

Mason nodded. 'Get some kip,' he said. 'We'll sleep for a couple of hours and then we're going for a run to help clear our minds before the trip.'

'A run?'

'You were fit once, weren't you?'

'Don't you want to leave immediately?'

'I don't want to leave at all. My instinct is to stay with Sarah. But my being here doesn't seem to be helping my sister very much. That said, I don't think important things are very often, if ever, achieved in haste. And to be really honest, if I don't sleep first and then burn off some of this tension, I'm likely to hit something. And you are the clear and present target.'

'I haven't got any kit.'

'I'll lend you some,' Mason said. 'I'm fucked if I'm running on my own. And running kit, mate, is the very least of your problems.'

They took the train to France from Ashford and caught a connecting TGV, mostly full of skiers. On the journey, Mason told Seaton about the condition of the other surviving girls from the ethics seminar. He'd established contact with the families of the English girls in the aftermath of the funeral he'd clandestinely witnessed. Both were in hospitals, sedated and on suicide watch. The American student, older, apparently tougher, had been restrained by air stewards trying to open an emergency door on a flight home, six miles above the Atlantic. She was wearing restraints in Bellevue, now, her distraught parents swapping vigilant shifts outside her room.

The TGV was quick. But Chamonix was the Alps. It was forty-five chilly and discouraging minutes before they were able to find a taxi prepared to take them to the address above the village provided by Malcolm Covey.

'How do we know he'll see us?'

'Covey said he'll be expecting us.'

It was cold inside the taxi. Colder outside, as they climbed higher and the air got thinner. Seaton rubbed his glove against the condensation on his window. It was a borrowed glove, one of a pair of Mason's skiing gloves he'd been lent for the journey. Splashes of snow looked luminous between the trees in the pond of view the knuckles of his hand had rubbed against the glass. He shifted against the car's upholstery. He felt his leg and back muscles, stiff and tender after their run of the morning. The run had been long and hard. Mason was as well-conditioned as he looked. But the unaccustomed exercise had left him feeling better than he could have imagined. The car started to climb a steep gradient that pushed him back in his seat. He watched condensation encroach on his diminishing pond of view. It bleared to a puddle. They were rising through the tree line, the boughs coniferous and dense. Through the windscreen, in yellow headlamp glare, snow twirled downward in slow thickening flakes. Music crackled into life on the cab radio, the Quintet of the Hot Club of Paris, the gypsy virtuoso Django Reinhardt nimble on the frets of his guitar.

'*Merde!*' their driver said, stabbing buttons on the dash. Behind him, in the light from the glowing radio, his passengers swapped a glance.

They were left on the cobbles of the monastery courtyard by the cleric sentry who answered Mason's pull on the doorbell. It was snowing more heavily now, wet flakes that clumped on to their shoulders and bare heads as they waited. Seaton's impression, looking at the dark arches and the walls above them, was of stone chilled to indifference by centuries of winters like the one on the way. It was a bleak and ancient building. Yellow patches against the brooding mass of the place, sparse and without warmth, suggested candlelight burning through the windows of odd cells and cloisters. Seaton shivered. But only with the dampness and the chill. There was no sense of menace here. That was entirely absent. There was none of the feeling he had felt first in his own flat, so strongly in the humanities block at the university in Surrey; nothing of the subtle foreboding he had felt even in Richard Mason's house at the edge of the sea in Whitstable. This retreat was a true refuge. How far you had to come to feel safe! He shivered again, aware that Mason was studying him.

They were shown into a large room lined with leather- and

vellum-bound books. A fire of pine logs burned in an iron grate and made the air sweet with the scent of resin. The smell brought a pang of hunger to Seaton's stomach. They had shared breakfast on the train from Ashford but had eaten nothing really since. A cleric came into the room dressed in the brown fustian and rope belt of a Franciscan monk. He was carrying a tray. He gestured for them to sit in chairs to either side of a wooden table and placed bowls from the tray in front of them. The bowls were filled with a thick dumpling stew. He put down a platter, heaped with chunks of bread. 'Eat,' he said. 'Please, gentlemen, eat freely.' His English was harsh with mountain vowels. 'You are to meet with Monsignor Lascalles. You will need for your bellies to be full.' He laughed at whatever joke he thought he had made and poured water from a pitcher into pewter goblets for them before turning to go.

'Without wishing to sound ungrateful,' Mason said, 'when it comes to monks, I've always had a preference for the Trappists.'

Seaton sipped water from his goblet so cold it bit into the nerves of his teeth. Mason tore bread with strong fingers and shoved a piece into his mouth and chewed. Seaton thought he should try to make conversation, make a joke of his own, make light of the circumstances. But he couldn't think of anything funny to say. And Mason seemed to be avoiding his eyes. He was suddenly struck by the feeling that Mason was nervous, meeting the old priest. So, like his companion at the table, he ate in silence. The only sound in the room was occasional sharp cracks and bursts from the grate as heat exploded pockets of resin under the bark on the burning logs. Both men concentrated on their food until their bowls were empty under resting spoons. Then the handle turned in the door and Lascalles came in.

They stood. The priest bowed his head briefly, twice, once

in courtly acknowledgement of each of them. He wore a soutane to his ankles and his head was bare. His white hair was cropped severely short. He was tall in the soutane and looked very thin. When he walked towards them, Seaton saw that he wore old shoes, vigorously polished to a painstaking lustre. And he felt a completely unexpected and hugely strong wave of pity for the old priest. For his fragility and his proud unflinching faith.

He wondered would the three of them somehow prevail. Fate linked them, perhaps even predestination. There was something Gothic and strange, and at the same time recognisable, about their situation in this remote and Catholic keep, with its roaring logs and walls of scholarly vellum. It reminded Seaton of the fictions of Rider Haggard and Conan Doyle and Bram Stoker. Three men, civilised and formidable, gathered to plan an assult on the forces of evil armed with valour and learning and staunch moral rectitude. It was a plot that seemed reassuringly familiar from the torchlight reading of his youth under the blankets of his bed. Except that he had been to the Fischer house. And the reality of it was so black and hopeless with evil that it made a nonsense of the cosy collusive fantasy he was tempted to indulge in now. You weren't staunch in the midst of the slippery chaos dwelling in the gloom in the mansion in Brightstone Forest. You were helpless. You were prey.

He looked again at the priest. The skin was like taut tissue paper over his facial bones. At one temple, in the firelight, an artery beat feebly with the thin blood that fed his brain. His faith endures, Seaton thought, but whatever strength and vitality he once possessed can only be a decades-old memory to him. Lascalles was dying.

He looked at Mason, with his distrustful eyes and sullen cheekbones; Mason, lithe and powerful, with the look on him of an angel about to fall. There was strength in Mason, right enough. But it seemed to be entirely of the bludgeoning sort. He'd asked Mason how he'd planned to keep his sister sedated and therefore safer while they were away. Morphine, Mason told him, sourced from a tame doctor in Herne Bay. How do you tame a doctor, Seaton had wondered out loud.

'You make him grateful. He had a problem with a gang of seafront B&B scumbags, living on benefits and demanding methadone scripts with menaces. It got worse after he went to the police. He contacted me in desperation after they beat up his twelve-year-old kid.'

Seaton had laughed. 'How many kneecappings did you actually have to perform?'

'Only the one,' Mason told him.

Seaton hadn't been able to tell whether he was joking or not.

Now, he felt a chill as cold as mountain water seep into his soul. He thought about the long corkscrew of descending turns on the snowbound road beyond the monastery walls, separating him from the skiers sharing Glühwein in their pretty cabins a thousand metres down the slopes from where he sat. Here, he was in the domain of the crag and the blizzard, high, where avalanches gathered their profound and fatal enormity. He felt lonely. It was not an unfamiliar feeling. In truth, he had spent every waking hour of his last twelve years in lonely conditions of varying intensity. But even by his own dismal standards, here and now, he felt very isolated. And it wasn't just loneliness, was it? What Seaton really felt, what really isolated him, was fear. That was where his Rider Haggard fantasy really fell apart. He wasn't valorous and staunch. He knew it, in the company now of these two brave men. He was a coward, mortified, alone.

In the room, the silence was broken. 'We've met before, Father,' Mason said.

Lascalles smiled at him. 'Twice,' he said.

Mason looked nonplussed. 'Twice?'

'On the first occasion, you were very young. I am not offended you do not remember. But I remember, for the joy and the relief the moment brought me. I baptised you, Nicholas.' He smiled again, more broadly. He gestured for his guests to sit. They sank back on to their chairs at the table and he sat himself, in an armchair facing them. 'I see I have your attention. But we need to begin at the beginning, do we not. And I suppose the beginning for me was when I met Wheatley, at the front, at the place history has come to remember as Passchendaele, in the autumn of 1917.'

His faith had been severely tested even before the outbreak of war. He had been a novice priest when a great passenger vessel foundered five hundred miles from Newfoundland at night in the freezing Atlantic. He had read the newspaper account with greedy incredulity; unable to believe a merciful God could allow so many so young and innocent to perish in such hopeless circumstances.

'April of 1912,' Lascalles told Seaton and Mason. 'I was a boy of seventeen when the *Titanic* went down. My vocation was almost sunk with the doomed ship.'

But he was young. And the young have enthusiasm. And his enthusiasm renewed his belief in something more exalted than a world of profit and sensation and the imperial hunger of nations. So the outbreak of war in Europe hardly intruded on his own intense speculations on the true meanings of the Gospels. Or of his intense joy at discovering the poetry of his fellow Jesuit, the Welshman Manley Hopkins. In the spring of 1916, he was ordained a priest in Rome by the pontiff himself.

But it transpired there was little time to rejoice in Eternal Truth or debate theology with other learned servants of God. And there was even less time for poetry. By the summer, Lascalles had been seconded as chaplain to an infantry battalion of the French army. By the autumn, he was reading funeral rites over mass-burial pits filled with quicklime as they interred French dead by the hundreds, by the day, during the battle for Verdun.

'Do either of you know about what happened there?'

'I'd say Paul here is more of an Easter Rising man, Father,' Mason said. 'For him, 1916 is all about Patrick Pearse and Michael Collins and the occupation of the Post Office in O'Connell Street.'

'It was still called Sackville Street then,' Seaton said. 'But you're right enough. I don't know anything about Verdun.'

'It was the collective name for a system of supposedly impenetrable fortresses,' Mason said. 'They were built by the French to discourage German thoughts of invasion. The flaw lay in the massiveness of the fortifications and the number of men they committed to a static defensive role. By 1914, all the more astute German commanders knew that Verdun could simply be bypassed by a modern mobile army. But the German Chief of Staff, von Falkenhayn, knew the French would feel obliged to defend it. It had come to represent national pride. A full assault would commit the bulk of the French army and make them an easy target.

'Since the progress of the war had made Verdun a salient in the French line, it could be attacked by heavy artillery bombardment from three sides. The French still refer to Verdun as the last great battle. But, in reality, it was a slaughter, only really distinguished by the number of dead it claimed.'

'The siege began in February,' Lascalles said. 'It finally petered out in October. By then a million men had been killed or wounded in the battle.' He paused for a moment, remembering. And remembering vividly, Seaton thought, from the shadow inflicted by the recollection on his face. 'By the autumn I was counselling the still-living, comforting the wounded and burying our legions of dead entirely by rote. I believed in nothing. Cruelty and chance and sometimes absurdity dictated human life. Instinct and cunning permitted survival. There was no afterlife. There was no hope. And certainly, there was no God.'

There was silence. Mason broke it. 'Why did they send you to Passchendaele?'

'You might think because Falkenhayn had familiarised me with slaughter. And because your General Haig planned another. But the truth is, the British had sufficient chaplains of their own, in all denominations. They had no practical requirement for a French priest who no longer believed.'

Seaton said, 'So why did you go? Why were you sent?'

'Wheatley,' Lascalles told them.

Twenty-Four

He had heard the story before being seconded, because rumour spread fast along the front and different languages proved little obstacle to the proliferation in wartime of legend and myth. So he had heard, in the mess, the story of the English artillery officer whose men had become too unnerved to serve any longer under his command. It was an odd situation, because the mutinous artillerymen were campaign veterans, battle-hardened gunners who prided themselves on their professionalism in the field. It was not the usual matter of cowardice or shell shock or exhaustion. Instead, the story was that they had seen something that had subsequently made several of them risk execution for mutiny rather than continue to fight in their particular unit. And they were adamant, these men. They were adamant even in the peculiar light of what they claimed to have seen.

The officer concerned had been hit by an enemy shell. The violence of the blast should have blown him into vapour. But in the aftermath of the explosion, as soil and debris rained back on the smoking earth, he was seen to clamber from the shell hole, ragged and smouldering, but intact. Incredibly, he seemed entirely unscathed.

'I walked over to him,' a bombardier facing an insubordination charge was quoted as saying. 'It was dusk, but you could see pretty well. Better than I would have liked to, it turned out. What I noticed straightaway was that he didn't move right. He wasn't staggering, like you see the wounded and the dazed stagger on a battlefield, looking like men seeking somewhere comfortable to fall. Instead he had this stiffness about him, like you see with a strung puppet in a pier-end show. And when I got closer to him, a flare burst directly above us and I found myself staring right at his eyes. You couldn't look into them. They were dead. They had the sly sparkle you see in the glass eyes of a ventriloquist's doll. But they were quite deprived of proper life. I pulled up, still with the field dressing in my hands I'd torn from my pack to treat him with in the event there was anything left of him to treat. In the fading light of the flare, you could see his movements becoming smoother and more convincing. More human, if you will. I was still rooted to the spot by the sight of him. And then, as he brushed mud and ash from the rags that were all that was left of his uniform, he cocked his head with a jerk that made me jump and smiled at me. And the smile was the smile of a man deprived of his soul. I can't put it more truthfully than that. And I can swear to you on a Bible I had not taken a drink. I remember the word from Sunday School. The word is abomination. What I saw that evening at the front was nothing more or less than an abomination.'

'When my colonel showed me this statement, I was intrigued by it,' Lascalles said. 'Its contradictions were odd. Here you have a corporal who is clearly a veteran of combat, bravely attempting to assist his officer in the middle of an enemy bombardment. He is experienced and he is courageous. And something makes him insubordinate.'

'And terrified,' Seaton said.

Mason sipped water.

'Forgive me,' Lascalles said to his guests, smiling. 'Allow me to offer you something stronger to drink.'

The British requested Lascalles because they needed an expert in magic. An authority in the subject was required to dispel the rumours circulating about the artillery officer it was said had bartered his soul for survival in battle. Soldiers were superstitious. Stories like the one about the Angels of Mons were encouraged, even fostered by the High Command because they suggested that the Almighty fought on their side. But this business was different. Officers were there to lead by example and to be believed in. They could not very well sacrifice this one to appease a single unit of uneasy men. But the fortunes of the war made it difficult in 1917 to end a mutiny at the end of rifle barrels. Firing squads were bad for morale and the planned assault at Passchendaele was going to be difficult enough, without further damage to the spirit and commitment of the troops.

The Jesuit Lascalles had gained his expertise in the subject as part of his studies. He had researched witchcraft in rural France. He had witnessed an exorcism performed in Madagascar. He had studied apparent accounts of demonic possession in Suez and French Equatorial Africa. He knew enough to suspect that the occult was both pernicious and widespread. But he was agnostic about its authenticity. He did not believe in the miracles of God. So he could hardly believe in the miracles of Satan.

His meeting with the English officer took place in a dugout about a mile behind the line. It was November of 1917 and the afternoon, like every afternoon, was spent under the dark pallor of the bombardment. He went there unescorted. The duckboards were treacherous under his leather-shod feet as he tried to pick his way through the labyrinth of support trenches with a hand-sketched map guiding him. It was raining and the map was limp and wet in his hands and the ink on it ran as he tried to navigate. He was half-lost and very conspicuous in his grey French field uniform and blue-trimmed cape amid the vigilant sentries and well-drilled teams and toiling packhorses of the British rear. This was the idea, of course. His arrival was well-witnessed. And he could see from the expressions on the men's faces that they all knew why he was there.

He found Wheatley alone, turning over a tarot pack, his quarters lit by a paraffin lamp artfully hung so that Wheatley's features were mostly concealed in shadow. He saw that the English officer wore a greatcoat with the collar up and a muffler and leather gloves. It was cold, of course. It was a raw November, cold and always damp, in these tombs hewn for the shelter of the living, in the ground.

'Whisky, Father?'

Lascalles accepted. He did not drink whisky. He had wanted to see Wheatley's hands. But in this he was disappointed. The bottle and glasses were reached for from their shelf and the drinks poured with the gloves still on.

'So. What in heaven's name can I do, I wonder, to assist a Catholic priest.'

'I would like to ask you, if I may, about your time aboard the sailing ship. Before the war. Where you went. What you did. Who you met. And what you might have learned.'

Wheatley was silent for a moment. He said, 'I learned to cross an ocean without spending every waking moment vomiting over the side. I think that was probably my single greatest accomplishment, Father. And, of course, I learned to tie a fairly impressive array of nautical knots.'

Lascalles nodded. He looked at his glass on the table they shared. If anything, it was getting gloomier in the dugout, the wick of the storm lamp hung behind Wheatley burning ever shorter and its flame more feebly. There was just enough light for Lascalles to see the liquid in his glass tremor with the shock through the earth of great and distant shells exploding.

'You don't believe in magic, Father Lascalles,' Wheatley said. 'No more than you believe in God. No more than I do. This meeting is a charade. I think you should do the dignified thing. Give me a clean bill of spiritual health. Then go home and struggle with your own absence of faith.'

Lascalles took his matchbox from his pocket and shook free a match and stroked it sharply against the rough side of the box. He smoked a pipe in those days and his English waterproof matches were the long-shafted, brighter-burning sort designed to kindle a reluctant bowl of pouch tobacco. Wheatley held out the flat of a palm to shield himself from the glow of the flame and Lascalles saw two things. He glimpsed a couple of the bronze symbols strung from the runic bracelet on Wheatley's exposed wrist. And he saw the skin on Wheatley's brow, below his cap, above the raised gloved fingertips hiding his eyes from the flare of sulphorous light.

'His skin was white, the colour of soft cheese,' he told Mason and Seaton, both sipping wine now, instead of water, from their goblets. 'And it was moving. It was stretching and pulsing as though tiny worms wrestled beneath it as it repaired itself, regained its life and cell structure. There seemed something both urgent and furtive about the process. It was hideous. Seeing that, knowing the significance of the symbols strung around his wrist, I knew that the bombardier whose testimony I read had been telling only the unembellished truth.'

'Did Wheatley say anything?'

'He said, "You've the manners of a potato farmer, Father. I've been disfigured by a gas shell and don't wish to be stared at until I'm properly healed." And then he laughed. Of course, he laughed.'

'But you'd exposed him,' Mason said.

'My son, it was I who had been exposed. I had strutted through the English trenches to our assignation, the master of situations. For over a year by then, my secret scepticism, my clandestine but total lack of belief had protected me. I was immune to the dangerous optimism engendered by faith. I understood the meaninglessness of war and life. I had long ceased entertaining hope. I was perfectly equipped for survival. And then I saw what I saw that afternoon and was confounded. And exposed.'

Seaton said, 'What did you say in your report?'

'Only that I could not wholeheartedly recommend him.'

'And what happened?'

'I believe he was given a medal, decorated and then transferred. You have to understand the circumstances. Canvas field hospitals adrift in seas of mud, staffed by boy doctors recently qualified in the genteel examination rooms of Edinburgh or Oxford. Young men engulfed in horror. And the Germans did use experimental ordnance. Both sides did. His story would have been more plausible than the truth. That's assuming he was even subjected to an examination. I cannot tell you if he was. I can tell you that I never saw him again and remained, in a curious way, always grateful to him.'

'He restored your faith,' Mason said.

'He did, Nicholas. He proved to me there is a Devil. And what on earth would be the point of a Devil, my friends, without a God?'

Mason excused himself. He said that he wanted to smoke and would feel more comfortable doing so outside. Lascalles assured him that smoking was a tolerable vice in the room they were in, but Mason was emphatic. It was a lie. He had no cigarettes on him and no intention ever of smoking another one again. He had smoked all he had in Whitstable and bought no more on the TGV, where supplies in the buffet had been plentiful and cheap. The truth was, he had been shocked by how short of breath he'd felt on the run in the morning with Seaton. A decade of alternating between self-pity and fear had done little evident harm to the Irishman's lungs or legs. His bank balance and love life may have suffered, but his fitness was impressive and his pain threshold surprisingly high. It had taken seven tough miles to bleed the competitiveness out of Seaton and the experience had left Mason short-winded and somewhat disgusted with himself. He liked to win. It was a matter of pride. And he liked to be in the best shape he could. That was a matter of survival.

He walked through a chilly vestibule that smelled of wood polish and holy water. The priest had offered them wine but, as with the food, had taken none himself. Mason well remembered how spartan had been the conditions they had found him in, huddled over his rosary, at that riverbank in Africa. Here, he suspected that Lascalles lived even less indulgently. Was it habit? Was it penance? The opulence of the library they had been shown to was strictly for public consumption. This seminary sang with the hard and vibrant piety of self-denial and rededication. He knew without having to see them that Lascalles' quarters here would in no way reflect the man's pastoral history or present distinction. They would make no concession, either, to frailty or to age. His choice would be a stone cell and a truckle bed and maybe the luxury of a bucket under it to piss in during the night. Lascalles was not here, as Seaton had assumed, to count out his last days in smug contemplation of his own past spiritual glories. Lascalles was here to purify his soul and face his maker and His judgment.

It was cold in the courtyard. The snow was soft and powdery under his feet in the cold. It had stopped snowing. But there were four inches of fresh powder light as spun flour under his feet and Mason wished for a moment, with all his heart, he was occupying one of the chalets in the town below, looking forward to taking the cable car to the top of the glacier in the morning. He closed his eyes and pictured the long tricky traverse and the steepling off-piste descent he had skied down so often from the top of the glacier, descending through the pale wilderness, with its blue shadows and silences. Turning ever downward. Down the remembered valley into Argentière.

He knew the mountains, too. He had climbed Mont Blanc and the Grande Jorasse and the Matterhorn as part of his training. It had been challenging and interesting to learn to do. And Mason had enjoyed the technical demands and accomplishment of each of his climbs. But he had loved far more to ski. With his eyes still closed, he felt as though he was very nearly grieving for the sensation of it now. Jesus. It was almost as though the Irishman's sadness was a contagion, as though Paul Seaton's persistent melancholy had crept uninvited into his own psyche.

He opened his eyes. But the mood would not lift from him. He thought for a moment about the Irishman's lost unreconciled love. Lucinda had been her name. He'd had lovers of his own, but he didn't think he'd loved any of them the way Paul Seaton had so briefly and poignantly loved Lucinda Grey. He'd had more than his share of drunken one-nighters. He'd had a fairly prolonged passionate romance in Germany, interrupted by the professional complications of postings and leave. And he'd embarked on a dangerously stupid affair in Ireland with the wife of a Provo quartermaster. He'd done it simply to spite the man, a murderous player regarded as untouchable for 'operational' reasons no one ever properly explained to Mason. But he'd become very fond of Sinéad, with her grey eyes and her lethal temper. She'd never have left the bastard, though, regardless of the circumstances. The love of her two young kids welded her to the marriage.

If he thought about it, nearly all of Mason's significant relationships had been with other men. He'd taken lives and he'd saved them, too. More of the latter, he hoped, than the former. He had hated his enemies and he had sincerely loved his comrades. And he had shared his own life most intensely when its very survival had depended on their loyalty and their courage, and their coolness under fire, with his brothers in arms.

Except for his sister. She was the exception to his soldierly rule. He loved his sister very much. He loved her more than he loved anyone. He loved her innocence and possibilities and the incandescent brightness of her nature. She was a one-off, was Sarah. When they made her, they broke the mould. He knew that a big part of his love for her was selfish, because the thought of facing the world without a blood relative left living was a terrifying one. It meant familial destruction, stark isolation. It gave that dark word, loneliness, the depth of an abyss. His mates loved him, if they loved him, through his deeds and wisecracks. Sarah just loved him. And he loved her. And it wasn't entirely a selfish love. It couldn't be. Because Nick Mason knew that he would give his life protecting hers.

Sell, he thought, rather than give. Sell was by far the more accurate term. And not cheaply, either. It had started to snow again and he looked upward and blinked against the heavy flakes drifting down against vaunting walls. Nick Mason would never have given his life. That was alien to his nature. But he would sell it for his sister's sake. And he knew that whoever tried to take it would be obliged to pay a painfully heavy price.

He sighed. It was a nice thought to go back in on, that, after the satisfaction of his fictional cigarette. It sounded just the right note of defiant machismo Paul Seaton would have expected from him. He suspected that Seaton didn't rate him, thought him little better than a boorish stereotype. But that was okay. He didn't really rate Seaton, not in a fight, he didn't.

Seaton's bottle had gone a long time ago. It wasn't his fault, but it was a fact, nevertheless. Seaton was shot. They were going to have to go to the Fischer house and confront the thing that held the three surviving girls in thrall. Theirs was a desperate enterprise, compelled by need but with scant chance of success. Mason could feel in the reluctant recesses of his soul that this was going to be much more dangerous than his encounter in Africa had been. And he knew in his soul that he had only been the victor then by a breath.

What worried him more than the frailty of his ally, though, was the Havana-loving enigma, Malcolm Covey. Covey possessed an oily omnipresence. He was slippery and clever. And the vague unexplained ambiguity of him was disconcerting. Mason had started to feel a faint menace at the mention of his name. He would have to ask the priest about Covey. Seaton could be appallingly stupid, for someone reasonably bright. But there were no flies on Monsignor Lascalles. Not yet, there weren't. He turned a circle on the balls of his feet, taking in the heights of gloomy stone and the pale void of falling crystals above them. He pulled in a breath that stiffened his lungs with cold, and followed his own fading footprints back inside.

He met with silence on his return. But it was a companionable silence, there in the library. He knew that Seaton and the priest knew that he had not escaped its enclosure for a cigarette. But he knew equally that in the scheme of things, his small deception mattered to neither of them.

'Something else happened, didn't it, Father? Something else happened in Wheatley's dugout that you didn't tell us about.'

'It was unimportant, Nicholas.'

'Tell us anyway. Knowledge is power.'

Lascalles smiled. 'Faith, my son,' he said, 'is power.'

'Nevertheless.'

The smile twitched on the priest's face in mellow firelight. The flames from the grate were fading in their fierceness now. But Lascalles' expression showed that his memory burned bright and undiminished. 'His dugout was sturdily revetted. There was a cot with an army blanket, the card table between us and the chairs we sat in. He had books on one of two shelves. Cans of bully beef and coffee and his whisky bottle sat on the other. In the corner, on an upturned packing case, was a Victrola phonogram. In other circumstances, the scene might have seemed almost what you English describe as cosy. But even without the other factors present, the pervasive smells of cordite and lice powder, and the small breach in the roof planking from a recent mortar attack, would have prevented that smug illusion. And something else. Something shared the table he sat at, next to the cards displayed from his pack. It was a Webley revolver, the grips missing and the cylinder torn out of it. He must have been wearing the weapon when he was hit. There it lay, like some skeletal relic, mute proof of the power of an explosion no one mortal could have survived.

'I wore the uniform of a captain during my secondment during the war. On entering Wheatley's quarters, I had taken off my cape. There had been no invitation to do so. But I had been anxious to occupy as much of my subject's time as possible. Anyway, the garment was hung on a peg. As I rose to put it back on, Wheatley did not, as would have been common courtesy among men of his rank, rise with me. He stayed slumped in his chair. Abruptly, the Victrola began to play.'

Seaton said, 'Do you remember the music, Father?'

'I recognised it instantly. I did so despite my incredulity. You must remember that, in 1917, gramophones were very primitive contrivances. Certainly they did not possess the capability to turn themselves on.'

'What was the music?'

'An obscure song by a Vatican composer, written in praise of the Almighty, rightly infamous as one of the few songs recorded by the last surviving castrato.'

Seaton said, 'Did it sound normal?'

The priest scoffed. 'If a castrato ever sounded normal. And then for a few bars only. The melody became corrupted by a sort of syncopation. I was fastening the collar of my cape, effecting to ignore this sinister pastiche. Satan's little joke, you see. Choral music corrupted into what even I recognised as the American craze. It was music meant to be sacred, played as ragtime.'

Mason looked up at Lascalles. 'You've been an adversary of the devil for a long time,' he said.

But Lascalles did not comment on the observation. Instead he said, 'Are you not curious about your baptism?'

'I think I've guessed most of it. When my father was trading in Africa, I think he became involved in magic. Juju. Powerful magic. It's why the house by the sea he bought in Whitstable is not the safe sanctuary from disturbance Paul thinks it ought to be. I think you saved my soul and I expect my father was grateful. But you believed he passed something to me. Let's call it a capability. I think you have followed my career. Christ alone knows what influence was put to use to enable you to do it, but that's what you've done. And I think what happened with the Kheddi was a sort of audition. You summoned me there. It was your little test.'

'Not mine. Yours. And you passed it.'

'Bullets killed the Kheddi, Father.'

'Bullets fired from your gun. It was not bullets that destroyed the demon, Nicholas. You did that.'

'I'm not as good at guessing games as Nicholas is,' Seaton said. 'I haven't had the same expert grounding in subterfuge as our intrepid soldier boy. I can't guess who Malcolm Covey is. Or what part he really plays in all this. I'm afraid you'll have to tell me.'

Lascalles looked at him. And Seaton felt a flush of embarrassment. Absurdly, he'd felt jealous when the priest had referred to Mason as 'my son'. And Lascalles had done it twice. He felt childishly resentful of the history the two men shared. He felt excluded. And now he felt that Lascalles could see his resentment written plainly on his face.

'Klaus Fischer died in Buenos Aires in the spring of 1983,' Lascalles said. 'He had reached the age of eighty-eight. It was a long life. Such a man would have compelling reasons for going to his death reluctantly. But die he eventually did, twelve years ago, peacefully it was reported, in his sleep. Five months after his death, you were visited in hospital by a man who seems to have shared many of Fischer's characteristics.'

Seaton nodded.

'Not in his dotage, of course. But in his formidable prime. Think of the girth, of the flamboyant attire and the cigars. Think of that teasing expertise on the subject of the occult. Did he enjoy music?'

Seaton thought about this. 'I only went once to his home. I was renting a bedsit in Dalston, scraping together the fare to get me away to the States. I was obliged to list my address with the hospital and he must have got it from them because one morning the postman delivered a note from him inviting me round for tea. As I say, I went only the once. He owned a large flat in a mansion block in Victoria. He showed me his listening room. He possessed a stereo system that must have cost him several thousand pounds.'

'It's impossible,' Mason said.

'Jesus,' Seaton said, 'the hypnotism.' He had remembered the words of Pandora's journal, the hypnotic power she had witnessed in Fischer, confined to the boat cabin with him on their wretched crossing. He put his head in his hands. And the priest crossed the distance to him and put a hand on his shoulder and squeezed.

'*Courage*, my son,' he said. It is not your fault. Nothing prepares us for such encounters.'

Mason said, 'You really think it's him, Father?'

Lascalles shrugged. 'I can tell you only this for certain. Before 1983, there is no record of the existence of a Doctor Malcolm Covey.'

'They're so clever,' Seaton said.

And Lascalles frowned. 'There is no "they", Paul. We face only one adversary.'

'I've seen them, Father. They have tried to do me harm.'

'Manifestations.'

'Is Covey a manifestation?'

'Paul,' the priest said. 'I would say you are named in honour of the appropriate saint.' Steel had replaced the avuncularity in his voice. Both of the men in the room with him tensed. It was very late by now, approaching two in the morning. But Father Lascalles seemed to be strengthening with the hours rather than having his age betray him with fatigue. 'Fischer burns in hell,' he said. His voice was like a file reducing iron. 'They burn in hell, all of those who served him at the time and in the place we are discussing. Covey may or may not be a man. But he is a mere servant, a puppet. We face the foe we have faced since the Fall. Him only. To forget this fact would be fatal for both of you.'

He turned and walked over to one of the bookcases and put a hand into a pocket-slit sewn into the side of his soutane. The hand emerged with a pair of spectacles. He unfolded their wire arms and put them on, and fingered spines along a bookcase shelf. It was obvious to Mason that, even with the spectacles, he was searching blind, waiting for his index finger to recognise the texture and breadth of the spine he was seeking. It only took a moment, really. His hand stopped and he pulled out a small volume with marbling on its cover. The sight of it made Seaton gasp audibly. Mason felt a stab of sympathy for the Irishman. For him, this was turning into a night of revelation.

'Yes,' Lascalles said to Seaton. 'As you have observed already with your sharp eyes, she was in some ways a creature of habit. She always bought the same notebooks in which to inscribe her thoughts. You need to read this, Paul.' The priest's voice was gentle again, compassionate. 'Reading this will answer questions I have not.'

Twenty-Five

6 October, 1937

I do not accord that date any particular significance. It is exactly ten years since a rather younger and vastly more innocent version of myself last committed thoughts and events to paper. They were trite and shallow thoughts and they were terrible events. And I have written down virtually nothing since. But the anniversary is not what prompts me to pick up my pen this morning and detail my intentions. That date is no more, really, than a grim, slightly troubling coincidence.

Yesterday, for the first time in months, I read a newspaper. It was in a dentist's waiting room in Weymouth Street. It was a routine appointment and I had forgotten to bring along something to read. *Punch* has never been greatly to my taste and I have come to loathe the fashion magazines. So it was the day's paper or it was nothing. And I came across an opinion piece, which focused on the situation in Germany. The members of the Führer's inner circle were each described, in detailed and highly flattering terms. Göring was there, of course, resplendent in a uniform I imagine he designed himself. The author of the article was an English historian with a professorship at Oxford. Like many academics, he seemed fascinated by the notion of the man of action. He described Göring's feats as a member of the Red Baron's Flying Circus in the war. And, of course, the tone was eulogistic. He wrote of Göring's prowess as a huntsman. And he refuted indignantly the persistent rumour that the Reichstag fire in '33 was started not by the Communists, but by Hitler's loyal acolyte Hermann Göring. All in all it seemed to me a shallow sycophantic piece.

I don't care about the Reichstag fire, or the part Göring may or may not have played in setting it. An act of arson cannot be blamed or credited for what has happened in Germany. The Nazi Party would have come to power regardless. There was a relentless inevitability about their rise. They are like a whirlwind which certainly Germany, and perhaps the whole world, will reap.

But I looked at the picture of Göring, gloating and imperious. And I thought about Wheatley, with all that acclaim and wealth his books are now bringing. Fischer; the Hollywood mogul; all of them have prospered. And I allowed myself to think back to the terrible events of ten years ago. And the recollection brought in its aftermath a compelling need in me to find out finally something about the poor doomed boy they abducted. Alive, he would be coming to maturity now. But his adulthood was stolen from him. He is dead, because they killed him. What sort of character was he? What sort of man would he have become? I saw dignity and courage in the very little I was allowed to see of him. But I felt the need, now, overwhelmingly, to know more.

This wish to learn who Peter was seemed both respectful and appropriate. And it came upon me with the weight of obligation. Guilt is a powerful emotion, but I have lived with guilt, insidious and futile, for a decade. This was a vastly stronger and more positive urge.

A day has barely gone by that I have not thought about how close we came to escape. But after reading the newspaper yesterday, after seeing Göring strutting in his cape and boots and baubles of high office, I began to wonder finally, too, about the possibility of retribution. They should be punished for what they have prospered so obscenely from. One day, they will each be called to account for their crimes before God. But they should be punished now, in the secular court, exposed and condemned as the murderers of an innocent child.

Child abduction is not a common crime in England. It was not a common crime ten years ago. There is every likelihood that when Peter was taken, the police were alerted to his disappearance. An eight-year-old could not simply be allowed to vanish in this country in 1927, regardless of how impoverished his family circumstances might have been. A mother will not quietly relinquish her son. It goes against nature to do so. My wretched life has made me a reluctant authority on abomination. For a parent willingly to give up their infant to malevolent strangers would be exactly that. So it is likely the police were alerted. And when a preliminary search proved unsuccessful, an investigation would have begun. And that would surely have meant a report in the press. I don't mean a story in a national newspaper like the *Daily Herald*, which printed yesterday's apologist drivel about the Nazi High Command. But it would be the public duty of a local newspaper to report a local disappearance, give a description, perhaps even, if one existed, print a photograph of the child gone missing.

I know that the obvious thing to do would be to hire a private detective to help me in my search. Seeking professional help is surely the most sensible course. But the thought of involving some grubby ex-detective, more used to spying on adulterers, to exposing squalid assignations for evidence in divorce cases, seems altogether abhorrent. The circumstances involve too much unreconciled grief, too tragic a loss, for me to be willing to engage a paid mercenary to assist me. If I'm to do it at all, I'm to do it on my own. My sources must be the Public Records Office and the British Museum, where I believe there is kept a copy of every publication ever printed in the British Isles. My strongest clue is Peter's accent, which in the precious few words we exchanged, I am sure, betrayed the Celtic lilt of Wales.

My first obstacle is a very practical one. I have no pass allowing access to the British Museum Reading Room. I am not a student or a scholar or a paid researcher. It is a decade since I can claim to have practised any profession. There are, ironically, examples of my own work in the great archive I seek to search. But I could not get through the door to ask to look at them, even in the unimaginable event that I should wish to do so. This is a difficulty. But I am resolved now and will not be deterred.

6 October, 1937, later

At four o'clock today I walked the distance from the flat to St Luke's Church in Chelsea for an hour of instruction. It was a sooty autumnal afternoon of wet pavements and lingering tobacco smoke. The shop windows along the King's Road were yellow and dim in the dampness. Men made anonymous by their uniform garb of grey mackintosh and felt trilby walked women on precarious heels. The streets seemed improbably busy for a Wednesday. The shop displays seemed dowdy and undeserving, too lacklustre to draw trade. But, of course, the bustle is all illusion. Many tread the streets because they have no jobs to go to. All they are spending is shoe leather in their melancholy efforts to occupy unwanted time.

The road traffic pointed north was stationary. There is something splendidly democratic about a traffic jam. I saw a Delage with headlamps the size of soup plates and the streamlined body of a panther idling behind a filthy coal wagon that shook with every revolution of its decrepit engine. The coalmen sat on the back of the wagon, smoking vacantly amid the sacks of coal and coke and bags of slack, their faces and hands stained black like those of a minstrel troupe. The owner of the Delage sat behind his driver, reading the financial pages and making swift calculations on an abacus placed on the arm of his seat. He was jowly in his astrakhan coat collar, almost regally patient in the jam. I shivered. The coal-wagon minstrel troupe had reminded me momentarily of Al Jolson, the American film star, the celebrated lead in *The Jazz Singer*. They had innocently brought to mind the circumstances in which I first became aware of the film.

A milk cart was responsible for the hold-up. Its horse had apparently bolted and turned the cart, sending zinc milk churns tumbling and spilling over the macadam. Milk ran and dissipated, the colour of weak coffee in the gutters, by the time I passed this spectacle, the nag now still, flanks steaming innocently in the rain as an ostler stroked its head and a policeman gathered details from the poor milkman into his notebook under the cover of his rain cape. Car horns hooted behind them, but they did so despondently, as if reconciled. I crossed the road where I always cross it, by the bakery. Catholicism will forever now, I think, evoke in me the smell of freshly baking bread. This is a good thing. I can think of few smells better fitting the liturgy. And those others I can think of are meagre or sad, while bread is comforting.

Monsignor Lascalles provided the answer to my problem concerning access to the Reading Room. I did not tell him why I wanted the card. On completion of my instruction, when I am accepted into the faith, I might ask him to be my confessor and tell him everything. I would need to be resolute to do so. Whatever his training, whatever his experience, I know that in confessing to him, I would lose a friend and disillusion a virtuous man. My weakness with my instructor is that I want him to like me. Vanity and intuition together insist that he does. He was a man before he was a priest and with his sinewy strength and saturnine handsomeness, the man inside the soutane is still starkly apparent to me. He is serious concerning the instruction and sometimes even grave. But afterwards he is relaxed and smiles and he has the fatalistic humour singular to the French. I do not want to disappoint him. And yet I think it inevitable that, one day, I must.

I explained my dilemma as we drank coffee in a vestibule in a wing adjoining the consecrated part of the church. Here, a woman must still keep her head covered. But a guest is allowed to smoke. So I smoked gratefully under my mantilla. The Monsignor does not smoke. He smoked in the war, he told me, when everyone did. But he has since given up the vice. I suspect smoking is only one of many small pleasures his vocation has compelled him to relinquish.

I told him I wanted to gain entry to the British Museum in order to conduct a private research project. But that I needed urgent access, rather than having to wait for the wheels of bureaucracy to turn. I phrased it to him this way deliberately. The French have a familiarity with bureaucracy that makes most of them detest it. He seemed to ponder for a moment. The Monsignor's face has a lean highborn look, well-suited to thought. And then he brightened and smiled.

His Eminence the Cardinal employs two voluntary researchers, he told me. One of them is a woman. Both possess just such a card.

Won't the subterfuge involve lying, Father?

He cocked his head and his eyes twinkled. He has grey eyes. There is no real softness to them but, like their owner, they can be kind. The name on the card is that of Susan Green, he said. You have committed no sin I can readily call to mind if the guardians of the Reading Room assume the name is yours. I shall see the card is delivered to your home in the morning.

7 October, 1937

I have found him. I am sure it is him. If so, they chose shrewdly. I left the museum already making plans in my head for my journey. There are garages in Great Portland Street where any respectable person with the means can hire a reliable car. The journey will be fairly arduous, along remote roads I have never driven. But I was a good fast driver in the days when I owned a car and drove regularly. To think, the woman I once was owned a red Bugatti. When I look back at myself in those days, at what I did and hungered for, I gaze disdainfully upon a person I barely recognise. But she was me. And I am responsible for everything she did. Buying the Bugatti was, I suppose, the very least of it.

Now, my sensibly shod feet and the Underground are usually sufficient to get me about. I'm parsimonious with taxis, shameless when it comes to taking buses and trams. Humble pursuits help in our attaining a state of grace, the Monsignor says. Having left the museum building in Bloomsbury, almost without thinking, I began to walk in the direction of Foyles bookshop on Charing Cross Road, where I knew I would be able to buy the maps to plot my journey in detail.

Even on a wet autumn in early evening, I generally enjoy Charing Cross Road. When I reached it, the lights in the long and ramshackle row of bookshops on its east side were burning brightly under flapping canvas awnings that almost stretched the width of the pavement. A chestnut-seller stood with a burnished uplit face above his glowing brazier. Even with the swelling evening traffic, I could hear the bellow of the costermongers at their stalls a block away off Cambridge Circus. Foyles, across the road from me, was a bright yellow palace of books in the fading light. There is something thrilling about coming across the spectacles of London like this, something that even the most jaded Londoner can appreciate. And ordinarily I would have felt the familiar excitement of it myself, emerging upon it from the austere and gloomy streets of Bloomsbury. Except that I couldn't, because I had the very strong intuition that I had been followed there from the museum.

I had reached the edge of the kerb. I was obliged to wait for a lull in the hurtling traffic. A red bus carrying a sweeping advertisement for Gillette Safety Razors in silver and green across its top deck braked in front of me to allow passengers on to the tailboard from a bus stop to my right. Now I was trapped. For an absurd moment I imagined a heavy hand on my shoulder and the whisper of Cockney authority confiding, *Madam, we know you're not Susan Green*. I even turned around. But all I saw was the oblivious march of September pedestrians in raincoats under raised umbrellas. When I turned back again, the bus had pulled away and Foyles beckoned.

I will set off tomorrow morning. I have telephoned to arrange the car and they are going to fill the tank with petrol and the radiator with water and check the tyres and the engine tonight. I have arranged to pick the vehicle up at 8 a.m. They were very enthusiastic for me to try their latest model. I told them I didn't care a jot about the manufacturer or year so long as the car is reliable and its colour black. I want to be as inconspicuous as I can be. At the risk of falling from the Monsignor's grace, I know that nature contrived to make me a conspicuous woman. It might be committing the sin of pride to allude to this. But really, I think it is only stating a fact. I have never required a crimson sports car to turn the heads of either sex.

Perhaps I should have told them that I do not wish to hire a German car. After Foyles this evening, I walked down past Sheekey's fish restaurant and along Bedfordbury for the Strand and Embankment Underground station. There was a boy at the station entrance, hawking the *Evening News*. I glanced at the front-page headline. President Roosevelt has made a speech calling on American Nazis to be more tolerant of other political groups. But tolerance is not a part of the Nazi ideology. The iron broom Hitler talks so fondly about, leaves a trail of blood when he uses it to sweep. Tolerance to them is no different to weakness. That is why appeasement is such a paradox. It can only encourage what it delays and seeks to prevent.

Rather than going straight into the station and taking my District Line train, I walked across to the Embankment and watched the river for a while. I have always loved the river. The night was gorgeously clear and the Thames was at full tide, its oily surface lapping against the mooring rings which depend from the mouths of sad bronze lions' heads, set in the stone of the bank and grown green in their watery toil. I watched a pugnacious tug pull a long line of barges filled with bitumen or coal upriver while its steersman puffed on a pipe and sipped at something fortifying from a metal flask in his wheelhouse. The sail of a barque sucked light like a vacuum sucks air as it passed blackly across the gas lamps and braziers illuminating the wharves of the far bank. At Cleopatra's Needle, I stopped and turned back and watched as engines departed Charing Cross Station for points southeast across the river bridges with jubilant screams on their steam whistles and firefly sparks dancing in their furious manes of smoke.

The Germans will bomb London. That is what a man from the Ministry of Defence said on the wireless a few evenings ago before he was forced to resign from his job for the crime of 'warmongering'. Thus was a civil servant disgraced and deprived of his pension for the crime of telling the truth. I know of two bad men who will profit from the war. Göring, of course. And Fischer, the monster whose factories manufacture the bombs they will use to disfigure and even destroy the city I live in and so cherish. Perhaps I can help heap disgrace on them both before war breaks out. And in the meantime, I can boycott German automobiles. A feeble joke, but it made me smile, just now, as I wrote it. I had forgotten how fulfilling sharing one's thoughts in secrecy can be. When I complete my instruction and convert to Catholicism, I am sure I shall be one of those awful women who attends confession every week.

Before going for my train, I sat on a bench at the side of the river and smoked a cigarette. And I was possessed again by the odd feeling of being watched I had felt earlier on Charing Cross Road. Then it passed and I was able to enjoy my vice if not in a state of grace, then at least in the great capital's magical state of crowded seclusion.

<u>10 October, 1937, London, dawn</u>

I am exhausted and yet quite unable to sleep. I reached home in the small hours after a journey I can barely remember. All I can think of is what they looked like when they caught us in our attempted escape, cold and bedraggled on the beach, lost and looking for a ferryman to pay or a boat to steal so that we could make our escape from Wight. I had given Peter my coat by then to cover the rags they kept him in and to try to keep his undernourished body warm. We had been looking, of course, for the boat beached by Wheatley. But I had not been able to find my way back to it in the sea mist that descended to wrap the island following our flight. They loomed out of the vapour, three men in overcoats and evening wear, silk mufflers around their throats and top hats giving them menacing height in the gloom. They were laughing and one of them, Crowley I think, was wearing a monocle. Smell is a very acute sense on an empty stomach and they smelled of cigars and camphor and brilliantine and the smell made me retch thin bile on to the sand. And they laughed louder, pulling my coat from the thin shoulders of the boy, throwing it at me, turning with him, taking him away for the last time.

What I have found should be sufficient to prompt an investigation, even after all this time. There may even be concrete proof, at the Fischer house, of their murderous offence. I believe it now lies abandoned. Regardless of that, I think I have uncovered sufficiently compelling circumstantial evidence to build a case against them. But the past few days have taught me that I cannot continue with this alone. I need to confide in someone trustworthy and wise. I need cool and detached advice on how best to pursue the matter. Should I go to a lawyer now? Would I be more sensible making a statement to a detective at Scotland Yard?

I am tempted, of course, to tell the Monsignor everything. He is so clever, with that fastidious cleverness that comes of being a Jesuit and a Frenchman. I no longer care that I should disappoint or disillusion him. The need for justice overrides my foolish vanity.

But the Monsignor is a Catholic and a foreigner. Neither characteristic is seen as entirely respectable. This is especially true now the country is so fraught with thoughts of war.

There is my cousin, Edwin Poole. He is younger than me, and I see precious little of him. But his career at Lloyds thrives. He is a member of all the best clubs. He takes a box each season at Covent Garden and gives lavishly, if a little too conspicuously, to good causes. The idea of a family scandal might appal him. And I know he knows Wheatley slightly. But I need to speak to someone. And a blood relative, who makes a successful living calculating risk, who depends upon discretion for his very livelihood, might not be the worst choice of confidant.

I need to go to bed. I am desperately weary. But I cannot get the smell of camphor and cigar ash out of my nostrils, or the topper gleam of beaver skin through fog, out of my mind. I hear their jeering laughter, the venom and contempt of it. I can see the tobacco stains on their teeth, the black gold of Fischer's capped incisor. There is the sheen of patent leather in the flat light on their shoes. Crowley wore spats, too, I remember. They were wet and dirty at the skirt with scum trailed from the tideline. Poor Peter, insulated in mist and horror from the love and safety of his orphaned life.

God forgive me.

Peter, forgive me.

I must take back the car in the morning. I shall speak to my cousin first thing tomorrow.

Twenty-Six

Seaton had read her account out loud so that Mason might hear it, too. And it was Mason who spoke first when Seaton had finished and slowly brought the covers of the little volume back together in his hands.

'She was in love with you, Father.'

The priest spoke with his back to them. 'She was very beautiful. And she was abundant with intelligence and life. And I was a little in love with her, I think.'

Seaton said, 'Where did you get the notebook?'

'She gave it to me herself. She presented it to me bound in brown paper and string secured by sealing wax. She said I was to read it only in the event of her death. Otherwise, she said, she would be back to collect it from me within a fortnight or so. The occasion upon which she gave me the journal was the last on which I ever saw Pandora.'

'It was her last confession,' Mason said.

'She never got to make her first confession,' Seaton said. 'She never finished her instruction, was never accepted into the faith. Edwin Poole saw to that.'

'Nevertheless, Paul. I think that in every important particular, Nicholas is right.'

'Did she have a premonition of her own death?' This from Mason.

Lascalles hesitated. 'The last time I saw her, she was serene. She handed me the package containing her journal with a smile. But the precaution speaks for itself, I think. She was reconciled to her course of action. Perhaps she was even confident of the outcome. But she was never in doubt about how malign and formidable were the forces she was challenging.'

'She called you *Monsignor*,' Seaton said. 'So did the Franciscan who brought the food in here earlier. It suggests a Vatican rank.'

'I am a priest.'

'One who could summon an instant favour from a cardinal.'

'I had a telephone. A cardinal is a priest before he is a prince of the Church.'

There was silence in the library.

'It wasn't malnutrition, when they found her body in the river,' Seaton said. 'She wasn't starving, she was fasting. It was penance.'

Lascalles took out his rosary and kissed its crucifix. Mason thought that there were tears in his eyes. But in the unsure light of the dying fire, it could have been age. Or fatigue.

'I'm going to find Peter,' Seaton said. 'Pandora found him with a purloined library pass. I was a reporter once and good at it. I'm going to find him, find out who he was.'

Seaton's tone of voice here was new to Mason. There was a certainty to it. So Mason spoke tactfully, 'It was nearly seventy years ago, Paul. And it won't bring the boy back to life. Or her.'

'We need to know why he was singled out and taken.'

'*They chose shrewdly*,' Mason said, quoting Pandora. 'He was probably a workhouse foundling, some poor infant soul no one cared about.'

Seaton shook his head slowly. 'I don't think that was what she meant. I think there was more to it. And I think that when I've found Peter, we'll be ready for the Fischer house.'

Mason looked to the priest. 'Father?'

Lascalles was looking at Seaton. 'I pray that God is with you,' he said. 'I pray that He is with both of you.'

Seaton was at the British Museum by the following afternoon. Mason got off the train at Ashford, where they had parked the Saab on their outward journey. He would drive it back to Whitstable.

'How long is this going to take?'

'As long as it takes,' Seaton said. There was no point discussing it. Mason thought he was wasting his time. Seaton thought it might actually be worse than that. He was following hunches again, felt the old familiar compulsion that had lured him before into catastrophe.

'I'll contact the families of the other girls,' Mason said. 'Maybe visit them.'

'You can offer them some of your stolen morphine,' Seaton said.

Mason looked at him.

'I'm sorry. I'm sorry, Nick. That was uncalled for. But this should only take a couple of days. Sit tight. Wait for me.'

Mason shook his head. 'Sarah's in good hands. I have to do something.' He was quiet for a moment. 'It's Tuesday. Be back by Friday. That's as long as I'm prepared to wait. With or without you, that's when I'm planning to go to the Fischer house.'

'And do what?'

'You're Irish, Seaton. So I'm sure you've heard of Semtex. I'll wire the place, blow it to fucking kingdom come.'

Seaton walked from the terminus at Waterloo over Waterloo Bridge to Aldwych and along Southampton Row towards Bloomsbury. They'd slept a couple of hours on truckle beds in the Jesuit keep and then been driven down the mountain by the Franciscan, chuckling at the wheel of a VW van as it slalomed on narrow tyres through the hairpins, racing to get them on the first available train. Now it was mid-afternoon, and he was in London, walking autumnal streets to a familiar destination. Old copies of the *Western Mail* would have been transferred to microfiche back in the 1980s. He could think of no reason why the library's run of copies would be incomplete. He would comb every page of every edition from the beginning of September 1927. The certainty had set in him that he would find something. It burned like a small fire in his belly as light from the sky along Southampton Row retreated and deepened and the shadows softened and he turned, almost by rote, into Museum Street, under the threat of advancing rain.

A Welsh accent spoken by a child, seventy years ago, meant Wales. Britain was a kingdom then, without mobility or flux. The working classes only travelled when they marched or climbed into cattle cars as conscripts to fight in imperial wars. Most people lived and died in close proximity to where they were born. Only the privileged few, like the public schoolboy Young Mr Breene had been, were afforded the luxury of casual travel about the country. Peter's disappearance had provoked no widespread response. To merit that, back then, you had needed wealth or status or the notoriety of the poor kidnapped Lindbergh baby. Peter had been of the common herd. His Welsh voice had distinguished him for the first time outside the land of his birth, only after his abduction from it. Seaton felt curiously certain of that.

And so he found him almost straightaway.

The first story was a filler, filed by a court stringer and offering no names. Carried in the edition printed on 4 October, it merely said that an eight-year-old orphan had gone missing from the fishing village of Aberdyfi in Gwynedd. It didn't even determine gender. But Seaton knew who it was. As Pandora had observed in her journal, child-stealing was in those days a rare crime.

The second story appeared on 20 October and was well-fleshed-out. It appeared under the byline of Philip Beal, credited as the *Mail*'s Senior Crime Reporter. A portrait was constructed of the boy, using quotes provided by his parish priest and the headmistress of the church school he attended. According to Miss Marjory Pegg, Peter Morgan was honest, obedient and blessed with a sunny disposition. He was an enthusiastic football player. He was also, she maintained, an immensely gifted student. Miss Pegg was adamant that Peter would not have gone off willingly with a stranger. She was not specific about the nature of his academic gifts. Or if she was, her further comments had not survived the subs, busily cutting stories to length in the *Mail*'s Cardiff newsroom.

Seaton didn't put much store in the description of the boy. It was an old trick. Reporters had always colluded with the police in doing this. The more vivid and attractive the portrait of the victim, the more emotionally embroiled in the story the reader became. It was a tried and tested ploy in nudging unknowing witnesses into remembering something important they might have seen.

More significant was the status of the writer. Three weeks after the boy vanished, the *Mail* had known it was dealing with a crime. A child abduction; then as now, it was among the very gravest offences anyone could commit. Nobody nursed the illusion that they were dealing here with an accidental tragedy; a small boy dying of exposure lost in the wind-scoured hills that rose behind the village. Peter Morgan had been stolen. Then he had been murdered. And no one had ever been called to account for these awful, planned, sequential crimes.

Seaton rubbed his eyes with the heels of his hands and read the story a second time. He switched off the microfiche projector. The hot whirr of its fan faded as the light went out and the inked columns on their yellowed page from a newspaper printed a generation ago were lost again to darkness and history. He pulled back from the viewfinder and looked up at the walls of the Reading Room and blinked. He looked at his watch. It was a quarter to five. He straightened a leg and patted his trouser pocket to reassure himself he had the change he required for the calls he needed to make from one of the payphones in the library vestibule. And he looked around him.

Pandora Gibson-Hoare had sat here, in this very room, and read the same words he just had and then walked to Charing Cross Road to get her maps to plot the journey made in her forlorn quest for retribution. And she would have needed maps. There had been no motorways to shrink the country then. The roads linking the cities of Britain were tenuous in those days, potholed and narrow and, when the sun went down, entirely dark. In Seaton's imagination it seemed an awful, alien place; coal-fired, gas-lit, empty-skied, monochromatic and unmoving in its polarities of slum squalor and brittle high-born privilege. How Britain and the world with it had changed in those seventy years, in that human span, that single lifetime of which Peter Morgan had been robbed. Anger stirred in him. And Seaton knew he was sharing the same indignant rage Pandora had so vibrantly felt.

Like her, too, he had the strong sense of being followed when he left the museum. He walked back to Waterloo and bought tickets with some of Malcolm Covey's money for the train journey to Aberdyfi. The Saab was in Whitstable. It would be quicker to go by rail. You took a northbound express from Euston and changed at Birmingham for West Wales. The Aberystwyth train stopped at Aberdyfi between stops at Machynlleth and Barmouth in its slow and scenic journey along the Welsh coast. If he set off early enough in the morning, he would be there by tomorrow lunchtime.

He was followed stealthily and felt the pursuit cease only when he left Waterloo Station after buying his train tickets and turned from Waterloo Road into Lower Marsh on the route back to his flat. He paused on Lower Marsh. The shops were closing. Their shutters were coming down. A large weak part of him wanted to spend more of Covey's cash on a room for the night at the Novotel on the south side of Lambeth Bridge. It was a new and anonymous place, too glossy and recent for ghosts. But with the same certainty that told him he was no longer being followed, he knew now that it was safe to return to his home. There would be no more games tonight; no clangour of cathedral bells, no disembodied songs leaking from the guts of broken players. The real business was almost upon him. The trickery would begin again, the chilling mischief, only when he reached the Fischer house.

Light diminished along Lower Marsh with the lowering shutters and detritus stirred in the gutters, tissue paper shivering around pieces of bruised fruit dropped from the morning market stalls. He thought about Mason with his Semtex bluster on the train, and the pain over his lost sister which provoked it. He wondered what would Mason be doing at that moment and felt a feeling like a wrench in him of pity and foreboding for the man. Wind gusted and the gutters flapped. The street was dark. He sniffed and caught the faint dissipating whiff of cigar smoke on November air.

Twenty-Seven

Aberdyfi was a shallow rank of terraces rising with the steep incline of the land and facing the mouth of the Dyfi estuary. Penhelig, where Peter had actually come from, was a cluster of dwellings tacked on to the southern end of the village. Everything was of a type, of a period, as though the place had drowned in sepia or become cursed and frozen in time. It occurred to Seaton that this was because the village was in Snowdonia. Since the establishment of the National Park, it would have been impossible to build anything new. It would have been illegal to demolish anything not completely derelict. It was a fact he thought might help him in his search for secrets from the past. Aberdyfi quite deliberately celebrated the past. It was where the village lived and, when the tourists came in the summer months, thrived. The place seemed, more than anything, a monument to itself. The present was circumscribed, here, tolerated only if it did not necessitate physical change.

Peter had been baptised and raised in the Anglican Communion, in what was, in his childhood, the newly established Anglican Province of the Church in Wales. His school had been a church school. His birth had been registered in the Parish of St Luke's. And Seaton had spoken to the vicar from a British Museum payphone to arrange a face-to-face talk and to seek permission to take a look around his church. He'd lied about the reason. A cold call did not invite discussion about an infant tragedy. He'd relied on his rusted talent for invention to find a pretext.

He walked along the seafront to Penhelig under the drum of insistent rain. Cloud in a grey mantle concealed the peaks of the hills to his left. To his right, he passed a cluster of small fishing boats and yachts in Aberdyfi harbour. Craft sat still at anchor. It was very quiet under the rain. There was not enough breeze even for their rigging lines to slap the masts of the boats dragged up above the tideline on the sand. Within a few minutes of disembarking at the station, Seaton was completely soaked. He had not been so drenched since the evening he had got off a London bus, shivering with presentiment, on Lambeth Bridge. That was the night he'd met Malcolm Covey in Zanzibar. In the rain on the Aberdyfi seafront, it seemed an awfully long time ago. In calendar time, it was still less than a week.

He dumped his overnight bag on the bed in the room he'd reserved by phone at the Penhelig Arms. It was a nice room. It was more of Covey's cash. The inn was sited on the coast road and his small window faced the grey rain-stippled estuary.

St Luke's was an ascent up a steep tree-lined lane that yellowed to a wash of gravel and gurgled in the ditches flanking the lane as he climbed. The church was high above Penhelig and lost from sight in a fold of hills until he saw the slate spire, almost upon it. The door to the church was open and lit from its porch in the general gloom of trees and sky. There was no priest, though. The Reverend Madden had been called away to see a sick parishioner. Seaton was met instead by a Mrs Reeve, who explained this to him. He had long ago, as part of his training in his old profession, disciplined himself against writing off people as types. But he had Mrs Reeve down straightaway as the sort of spinster who fusses around church flowers, spraying beeswax on pews, cleaning the font.

'You'll be the writer, Mr Seaton,' she said.

He had Covey's fake accreditation dampening in his coat pocket. But it had no useful application here. And writers didn't need qualifications. They just needed subjects to claim to be writing about.

Mrs Reeve had a cloth between her hands and her hair pulled back in pins away from her face. She was middle-aged, all spectacles and bland parochial disapproval. And then she smiled, and it seemed to him as though the summer sun came out.

'Writing a book about Marjory Pegg, are you?'

'Researching one.'

'By all accounts the woman was a saint, the work she accomplished at the school. Can I get you a cup of tea, Mr Seaton? Or there's coffee, freshly brewed.'

Seaton squeezed the raindrops from his eyebrows with his thumbs. 'Coffee would be grand,' he said.

By all accounts. So the two women had never met. But that would have been a bit much to ask for. Marjory Pegg had been forty-three at the time of the disappearance, according to the crime reporter Philip Beal. And Beal had struck Seaton as a pro. Such facts as he had been able to establish, he would have been far too methodical to write up imprecisely.

They drank their coffee in a tiny room off to the left of the church altar. The room smelled of cut flowers and was lit by a naked bulb against the gloom allowed by one small stained-glass window. Rain gurgled and spilled over swamped guttering on to the ground outside. Mrs Reeve produced a framed picture. It showed eight pale children standing to attention in front of a stone building in a schoolyard. Seaton knew it was a schoolyard because the lines and numbers of a hopscotch game were still etched faintly on the flagstones in front of the class. The children were flanked by a neatly dressed woman and a thin elderly man in a clerical collar.

Seaton assumed the man was one of the Reverend Madden's predecessors. He studied the woman.

Marjory Pegg was tall and bareheaded in the picture. Her thick silvery hair was combed back into a bun. She wore a plain pinafore dress over a striped shirt buttoned to the wrists and collar. Pinned to her breast was the sort of watch worn on a ribbon or chain by a nurse. Seaton could clearly see where the schoolteacher's stockings had been darned under the knee. And her shoes, plain and immaculately polished, were thick with the resoles of careful repair. She was smiling in the photograph, into the sunlight that gave the picture its vivid sharpness and detail. Her eyes were squinting against the brightness. But this did nothing to harden her expression. She looked kind and cheerful. And she looked immensely proud of her charges, with their tousled short-back-and-sides haircuts and their short-trousered uniforms.

The brilliant clarity of the shot gave the photograph between Seaton's hands an impression of immediacy, of modernness, as though it could have been recently posed and taken. But this illusion was swiftly dispelled. The boys had the young-old faces of children who had endured the hardship common to their class and time. These boys did not look strangers to cold or occasional hunger or the visitation of grief. Their eyes had a tough, wary innocence. Seaton studied expressions possessing complexities he reckoned altogether lost to modern youth. These were children of their age; at once buoyant and carefree, cautious and bruised. None of the group could have been more than about eight years of age. But there was nothing in the picture to distinguish Peter, if he was among them, from the rest.

Seaton was reminded of Fischer's crooned platitudes about polio and rickets. But there were no calipers bolted to the legs of any of the boys. And none leaned on a crutch. He was reminded of Mason's bleak dismissal of Peter the workhouse foundling. But Miss Pegg's brood were of a muchness. This was a jaunty band of brothers, a healthy hardy litter without a runt.

'You're frowning, Mr Seaton.'

'I'm just wondering, is one of these boys Peter Morgan?'

The picture was taken from his hands. On Mrs Reeve's face, the sun went into eclipse.

'I'm sorry.'

She stood. 'You're here under false pretences. You lied to the Reverend. I'd be obliged if you'd leave.'

'Please, Mrs Reeve. My interest is far from merely prurient.'

'I'm sure. And I'm sure your time is precious. And since I know nothing about any boy called Peter Morgan, you are wasting it here.'

She still had the framed picture in her hands. They were shaking slightly. The smell of flowers in the small room was underlaid by water, stagnant in a vase or backing up from a drain somewhere, brackish, choked by leaf-fall. The sound of rain spewing from the gutter outside was incredibly loud. Seaton thought he heard a chord of organ music stir from somewhere outside the door separating them from the aisle of the church and he shivered and goosebumps pricked and raised themselves on his flesh. He steeled himself for the clump of a team of horses, for the snorts and gasps against the bit, under their black mourning plumes.

'Leave,' she said. She had the picture held in one hand, her pride in the saintly Miss Pegg forgotten, redundant.

And there was no organ music. It had been his imagination. The time for games was past. He was the only one still playing them, and he was ashamed of his little deception here. Ashamed. He bowed his head and reached for the door handle and walked before the altar and along the silent aisle and past the font, out of the church porch.

He found himself among graves. It was still light, though

the evening darkness was fast enough descending. He had blundered to the right instead of the left and the route down the hill to Penhelig in his haste to get away. When he looked around, he was on a small plateau to the rear of St Luke's. The headstones were modest, rain-stained sandstone and dull granite rather than marble. The grass was recently cut. The shadows of the graves stretched over the grass in low sunlight. It was still raining from above him, but over to the west, out over the sea, the cloud had thinned in a fiery horizon. Seaton looked at the headstones. After a moment, he found the grave belonging to Peter Morgan's father. By Public Subscription, it said on the granite, chiselled and still somehow free of moss after seventy years. His name was etched into the stone below a handsome carved relief. It was a small stone. But Seaton thought the people of his village had done the memory of Robert Morgan proud.

Seaton knew from the account written up by Philip Beal that Peter's father had been the cox of the Aberdyfi lifeboat. He had perished in a storm after the lifeboat capsized, attempting to reach a foundering cargo vessel in Cardigan Bay. That had been in 1925. He had been thirty-seven years old. It had been the sort of small tragedy familiar to seafaring communities. It had deprived Peter Morgan of his father at the age of five. It had inspired the piece of commemorative art carved and rubbed into granite that Seaton looked at now, flushed with low November sun, the sound to the rear of him of rain dribbling through church gutters, the tended grass wet under his knees as he ran respectful fingers over the relief.

It showed a lighthouse mounted on a rock. Its single beam spread to the right across the stone. The dead man's name had been written in the beam. And under it, the lines:

A BRINGER OF HOPE
LOST BUT REDEEMED
IN GRATITUDE

Well. The Aberdyfi boat would have saved a lot of lives. It was why they were built. It was the reason their crews went out.

Seaton got to his feet. His legs ached. Dusk was creeping now among the graves. Most of the headstones were crowded with names. Morgan's ancestors had been buried elsewhere. He had come to Aberdyfi from Barmouth, where he had himself put to rest the bride who died bearing him his son. He had come to Aberdyfi to escape grief. But they had done him proud, his adopted people, with their tribute, with this refuge on the plateau in the quiet and the late light tucked to the rear of the old church. It seemed to Seaton as good a place as any to be buried. It was a place of peace and sanctity where a noble soul could sleep untroubled.

The barman at the Penhelig Arms was disappointingly young. Seaton would find no enlightenment there. He took his pint of Banks's bitter over to a table by the window. In the morning he would try to talk to the Reverend Madden. He had lied, but the clergy were generally forgiving. Tomorrow he would tell the truth, if not the whole truth, admit his interest lay solely in the abducted boy. He had lied because closed communities were apt to conceal their crimes and the disappearance was exactly the sort of appalling event to provoke collusive, clannish secrecy. He had hoped to stumble upon the subject of her vanished pupil as though inadvertently, discussing the unsung qualities of the admirable Marjory Pegg.

It had been the wrong approach. The crime had taken place so long ago, almost no one could be left alive to remember it. It was a remote enough event to qualify as history. Confronting it head-on, asking his questions openly, was not now likely to provoke pain, or resentment at unwarranted intrusion. He had made a crass mistake. But would put it right in the morning.

He took another, welcome sip of beer. Through the window, distant across the estuary, he could see the twinkling lights of a town, remote before the black hills massing in the night behind it. He didn't know the name of the town. He didn't know anything. And he was unlikely to find anything out. The old St Luke's school building was a ceramics studio now. It looked the same from the outside, but was filled with bags of clay and potter's wheels and kilns creating souvenirs for Welsh resorts whose visitors had a taste for indigenous crafts. The school records had long been destroyed. And Madden would not speak to him. Not now. Why on earth should he?

Seaton picked the menu up from his table. There was a dining room at the pub, a kitchen with a good reputation. More of Covey's money. Lamb featured heavily among the signature dishes. He would order a hearty casserole for which he could find in himself no appetite whatsoever.

The pub door opened and a woman walked in. He had to look twice before recognising Mrs Reeve. Her hair had been combed out and she was wearing lipstick. She had on a tailored coat and a scarf, finely woven out of wool. Seaton thought the scarf probably cashmere. She sat down opposite him and began to pull off a pair of leather gloves.

'Are you a policeman?'

'They don't investigate seventy-year-old crimes.'

She nodded. 'What is your interest?'

Seaton sighed and gripped his glass in his fist. Where to begin.

'Just tell me this. Is your interest likely to result in exposure? In retribution? In what is fashionably termed closure?'

He'd had the woman in front of him buttoned into a floral

overall, mopping imaginary spillages from the St Luke's font in a spinsterly attempt at attaining God's grace. Sometimes luck confounded judgment.

'Exposure is unlikely, Mrs Reeve. But I would hope with all my heart to make the guilty pay and bring a sad business to an overdue conclusion.'

She looked at the table, where her gloves rested now like clasped hands. 'That will have to do,' she said. She sighed. 'You've something of the priest about you. Catholic and defrocked, in case you mistake that for flattery. It could just be the Dublin brogue. But you've a basic goodness about you, I think.'

He said nothing. He sipped Banks's beer.

'I'll have a large whisky, Mr Seaton. No ice. I take my whisky with a dash of soda water. We'll have a drink. And then I'll ask you to accompany me to my home where I'll tell you what little I know about the sorry matter of the stolen boy.'

Mary Reeve lived in a house on the Aberdyfi seafront, left to her by her uncle. She had always lived in the village. She owned and ran a shop there selling antiques and curios. She had lived in a flat overlooking the shop. Most of the summer visitors were repeat trade and the shop did well, looked out for sentimentally by customers whose trinkets casually bought there had become, with time, cherished mementoes. For the last five years, she had lived in the house where Seaton sat with her now. Her uncle had been the golf professional at the links course just to the south of the village. Seaton had seen the flags marking a couple of its holes from the window of his train coming in. Her uncle, William Reeve, had been at school with Peter Morgan.

'Where did Peter live? Was there an orphanage?'

They were in her kitchen. Seaton suspected it had seen some changes since the death of William Reeve. They were seated at a hardwood table with a deep reddish grain. Her cooking range was shiny and German and new, and the steel utensils in her kitchen hung from butcher's hooks. Mary Reeve didn't bring her bric-a-brac home.

She smiled. 'There were no Social Services back then, Mr Seaton. There was no Welfare State to build institutions for fatherless boys. There was only charity. And it was random. And, by all accounts, it was pitilessly cold.'

'So what happened?'

'Marjory Pegg took him in. Her stipend was modest, of course. But she loved him. And the collection plate of a Sunday in St Luke's was felt by most of its parishioners to be a worthwhile obligation.'

'So the parish paid for his keep?'

'In strict terms, yes. But the people here wouldn't have put it like that. They'd have called it caring for one of their own.'

'What kind of boy was he?'

She shrugged. She stared at her hands. 'He was taken thirty years before I was born. So this is hearsay. But it's the most truthful hearsay you're ever likely to get. He was good at football and cricket. He liked to read adventure stories. He made friends easily. I don't doubt in the autumn, he scaled the wall and stole the odd apple from Bradley's orchard.'

'They all did that?'

She smiled. 'A rite of passage.'

'So,' he said, 'an ordinary boy.'

Mary Reeve looked at him. 'Let me tell you about my uncle.'

William Reeve had left school at sixteen and gone to work as a railway clerk in Machynlleth. He caddied in his spare time to help save for his own clubs and course fees. By twenty, he was a scratch golfer and went on to win several amateur tournaments in Wales and the northwest of England. In 1940, at the age of twenty-two, he was called up to fight in the war. He saw action in Italy. He was eventually commissioned and rose to the rank of captain. He was awarded a DSO. And he did not leave the army until three years after the end of the war in 1948.

'My uncle said his rank owed everything to the army's need to field potential winners in inter-service sporting tournaments,' Mary Reeve said. 'But he couldn't joke the medal away. He was a brave, kind, modest man. I suspect he was a formidable soldier in the execution of his duty. But he chose an unusually quiet life, once the choice was his to make.'

Seaton said nothing. Sometimes it was the best way of all to ask a question.

'I've often wondered whether it was his choice, entirely. The limitations. The strictures. Oh, they seemed self-imposed. But you can't help wondering, speculating. I very much suspect my uncle lived a life curtailed, Mr Seaton.'

Now, he did ask a question. 'Why?'

It was very quiet in Aberdyfi, in Mary Reeve's handsome, stone, inherited house. Her refrigerator trickled, self-regulating. And a quartz kitchen clock ticked spasmodic seconds on the wall. But there was none of the noise a city dweller, like Seaton was, would readily associate with life. There was no human noise. There was no passing traffic on the road outside.

'Come with me,' she said. 'I want to show you something.'

William Reeve's study was lined and mounted with more golf memorabilia than Seaton would have thought it possible for one room to accommodate. Properly displayed, he thought there might be sufficient artifacts to fill a small museum. There were wooden shields with brass plaques screwed to them and silver trophies topped by cast or sculpted figures in plus fours. There was a cracked and yellowing collection of balls, buckets filled with shafts, the leather smell of old grips and varnish and linseed oil. But the room was a room, rather than a shrine. It was a monument to the game, not to Reeve himself or his golfing accomplishments. There were photographs, but their subjects all had the familiar look of sepia champions from some golden age of a game about which Seaton had only a vague passing knowledge.

Mary Reeve spoke with her back to Seaton as she rummaged in a bureau in the furthest corner from the door.

'When my uncle was thirteen, his father took him as a special treat to Hoylake to see the final rounds of the Open at Royal Liverpool. They sneaked under a rope into the gallery and saw Bobby Jones play the back nine that won him the championship. Nineteen thirty. It was Jones's last championship round in any tournament.'

Seaton said nothing. She straightened and turned around. She held a velvet bag in her hand, shaped by the flat rectangular object it concealed. A slim volume? Another picture?

'My father called Jones a peerless talent, the best golfer he had ever seen, the greatest player ever to hold a club between his hands.'

The bag was black and felt and had a tasselled drawstring. She loosened the string. 'He saw greatness, at Hoylake, my uncle told me once. And then, very quietly, he told me about the miracle called Peter Morgan with whom he'd been to school.'

She pulled the cloth free and let it drop to the floor. He saw that she held a small chalkboard in her hand. She gripped it by its wooden border in her fingers, delicately, so that her fingers did not touch the slate itself. She brought it across the room to him, into the light, holding it up, turning it between both hands to show what it displayed to best effect.

It was calculus. Four lines of dense equations had been

scrawled across the slate. The chalk in which the equations were described was so old it had yellowed. The oil mixed with the chalk in the pressing process, to stop it crumbling on use, had decayed and yellowed to a faint stain on the black stone. Examining the characters, Seaton saw that it wasn't really fair to call the equations scrawled. The numbers and signs were bold and confident, the work of a small hand hurrying to keep pace with the intellect dictating what it described. He was looking at the work of a mind functioning at cyclonic speed and power.

'He was good at football and cricket. He stole apples from Bradley's orchard,' Seaton said.

'Yes. And this. He was this too,' Mary Reeve said.

'Was it recognised?'

'Oh, they came from far and wide to court him. Doctor Carter from Cambridge and a fellow from Trinity College and even a chap from the Sorbonne. Professor Covey came up from Oxford at the wheel of a Delage.'

Seaton almost staggered on his planted feet. 'Malcolm Covey?'

'He took some of the boys for an ice-cream. He took my uncle. They were treated to double scoops, lashed with raspberry sauce. But you couldn't buy Peter Morgan with a cornet, my uncle said. He was intent on medicine, was Peter. The boy was Edinburgh-bound.' Mrs Reeve turned and bowed and picked up its shroud and clothed and put the relic back in the drawer of her uncle's bureau from which she had taken it.

There was a clock in here, too. But it wasn't quartz. Seaton could hear the swing of its pendulum. He looked at it now, following the sound. It was mounted above the bureau and he could see the pendulum flicker in its glass-fronted chamber. Its face was porcelain, numbered with roman numerals. Its hands showed the wrong time. It had stirred itself into life, as old clocks in old rooms were sometimes apt to do.

'What happened to Marjory Pegg?'

Mrs Reeve stiffened with her back to him. 'She took her life. She loved Peter as a cherished son. She hoped for eight tormented months in the silence following his departure from here and then she could endure the torment no more.'

'You said your uncle's life was curtailed. It's a strange word to use.'

'But precise, Mr Seaton. Peter had seven classmates. Two were killed in the war. One died at Normandy and another later in Borneo. But none of the seven ever married. And needless to say, none ever fathered a child.'

'I see.'

She laughed. 'I doubt it.'

'Why did you change your mind, Mrs Reeve? About talking to me?'

And now she turned. 'When you left the church I climbed the tower to watch your departure. I didn't really trust you to leave, I don't think. And I saw you among the graves. It was clear you had lost your way in finding them. And then you discovered Robert Morgan's grave. I saw you kneel and cross yourself. I think you wept, Mr Seaton. I saw you wipe your eyes with the heel of your hand.'

'It could have been rain.'

'It could. It could indeed have been rain,' she said.

Twenty-Eight

The rain itself cascaded on the half-mile back to the Penhelig Arms. It was twenty past ten and the last lamb casserole had long been and gone. It didn't matter. He still wasn't hungry. He peeled off his soaked clothing and showered and went to find fresh underwear in the bag still unpacked from France on his bed. He unzipped the bag and felt the bulk of its hidden cargo between his folded clothes immediately. Black, voluminous in finely printed pages, it was an old and much-used missal. He held it in his upturned hand and allowed it to open itself against the spine. It did so on a dark green bookmark. But it wasn't a bookmark at all, when he picked it out. It was a British Library pass, carrying the faded stamp of the British Museum and made out in ink turned violet by age to someone called Susan Green.

He dropped the pass back into the missal and noticed with a frown that it marked the start of the funeral liturgy. Closing and turning the book in his hand, he looked at the embossed cover, the heraldic defiance of a Maltese Cross still visible, stamped in the hide. He opened the missal to the flyleaf. Lascalles' name was written there, and under it the date of his ordination. And there also, in much more recent ink, was written a telephone number and the prefix for France.

There was a phone in his room. He dialed the number. More of Covey's money tolled across Europe through the night as Seaton waited for an answer. The phone at the other end rang forever. When it was answered, the Franciscan was not roused, in greeting Seaton, to his familiar chuckle of bonhomie. 'Ach, you have almost killed the Monsignor, you and your *gefallene Engel* friend.'

The mountain accent was hard, mulish.

'Please, Brother.'

'He sleeps.'

Seaton closed his eyes. 'Then wake him.'

He waited through another eternity of Dr Malcom Covey's metred time. Or was it Professor Covey's largesse, measured out in children's treats and legitimate travel expenses? He could see Covey, right enough, at the wheel of a vintage Delage. He could see the white walls of the tyres and smell the hide on the seats. But he had met Malcolm Covey, shaken hands with the flesh and blood of him. And he knew with a certainty that Covey was a man. Fat men didn't wrinkle like the thin. But Covey, fat as he was, was surely nowhere over fifty. Seaton closed his eyes. Figures and algebraic letters danced and flickered in chrome yellow on the blackness of his lids.

'Paul?'

'He was a genius, Father. Their boy. Their sacrificial. He was taken precisely because of who he was.'

'Not who he was, Paul. He was taken because of what he would have become.'

And Seaton understood. His legs dumped him, strengthless, on the bed next to his bag. He understood. He had to fight to breathe. He held the reciever of the phone against his ear, suddenly dumb. It was the vaccine Peter Morgan might have developed. It was the surgical procedure he could have pioneered, the disease for which he would have found a cure. They had bartered with the Devil over the good for mankind in him. Their sacrificial had been chosen with precise and infinite care.

'And the girls?' Seaton did not recognise his own voice.

'What do you think?'

The peace treaty that one of them would broker, Seaton thought. The campaign against some awful endemic corruption. The life-changing charity that one of them might found.

'What should I do, Father?'

'Bury the boy. Make him safe. Put him, finally, to rest. Do this and I believe the evil emanating from that place will altogether cease.'

'I'm not a priest.'

Lascalles laughed. It sounded awful, the lonely amusement of a dying man, a last consolatory gasp at life. 'You are what you are, Paul,' he said. 'Being what you are, I have every faith that you will find a way.'

The phone went dead. Seaton knew that he could spend the entire night redialing and its cloistered ring would still remain ignored in the mountain keep. He had everything that the Jesuit Lascalles was going to give him. Give them. He sleeps, the Franciscan had said. And soon his body, at least, would enjoy the profound rest of the dead. He had survived to the age of a hundred, waiting for the promise of what Seaton and Mason had been chosen to accomplish. He had endured patiently from the moment he had broken the seal on Pandora's confession and discovered the secret for himself. Now he considered his work accomplished. There was nothing in his own mind or conscience left to bind the old priest to the earth.

I have every faith that you will find a way.

Except that Seaton didn't for a moment share that faith. He tossed the old missal back into his bag, knowing it was the Jesuit centurian's dying bequest to him, certain it was going to be nowhere near what was required.

He called Mason.

'They're the same,' Mason said, in answer to the unasked question. 'The Americans let their girl come round. She chattered volubly enough, at first. But in the persona of a cigarette girl from a Chicago speakeasy. She seemed to think she worked for Al Capone. Her poor parents were encouraged. Then she began to scream about some guy called Harry Greb. And the Bellevue medics doped her up again and got a clamp into her mouth to stop her biting through her tongue in terror.'

Seaton gripped the receiver tight. His hand was shaking. He felt the phone tremble against his cheek.

'Useful trip?'

'We'll know tomorrow,' Seaton said. 'We'll find out then, so we will.'

Mason grunted and hung up and Seaton remembered that the Franciscan's fallen angel had never greatly cared for the Irish.

They took Covey's Saab, with its canvas roof and jittery, sometimes disobedient, radio. It was an act of defiance and a signal to their adversary. Mason checked briefly on his sedated sister and filled the car boot with various ominous-looking canvas bags. The Saab would be far less suspicious a vehicle to transport Mason's ordnance on the Wight ferry in, than his own Land Rover. That was the soldier's logic.

'I don't think you can kill it with a gun,' Seaton said, watching Mason load up the boot.

'The thing that came after you splintered the stairs with its tread, for Christ's sake,' Mason said. 'It had weight and mass. It's corporeal, at least some of the time. And it's a fucking big target, by the sound of it. Trust me, Irishman, it'll take a round.'

The sun had come out. It was just after four in the afternoon and below them, beyond the shingle, sunbeams glittered through broken cloud on the shifting green surface of the sea. The air was suddenly fresh with salt. A breeze ruffled Seaton's hair. He got into the car and looked at the backs of his trembling white-knuckled hands. It wasn't terror that made him shake. It was anger. And it was almost surprising. He could not believe the fury he felt over a sixty-year-old murder. But he did. He kept thinking of the empty journal pages and her body on the strew of pebbles at the river's edge, cold, daubed under a tarpaulin with river filth. She had been exquisite. And passionate. And on her own humble path to redemption. And she had been slain with brutal degradation and derided for decades following as a suicide, shambolic and dispossessed. He railed at the waste and furious injustice of it.

He wanted to trap the slippery emissary, Covey, corner him in a place he couldn't bolt from and kill him with his hands. He had educated hands, had Paul Seaton. And though much of his conditioning had slipped away through self-neglect, his hands had never forgotten the painstaking lesson they had learned in his tender youth. He wanted to corner Malcolm Covey and beat him until he squealed and whimpered and then continue beating him until he stopped breathing altogether. He clenched his hands into fists, unaware of doing so, the nails so tightly pressed into the palms that the skin broke and blood oozed on to the pads of his curled fingers. He was oblivious to it. He was eager to meet Malcolm Covey again. Of course, he was still afraid. But he thought that he felt altogether more anger, now, than dread.

About the boy, he could allow himself to think barely at all.

Nick Mason closed the boot lid on the Saab's lethal cargo and looked at his wristwatch.

He was uncertain about the Irishman. He had not thought it possible for cowardice and courage to coexist as they seemed to do in Paul Seaton's troubled nature. Soldiering, he'd seen much cowardice disguised by bluster. And he'd seen courage often enough tempered by fear. He'd felt fear himself, shaken off the disabling grip of it, defied its capacity to disarm a man in combat and carried on doing what he was lethally trained to. But he had never before encountered anyone like this. He looked at the man now, Seaton oblivious to his scrutiny, face set in the interior mirror, eyes hard on the road and jaw clenched tight in resolution. He'd seen too much, had Seaton. He'd seen things men should not. And the experience had terrified and wounded him. And now here he was, against all reason, going back for more. Seaton had been more haunted than hardened by whatever battle he had fought. But here he was, resolved, determined.

For himself, Mason felt only a sort of gloomy fatalism. Despite the baptism he could not recall, he observed no faith and followed no religion. He had chosen his own vocation as a fighting man. He enjoyed the uncertain and uncompromising nature of what he did. Beyond that, though, there was only what the present circumstances demanded of him. He loved and wanted to secure the life and sanity of his sister. He would do whatever was needed of him. He had never before been found wanting. He would not be found wanting now.

He suspected that the priest might have been right about the killing of the thing in Africa. He'd felt a power and potency in him when he'd squeezed the trigger like nothing he'd felt before or since. He'd told Seaton he'd been spooked and jumpy in that butchering, butchered chieftain's hut and certainly that was half-true. He'd been spooked, without a fucking doubt. But when his bullets ripped into the thing that had climbed behind him from its throne and he saw it tumble, cleaved, to the ground, he'd felt exultant.

He didn't feel exultant now. He felt foreboding. The Fischer house wanted him, had lured him for the magic endowed in Africa by whatever dark mischief his father had indulged in.

But mostly, Mason suspected, of the two of them it wanted the Irishman much more.

Malcolm Covey, Fischer doppelgänger and slippery fixer, had orchestrated their impending, iminent trip. Covey it was, who had nursed Seaton through his long and demeaning disintegration. A dozen years after, it was Covey who had known of Seaton's whereabouts in the chaotic aftermath of the visit paid the Fischer house by the seminar group. The Irishman had been living the sorry life of a forgotten fugitive. But Covey had somehow possessed his unlisted number.

Now, Covey's subtle guidance was steering them both towards the same opaque destination. He had approached Seaton far too improbably well-informed about what had gone on with the student party for it to be otherwise. Had Covey set up the business with the chest in Gibson-Hoare's attic? Certainly the original journal had been ridiculously easy for Seaton to find. Gibson-Hoare, a man versed in the secrets of antiques, would surely not have missed a thing so poorly hidden.

So Covey had sent Seaton on his first innocent visit to the Fischer house. And Seaton had escaped, which had not been at all what Covey had intended. And now Seaton was going back. At Covey's urging, he was going back. It was all about Seaton, wasn't it? He himself ranked not much above set-dressing in the overall scheme of things. But why? Was Seaton himself not given to wonder? He looked at the Irishman again. Seaton's focus was firmly on the road, his thoughts concealed behind the tight eyes and clenched jaw. What possessed the Irishman? More pertinently, what was it that this Irishman possessed?

Mason shook his head slowly and reached a hand into his jacket pocket. His fingers closed on the sharkskin grip of his jackknife. There was comfort in the familiar weight and shape of it, the recognition. The touch of it spread a feeling through him not dissimilar to gratitude, or relief. He would do that, for now, for want of a choice, he decided. He would take what small comfort was available to him from what he recognised, from the precious little that he fully understood.

Their crossing was made in bleak driving rain that stippled the grey Solent and made sombre monoliths of the forts rising from the surface of the sea. There was no other shipping traffic visible to them as they huddled under a dripping awning on the promenade deck of the ferry, sipping coffee. When they got to the dock at Fishbourne, the weather worsened, rain drumming an insistent tattoo on the canvas roof of the Saab. Seaton switched on the lights to see and the wipers washed waves of water from the cascading windscreen. This time, at the wheel of a car on empty autumnal roads, he did skirt the perimeter of the forest. And he approached the Fischer house from the south. They flapped and jounced through soaking trees along a forestry trail until their headlamp beam picked out a single gatepost surmounted by a stone griffin still wearing the weathered remnants of a snarl. Seaton slowed. He saw the second gatepost, prone and snarled in ivy. And he shifted from second to first and picked a path between the two, forgotten gravel firm under his tyres on the twisting drive to Fischer's abandoned mansion.

Mason spoke. 'What will we find?'

'The seminar group were armed with keys to padlocks securing the one gate in the barrier they found surrounding the place. They discovered a ruin, fortified by chain-link fencing and barbed wire. That's what their lecturer remembered, before the confusion and the chaos overcame them. I expect our welcome somehow to be warmer than theirs was.'

'That's my feeling, too. But we're armed with a whole lot more than padlock keys.'

They found no fence to exclude them. The house lights were burning. They were not bright, but they were undeniable. Seaton willed himself to raise his eyes to the tower, before their approach lifted his view of it above the windscreen of the Saab. There, light glowered, blinking reddish through the thick uneven panes. Beside him, he could see Mason load and reload twin magazines for a short snub-barrelled weapon he'd pulled from a bag in the the boot during a roadside stop he'd insisted upon only a few minutes after they'd disembarked. The tower receded over the roof of the car with their approach. Seaton saw now that canvas shrouds were stretched over the curves of majestic cars on the sweep of drive fronting the house. In a tear in one of these he caught the glimmer of chrome and black-waxed bodywork. The soldier to his left was breathing hard and winding coloured adhesive tape around his clips of bullets. It occurred to Seaton that a decade earlier, when vanity and self-consciousness had played the role in him they will among the young, he'd hoped for a significant cameo, at least, in the spectacular movie of life. Be careful what you wish for, he said to himself now, as he drew the car to a halt and got out and approached the door to the Fischer house through the graveyard of limousines, in the heaving thrum of the rain.

Twenty-Nine

He found himself alone when he reached the door. No matter. It was too late now for retreat or prevarication. He pushed, but on this occasion he found the door firmly locked. He hammered on the knocker. After a moment, his knock was answered by a tall figure dressed in the livery of a butler.

Above the servant's spoiled face, the plates of his skull looked as though a clumsy infant had reconstructed them. Old brain-matter stains still tarnished the bone. From behind him, in the house, Seaton heard the drift of music and faint laughter. The man held a covered salver. He bowed to the visitor.

'Hello, Giuseppe,' Seaton said. The butler gestured him in and then stooped forward confidentially. His breath was cold with decay, his voice the whispering saw of a Chicago ghost.

'I should warn you that Mr Greb has been drinking, sir.' Giuseppe cocked his ruined head towards the stairs. Seaton willed himself to look. They were carpeted with a plush pile that receded into blackness after six or seven steps. The house had changed in other ways. The vestibule had been improvised into a sort of ballroom, tables pushed in a circle against remote walls, the figures seated at them formally dressed, indistinct under the fractured splash of odd glitterballs. But watchful.

'His mood at present is convivial enough,' Giuseppe said. 'But we all know how easily Mr Greb's aspect can darken.'

Seaton was wondering what lay under the lid of the salver.

'If you would be so good as to follow me, sir, I would

like to take the liberty of reuniting you with an old and valued acquaintance.'

Seaton followed the dead factotum around the perimeter of the room, picking his way between tables, trying not to look at the faces of the guests, each as lifeless as Fischer's man and watching him with empty curiosity. They gained a corridor and walked along its length of uniform doors. Light from under one in a feeble ribbon on the floor distinguished it. There was music along the corridor, grimy with needle-dust, busy with remembered static. It was the John Lennon song 'Imagine', sung in a baritone growl to barrelhouse piano accompaniment. Seaton took it to mean that Nicholas Mason must be somewhere in the house.

Giuseppe opened the door and stood back from it. Lucinda Grey, surprise showing in her once-lovely features, looked up from where she sat over her sewing machine. Her pale body was clothed only in an underskirt and bra. When she pressed on the treadle of the old machine, Seaton could see her kneebone flap through a tear in the skin of a wasted leg.

'I'll be joining the party the minute my dress is finished,' she said. The flat, familiar vowels of her northern accent were heartrending to him. But there was no garment under the needle and no thread on the spindle to sew one with.

'Oh, Lucinda,' Seaton said. He was trembling suddenly, overwhelmed with shock and grief. He had not prepared himself for this. He had put Lucinda Grey away in the safe refuge of his mind where the sun always shone on her lambent skin and she could go on forever being twenty-one and beautiful. Surely her life could not be over. Surely not her. He groaned.

'Why did you have to die?'

'Dying is easy,' she said. 'Living was the complicated part. You remember the night you wouldn't come to the opening of that bar David Haliday had painted?'

He nodded. And he noticed the shape of someone else, indistinct, in the corner of the room. It didn't matter. Only Lucinda mattered.

'We went on to Tabu, that night, Paul, after the place with David's murals. And I snorted heroin. I was low because you hadn't come and someone had a wrap at Tabu and I snorted a line of it. And the disappointment melted away. And I felt I was floating on air.'

He remembered. He had met her coming home. He'd had Pandora's journal hidden in his pocket. She had looked like she was floating on air as she came around the corner into his vision on Lambeth High Street.

'I went back to York, after you. Couldn't deal with London any more. And the low feeling got worse. And heroin was very fashionable then. It took the pain away, Paul. And it was cheap.'

'Oh, Lucinda.'

'Did you not wonder why we never ran into one another? Even accidentally? I don't think you could have helped me. That said, of course, it never occurred to you to try. But the overdose was accidental.' She frowned. Her eyes were coloured an absent, recollected green under the dead strands of her fringe. Her bobbed hair, its texture once satin, had been turned by death into a coarse wig. 'At least, I think it was accidental.'

The figure emerged from the corner. It was Patrick, as Seaton had guessed it would be. He had thought for a moment that his own anticipation might prepare him. But it did not. When he saw his brother's face, lost and sorrowful in death, he began to weep. He had missed him so. Behind him, Fischer's man coughed politely. 'Sir?' Giuseppe said. He had taken the lid off the salver. He held the salver out. A gun lay on it, an ancient Webley revolver pocked with shrapnel scars. It had new grips on the stock and a shiny new nickel-plated cylinder. The hammer was cocked and Seaton saw the seat of a bullet, snugly poised in the cylinder's uppermost chamber.

'What happened, Patrick?'

'It's hard to say.' There was something wet and noisome in Patrick's chest. He coughed, and the odour from him was dank and cold. 'I didn't come up,' he said. 'It just seemed easier not to.'

Less complicated, Seaton thought, nodding, his hand reaching absently for the butt of the gun on the salver proffered by the ghost. Life could be unbearable, at times. He heard a baritone snigger and a chord shift in the song.

'You'd be as well to finish up, sir,' Giuseppe said. Lucinda and his brother were sullen, watching him. 'The mood of Mr Greb might turn sour at any moment. And then where would all of us be?'

Where indeed. Seaton lifted the revolver from the plate. It had a reassuring heaviness in his hand. He put the barrel into his mouth. It seemed so natural a thing to do.

'Very good, sir.'

He would escort Lucinda to the ball. Patrick would be there as well. They would have fun, like they used to do. They would have fun, that light and fondly remembered feeling he hadn't encountered in years. It would be just exactly like old times. They would drink Lambrusco on the rooftop at St Martin's. There would be tennis in the park and picnics. He could feel the welcoming warmth of the sun on his back on the bench by the cherry tree and smell its forgotten blossom. His finger curled on the tension of the trigger and he closed his eyes.

'Imagine' grew suddenly enormously loud and there was a slap on his arm that jerked the Webley out of his mouth and his grip. The gun fell to the floor and the hammer came down and the report crashed loudly through Seaton's head. He blinked. Mason stood in front of him. He had camouflage cream smeared across his face and weapons and ammunition strung from bandoliers and webbing across his combat fatigues. Seaton looked around. They were in the vestibule, the house derelict, the stairs behind Mason naked and decrepit. There were no lights lit in the house now. And in the unremitting rain outside, there was no moonlight. Seaton could hear the rain beat fierce on the panes of the windows. What little he was seeing, he was seeing only in the beam of a torch attached to Mason's combat jacket and pointed at the ground.

Mason slapped him, hard. 'What's that in your pocket?'

'The missal Lascalles gave to me.'

'What do you need to do?'

'Find the remains of the boy. Give him the burial to which he's entitled.'

'Don't wander off again, Paul. It's too dangerous.' Mason looked at the revolver, smoking slightly, smelling strongly of cordite, and lying between their feet on the parquet floor. He kicked it away into the gloom. 'Something to do with Covey and the hypnosis, I expect.' He licked his lips. His eyes skittered like the kicked gun. 'You were very suggestible,' he said, quietly, as though to himself.

Seaton looked at him. Mason was a soldier. And he didn't know what to do. He had just saved Seaton's life, but there was no standard operational procedure to follow, now, in the blossoming madness of the Fischer house. He was festooned with destructive weaponry. And he was completely impotent. Seaton thought Mason too brave and disciplined to panic. But the next step had to lead somewhere. And it was entirely up to him. He looked around and saw that the central staircase now went down as well as up. Shame burned through him at the way he'd just been exposed by the forces in the house, stripped naked, lured to the brink of willing self-destruction. But he hadn't the time to suffer the shame, to castigate himself. He was compelled to act. If he didn't, they were damned anyway.

There was a noise from some remote floor above, a dry chuckle like the scrape of lazy chains.

'Mr Greb,' Seaton said. 'Their beast has awoken. We have to recover the boy's remains before it's properly aroused.'

The voice above them tightened and then broke with a roar.

Mason gripped the machine pistol hanging across his chest and looked back towards the dark maw of the descending stairs.

'We need to find the games room,' Seaton said. 'It was all a game to them, Nick. Always. They were the players of a diabolical game. Serving a playful master, they were obliged to be. And that's our clue. We need to be in the basement.'

They descended stairs, carpet remnants sticky under their feet. A corridor followed. The bellowing fury above them faded slightly. But that was no comfort. The corridor was catacomb-like, dank and dripping. Seaton felt more deeply entombed with every step.

'In here,' Mason said.

They entered a billiards room. It was low and narrow and four tables had been arranged along its length. There were racks of cues. There was a shelf heaped with rotting boxes of board games. Baccarat counters and casino chips formed greedy neglected piles. Music was playing. Seaton thought he recognised Frank Rosolino's mournful trombone. The sound was euphonic, soft at its sonic edges, as though played through an old-fashioned valve amplifier. The lights over the tables, one by one, switched on with a weary fizz.

There were framed pictures on the walls and Seaton saw that, of course, they were Pandora's photographs. They were the lost archive, retrieved and printed up and mounted and hung in here. Passing them, Seaton identified Aleister Crowley, something preternaturally old in the sunken skin around the eyes and coarsely textured about his complexion. His shoulders were bunched under the black vanity of the silk embroidered robe he wore. His neck was a wattle of flesh. The eyes themselves were only partially focused, as though mostly lost to some wild and sly avenue of speculation. It was the study of a man who had lived too much and far too extremely. He had dug too deep into what wiser and less ambitious men avoid. The experience had left him frayed, had dispossessed him, it seemed, of his vitality and senses. As Seaton passed by, the portrait's eyes followed him and the lips cracked a confidential smile.

Wheatley was almost beatific, by comparison. He had a pale face too pudgy for distinction and his glossy black hair was centre-parted, after the fashion of the period. He wore a for the camera smile that seemed strictly the minimum of effort required by the protocol of the moment. There was something about the eyes, though, that gave their owner away. They were focused on the photographer, rather than on the lens. And although they were dark eyes, lacking naturally in transparency, the lust in them for Pandora was nakedly apparent. Seaton paused in front of Wheatley's picture. He looked for telltale scars from the explosion in Flanders that should by rights have completely obliterated all trace of the man. But the magic had been strong and complete and there were none. His complexion was innocently smooth. It had taken a lifetime's indulgent thirst for the best vintages in his well-kept cellar to kill Wheatley. He had been almost eighty when his liver eventually failed, and death was finally permitted to claim him.

Fischer was confident and debauched. His was the picture of a man smugly and completely given over to evil. Seaton knew he was looking at the darker and more sinister progenitor of Malcolm Covey. This was apparently what Covey was destined to become. Had Covey looked like this at their first encounter, he thought, he might have screamed as he did on the afternoon he became lost in the forgotten turns of the hospital maze. What was the difference between them? Covey was more human, Seaton decided. There was not much left that was human any more in Pandora's last portrait of Klaus Fischer. It was the depiction of a willing monster. They had all been monsters. What they had done had been monstrous, too.

There was baize still on the billiard tables. It was frayed and faded to yellow under the lights. When they reached it, Seaton saw that the far billiard table was spread with an ancient stain. It was a thick, black excrescence that had once welled across the baize and dribbled into the pockets.

'Steady, Paul,' Mason said.

But there had been no way to steel his resolve for this. Grief shuddered through him. He felt the grip of comforting fingers on his shoulder. He stared at the stain on the table. He groaned and his breath faltered and he touched the ruined baize. From far above, he heard the beast's cavorting laughter. Tears blurred his eyes. The blood had been everywhere.

'Marvellous!' said a voice.

There were two figures by the entrance to the room. They were attired in evening wear and white silk mufflers and top hats. The glass of a monocle glittered above the spoiled grin of one of them. Even from forty feet distant, they smelled of cigars and brilliantine. And they stank of feral rot.

'It's Crowley,' Seaton whispered. 'And Fischer.'

'Crowley and Fischer burn in Hell,' Mason said. His voice was raw with scorn. He hawked and spat on the floor.

'Golly,' the Crowley apparition said. 'You're no fun.'

Mason spat again. He gripped the weapon across his chest.

The figures began to fade. They had receded from sight

almost entirely when the Crowley apparition said, 'You've angered Mr Greb. And Mr Greb will settle with you shortly.'

'Why is it called Mr Greb?

'Harry Greb,' Seaton said. 'A prizefighter Fischer's manservant knew in the days when he worked for Al Capone.'

Mason nodded. He shone his torch at the floor. He held the beam poised over a section patched and paler than the rest. He took something from the pack on his back and opened it and handed it to Seaton. It was an entrenching tool. He nodded at the ground. 'A layer of concrete over hardcore and then earth,' he said. 'Tough going, but it could be worse. I've scraped graves on battlefields from less hospitable ground.'

Seaton looked at his own soft, unaccustomed hands. And a voice that caused the skin on his head to itch and crawl icily called down all the way from the top of the stairs to reach them where they stood.

'My name is Harry Greb. I licked Tunney. I licked Tunney good! And I'll lick any man, alive or dead.'

There was a pause. 'Are youse coming up to fight? Or am I coming down for youse?'

Mason handed the entrenching tool to Seaton. Seaton took it. Mason fingered the weapon around his neck. He was sweating, the breath coming shuddering out of him.

'You can't go up there.'

'It's coming down here, if I don't,' Mason said. He said it flatly. He was dealing with fact. 'You have to recover the child's remains and get them out of the house. You have to do as Lascalles said and bury the bones beyond the influence of this place.' He nodded at the entrenching tool. He licked his lips and looked at the ceiling. The house was warming with the baleful threat of the thing above. In the basement, it was becoming harder to breath. 'Now fucking dig, Seaton. Dig like your life depends upon it, which I very much suspect it does. You're an Irishman, aren't you? You're a Mick. You're a Paddy. So it shouldn't be beyond you to dig a fucking hole.' He grinned. He walked towards the entrance of the room. He was breathing hard, sweating, a sheen of fear on his face. He was clearly and mortally afraid. But he would go, because he was brave as well as frightened. His bravado was there to try to conceal the fear. But Seaton saw that the fear could do nothing at all to mask Nick Mason's appalling courage. He would go. Of course he would go. This was what he did. This was who he was and had always been. He was a fighting man. And so he would fight and try his best to win.

In the doorway, he paused. 'If I don't make it, keep an eye on Sarah for me, Paul. Don't get any ideas about her, though. So much as put a finger on her, and I swear to Christ I'll fucking come back and haunt you myself.' He turned.

'Wait,' Seaton said. 'Wait. I know something about boxing. About its history.'

There was a thud above them. It was hard to tell how far.

'Mate. There's no time for this.'

'The devil enjoys games, does he not?'

There was a mauling, capering sound from above.

'It thinks it's Harry Greb. And Greb was truly formidable. The first time they met, he slaughtered Gene Tunney. He was more than a match for Dempsey on every occasion they sparred together. In his entire career, he was only put down the once. But every time he climbed through the ropes, he took a secret into the ring with him. Harry Greb was blind in one eye,' Seaton said.

The thing upstairs moaned and scrabbled and they heard the screech of rent timber.

'That isn't Harry Greb,' Mason said. 'I only wish to Christ it was.'

'But it thinks it is. At least some of the time, it does.'

Mason looked at him. 'Completely blind?'

'Profoundly so.'

'Do you remember which eye?'

'I do. Sure I do. It was the right.'

Mason frowned and nodded. He walked across the room and the two men embraced one another.

'There's a stream to the south of the house. I'll bury the remains beyond it. I'll cross where it narrows and meet you on the other side of the stream.'

There was a heavy scrape from above as the thing at the top of the house took its first step down to them. After finding its voice, it had assumed some sort of shape. Puffs of old plaster dust were shaken out of the games-room ceiling around its wooden supports. It's grown, Seaton thought. It's got bigger since the last time I was here.

'Dig, Paul,' Mason said, quietly, from the doorway. 'For Sarah's sake. For the sake of all our souls.' He chambered a round in the weapon across his chest and kissed its muzzle. 'Dig,' he said. And he was gone.

Seaton spread his feet and raised the entrenching tool above his head in the grip of both hands and smashed the pointed tip against the ground. Again and again he drove the tip against the stubborn crust of concrete on the games-room floor. I should have spat on my hands, he thought, breathing hard, aware of the fierce heated friction of the shaft. But his mouth had been too dry with fear for him to have found the required spit. There were raking bursts of gunfire from upstairs, crumps of sound that Seaton thought might be stun grenades. The odour of combat drifted down to him, hard and metallic-smelling. He heard the bestial roar of something surprised, maybe even hurt. But sorely enraged.

Seaton grunted and dug. He was through the crust, using the blunt of the entrenching tool to rake stones from the soil, deepening the impression in the cool loam underneath.

He could tell from their odd dry tingle on the shaft of the tool that his palms were flayed. No matter. Should he survive, the skin of his hands would grow back. There were more noises from above. The entire house seemed to screech and shudder. It shifted. Floors buckled and walls bellowed inward and outward with shock and repercussion. Noise came in savage and frenetic squalls and faded abruptly. Drafts erupted and rippled and were gone. The music, though, had entirely ceased. Its absence was unnerving in the house, in the fine, falling precipitation of dust induced by Mason's fight. There was a rumble and a roar from a landing above. It was a cry of primeval triumph.

'On my way, Irishman,' said a rough voice. 'I'll be down to you directly.' Mason was dead. He had lost the battle he never could have won. Seaton heard the thing that had defeated him saunter and crash downwards. He thought he heard music again; Al Bowley, The Hot Club Quintet, something faint and frenetic and almost comically irrelevant. He saw a bone gleam palely in the loam, not much bigger than a rabbit bone, and he choked on sobs and cursed a miserable God that he hadn't been given the time to complete the task he knew now to be his sole and urgent obligation. He looked at the entrenching tool, its shaft sticky with his own gore between bloody hands. It was no sort of weapon. He would fight with it anyway.

The thud of hooves was imperious down the stairs. Seaton stood upright and hefted the tool. And then there was a cry and it was human, Mason's fierce cry of defiance as he raked gunfire into the beast once more in a desperate rally somewhere above. He was exacting his vengeance for his sister's suffering, was Mason. More than that, the fallen angel was selling himself to buy his sister some sort of salvation.

A dark universe crashed and shuddered in pain and rage above his head and from somewhere in the games room,

Seaton found a velvet bag containing billiard balls and emptied it and crouched and sifted loam for precious bones to carry away. The sounds of conflict subsided above. He filled his bag. Unhurried and tender, thorough and methodical, he filled his velvet bag with all the precious remains the black soil surrendered to his combing, sifting fingers. And then a weight subsided in him and he knew he had them all.

He felt the fight above was truly over, now. He felt sadness and pity at the death of his valiant friend. He admonished himself for the pity. It was an emotion he was prey to. It was one Nicholas Mason had never had need of. He listened for Mr Greb, but heard nothing. He carried the bag into the corridor. There were many doors in the gloom of its considerable length. But there was light under only one of them. It was pale in a narrow strip and softly inviting. He tried to rub the soil from where it had stuck to the raw of his hands. He listened for the approach of Mr Greb. Still nothing. Licking its wounds, perhaps. Slowed and even hurt by its desperate adversary. He needed to get his bearings and couldn't do so in the darkness. He moved with the bag in one fist to the lure of the light.

Thirty

The door opened on to a school classroom lit by opaque globes of glass suspended from its ceiling by electrical wires, the wires covered by black fabric woven into plaits. Miniature desks occupied four precise rows. The desks were built in pairs and each had a bench seat attached. The desks had white porcelain inkwells set into them and carved grooves above the hinges on their tops in which to place pencils and pens. The classroom wore the mingled odour of chalk dust and wax polish and wet gabardine wool and carbolic soap. It smelled of childhoods spent in the secure discipline of long ago. They were weathered and scored and blackened at their edges, but there was no graffiti carved into the desktops. There was a neat pile of prayer books or hymnals on a shelf in a bookcase to Seaton's right. Their black cloth spines were threadbare with devotion. It was night, because outside the narrow windows all was dark. Seaton had entered from the rear of the classroom. The row of windows was in the wall to his left. In the electric light, landscape pictures looked lurid and childish in poster paint on coloured paper tacked to the walls.

Marjory Pegg stood at the front of the classroom with her back to him. Her hair was splayed, grey and unkempt, across her shoulders. She was chalking a sentence in neat script on to the blackboard. The characters were too small for him to be able to recognise individual letters and so distinguish words. The light was feeble. It was very dark outside. And from the back of the class, under the dim yellow globes hanging from the ceiling, he could not make out the writing on the blackboard.

There was a door with frosted panes in its upper half to the left of the blackboard. Seaton knew, without looking, that the door through which he had entered just now had gone. It had no logical place here. It had been a part of the Fischer house. And he wasn't there any longer. He was in Peter Morgan's village school at Penhelig. He could hear the ticking of the radiator on the wall under the row of windows to the left of him as its pipes contracted and cooled. On the draught from under the door in the classroom corner, he caught the dead-cinders whiff of a coke-fired boiler allowed to go out.

He suffered a start of blind panic at the thought that logic might have stolen the bag from him. But it was there, in his right hand, the velvet tacky in his tender grip.

The teacher shuffled and turned to face him. She was dull-eyed in death, her complexion cold and the flesh of her arms blue and ragged where she had opened her arteries in long slashes to let the blood escape. It was the way you did it if you really meant it, Seaton remembered old Bob Halliwell saying to him, once. You didn't slash haphazardly at your wrists. What you did was cut deeply into the tender flesh from the crook of your elbow to the heel of your hand. You cut the blood vessels lengthways so they could not be cauterised and staunched.

From the front of the classroom, Miss Pegg raised her head and looked at him. Her movements seemed clumsy and somehow reluctant. The classroom was authentic with detail, down to the spotless condition of the inkwells, each obediently rinsed as the final ritual carried out at the end of each dutiful school day. But its teacher was a troubled, troubling figure, lurching and scary, wretched with lack of life. Her feet made a slithering sound when she shifted. From the back of the class, Seaton could see that they were wrapped in bits of newspaper bound by rags. She smiled and her mouth was a chasm of decay. He remembered the shoes Marjory Pegg had worn in her picture, punctilious with repair. Had she become destitute after the events described? Perhaps she would tell him. He wanted, less than anything just then, to hear the apparition speak.

Watching her, he remembered something else. Wheatley had made the remark to Pandora on the way to the Fischer house scullery as they went to scrounge coffee early on a November morning in 1927. He had said that suicides could be very useful to the beast they intended to spawn. He hadn't bothered to explain to her precisely how.

Light twinkled through the windows. There was a pattern to it, a line of progressing dots of brightness, evenly placed, each about the height of a man. Seaton knew what it was. It was the helmet lamps of miners on their trudge to the pithead for their shift. Miss Pegg turned her head to the lights and she dropped her chalk to the floor with a small clatter and held her hand over her open mouth. They were singing, the miners. It was something heartfelt they were singing, something rousing, inspirational. Was it 'Men Of Harlech'? Had there ever been coal deposits to bore and dig for in this part of Wales? Seaton struggled to remember. He hadn't thought there were. He thought there might be slate quarries within marching distance of Aberdyfi. But he didn't think there were pits.

Marjory Pegg, her hair an unkempt shawl across her shoulders, rocked on ragged feet. To his right, next to the bookcase, Seaton saw that a row of coat hooks had been screwed into the wood. The pupils had collected their coats before their departure, of course. Except for one. A child's raincoat, blue with a belt trailing from sewn loops, hung on the nearest hook. There was a blue scarf hung over the coat. And above these items, a blue cap with a single hoop of white and a badge embroidered in silver and red, neat above the peak. Then there was nothing until the farthest hook, at Miss Page's end of the classroom. A cane hung by its curved handle from the farthest hook. The cane was about three feet long and the final eight inches or so of its jointed length, to the tip, were stained with some dark stuff that had dripped into a small puddle on the floor beneath. Seaton's eyes shifted and he saw that the teacher was watching him, had noticed him looking at the cane. He could no longer see her eyes. They were just hollows now, filled with unreadable shadow.

Had the light dimmed? It must have done. It wasn't 'Men Of Harlech' they were singing outside. It was something maddeningly familiar and at the same time strange. But it wasn't 'Men Of Harlech'. And looking through the window, he was no longer sure that the procession of lights came from the lamps on miners' heads. They seemed too violent and uncertain, torn out of the general blackness, more like naked flames. In the charged stillness in the classroom, Seaton heard blood drip from the tip of the cane into the congealing puddle under it. And the teacher moaned. And he launched himself and bolted past her and threw himself at the classroom door, praying for the night breath of Brightstone Forest in the rain and escape.

Except that the door opened on to the saloon bar of the Windmill pub in Lambeth High Street.

The pub interior was almost exactly as he would have remembered it. It must have been after closing time, though, because there was no one behind the bar itself and present, only a trio of late customers, playing cards around one of the bar's small, circular wooden tables. All three players were attired in evening wear. They smelled strongly of Turkish tobacco and cologne, something old-fashioned and expensive.

Tabarome, perhaps. Or Mouchoir de Monsieur. The scent mingled leather and lavender. But there was a taint to it, a base-note of sweet decay.

Sebastian Gibson-Hoare merely nodded at him. Young Mr Breene stood. The third man did not glance up from the cards. 'Allow me to introduce you,' Breene said.

'No need,' Seaton said. 'Mr Gibson-Hoare and myself have previously met. The murderer, Edwin Poole, I have no wish to become acquainted with.'

'Very good,' Gibson-Hoare said. He chuckled. Poole still had not looked up from his cards. 'You spotted the family likeness?'

Poole did not much resemble his cousin and victim. He had the vapid monochromatic handsomeness of his time. His hair was sleekly oiled and his jaw smooth from a professional shave, expensively administered. Outside, the torches flickered with the burn of pitch and there were screams and glass shattering and the lusty voices sang. Seaton had finally recognised what it was they were singing, at the same moment as he read the words on the blackboard, bolting from Peter Morgan's classroom. It was the 'Horst Wessel Song'.

'What on earth do you think that commotion is outside?' Breene said to him. He had sat back down.

'It's nothing on earth,' Seaton said, thinking, its Göring and his wolf pack, marauding through the past these men had all of them helped contrive.

'You were never a fighter pilot,' Seaton said to Breene. 'Archie McIndoe didn't reconstruct your face. Some black-magic ritual that went wrong, was it, the scarring? Some sick ceremony that didn't come off quite as you'd intended?'

Breene just looked at him. Gibson-Hoare chuckled.

'You must all be very proud of what you've accomplished.'

'Oh, you've no idea,' Breene said. 'My goodness. The fun we've had.'

Spare the rod and spoil the child, the teacher suicide had written on the blackboard. Seaton said, 'How often is she obliged to beat the boy?'

And now, Edwin Poole did look up from the study of his hand. 'As often as Mr Greb requires it,' he said. He looked at the bag in Seaton's fist. 'Why don't you rest your burden. Put it down somewhere.' He gestured vaguely to a corner with his eyes. 'You're among friends, old man. You can relax.'

But Seaton had no intention of letting go of what he held. Poole was handsome, callow, unlined. Unlike the other two, raddled spectres at the table, he had apparently died young. He reached into his coat pocket and pulled Wheatley's revolver out of it and put the weapon on the table. 'Are you after being a gambling man at all, Mr Seaton?' His stab at the accent was better than fair. But then, they were all of them skilled at mimicry.

Seaton looked at the revolver. The habitués of the house were showing an ominous, stubborn fondness for the weapon. 'Malcolm Covey is Klaus Fischer's son, isn't he?'

'Don't you go minding all that, Pauly Boy,' Gibson-Hoare said. 'Now are you, or are you not, after having a little flutter here at the table with your ould pals?'

'I'm not.'

'Ah, come on with you.'

It was quiet outside now. Inside the pub, the tape behind the bar had started to play. Marvin Gaye was singing 'Abraham, Martin and John'.

'Coolie music,' Breene said to him. 'Sure, you're fierce partial to it, so you are.'

'Play with us,' Gibson-Hoare said.

'What would be the point?' Seaton said. 'You cheat.'

'Doesn't everyone cheat now,' Breene said.

'The point,' Poole said, 'is the stakes. Your ould pal Nicky has breathed his last breath. And you! Mr Greb is after being furious with yourself. Your prospects are looking gloomy, lad. But Mr Greb is terrible prey to his own obliging nature. And he'd give even the likes of you a sporting chance of survival.' Poole had gathered the cards and he shuffled them above the tabletop between both hands, expertly, now, as he spoke. His facility with the cards, in death, was almost mesmerising. It was a skill contagious with the thrilling affliction of risk. 'Let me explain how this simplest of games is played,' he said. 'We each choose a card from the pack. Draw any but the lowest card, Paul, and you can walk out of that door and into the rest of your natural life.'

Seaton hesitated.

'Come,' Poole said. 'Join us.' He was serious now. This was a serious offer. The pantomimic Irish brogue was absent from his voice. 'The odds are very generous,' he said. His own accent was uncanny, a phonetic relic, the received pronunciation you might hear in a wireless broadcast recorded seventy years ago.

'And if I draw the lowest card?'

'You do the honourable thing,' Gibson-Hoare said. 'It's why the gun is on the table.'

Seaton nodded. Poole stared at him. Marvin Gaye had been superseded by Billy Paul and 'Me And Mrs Jones'.

'The year out there is 1983,' Gibson-Hoare said, softly, nodding at the door of the pub. 'It is springtime. The cherry tree in the little public garden across the road is ripe with pink and fragrant blossom. It is four o'clock on a Saturday afternoon. Lucinda Grey is sitting out there on the grass, reading the very latest edition of *Vogue*. She is lovely in a pale, pleated linen skirt and an ivory blouse, both of her own design. She is waiting for you, Paul. The tennis court is booked for five. You are sharing lasagne and a bottle of Frascati for your supper.'

Seaton looked towards the door. Above its frame, in the

line of clear panes that topped all the frosting and engraving of the coloured glass in the pub's facade, he could now see a sickly spread of pewter light.

'The year is 1995,' Seaton said.

'You're mistaken,' Gibson-Hoare said. He said it gently, like a sad but essential reproach. 'Tomorrow night, you will meet Greg and Stuart. Mike has promised to come. And Patrick will be there.'

'Step out of that door, Paul, and you'll be twenty-three years old again,' Poole said, 'in a world as young and unsullied as yourself. Put down the bag. Relax. Trust us.'

'I need a drink.'

He reached over the bar and put a pint glass under the Director's tap and pushed the pump from the wrong side until the glass was full. He straightened up and raised it. The beer was black and smelled brackish, as though brewed from a source grown stagnant.

'Sure to hit the spot,' Poole said, idly, from behind him.

'Bejaysus,' Gibson-Hoare said, the roaring boy again, Brendan Behan to the syllable, now Seaton had his back to them. 'There's nothing on God's good earth touches a drop of the Liffey water.'

'Who was the girl, Poole, when you were posing as Antrobus? Who was the girl with you in Perdoni's, the two of you watching me that morning?'

'One of Crowley's cast-off acoloytes,' Poole said. He sounded bored. 'She entertained me, briefly. And then I grew as tired of her as he had.'

'Where is she now?'

'Depends on your perspective. She's where I left her. At the bottom of an Antwerp canal.'

Gibson-Hoare sniggered.

'Or she's in the lavatory here, powdering her nose.'

Seaton looked around in the thin forgotten light seeping

through the clear panes from whatever Lambeth lay under their spring sky of nightmare. Where the pub walls met the ceiling there were splotches of mould spreading. It was as though he had entered a world malevolent with decay. Outside, it would be careless and worse, wretched duplication, pastiche and chaos. He put his drink down on the bar and steeled himself and lifted his eyes and looked at the three of them through the mirror behind the bar.

He'd discovered in the tower on his first visit to the Fischer house and had it confirmed often in the hospital, that reflection was never kind to them. Now, in the Windmill mirror, their clothing was reduced to wormy rags and moss pitted the dead flesh of their faces. All three were looking with their corpse eyes at the bag he held in his hand. Even in death, he could see that the rictus of terror gripped their collective gaze. He looked down at the worn and faded velvet of the sack. It bulged gently and felt pitifully insubstantial.

The strings backing Billy Paul did not now sound so lush or lachrymose. They didn't sound very much any more like strings at all. The notes sounded less drawn from a violin by a bow than ground out by a handle turning a street-corner organ. The music had turned harsh and mechanical and the melody perished in the dead pub on every phrase. Seaton shivered. It was not, out there, the spring of 1983 he had lived through and remembered. He pictured weary slums spreading southward beyond the pub doorway under a soot-spangled sky. The faces of the people dwelling in them were pale and pinched and wretched. It was cobbled and damp and the tenements sagged and the vermin writhed in the plaster lattices and mattress ticking, in the absence of light and heat and soap. It was a wasteland of polio and rickets, of hand-me-downs and head-lice and unremitting, gnawing undernourishment. It was a place of long-perished hope. Joy there was the scant ghost of hopscotch games in chalk washed from the pavements by rain. It was a locality entirely lost to faith. It was the South London of Edwin Poole's jaded imagination, or his nocturnal travels. Some nagging instinct told Seaton that Poole had been no stranger to the night exotica luring toffs to the dockside dives of Wapping and Rotherhithe seventy years ago. But the North Lambeth lurking beyond the pub door was not exotic. It was a wasteland of the Great Depression, a vaguely remembered and reconstructed limbo, holding scant attraction, ever, for anyone. It owed itself to Poole's disdainful glances, through the cold blear of cab windows, on his way to, or home from, somewhere else, long ago. It was fearful and grotesque.

The pub, though. The pub was almost perfect. They had taken a memory from his most treasured time, plucked and traduced it. And he thought he knew how. It had been Covey's achievement. A willing subject, every bit as suggestible as Mason had assumed he was, he must have told Malcolm Covey all about himself in the secure, intimate betrayal of the hypnotic state the bogus doctor lulled him into at the hospital. How many sessions had there been? They had stolen from him, looted the locked closet of his most secret emotions. And the realisation brought with it not just indignation but confusion, because although he was sure of the how, Seaton had not the remotest understanding of the why of what had been done to him. Why? In God's name, why pick on him?

The smell of the beer he had drawn was a rotten, brisk rebuke in his glass on the counter in front of his nose and the music wheezed towards its conclusion in his ears.

Spare the rod and spoil the child.

He hefted the poor, velvet-clad remains he gripped in his hand. Oh, well.

He turned around and walked across and pulled out a chair and sat down with them at their table. He rested the bag in his lap. 'I'll go last,' he said.

Gibson-Hoare picked first and drew the jack of clubs. Seaton tried to concentrate on the game. It was a simple enough game. And he needed to be cool and he had never needed more to have his wits about him. But in his mind he saw Lucinda, the patella bone flapping through skin when she worked the treadle of her sewing machine. And he felt the fury shake him like a stampede.

Breene picked. He drew the nine of hearts. Seaton tried to calculate odds as he thought about Mason's sister, bruised and unconscious in bed in Whitstable, having been dragged naked from the sea in a sheet by her weeping brother.

Edwin Poole drew with pale and expert fingers and he flipped over the queen of diamonds on to the tabletop with a snap. And all Paul Seaton could see in his mind was a woman with her throat expertly slit, stranded on the mud on a foggy, long-forgotten dawn at Shadwell Stair.

He expected his own hand to tremble when he drew. But it did not. With his left hand, he turned the drawn card and showed the two of spades. And Poole smiled at him. A gold incisor snagged the smile on its owner's lower lip. Seaton noticed that the music had stopped. Billy Paul had finished singing his maudlin tribute to the wife of another man. He dropped his card. He put his right hand on the stock of Wheatley's revolver. And using the thumb of his now idle left, he flicked the deck and the cards flipped in neat procession and he saw that each and every one of them was the two of spades. He smiled back at Poole and shrugged. He lifted the revolver up from the table towards his head. It was such a heavy tool. It lacked the essential attribute of balance. It was altogether a clumsy instrument. You could handle it forever and its ungainly weight would always go on surprising and dismaying you. It was so quiet in the Windmill saloon, you could have heard a drop of blood drip from a chastising cane to the floor, he thought, pulling back the hammer, pressuring the trigger, lowering the weapon and putting a bullet into the right eye of the grinning spectre of Pandora's murderer.

'Everybody cheats,' he said. He continued to pull the trigger.

Thirty-One

He was back in the vestibule of the Fischer house. He was on his feet. But the gun was in his hand and it was smoking and when he touched the barrel, it was hot. He tried to look at the cylinder to see how many of the shells it housed were now spent but, in the darkness, could neither calculate nor remember how many shots the gun had fired. It did not matter very much. You could not kill a ghost. Not with a gun, you couldn't. He put the Webley on the floor. Some intuition told him that whatever hope he possessed in this bleak and singular predicament, it did not lie in a gun.

Transferring the bag from his left hand to his right, he walked out of the front door. He descended the steps to the grounds, fully expecting Giuseppe's lanky cadaver to emerge from the shadows, voice full of melancholy warning, trying to draw him back. He heard the rain. He heard the crunch of wet gravel under his own feet. He did not hear Giuseppe. He heard a groan he thought might be Mr Greb passing through the vestibule on his way to devour him. And his heart thudded and dread drenched and scalded him in the falling rain. But when his mind made sense of the sound, it was the wail of some old blues singer. It was Bessie Smith, or maybe Leadbelly, the pain of their lamentation roaming the empty house, freed from a shellac disk revolving under a needle and played there long ago in a time of evil and incalculable despair.

He thought he felt the bag shift in his grip. But he knew it couldn't be so. He was crying, now, he knew. He was sobbing in the rain and darkness with fear and grief and rage, all mingled. He kept on walking. He turned and the lights of the house were dim and grown quite distant behind him. He wiped tears and snot and rain from his face with the back of his free hand. It was very dark. It was time to get his bearings, locate the stream, find the relative sanctity of the far bank for the burial. He cursed himself for abandoning Mason's entrenching tool in the basement of the house. No matter. He would dig with his ruined hands. They would have all the time in the world, his hands, afterwards, for repair.

Looking around, he sensed the density of foliage rather than empty space. Yet his path had been unimpeded. It was a confusing contradiction that made him stop. He extended a hand and touched the obstacle of a rough, dense hedge directly in front of him. The leaves of this obstruction were fleshy, springlike, dry in the deluge. And he laughed, bitterly, knowing where he was. He was in the derelict maze at the hospital to which he'd been sent a decade ago. It had the smell and stillness and familiar, overgrown threat. The velvet bag in his hand seemed to shiver and fret again and he thought; nerves. My nerves. My ould nerves are shot to shit, and little wonder. I'm nowhere near up to any of this. And he sensed the brush of pursuit, closing in on him, from somewhere in the maze to his rear.

Seaton became aware, with appalling dread, of who it was now approaching him. It was not Mr Greb. Where the beast would have marauded, parading its strength, his pursuer now larked and crept. Jesus, he thought, knowing who it was, or more accurately, who it had once been.

The nurse from Dundalk who had strayed into the maze with him that afternoon in the hospital grounds had done so with a serious fancy for the young Paul Seaton. He discovered this a week after his rescue from it, when she entered the cell they had put him in to recover from his breakdown and, careful not to loosen his restraints, straddled and mounted him after an intense, smirking period of arousal. He was easily aroused. He was twenty-five. It was the first sex he had experienced since Lucinda Grey had abandoned him. By the time he was entered into her, he detested her. But he was unable to voice any feelings he might have had, a rubber clamp having been put into his mouth to prevent his occasional seizures from allowing him to bite off his own tongue.

She must have died. She must have died to be pursuing him here, decaying, flirtatious.

'Doctor Covey is ready for you, now,' she said from behind him. There was gravel in her voice. She giggled. The velvet of the bag rippled gently against his thigh. That happened, he thought, amazed. That did occur. I felt it.

'He's in the dining room,' said the dead nurse from Dundalk. He could feel the cold soughing off her with the chill of the wind off a lake at night. 'The doctor thought that you might enjoy dinner together.'

Seaton sighed and turned. And there was nobody there. He began the walk back to the house. He felt more resigned than afraid. Fate had always meant for it to end like this, he realised. He would never have been allowed to take the coward's way out. It would have been cheating fate. And fate, above all else, would not be cheated.

'It would have been cheating yourself, too,' he said, under his breath. He gripped the bag, entirely ignorant now of the pain that doing so inflicted. He looked up at the lozenge windows of the tower, where lurked the beast that had killed his courageous friend. He thought about Malcolm Covey and the life Covey's machinations had deprived him of. He trod wet ground, and the house and his confrontation there in the room where their ceremonies had been held drew nearer.

'Old chum,' Covey said, when Giuseppe, liveried in cloth and gilt splendour now, opened the dining-room doors and announced him with an obsequious bow.

Covey was seated on a sort of throne. He had on a cloak with a goat-head fastening embossed in ebony and gold. There was a broach pinned to his chest with runic symbols carved into its ancient metal. His armour, Seaton thought, almost absently. He's come here well-protected. There were rings on most of his fat fingers. The fingers drummed and clinked on the surface of the high table he sat at. He looked dark and furious and the table itself heaved with food and accoutrements. It was heaped high with elaborate dishes and clustered with bottles of wine and liquor and spilling flower vases. But the meat on the suckling pig in pride of place smelled rank and the fruit was bruising in its burnished bowls. Petals lay on the tabletop from blooms curling and already dead. This was the place where they had held their feather and horn banquets and the contamination of it stank through the decades to Paul Seaton with the virulence of plague. He looked at Covey, who had aged a good decade since that night not so long ago in Zanzibar. But perhaps that was just the light. The room was illuminated only by the two ornate tabletop candelabra, their candles red, dripping wax like gore and giving everything in the room a bloodshot cast.

Seaton sat down. It was a long table. He sat carefully out of Covey's physical reach. 'You'd have to wonder why, Malcolm,' he said. 'You really would.'

'Power,' Covey said, flatly. 'Authority. Influence. Wealth. Nothing you would ever, truly, comprehend. So let's not bother with philosophy or morality or ethics, let's cut to the chase. You have something in that bag on your lap that doesn't belong to you. Return it, Paul, and I assure you we will part as friends.'

'If I don't?'

Covey's smile flickered, bloody in the candlelight.

'Mr Greb will shortly join us. You would not wish to encounter Mr Greb.'

Seaton nodded. This was true enough. Except that the house was quiet.

'You know what I think, Malcolm? And this is only my supposition, mind. But I've a sneaky suspicion your beast is hurt. It killed Nick Mason, right enough. And in time you and Mr Greb will be all the stronger for possession of the magic Nick's father endowed him with. And that's just as you foresaw and planned it. But he was altogether tougher and more resourceful than you thought he'd be, was Nick. And right now, Harry Greb is feeling badly from the fight. He's taken a standing count, so he has. It's my belief he'll be in need of a rest before he comes for me. To my mind, for the present only, it's down to the two of us.'

There was a slouching sound from above, as if in contradiction of what Seaton had just said. And Covey smiled and glimmered. But the sound had betrayed itself in Seaton's mind with lack of appetite. Mr Greb would recover. The beast would gather itself. But it hadn't quite done so yet. Covey took a toothpick from a barbed display of them on the tabletop. And Seaton remembered the magic the man's father had contrived in the bar in Portsmouth to break the back of a belligerent sailor.

'I want the bag in your lap. It doesn't belong to you. You've stolen what it contains. Return it and you will leave here healthy and sane. Give it to me.'

'Ah, Malcolm. Why don't you go and fuck yourself.'

The thing above them, gathering obvious strength, murmured and shifted.

Covey bit the toothpick he'd been playing with and Seaton felt pain blister and grind through him. And the bag soughed in his lap. And he knew, finally, that he would fight with the persistence with which his dead and valiant friend had fought to give the boy the burial he deserved.

'Why me, Covey?'

Covey shrugged. 'Give me the bag.'

And the thing above them found its feet and began to shift down the stairs.

The bag rippled in Seaton's lap. Covey took the toothpick from between his teeth and held it out towards a candle flame. Seaton's clothing was soaked. Lascalles' old missal was pulp in his jacket pocket. There was a hiss of steam from his sodden cuffs and the heat through him was bright, burning agony.

'Give me the bag.'

'Never.'

Behind him, Seaton heard the beast burst into the room on a draught that extinguished the candles and pitched them into darkness. It howled and the bag rippled in his lap. Covey cursed and the beast panted and stank at Seaton's back with fury. He heard Covey's fingers scrabbling on the tabletop, for a knife? For Wheatley's revolver? Behind him, he sensed Mr Greb gathering, poised for attack.

Matches. Covey was searching for matches.

Seaton laughed out loud. He had remembered something. He had remembered something vital he had probably been schooled by the man opposite him to forget. 'I'll give you light,' he said.

And Malcolm Covey screamed.

Seaton put both hands over the bag. He felt the nap of velvet over its sad, small protrusions. He closed his eyes and the darkness behind his lids was cleaved by brightness. 'I'll make you safe, Peter, so I will,' he said.

He held the beast back with a part of his mind in the way he now remembered he had done it before. He'd used a great amount of his power, then, instinctive and untried. It had been a moment so cataclysmic that the forest itself had been stunned to silence and its birds had shed their feathers on the wing. The Irish myth of running water hadn't stopped Mr Greb. He had done it. And vanity had caused the collapse in him that followed. Not content with felling the beast, he had approached it where it lay. And he had looked it in the face. That was a mistake he would not repeat.

It was behind him now, mewling, manacled by a single, ironbound thought. And Covey was scraping matches against the side of a box in a bid to repeat his spiteful trick of a moment ago. But none of them would ignite, because Seaton wouldn't allow it. Wheatley's gun was on the table, sure enough. But Covey would find he couldn't pick it up. Seaton's mind had welded it where it lay. Covey was crying. He was sobbing, fumbling with the matchbox, dropping matches in the dark. Seaton smiled. He still had his eyes closed. He found that he could see perfectly well without the use of them. But he had far more important business to attend to than Malcolm Covey, with his shallow tricks, his tawdry ambitions. Seaton had made a solemn promise to the boy. He intended to keep it.

The velvet thrummed under his touch. His mind travelled to a plateau next to a church overlooking the sea. Trees provided seclusion and shade and there was the late glimmer of sunshine on the water. Robert Morgan's gravestone rose from the cut grass. Paul Seaton called on his power. His power was keen and almost unused and he dragged deep and so martialled and gathered the sum of himself. He concentrated. And it was as though the physical world conspired and colluded with him, belief confounding fact, matter shifting on the strength and clarity of what he willed. With profound resolution, with great tenderness, Seaton willed all there was left of Peter, the precious whole and the heal of him, to lie between his father's arms, safe forever, bathed in the granite beam of his father's light.

He sighed and lowered his head. The bag on his lap lay empty. The beast behind where he sat was gone, the baleful magic that had conjured it, abruptly and entirely defeated. He felt the house sag with perished illusion into the neglected ruin it should long ago have become. He opened his eyes and looked at Malcolm Covey over the spoiled food. Covey looked sad and careworn in his cloak and rings and symbols, deprived of his music and ghosts. He was rolling a cigar between his fingers. But he couldn't smoke it. None of the matches spilled on to his banqueting table would strike.

'Now I understand.'

'You understand nothing,' Covey said. 'What a waste. What an appalling waste. Damn you.'

'I could kill you.'

'You could do anything. But you won't.' He shook his head and looked at his redundant cigar. 'What a waste.'

In Klaus Fischer's mansion, the walls were scabrous and pockmarked now where pictures had hung. Rain pattered unimpeded through gaping holes.

Seaton stood and turned and picked a careful path through debris. He walked out of the ruined house into the night. He walked in rain until he was a distance away from it in what he judged to be the direction of the shore. He could not bear the idea of getting back into Covey's Saab and staring at the empty passenger seat. A strong intuition told him he would reach the shore and find a boat. Pandora had not found a boat. But he was confident that he would. He turned back once to look at the house, just before the trees grew so thick as to obstruct his view. He saw light on the glass of one of the tower's thick windows. But it was no more than a hint of moonlight and even from here, he could see that the pane was broken. The house was broken, derelict, bereft of the corrupting power it had possessed.

He had thought briefly about killing Malcolm Covey. Of course he had. But he had remembered what Nick had said in the basement about saving Sarah Mason and their souls. He thought Sarah Mason would be okay now. She would suffer grief at the loss of her brother. He knew what it was, himself, to lose a sibling. But Nick had courted death throughout his life and Sarah must have prepared, at some level, for his absence one day from hers. The dreams would cease, sanity would return and the chaos, now the ghosts were gone, would gradually be forgotten by her and by the other girls. It was Mason's caution over souls that most concerned him, and his own soul in particular. He had discovered something potent in himself. But he felt it would be very wrong to squander this awful discovered gift of his on trivia or spite. And though Covey had damned him, it was Covey who was surely damned. The man deserved the leisure of the rest of his life to ponder on the course of his deliverance when dead.

Seaton was nearing the edge of the sea. He could hear the dull percussion of waves breaking under the rain. And there was a boat, a rowing boat with oars, beached above the tideline when he reached it. It belonged to the house. He was confident the house would have no further use for it.

And then he sensed and turned and saw her.

Pandora stood twenty feet away, poised and beautiful, watching him. Her hair was an abundant glossy tumble around her face and spilling over the ermine collar of her coat. She stood there, tailored and immaculate. And he was aware in the yearning pull of the breeze of the scent she wore. He had always known he would one day see her, like this. The certainty had insinuated itself over the passing years. He had half-known it on a sultry summer day in Arthur's café at Dalston, sharing lunch with Mike Whitehall a lifetime ago. He'd been even surer, when he reached the clearing where Fischer's guests had duelled on his first clueless blundering visit to the house in Brightstone Forest. Had he really seen her that day? If so, she had been but the remotest suggestion of herself on the very perimeter of his vision. Now, she was its only subject. And he could fully see how she had left a trail of broken hearts and bewilderment in her wilful, singular wake. Her hair wisped at its edges in the wind from the sea and her coat collar ruffled as though stroked invisibly. Her mouth was dark rapture sculpted into flesh. She moved her head and he caught the lustre of pearls around her pale throat. Pandora nodded to him once and smiled slowly.

Seaton smiled back. And she was gone.

He rowed himself off the beach with his ruined hands. He could endure a lot of pain. It was one of his recent surprising discoveries about himself. Out beyond the beach, the sea was flat. The oars slapped water against the boat with the rhythm of his pained and steady rowing. He was headed for the red flash of a navigation buoy. When he reached that, out beyond the headland, he would see the lights of Portsmouth wink across the Solent. He rowed in rhythm and pain, purging his lungs with the salt freshness of the sea. And eventually, he heard the hollow boom of water against the metal sides of the buoy. He heard the pull and sigh of its moorings. The rain had stopped and the cloud had thinned and he saw algae green in phosphorescence on the great welded cone of the buoy, floating now in front of him. He steered around it, the oars heavy and cumbersome in the raw grip of his hands. But the current was aiding his progress. In a moment he would round the point and see Pompey and light. He had endured a considerable period of his life in darkness. But the light was close now and Paul Seaton felt he might have earned the right, at last, to live in it.